P9-CFZ-398

YOU

CANNOT

MESS

THIS

UP

YOU
CANNOT
MESS
THIS UP

A True Story That Never Happened

By

AMY WEINLAND DAUGHTERS

SHE WRITES PRESS

Published 2019
Printed in the United States of America
ISBN: 978-1-63152-583-4
ISBN: 978-1-63152-584-1
Library of Congress Control Number: 2019938259

For information, address:
She Writes Press
1569 Solano Ave #546
Berkeley, CA 94707

She Writes Press is a division of SparkPoint Studio, LLC.

Book design by Stacey Aaronson

To Kimber & Rick and Will & Matthew
For making both of my childhoods memorable.

Thanksgiving Day

Thanksgiving Day,
The Day we feast.
The day we pray,
And eat the beast.

The Pilgrims came,
To become free.
Of the English,
For You and me.

—Amy Weinland, 1978

Chapter One

PIPER COMANCHE 400

L ife goes by so fast . . .

It's something I had heard so many times that it had lost its meaning, suffering death by violent repetition. Maybe it's why the younger me never really believed it any more than I was worried about wrinkles, the rising cost of retirement, or that disturbing rumor that women's bodies magically expand at forty-five.

No, that crap wasn't going to happen to me.

And then, before I knew it, in the dreaded blink of an eye, I went from being John Cougar Mellencamp's youthful, free-willed Diane—complete with dribbling slacks—to living the part of life that goes on. The part after the thrill is gone.

Life was more blurry than fast, slipping into a mesmerizing normality. Disguised as humdrum and mundane, the routine began to suck the enchantment and marvel out of everything, leaving me at times wondering if I ever believed in anything beyond what now seemed so real. Driving in an endless line of minivans, we pick up and drop off, fill and empty ourselves into oblivion. It lulls our imagination to sleep. It stifles our spirit and lays waste to the creative genius that exists in every human soul.

As happy as I personally was, I wondered if there wasn't more. I was in a good marriage to a good person, who was probably better at being married than I was. I had two beautiful, healthy children. Though my boys weren't perfect, relative to my ideal of it, they were loving and genuinely did their best to follow the line our family had drawn in the sand. I had all the trimmings and trappings, a late-model imported motor vehicle with sliding doors, a big house, a DVR, and a counter-depth refrigerator. It was all good. It truly was. But, that said, was this really the "it" I was destined to arrive at?

Maybe it wasn't so much that it was going by at light speed, but more that we were so infatuated with cultivating stability and comfort that we had stopped seeing what was really going on.

Being able to get anything, anywhere, at any time hasn't caused our creativity to flourish; no, instead, and ironically, it's squashed it, convincing us that creating isn't as valuable as sourcing. We'd rather be comfortable than happy, or maybe we've replaced happiness with satisfaction. Why risk eating at a place you've never heard of when you can be comforted by something called Jack Daniels sauce?

THAT chilly November morning was a titillating exception to the reality of modern life. At the controls of my sleek minivan, I drove the few miles that separated our Ohio home from the regional airport. Past the Target and PetSmart, past the Walmart and the Lowe's, the Kohl's, the Walgreens, and the Kroger. Past the Outback Steakhouse, the Chili's, and the UPS Store.

Though it was the same silver Honda Odyssey I'd operated efficiently since just before our second son was born and the same roads I'd driven up and down, endlessly, since moving to the Midwest in 2007, the feel of adventure hung thick in the brisk air. Following my faithful guide and best companion, the friend who did whatever I wanted, my iPhone, I turned into the parking lot of the Wright Brothers Airport. It was less of an air hub than a weird collection of metal buildings situated in front of a single runway flanked by a thousand little points of light.

Maybe it was George Bush's lost America.

Surveying the five or six different hangars, my first task was to locate which building I was supposed to enter to meet Mary. My phone couldn't help me now, so it was up to my own cunning and catlike reflexes to find the right place. I was semiconfident that I knew where to go, a specific chain link gate with what I hoped was the correct entry pad. If only I had listened to my husband when he was giving me the directions the night before, rather than thinking about a million other things that were more interesting than hearing him banging on about the specifics. That kind of stuff was never necessary, that is, until you needed to know.

Yelling into the speaker with zero confidence, if that was even possible, I identified myself as a departing passenger. Without a reply from whomever was on the other side, the fence began to shudder and groan, allowing me to pull through the gates. This had to be it. From there, I was directed to an unmarked parking area behind the barely identifiable passenger terminal, near where a wide variety of small aircraft were in the process of being loaded, unloaded, and serviced.

Though my husband had taken his share of flights on smaller planes, I had not yet had the experience of hurtling through the wild blue yonder in an aircraft smaller than a regional jet. Today, all that would change. After parking the van in an area that looked suitable, apparently there were no rules here, I was warmly greeted by Mary, wearing her unfailing smile and cheery disposition. I had known Mary for at least twenty years but had never had the opportunity to form a deep bond with her. Guiding me over to the plane she opened the passenger door and motioned toward my bags, "Here, throw them in the backseat." It was that simple . . . no security, no awkward disrobing in a cold room, and no showing of the liquids. I just drove up in the parking lot and tossed my crap into the actual plane. Clearly, I was a baller.

Climbing up, I swung the small door shut, immediately realizing that its light, almost flimsy construction mirrored that of the entire airplane, the one that would separate me from the atmosphere at 8,000 feet. The sturdiness reminded me of a boat —ready to launch at a nearby lake for a day of fun, sunburns, and awkward trips up and down the back ladder—as opposed to an actual aircraft. We could swim back or call for help on our cell phones if the old boat couldn't make it—in this case, the flying one, the consequences were far graver.

Maybe I shouldn't think about that.

As I watched Mary go through the preflight checks necessary to begin our flight to Houston, I suddenly appreciated her steady maturity. She was taking it all seriously, not cracking the jokes that I would have been compelled to, even if our roles were reversed and I was the responsible airplane pilot.

I had always liked Mary and respected her, but our relationship had long been metered by the fact that my husband worked for hers, an association that prevented any real closeness. This was unfortunate as she was smart, funny, well-read, and pleasant. I had always looked forward to seeing her at the long line of cocktail parties, enjoyed talking to her and considered her to be a beacon of light amongst the sometimes dimly lit bulbs of duty.

Following Mary's lead, I strapped myself in with what seemed like an underwhelming harness. It looked more like something out of a 1973 Buick than a modern-day jet airplane. "I'm ready to start the engines," she said, handing me a huge aviation headset, complete with a microphone that looked like something from a Time-Life Books commercial. "We can use these to communicate. Also," she added, "you can hear the chatter between ground control and me."

I hadn't really expected such a personal connection to our flight, much less something called "chatter." It was like I was the co-pilot. Wait! Who was the co-pilot? Who would fly the plane if Mary became incapacitated? Taking it the inevitable one step further, I willed it out of my brain, sending it to wherever my review of the flimsy cockpit door had gone. Instead of questioning her, I just nodded furiously, agreeing with everything she said. That's what you did if you were from the South, and a people pleaser, and truly terrified of conflict. It was a trifecta that should have ended in a therapist's office, but that would have been admitting something was actually going on. Vicious cycles never end the way they are supposed to.

FINISHING her prep work, Mary fired up the engines with a flip of a switch, and after a couple of additional official-looking movements, she taxied the airplane toward the runway. I had never known anyone who could taxi a plane toward anywhere, much less a runway. The best my regular set of friends could do was back a car into a parking space.

The small four-passenger plane handled far differently than a jet. Even on the ground, I could distinctly feel every bump and imperfection on the surface below, like we were traveling in a golf cart on a dirt road in East Texas, not necessarily the sensation you are looking for prior to being launched into the air in a metal tampon. The aircraft itself was apparently, at least to aviation buffs, a classic—a Piper Comanche 400, one of only several hundred ever made. It was an attractive plane, even at forty-something years old it was pleasing to the eye. Honestly, that's something you could have said about me. The plane and I were of similar age, both of us maturing in our own special way. Its red leather seats looked worn, and my tail rudder had expanded, though neither had deteriorated to the point that we weren't flight worthy.

THE journey itself, as originally planned, could have proven to be an interesting trek even without the flight on a small vintage plane. I was heading back home to Texas to meet with my family on some matters that none of us really wanted to consider. The meeting regarding my parents' estate had been on the books for some time and was conveniently planned around Thanksgiving, so I could be in town for the uncomfortable discussions and subsequent signing of important documents. My siblings and I had begun to refer to it as "Death Camp Thanksgiving," a reference to a weekend meeting my dad had conducted the previous fall. That's when the four of us, everyone minus my mom, holed up in a downtown Houston hotel for two nights while he laid out his entire financial portfolio. By the time Sunday morning rolled around, we all had been issued matching briefcases that contained "the plan," precisely detailing what each of us needed to do when he was gone.

As much as the three of us had one another's backs, and said (and sincerely meant) that we didn't really care about the money, we all cared about the money. I wondered what it, and any other honest discourse about topics previously untouched upon, might do to our otherwise agreeable family dynamics. We were reaching that age when all the stuff that had once seemed so far off was bearing down on us with inevitable dread and wonder.

SUDDENLY, and at the last minute, the key meetings for the Thanksgiving edition of Death Camp Weekend had been moved up to accommodate a lawyer's holiday plans, and I was lucky that Mary had been in Ohio and flying herself back to Houston in time for me to make the new appointment.

My husband, Willie, and our two boys, Will and Matthew, were to follow tomorrow, taking the flights that I originally booked for the four of us. Though a little apprehensive about the single-engine plane, I was grateful to have a way to Texas that wasn't going to require a one-thousand-dollar charge on my already holiday-worthy Visa bill.

Mary began accelerating the Comanche's engines as we turned onto the runway. My heart began to beat more quickly as we gained speed. I felt as if I was on some sort of secret mission . . . with hidden weapons strapped in a sensuous fashion to my legs and arms. In reality, all I was armed with on most days was a cheap toilet brush, some semi-explosive bleach cleaner, and my smarter phone. It was hardly the stuff that had miniseries written all over it.

AFTER what seemed like a slow three-mile ride down the runway, the airplane began to shakily lift off from the ground, and I experienced a palpable "Oh crap!" feeling. It had taken a considerable amount of effort for the small craft to get itself off the runway, meaning it couldn't take too much to bring it back down. What had I been thinking? This was ridiculous. What had my husband been thinking? This was clearly on him. If I died, it was his freaking fault. Idiot.

As we vibrated our way to higher altitudes, I could sense concrete risk, danger and fear. Being a novice, I was not able to delineate between the "good" and "bad" sounds and sensations. This was thrilling, and oh yeah, it was scary as hell. It was an experience that fed my soul, different from a commercial flight. I wasn't watching life, I was actively participating in it, and, excitingly, anything could happen. We could crash, I could ask Mary to "pull over" so I could use the bathroom, or we could just continue to drift around up here in the fluffy clouds—I had no idea, but it definitely wasn't a sure thing either way.

I settled into thinking about signing the serious grownup paperwork. Our situation was uncomplicated relative to stories I had heard regarding other families. Everyone got on well—or as well as could be expected as we matured and morphed into who we really were. My older sister, Kim, was a flight attendant. Single, she lived in a beautiful house, which she kept meticulously decorated with her savvy interior-design skills. Rick, the youngest, flipped properties in the communities north of Houston. He and his wife Jennifer, and their five kids, lived in an old house that they had moved from inner Houston to the rural family place in the piney woods of East Texas. As for me, I was a happily wed suburban housewife, a struggling writer, a college football fanatic, a mother and a girl who had been uprooted several times, most recently to the land of enchantment that is Centerville, Ohio.

We were all so different but had remained close and shared, for the most part, the same moral platform. The discussions regarding Mom and Dad's estate would no doubt be interesting, as we three approached the subject of finances differently.

Rick is the kind of guy who checks the gauge on the propane tank to monitor daily consumption. Kim, at the other extreme, would gladly cash in a portion of her retirement fund to go to Italy. I was somewhere in the middle. I wouldn't install a meter on my blow dryer, but I also wouldn't cash in my adult diaper fund for a Carnival cruise. If I was being honest—and this is my freaking book after all—I would say that I was more correctly positioned on the financial barometer than my genetic associates, who would probably assert the same thing regarding themselves.

As far back as I could remember, Kim had been the royal anointed one within our family. She reigned supreme throughout childhood, a dominance that had continued right on up to our mysterious passage into the adult world. She was the pretty one, strikingly beautiful since the beginning, and was born with a great fashion sense. She was funny, thoughtful, smart, and, as a bonus, she didn't look like she had just sniffed glue when we went to Olan Mills for a family photograph. Yeah, I had spent many long years being jealous of Kim for having the nerve to be everything I was not, but secretly wanted to be.

Her potent influence is still apparent, sovereignty illustrated by the silver-platter snacking service offered up every time she chooses to bless our parents' home with her presence. Don't visualize Dean's French Onion or Frito Lay Bean Dip, oh no indeed, it's more like artichoke hearts and six kinds of imported cheese baked into a soufflé, or fresh-blended tomatillos, canola mayo and tenderly sliced jalapenos served with tortilla strips fried in peanut oil.

They won't come out before she arrives, and as soon as she ceases consumption, backing away from the kitchen island, the buffet ceases operation. It was how she rolled, and regardless of how long she stood commandingly over her kingdom, spreading her wingspan over her salty birthright, she never gained a pound.

It was sick.

RICK was the male heir to the Weinland throne, the boy that everyone had waited patiently through two babies with lady parts for. Yes, his penis was a welcome sight to my young parents, weary from pulling off yet another diaper only to find yet another soiled va-jay-jay. Heralded and trumpeted into life as the next Weinland leading man, Rick handled the pressure with great success. He didn't ever buck the system or refuse to go along with everyone's expectations; he just simply made it clear, from early on, that he was going to do things differently.

An artist whose paintbrush was mainly a drumstick, and sometimes an actual paintbrush, Rick had music and the dream of a simple, unmaterialistic life. He was also the funniest person I had ever met. Hands down. His comedic timing was flawless. His approach was a magical mix of subtlety and obnoxiousness. One minute he was the most hilarious person in history, verbally and physically, while in the next, he became part of the background.

Rick married Jennifer as the new millennium dawned, signaling a new era for humankind and our family. Like he, Jen was cut from a different cloth. Musical, an eclectic foodie and frank, Jennifer brought an entirely different dynamic to our family. We the people, committed to fostering an atmosphere of denial, were called out on the carpet by Jennifer, usually for our own good and sometimes much to our strong opposition.

To illustrate the Jen-effect, the adult family was gathered around the table one night early in their marriage. We were dealing with some minor conflict, an issue that had produced a palpable level of angst. It had something to do with Mom (a.k.a. Sue), who was noticeably upset but not willing to express herself verbally. We all got that, and basically everybody was just waiting for it to go away, without any meaningful words. God, please tell us there weren't going to be any meaningful words.

Jen, who had only said her "I do's, I don'ts, and I wont's" a couple of months earlier and didn't understand the rules of engagement, or thought they were ridiculous, or thought that since she was now having shower sex with my brother that it gave her new street cred, boldly broke the coveted silence. "I think we should talk about how we each feel about this, starting with Sue," she began, cracking the foundation our lives had been lived upon for so long. "Sometimes, I don't want to talk about my emotions and I think it's about self-confidence . . . Self-confidence is something many of us in this room have struggled with or are struggling with. If we talk this out it will be better . . . much better."

Really? Better? What does *better* mean? What in the hell was she doing? Didn't she understand how this was supposed to work? Surely there was some sort of pre-nup she and Rick had signed: "WE DON'T TALK ABOUT HOW WE FEEL IN FRONT OF THE GROUP, ESPECIALLY WHEN WE ARE ALL SOBER AND ALL IN THE SAME ROOM . . ." If you had downed a couple of bottles of Chablis—or were in the process of doing so —and were on a dark porch in Galveston at one in the morning and there were fewer than four people involved (not including the people eavesdropping from a bedroom window), then it was cool, but not at 7:45 p.m. on a freaking Wednesday.

Until that moment, I had never seen so much shock, alarm and panic—in unison—on the faces of my immediate family. It was as if someone had taken all their clothes off and asked us to look at a menacing boil on their personal parts. Or had just announced their secret desire to marry one of our cousins—OK, that really did happen, but that's another story.

My husband, Willie, covertly set off his own pager, fleeing the room to make a pretend phone call. He'd been in the game for about seven years and knew better, plus his family didn't want to discuss their feelings either. Maybe that fact about my in-laws, their respect for denial, outweighed the fact that they all had gigantic heads. Those oversized heads never really seemed like a big deal until I got wheeled into the delivery room to give birth to their descendants. Then I recalled the circumference, through gritted teeth, repeating words that my father said made me sound like I wasn't an adult. In my opinion, once you've passed a few big babies through the canal, you're just as much an adult as anyone else, no matter what kind of words you use.

AS Jennifer reviewed those bystanders still standing, presumably waiting for an answer that would never come, Kim kicked me under the table and then gave me a "WTF?" look combined with the curious hint of a smile. Regardless of the alarm bells that were going off, it was kind of funny—in a sick, twisted way.

Dad, always a total people pleaser and masterful at avoiding conflict, looked at me, his dependable, serviceable child, and said, "I think Jen's right, let's talk about it." I, never wanting to disagree with the man I so admired, nodded vigorously enough to seem bought in but not enough to have my sister punch me in the stomach in the half bath.

As for my mom, the unfortunate direct target of feelings central, she clutched her Pekinese and ran out of the room, nearly hitting the door frame on the way out.

Silence fell upon the group once again, only this time it was laced with a heavy powdering of awkwardness. Mercifully, after what seemed like seven minutes of cruel quiet, my brother finally shut things down. "Well, it was good seeing you guys tonight," he said, as he took Jen by the arm and exited quickly and professionally. Here was a man who respected denial; he was raised right, like me.

We have never spoken of the instance since it happened— we never investigated our feelings, our actions, our reactions, or what any of it meant to our family dynamics. It wasn't that we didn't care, it's that we cared enough not to. Thank God for that.

AS for me, I was, and am, the classic middle child. I have always seen myself as not the first and not the boy, so, I was just me, and I never knew what that was, exactly. She was pretty, he had a penis, and, well, I was funny. Really, to be fair, she was beautiful, he had enough potency in his business to father five children, and I was hilarious.

It never seemed enough.

Whether I had adopted the persona, and accompanying baggage, of the middle child purposefully, or instead my position in the family was cemented by reality, no one knew, especially not me. Enthusiastic, a pleaser, considered humorous by some and obnoxious by others, I fancied myself a harnesser of the pen. I had for years tried to get someone to notice, and, when they did, I wanted them swiftly out of my business. I had minimal fashion sense and rhythmic skills that only I could see. My mind, though well-used, was not necessarily brilliant. Though not unattractive, I was pretty in a decidedly Tina Yothers kind of way, mixing *Family Ties* with Princess Fergie to come up with a bushy head of hair, a solid frame and a flat face. My early battle with beauty—for I am alluringly attractive in present day —may have been because I was wholly uncomfortable with makeup, hair doing, and fashion. It's not that I didn't care, it's that I wasn't born with that chip that instinctually tells you when and when not to wear pantyhose, which kind of bra to wear, and how and why to apply eye shadow.

My life wasn't perfect and I loved it that way. As I approached my later forties I had started looking backward less frequently but with a growing sentimentality. Perhaps I was beginning to forget all the curves and edges of my childhood and would one day be left with only a glowing, warm feeling.

That natural process had gotten blown up earlier in the year, when Dad was in town watching the boys while Willie and I took a work trip. It was an innocent conversation that lasted only a few moments, but I kept going back to it. "The biggest fights your mom and I ever had," he had said, sitting there with a can of Bud Light in his hand, "were about you. I tried to protect you . . ." he added, and then looked away. That's where it ended, when my younger son dashed through the room with our one-hundred-pound dog following close behind.

Though I didn't fully understand what he meant, I had never brought it up again during his visit and hadn't seen him or been home since. It was as shocking as it was casual.

WHILE Mary looked confidently ahead into the clouds, I exhaled and settled into my seat. Blind trust and the blaring noise of the plane began to lull me until I struggled to keep my eyes open. I would have never thought I could sleep in a small single-engine plane piloted by someone I barely knew, but somehow slumber caught me by surprise, and I was out. Open-mouthed slobber time was upon us.

Chapter Two

COORDINATES

I was awoken by the voices inside my head—this time they were real. I knew we must be near Houston because the chatter had ramped up. I felt fuzzy, which was not unusual as I was not prone to catnapping and experienced difficulty re-emerging quickly from daytime sleep.

I looked over to Mary, she smiled back at me knowingly—not like "nice slobber" but more like "hello, dear"—a look that was almost too intimate. As I continued to return to a cognitive state, I couldn't shake the feeling that something seemed different, though I couldn't put my finger on it. She looked different, I felt different . . . it even smelled different.

Glancing back across the cockpit casually, trying not to come across as a freaky stalker, I realized that she *did* look different. I wasn't sure what she had been wearing when we embarked, or what her hair had looked like previously, but she was definitely transformed.

Again, Mary caught me glancing at her, and again, she smiled at me, knowingly. Good God, she was cocking her head ever so slightly to the right, like a cute young pup. Maybe I was a freak, OK yes, I was, but still, something wasn't right. Looking quickly back down at my own lap to avoid her glance, I made a shocking realization.

My skinny jeans, boots and sweater had morphed into some snug-fitting plaid pants. The color combo was mesmerizing—a blaring yellow-gold background, like the harvest-gold refrigerator my mom had in the '70s—offset with a brown check and narrow white gridlines. It was as if a roll of Scotch tape had exploded on my legs. Then there was a turtleneck sweater, ribbed, I suppose, for my pleasure. It was the same yellow-gold as the pant. It was seriously tight and for some unknown reason had a zipper at the back neck opening. I couldn't see it, but I could definitely feel it.

Speaking of secret feelings, I suddenly realized that the sweater didn't end where it ought to. I couldn't be sure, but it seemed like the ribbed goodness kept going past its normal, pre-established boundary. What I'm saying is, it felt like it covered my panty. Yes, it seemed like it truly did cover the panty area, front and back. And, if I wiggled just so, I could feel snaps. In my crotch. This was indeed a pullover turtleneck, but it was also a snap-crotch half-bodysuit. I had never worn such a garment, or seen one in person, but I had come across something similar on a blog dedicated to offensive items from vintage catalogs.

Though my shirt might now stay perfectly tucked into my tape-dispenser pants, if engaged in the consumption of adult beverages later, and if I then waited too long to go to the bathroom, I might be at risk of peeing my pants whilst searching frantically for the escape hatch.

You see, my crotch was snapped shut.

Before I could even begin to feel the deep, desperate itch that only man-made fabrics can cause, the wheels of the Comanche touched the runway. I had never landed at the West Houston Airport, a smaller tract designed for, I had assumed, non-commercial aircraft, so I had no idea what to expect. Pulling slowly to a stop in front of the terminal building, I saw a sign welcoming us to "David Wayne Hooks Memorial Airport" which was not on the west side of Houston but instead located on the far northwest side. I knew that because it wasn't far from where I had grown up. It was the home of the "Aviator's Grill" which our neighbor had always claimed was the next best thing to Red Lobster. She had religiously eaten there once a week, and

I had always wondered what that was all about because she had no dealings in airplanes, or airports, or flying lessons. She had spent many an indulgent few moments regaling us, as she stood in her front yard in unbecoming shorts, with tales of her favorite dish, the "Loop De Loop" which was, apparently, a grilled chicken Caesar salad. She was a regular and even had a t-shirt that said "Aviator's Grill . . . Food Worth Landing For." As far as I knew, she had never landed for it, she'd only driven to it, in her Ford Country Squire station wagon, complete with wood paneling and that little fold-up, rear-facing seat in the way back.

Maybe there had been a change to the flight plan while I had been whacking my head against the window and slinging slobber across the cabin? Either way, I didn't feel comfortable enough to question Mary. She evidently knew what she was doing . . . after all, she was the certified pilot who had gotten us safely from point *A* to point *B*. She could taxi on a runway.

Disembarking from the plane, any hopes I still harbored for normalcy were completely extinguished. My shoes had changed, and even my luggage, which was being pulled from the backseat of the aircraft by a man with huge, bushy sideburns, was un-equivocally altered.

Mary's hair was alarmingly poufy, featuring a hard part di-rectly down the middle of her head. She was wearing a poly-ester, kelly-green pantsuit complete with a clingy dress shirt with an enormous bow at the neckline. I would have never said it to her face, but Mary looked like the hand-drawn model off of a dress pattern packet from a garage sale. She seriously looked like a homeroom mom, or like somebody who was about to whip out a cocktail and one of those Jell-O molds with meat floating in it. As she unbuckled her seat belt and stood just outside the plane, I could also see that Mary, who I'd seen in a wide variety of situations requiring a wide range of fashion choices, was rocking the high-waisted pant. Seriously, those pants went north-wards to where no decent pant should ever venture.

I didn't know what to think. Yet I still couldn't work up the nerve to ask Mary what was going on, she was acting so naturally. I didn't think I was dreaming, as I didn't get the feeling I usually experienced that kept me thinking "yes, this is a dream; this *is* a dream." That sensation always kept fantasy and reality carefully separated, so while I was experiencing something that felt real, I knew it wasn't (i.e. if I drive off this road it's not real, I'm not really going to die, **or**, if I have sexual relations with this policeman in tight pants, who is not my husband, nobody will ever know, because it didn't really happen).

This time was different. Something deep down inside told me this was real, not something I would wake up from.

AS I tried to figure out how I was supposed to carry all my stuff, Mary came around the plane cheerily and handed me a jacket. It was Houston in November, so while it wasn't cold, at all, it also wasn't hot. I put the blazer-like item on without even thinking. Looking down, I noticed that the brown in the jacket matched the brown in my plaid pants perfectly. These were what the Sears catalog used to call *coordinates*. Running my hands across the front, I realized that something had been placed in each of the large pockets—a small notebook and orange Bic pen on one side and a tube of lipstick on the other.

Walking through the small terminal building I noticed a deluge of other oddities—most of them involving exposed chest hair, wood paneling and orange carpet. The smell of burnt coffee and cigarettes was thick in the air. I trudged through the inside and out onto the triangular-shaped parking lot—zombielike—in a fog. There were a dozen or so later-model cars, predominantly American made and in a wide and awful array of colors and finishes. I stumbled along behind Mary, toting my ugly luggage with no wheels or extending handles. By the time I had managed to get midway through the parking lot, I was staggering, not so much because I was confused, and I was, but instead, because like most people, I was struggling to carry a three-piece suitcase set with only two hands.

The original plan had been that we would meet up in the airport parking lot (the West Houston one, not this one) with my father, sister, and brother. From there, we could continue on to our late-morning appointment with the attorney and financial advisor. There would be papers to sign. I couldn't sign papers dressed like this. Normally, I would have been up for it, wearing this kind of thing in public, but not for paper signing. Dad had always told us to dress up for document dealings, and though I was certainly "dressed up," I don't think this is what he meant.

Mary looked back at me, "You coming?" she shouted, still smiling, still head cocking. The best reply I could muster was a halfhearted smile and slight nod. She seemed so damn cheerful and confident, as if nothing unusual was occurring and that the whole world had not been suddenly turned upside down.

Had she seen the chest hair, I ask you, had she seen it?

Stopping at the last car in the lot, she turned again, almost too patiently, almost too happily. It wasn't that she hadn't ever been nice to me, it was more like she was acting like she knew me better than I knew she did. Finally catching up with her at the car, I stared down at it as if I had never seen a motor vehicle. It was huge, that is in length, but curiously short, like a low rider. It was silver with a maroon faux-leather top, so faux, it may not have even been vinyl. I loved cars, always had, and thought it looked like a Ford LTD, possibly a midseventies model, a long, sprawling four-door.

Utilizing an actual key, Mary unlocked the trunk so we could place our bags inside. It was massive—we could have both gotten in and still had room for all our bags, the spare tire, and one of my children, the big one. "Let's go," she chirped as she unlocked the driver's side door, again with a key, this one a different shape than the first. Once inside, she slid across and unlocked my side by pulling a long silver nail out of the top of the door.

Divided by the huge armrests, we were almost sitting in different zip codes. The seats were velvet-like, they and every inch of the interior the same maroon as the vinyl top. If I had not been so distracted by my obvious parallel universe predicament, I may have well been concerned about the red velvet material permanently sticking to my ridiculously tight polyester pants. Adding little maroon bits to my Scotch tape wouldn't have done anything to enhance my new look.

Mary looked tiny behind the enormous wheel. As impressive as it was that she could drive an actual airplane, I wondered if she could maneuver the gigantic car onto the main road. Somehow, she managed to swing it around and out of the parking lot like she had been doing just that her entire life. The life I knew nothing about.

We were on our way.

Though it sounds bizarre, I didn't even think to wonder where we were going. I wasn't going to lunch with my family. That was out. No Leslie's Chicken Salad, no #38 from the Margarita's in Huntsville or Conroe. Yes, no Old Mexico Style Tacos. And so, I sat deep in the plush plushness, like an idiot, still not able to muster up the courage to ask Mary what the hell was going on.

SLOWLY, but not slowly enough, we traveled the roads nearby the airport. Though the route seemed eerily familiar, it, and basically everything I could see, was surreal. I guess I was aware of where we were, but it just didn't make any sense. What was apparently reality was not registering. I needed to hurl. After about fifteen to twenty minutes of pleasing scenery that I couldn't allow myself to connect with, the kind of pastoral setting that doesn't reveal age, we drove toward a landmark I certainly could not deny was real; the brick edifice where I had attended kindergarten through fifth grade, Northampton Elementary School.

Seeming to magically read my mind and detect my connection with something familiar, Mary signaled and turned the massive Ford into the parking lot of the school. Pulling into one of the spaces in the empty lot, in perfect view of the tetherball poles, she put the car into park and turned to look at me.

"OK, Amy, now I'm going to try to prepare you for what you have to do today. I know that you are aware that our surroundings have been, well, altered, and you are correct about that. There are very few rules, but, you need to know that you cannot mess this up. No matter what you do, everything will appear to work out just as it would have anyway."

What was she saying?

I didn't understand and I'm sure my face reflected that, but Mary ignored this, along with reasonableness in general. "Amy, your role today is that you are a writer in Houston meeting with an editor, your meetings ran long and won't finish until after Thanksgiving. You are stuck in town over the holiday with nothing to do, so, you are going to visit some distant cousins who live in the northern suburbs of Houston. You will arrive today and you will leave tomorrow, just before the sun sets. You are Amy Daughters from Centerville, Ohio. You are the married mother of two sons, one in his teens and the other in elementary school. You are a stay-at-home mom who writes as a sideline occupation. You are forty-six years old. Basically, you are yourself and can speak freely about your life within limits which shall become clear to you." Leaning all the way across the wide expanse of the LTD, she grabbed my clammy left hand in hers and looked me directly in the eyes, stating unequivocally, "Amy, this is going to be all right, *I promise.*"

I was completely overcome with confusion and shock, but not familiar enough with Mary, the boss's wife for the love of

God, to yell "WHAT IN THE HELL ARE YOU TALKING ABOUT?!" So, instead, I opted for sitting dumbfounded and silent as she pulled the car back out of the school parking lot.

MY ROLE, MY ROLE, I can't mess it up!?!?

What was she saying, oh my Lord, she had just grabbed my hand in a meaningful fashion. She was definitely crossing the pre-established and sanctioned lines of engagement—there was no *hand holding* prescribed in this relationship.

Someone had laced my Starbucks, my Greek yogurt was tainted—my deodorant had been tampered with. THIS WAS NOT HAPPENING!

Chapter Three

THE FREAKING PEOPLE

*W*ell, crap. I guess I knew where she was taking me next, but I absolutely couldn't accept it as reality. Staring blankly out the window, I watched as she made another hard left.

Then it happened. Something registered and resonated deep within my suburban-raised soul. Even in my mentally unstable state, I could see that this was a glorious sight, miraculous and dreamlike.

It was like a glowing city on a hill.

It was the Northampton Subdivision in its absolute prime.

Venturing boldly, or involuntarily, into a land where sheer terror and confusion were delicately intertwined with pure enchantment, we passed through the still-pristine white brick gates of the subdivision, our subdivision. The white bricks were proudly adorned with their red heraldic shields dominated by a majestic *N*, the remainder of the glorious name spelled out in black Old English font.

Northampton was an upper-middle class affair carved out of the dense piney woods, thick underbrush, and peaceful meadows of far-North Houston in the late 1960s. When my parents, along with my sister and me, first moved the thirty miles from the I-10 corridor of Houston to Northampton in 1969, there were only three streets, the community eventually expanding to 5,000 residents a decade into the new millennium. As time went on, two clubhouse complexes complete with Olympic-sized swimming pools and tennis courts were erected.

These areas became the hub of social activity, the site for everything from swim meets to Fourth of July picnics, Brownie meetings to wedding showers. We rode our bikes to the "club" and spent the entire day there. Mom didn't seem worried—she never even asked us to check in.

I wished I could still pull off riding a bike in a bright yellow-and-pink string bikini, damp from the chlorinated water, the wind blowing my bowl cut . . . the smell of Frito pie drifting through the air. If I tried that now, I'd either be arrested or cause a terrible car crash.

As we started down the main drag, Northcrest Drive, we passed the enormous one hundred-year-old oak tree that had greeted Northamptonites throughout the ages. It sat proudly on the first of the long, green line of well-manicured esplanades that stretched the entire length of the main thoroughfare. Each was maintained individually by a teen or family, one lucky winner being awarded "Esplanade of the Month" every thirty days. Next to winning "Yard of the Month" or, perhaps, being presented the coveted orange band of the school-safety patrol, it was the highest honor in all of suburbia.

The familiar-looking homes were new and neatly painted, fresh and minus any hints of the green mildew and algae that would eventually spread across their fresh stucco. What hadn't changed was the massive amount of trees the builders left on each enormous lot, making it seem like the houses were an actual part of the forest as opposed to replacing it.

We passed the old club house, pool, and tennis courts, flanked by "Ye Old Firehouse" with its red siren mounted precariously atop its pointed roof. This was the original version of the Firehouse, before it ironically burned down in the middle of the night, requiring the nearest Volunteer Fire Brigade to come to the rescue, from their subdivision to ours. This no doubt gave we, the action-starved suburbanites of America, a story to share and savor.

"Remember that time our 'Ye Old Firehouse' burned down?" "Remember that time that what's-his-name's wife cheated with that guy at the Ho-Jo on I-45 and 610?" "Remember that time those kids put rotten eggs in all the mailboxes?" All of them, and many more, were suburban myths specific to Northampton. As unique as they were, surely similar tales were shared by the countless pockets of suburbia that dotted the country, nay, the world. This was our folklore, a commodity you could lay claim to even if you didn't have a banjo or a log cabin.

Taking the main road, we passed by the street names I knew from the banana seat of my bicycle. My heart sang out their sacred names: Allentown, Bayonne, Craigway, Darby Way, Elmgrove, Fawnwood, and Glenhill! I could still remember the surnames of most of the families that had occupied a coveted corner lot on the main street. There was Kristi Beauchamp's house, glowing in the morning sun, her mother's flower pots meticulously cared for as always. There were bird baths, metal swing sets, and cars parked inside of clutter-free garages. I knew kids who lived on each street, kids that by and large had started kindergarten with me and then gone all the way through to matriculation at the new high school that would be built over the tracks from the entrance to our shared subdivision.

A building that was now eerily missing.

For all the bad press the concept of suburbia gets from sociologists, historians, and even artists, growing up in Northampton was a pretty sweet gig, at least the part of it that other people could see from outside the colorful array of front doors.

FINALLY, Mary maneuvered a hard right onto the longest of the long side streets, Creekview Drive. Winding down that familiar way, I knew precisely where we were going, where we would stop, where this could and should all end—but I couldn't compute the big questions of "Why?" "How?" and "What (TF)?"

What I was absolutely sure of was that I couldn't handle whatever came next. I couldn't go there.

There wouldn't include just the house. No, surely this bullshit made-up fantasy came complete with the people. THE FREAKING PEOPLE! Dad, Mom, Kim, and Rick—they would all be there. Wouldn't they? And then it hit me. Oh, crap. If they would be there, then SHE would be there! LITTLE *AMY* would be there! Holy, Holy, Holy CRAP. How old was I going to be when I got there? In other words, how old was SHE going to be? Surely I wouldn't have to have that . . . HER—us—shoved down my throat.

Oh. My. God.

But destiny, or fantasy, or some form of mental paradox was calling us onward. Even though Mary had never been here, to my little corner of the past, and didn't have the GPS necessary to find it, she knew just where to pull off to the side of the road, making a slow stop in front of the biggest house on the block. I looked up and gazed unencumbered through the large car window at number 24314 Creekview Drive, my childhood home in all its glory and spanking new splendor.

We had moved here in 1976 when I was eight years old. Mom and Dad didn't sell the place until after I graduated from college. The last time I had driven by the property, it had been transformed by its new-millennium owners. The covered brick entry was gone, a second-story front porch had been added, the garage had been converted into a living space, and the entire color scheme and outer materials had been unscrupulously altered. All that remained intact was a set of the original windows, perched high on the third level. I sketchily remembered that a flood had occurred at some point in the near past, the creek from behind finally rising high enough to overcome the ever-vulnerable structure, requiring a massive renovation. It had been that disastrous one year in a hundred that we all hoped wouldn't happen on our watch, the reason the house was zoned in the flood plain in the first place.

But on this day, at this splendid but untrue hour, the years of aging were yet to occur. Yes, on this day it was perfect. It was pristine, it was unfettered and it was glorious. Holy crap, I was home when it was still our home, I was back when it was still back in the day—I was at the place where previously only my subconscious could take me. Looking wide-eyed, drooling mentally, my next thoughts were the most lucid that I had conjured up since landing at Hooks airport.

What did I have to do now?

And so, I turned to Mary, who had become the cruise director—my own personal Julie McCoy—for my fantasy voyage backward. And, like Julie's little Vickie, like a young grasshopper awaiting instruction from her Michigan-born *sensei*, I awaited the answer.

Mary turned to me with a look of compassion. "Amy," she said with grave preciseness. "It is ten thirty a.m. Thanksgiving morning, November 23, 1978. You are about to play the role I laid out for you earlier. I will leave you here and pick you up tomorrow at five p.m. They are expecting you. You have to go now. You absolutely have no choice. You must get your suitcases and walk up that sidewalk and ring that doorbell."

Her words were delivered with such force and gravity that I had no choice but to listen and obey. It was almost like what she said couldn't be questioned—she had been placed in charge by an authority who could alter time.

This was going to happen, regardless of how ridiculous it was.

MARY got out of the car with relative ease while I struggled to open my door—a massive, long, steel beast positioned awkwardly close to the ground. Somehow it managed to avoid whacking the curb completely, but the bottom grazed the concrete, creating an awkward friction. I met Mary behind the car, where she unlocked the trunk, again with the key, giving me my suitcase, the work-type satchel and what looked like a version of the cosmetic case my maternal grandmother had carried. Granny had called it a train case. This version was green, vinyl, and textured to look like leather, complete with visible stitching along the sides.

"I think you have everything," Mary said, peering into the deep cavern of the trunk and then slamming it down with a huge, hollow thud. I stood motionless, but she continued to move, turning toward the front of the car. Looking back and seeing me still standing there, she returned to where I was, with my bags on each side of me. She patted me warmly on the back, smiling broadly. "Good luck, Amy!" she said. "I'll wait here to see that you get inside!"

"I mean . . ." I began awkwardly, panicking as she moved toward the driver's side door. "How do I do this . . . How do I get a hold of you if I need something? Like, if I get in trouble or get sick . . . What will I do?"

"We won't talk," Mary said firmly. "You won't need me, you'll only need yourself—you are the only one who can do this."

"Can I text you?" I whispered, my voice trailing off. "If I have a question, about like, my role and all that?"

"You can't text here," Mary said. "It won't work. There are no mobile phones here, no personal computers, and no internet. No messaging, no emailing, and no texting. YOU are the only one who can do this and you will have questions, but, Amy . . ." Now it was her voice that trailed off. "You have to answer them, only you can answer them."

Then, once again, she cocked her head, like she was going to either say something profound or ask me for a dog biscuit. "It's less about the answers than the questions themselves. It's time to ask the questions . . ."

Questions? I thought. What questions? I didn't have any freaking questions and I didn't need the answers to questions I didn't want to ask, because there weren't any. I knew what happened, in there, in that yard, in that house, in that childhood.

Yes, it was a part of me, but it was over and really, it was insignificant, it was as normal and vanilla as the very suburbia that I was standing in. It was common. Seriously, come on, I wasn't Anne Frank, Anne of Green Gables, Anne Boleyn, Anne Hathaway or even Annie from that stupid musical I didn't like.

Nothing to see here, folks, move along to something else that mattered, not this.

"It's time," Mary cut in, coming ominously behind me, putting her hand on my shoulder. "You can do this, and you must." Eyeing her briefly as she nodded, smiling again in that disturbing yet meaningful fashion, I stood by the mailbox and stared at her, as if in a drunken stupor. I looked toward the house, back at Mary, and just stared. "You have to go now, Amy," she said firmly. "You don't get to decide, it's been decided. Believe me," she said, softening her tone ever so slightly, like she could possibly understand my dilemma. "It will be OK, I promise . . ."

Slowly turning toward the house, I looked up, and then after an additional look back at Mary, I started up the path to my house, or was it their house, who knew?

This is where the whole people-pleasing mentality worked against you, because if you ever go back in time you ought to at least put up some resistance, or ask some tough questions, or do something other than nod furiously and go along with the program. I had always gone along with the program, sometimes to my benefit, other times to my demise. Today it could go either way. That is, if any of this BS was even for real.

THIS *IS a dream, this IS a dream, this IS a dream*, I repeated in my mind over and over. Maybe if I clicked my sparkly red shoes— or vinyl Yo-Yo heels—together, I would be transported back to Ohio, or Kansas, or someplace in the future that was supposed to be the present. Half of me wanted it all to end right here, willing the wild aberration to stop before it went even a blink of an eye further. The other half wanted me to have the courage required to do this right and bravely face whatever was at the end of the sidewalk.

It was all there: the pine needle covered lawn, the tall towering pines, the holly shrubs, the flower beds lined with bricks left over from the construction, the long driveway. There is a special smell associated with a thick, lush lawn of St. Augustine grass, almost enabling you to taste its blades. It was exactly what came to mind when I read that verse from Psalms, "He makes me lie down in green pastures." The green pastures in my soul were always a thick bed of St. Augustine grass, laying in the yard, this same front yard.

The house was atypical even for the 1970s, as many of the doors, windows and other features had been supposedly pulled from a house in New Orleans by a builder who had originally designed and constructed the house for his own family. The builder went bankrupt, the house went on the market after construction (but before wallpaper, carpet, and other optional items were chosen and installed), and my dad, always game for a bargain and an unconventional living space (or unconventional anything for that matter) convinced my mom to buy the house, finish it, and move four streets back in the same neighborhood we had lived in since 1970.

The outside appearance was a fusion of English Tudor and 1970s American Contemporary, chocolate-brown wood and white stucco. It stood a full three stories high, unusual for our neighborhood. We were always referred to as the people who lived in the three-story house. An honor really.

Reaching the place where the sidewalk ends, I placed my shaking finger on the doorbell, pressed firmly, and waited for whatever lay behind the door at 24314 Creekview, Spring, Texas, zip code 77379. Good God, this was still the 713 area code . . . nobody knew anything about 281 here, or 832. In my time you had to dial ten digits, here it was only seven. God, there was still long distance . . . what if I needed to place a collect call to my husband?

Could you even still do that, and could an operator really connect me with the future, my real life, the one where I was sexually active?

Chapter Four

HELLO FROM THE OTHER SIDE

fter a few long seconds, providing me more time to realize this was all probably crap, the door began to open.

"Hello!" a middle-aged man who looked just like my dad said, thrusting his hand forward. "Happy Thanksgiving!" he continued.

I took his hand timidly and shook it, staring at I'm not sure what. "I'm Dick Weinland," he said. "And, well, I guess we are cousins! We're glad you could come for Thanksgiving!"

A meek "Thank you. I'm Amy Daughters," was all I could manage to reply, almost inaudibly, trying both to look, and not look, into his bright young eyes.

The man, my dad, was dressed in an outfit I remembered, a wide-collared golf shirt. It was brown, orange, and white, with a Snoopy character wearing sunglasses on the left man breast, where a Polo horse or Lacoste alligator would otherwise be. It was snug fitting and tucked into slacks, also clingy though I shouldn't have noticed. They, the pants, not the man parts from which my very existence had sprung forth, were secured with a brown leather belt with hand-tooled designs. Further to the south he was rocking a mock cowboy boot.

He looked so young. His skin was smooth, tan, and perfect—his hair was black and shiny, combed over with poufy, hair-sprayed care, featuring carefully groomed sideburns. If he had known who I was, his adult daughter with a C-section scar, I would have said with a well-earned hint of sarcasm, "Looking good, Dad . . . Looking good!" I would have also told him to please go up a size on the slacks.

Looking over my shoulder, Dad nodded and waved vigorously. I turned weakly to look back down the path—it was Mary waving, honking the horn, and slowly pulling the massive car back into the street to return to God knows where.

So there it was. She had left me here.

"Well, come on in and meet everyone!" the young Dad person said. And with those simple words, I crossed the threshold into a world that I barely remembered but was vividly and intensely familiar with. Standing on a large brown latch-hook rug with unidentifiable orange flowers—Mom had hooked that thing herself—I was overcome with a wash of emotion.

My first impression was how small it all seemed. At a swift pace I could reach the back of the house in an instant. Yes, I was sure it had shrunk. I was certain that my house (the one I never made a mortgage payment on) was bigger than the house I was standing in now. God, the two rooms I could see were shockingly modest. I had always pictured this house, and these rooms, as bigger than anything that I had lived in since. I could have only hoped to buy a home that was this palatial.

My thoughts were interrupted by the clatter of several people on the floor above us. "Someone is here!" one yelled. "Maybe it's that cousin woman, or Grandma and Paw Paw!" another cried out. Turning to my immediate left, I looked up a half-flight of stairs that led to small landing, turned left and disappeared. In an instant, three smaller people were clamoring down, competitively vying to be the first one to reach the bottom.

"Kids!" Dad said. "This is your cousin, Mrs. Daughters, she and her family live in Centerville, Ohio! This"—he put his hand on the tallest child's shoulder—"is our oldest daughter Kimber, she's twelve."

"Dad!" Kim retorted almost violently. "My name is KIM not KIMBER!"

He just smiled, not even flinching, and continued to the next, shortest child in line. "This is our son, Rick, he's eight." Rick, cocking his head just so, humorously gave a Fonzie-esque thumbs-up. I couldn't be sure, but he might have winked at me.

"And this is our number two girl, Amy, she's ten years old," Dad continued. I watched Amy squirm and dance about, with a full-fake smile and total unbridled mirth. She couldn't control herself. Her hands were wild, breaking not only Kim's and Rick's personal space barriers, but mine and Dad's too. She was a crazed, wide-eyed freak. Oh my God, she was nuts.

Admittedly, I glanced with pleasure at this smaller version of my older sister and younger brother, infused with a warm feeling to see my friends of yore, my companions, my lifelong comrades from the past and present. Their fresh faces glowed—the excitement of the holidays shown upon their youthful countenances. I could barely formulate their adult faces, but, they were there, yes, they were there. Even in my dilapidated mental state, I could tell that this was one of the greatest single moments of my entire life. Given time to properly absorb the wave of emotion, I could have sobbed openly.

But, looking toward the young Amy was a different story completely. Putting my finger exactly on the emotions I was flooded with would be difficult, but terms such as "uncomfortable," "hesitant," "uneasy," "awkward," "difficult," and a healthy dose of "painful" would be a good starting point. Honestly, I couldn't look directly at her. She was so wound up and she danced around in such an out-of-control way that I didn't know how to respond. Really, she was ruining this golden moment for me. Why couldn't I just look at Dad, Kim, and Rick without her trying to draw all the attention to herself?

Before I had time to consider any other deep, dark feelings bubbling from the bowels of my emotional basement, Dad cried out, "There she is, just out of the kitchen . . . This is my wife . . . Sue."

My God, it was my mother, my beautiful mom. Bursting forth from the past it was her, she who my life once revolved around, who held the keys to all things, oh Mom, oh God, holy crap, it's you.

She was gorgeous really. Her face sparkled, almost like it had been pulled tight over her facial bones, not a wrinkle to speak of. Her hair was carefully coiffed, and she wore a stunning burnt-orange pantsuit that, though absolutely horrible, somehow worked for her. This must have been during her self-described "Elvis" period, where she likened her physical appearance to the King. Really, she looked nothing like Elvis to me. I had to remember to tell her that when I got back home. With her hand outstretched to mine she said, "Hi! I'm Sue."

Taking it limply, I nearly passed out. I was literally dizzy, the room was spinning. "Hi, Sue, I'm Amy, thanks for having me," was all I could come up with. Mom was obviously less enthusiastic than Dad regarding my arrival, but she was nothing but gracious. I knew that the holidays had always been difficult for her. I also understood, even in my unstable condition, that my presence here, especially as an overnight guest, would not be a helpful element of any de-stress strategy she may or may not have planned while curled up in the fetal position in her closet last night.

Dad pointed up the stairs, almost as if he was intentionally spinning my attention in another direction so I couldn't absorb anything that was happening. "Amy, you must be tired from your trip. Let me take your bags up to the guest room. You can get settled in and then come down and join us."

"Yes," Mom agreed. "Kids, you let Mrs. Daughters get unpacked and she can come down when she's ready." Turning to me, she continued, "We are planning to eat later in the afternoon and, sometime between now and then both mine and Dick's parents will be here."

"This way, Amy, follow me and I'll show you your room!" Dad said.

And so, I followed him up the gold-carpeted stairway, tottering on the edge of sanity, needing a drink, needing to throw up, needing more than a moment to pull myself together. We went up one half-flight to the first landing and then turned, up another half-flight to the game room, which again looked absolutely tiny. The first thing I noticed when I made it to the second level was a wall-mounted intercom system, literally staring me down as I came up the last step and looked left. It was almost close enough to touch even though it was clear across the room. It was so familiar, yet foreign, but somehow was comforting, like an emotional anchor. The Nutone Intercom system. I might not have been able to call home, but for the love of God, I could contact the inside patio speakers or the kitchen with this little piece of technological genius. I saw more, so much more, but it was just too much to take in on top of meeting my hyper self downstairs, and my mother, Oh God, My Mother! MY FREAK-ING YOUNG MOTHER!

Up another half-flight to the second landing, we turned up the final half-flight to reach the third floor. I was going to stay on the top level, which contained only a bedroom, full bathroom and closet. This floor would eventually house each of us as we got older, just before we flew the coop, only to fly back again. Before we began using it regularly, we had always found the highly acclaimed third floor to be borderline spooky.

Dad entered the room first and set my bags down. "Well," he said. "You should have everything you need here. Come down whenever you are ready," he continued, "and we'll take you on a grand tour of the rest of the house!"

Yet again, I replied nominally, and he disappeared down the stairs below. As he left I had a sudden memory of him exercising on these same stairs, running up and down numerous times, sweating, panting, up and down, up and down. We three would run with him for a while but could never complete the number of trips he required of himself. I bet he may have done that precise task earlier this same morning, probably wearing something terrycloth.

Chapter Five

ARE YOU THERE, GOD?
IT'S ME MARGARET

So, here's the deal. I flew on a small plane with my husband's boss's wife. I fell asleep and woke up in 1978 wearing tight pants that made my butt look bigger than it really is. She drove me to my childhood home, in a huge Ford LTD, and told me—in my forty-six-year-old grown-up body—that I had to go inside and stay with my immediate family (including my younger self) for all of Thanksgiving and most of the following day.

That was it. It was simple. No problemo. Well that is, if you believed any of it could be FREAKING TRUE.

All I could assume was either I really had traveled on some sort of strange time continuum (crap, I didn't even know what that meant), or the plane had crashed and I was dead, or I was in a coma, taking full advantage of the IV drugs, or I was bound and gagged and currently in a state of hallucination heretofore untapped by the medical community.

Nevertheless, and regardless of how or why, I couldn't find a way to make it NOT real.

AFTER spending several minutes staring blankly at the textured wall—it looked almost like peanut butter slapped on a cookie sheet—it came to me, my next move. It was exactly the thing I should have always thought of first. Sitting at a chair by the built-in desk, I put my left hand over my forehead and eyes. I started to pray.

I had spent the last several months trying to foster a spirit of thankfulness, in all circumstances. "Well, God, thanks for this travel back in time . . ." Pausing, I wondered if this was some kind of huge God-thing or just some kind of huge mental breakdown. "I guess you've always known that I would like to go back in time," I continued, grasping for what I was supposed to say. "So, thanks for this time, no matter how painful, surreal and ridiculous it is . . ." Reconsidering my last statement, I pulled out my mental Liquid Paper. "I know it's not ridiculous, you know, if it was your idea . . . so, thanks . . ."

I trusted God implicitly, but still, this all seemed "out there." I guessed a lot of my hard-core Christian friends might think that it was some sort of evil hallucination, definitely not of God. But, if all things are possible, then why not extend "all" to its furthest limits?

The truth was, I was probably underestimating and judging all my people by trying to make it all about who would or would not believe this. How could I go from attempting genuine thankfulness while time traveling, to accusing people I loved of judging me? I wondered if there was counseling offered in these cases. Like maybe I could push a secret button, perhaps in the intercom, and be transported to a help desk, where someone could talk me down.

I settled for wrapping things up with God, always conveniently available 24/7. Only I never stopped to appreciate it— that is, unless I desperately needed Him, like if I was writing one of those stupid time-travel books and thought of it then, in retrospect to events that never even really happened.

"Please guide me through this and help me to learn whatever it is you want me to. And please be with my people back in the real world, if there is such a thing, while I am gone. That is, if I'm really not there. Really. Thank you. I know you're here, because you were here before, when this was real the first time. Amen. Really."

It was underwhelming, and manic, and confusing but, as usual, I hope He got where I was coming from.

I made my way to the bathroom and splashed cold water on my face. I didn't know why I was doing it, but that's what people did in the movies when they needed to collect themselves after some major trauma. What I didn't get is that time travel and being in a movie aren't the same thing, because in one instance you have a makeup artist at your disposal, while in the other, you don't. Before I knew it, not only had I traveled back to 1978, I had marred my over-mascaraed, over-blushed, and over-blue-eye-shadowed face. I really didn't know if I could achieve that look again on my own. In fact, I was really sure I couldn't achieve that look again on my own.

Crap. Double crap. I didn't need any of this.

Shuffling back into the bedroom, I flung my luggage onto the bed. I needed to find something, anything, to fix the latest mess I had created. The contents only mirrored the types of items I had packed previous to the 2014 version of this trip. It was old, vintage stuff that appeared to be brand new. Despite the time warp lag, I could still savor the finer things: a combination blow dryer and styler called the "Supermax"; Charlie perfume; beer-enriched Body on Tap shampoo; Miss Breck hairspray and Arrid Extra-Dry. It, the aerosol can of deodorant, was dominated by silhouettes of a man and woman apparently about to get it on, sexually—reminding me of those shadowy people from *The Electric Company* who spoke only in syllables.

"Sex—" one shadow would whisper.

"U—" the other would reply.

"—al" back to shadow number one.

"Heal—"

"—ing."

Then, there was what had to be the explanation for how my hair had gotten so light and fluffy; a jar of iridescent, emerald-green Dippity-do. The *crème de la crème* was a clunky Bausch & Lomb contact lens disinfecting unit. It was rectangular and white with a silver face. This could only mean that I was, at that very moment, wearing hard contact lenses that I would have to try and tweeze out of my eyes later in the night. I could vaguely remember the process of rinsing the lenses with one solution and then putting them in the case with another before inserting it into the little oven. Plug it in, push a button, watch the red light go on, go to bed, and voilà! The next morning the light was off, the contacts were suitably baked and ready to be placed, awkwardly, back in the eyes.

I wondered if I could cook a burrito at the same time.

Collecting a few necessaries and a vinyl makeup bag, I made my way back into the bathroom.

The third story was painted a piercing blue when we first moved into the house, a color my parents had toned down to a sky-blue. The bathroom had plaid, primary-colored wallpaper and linoleum flooring. Both rooms had built-in cabinets in a dark mahogany.

Coiffing my already well-coiffed coiffure and slathering all the makeup back on to the best of my ability, I looked at myself in the large, gilded-framed mirror. It was the most makeup I had attempted wearing since my sister overserved my face when I was a bridesmaid in one of my best friend's weddings.

Moving back into the bedroom, I grabbed my large leatherette purse, a light brown vinyl bag with stitches randomly strewn across the front, reminding me of Frankenstein's head. Inside, I found a coordinating wallet and then maybe the best thing I'd seen yet, a glass vial of Maybelline Kissing Potion. It was the roll-on lip gloss that I remembered as being the absolute rage in the '70s. It was flavored "Mighty Mint."

It hadn't struck me until just then that my iPhone and laptop were missing. Usually this would have signaled the end of the world, meaning I couldn't check my email, Facebook, and Instagram every fifteen minutes. Though I was shocked that it had taken me so long to notice, in this bizarre situation it didn't seem to have quite the same impact.

If I would have had any of these items, and an internet connection, I could have Googled "Is time travel real?" or "If your plane crashes can you go back in time?" or "What is toxic shock syndrome?" Then, I could have deliciously updated my Facebook status, finally coming up with something nobody could have competed with: "Gone back to 1978 as an adult! Happy Thanksgiving Everyone!" #polyester #timetravel #bowlcut #manbulge #missbreck #kissingpotion #sweethonesty.

But really, even if I could have done that, and even if people thought it was true, I would still only get thirteen likes. But that ridiculous lady I am Facebook friends with—who I've never even met—would get fifty-five likes for posting about how cute her cat looks when it gets wedged between the washer and dryer . . .

#UGH

Chapter Six

SERGEANT SNIPS

I had no concept of time and couldn't begin to know how long I had been sequestered on the creepy third floor. I didn't want anyone to think I was violating the toilet with some sort of time-travel affliction. That would really wind my mother up. I could almost hear her telling me on the phone back in the future, "First, she shows up at the last damn minute, wanting a place to stay, and then she makes a huge mess in the third-story toilet. You know your dad isn't going to clean that shit up . . . Oh 'Welcome!' he says, then he does absolutely nothing. Nothing, it's all up to me . . ."

Back down the first two half-flights of stairs, I stopped briefly in the game room. Again, it was so tiny, but otherwise as I had hazily remembered. My bedroom, or the young Amy's bedroom, was either on the left or right. I couldn't be sure, as I had used both of the bedrooms at one time or another. Continuing down, I paused on the last landing, treated to a mesmerizing view over the expanse of the ground floor. That's when all hell broke loose —crap, I had been detected by the overexcited Mini-Me.

Meeting me at the bottom of the stairs, Little Amy shrieked "Hi!" with overreaching glee. "You're so lucky, you're staying on the THIRD floor. I wish I could stay there, but I'm too young. You're not too young. You're older than me, but we have the same name . . ." All the time she was talking she literally danced around, moving her hands closer and closer to my person, obviously wanting desperately to touch me. She had serious self-control issues. Seriously.

"Do you want to sit down, we could talk some more, I could tell you about everything. And then, then I could show you everything, give you the *t o u r* . . . ?" Her eyes bulged more with every word, almost slobbering with elation.

"Sure . . ." I said halfheartedly, hoping someone, anyone, would show up and demand that she leave me alone.

She was exasperating, I was exasperating, and seriously . . . we were an embarrassment.

Leading the way, she sashayed through the formal living room and down the two steps into the sunken family room. The two rooms were separated by a black cast-iron fence, perched on the higher, carpeted ground. It had never seemed odd to me until this moment. Why would you possibly use an actual fence to divide the two spaces, especially given that you had the natural barrier of the steps? Though I had totally forgotten about it, I had never seen anything like it before or since.

Once down in the family room, which had the same faux-brick floor that stretched from the front entry, Amy led me to the far left corner where two bright-orange bamboo swivel chairs sat. Motioning wildly toward the second chair, she literally screamed, "Here, sit in one of our new chairs, we bought them at the Rattan Mart in Spring, by the Kroger!"

I nodded approvingly, sitting down on the rough tweed surface. It was as cozy as it was dangerous, sure to cause a nasty rash to whomever might dare to sit down in a state of nakedness. I had never thought to think that before, not understanding the nuances of adult nudity until after I moved away, at least from this house.

Little Amy plopped into the chair next to me. It suddenly struck me that the reason nobody else was in the room, the reason I was forced into aloneness with her, was because this was Thanks-freaking-giving. There was lots to do. The younger version of me was oblivious to this, yapping nonstop, going on about something at school, something from Mrs. Atwood's fourth grade class, something about Dreamsicles being available only on Friday.

Though I guess I should have been interested in whatever she had to say, I couldn't do it. I had just gotten to the point, at forty-six, where I could live with who I was now, and like it, or at least accept it. Going back all these years and seeing what sat in front of me, her, us, in full-on hyperness, full-on awkwardness, was too much, way too freaking much.

"Where is Mom, I mean, your mom?" I said, in as commanding a tone as I could muster given the situation. "I should try to help her with the dinner."

"Oh, Mom? She's fine, she likes to do everything herself," Amy said, apparently having Sue totally pegged. "But, I'll show you where the kitchen is anyway." Eagerly grabbing my hand, our hand, she pulled me up and lilted along as we made our way up the two steps into the breakfast room.

Looking down at her little hand in mine, I couldn't get over how tiny she was. She was rail thin, small-boned, and small-waisted. When was it that we became a big-boned, buxom, handsome woman? Was it something she ate, something we ate, after this? I wished I had my iPhone. I could have made a note to look at old photos when I got back, or regained consciousness, to pinpoint when her things became mine. But, wait! There was something! Digging around in my luxurious brown-blazer pocket, I pulled out the notebook and pen I had noticed earlier. Flipping to the first page, I pressed down firmly to get the Bic pen going, scratching out, "*Look at old photos, find out when it was I got big.*" And, "*Cast-iron interior fences . . . Was that really a thing?*"

Looking back down, I realized that Little Amy was waiting for me, staring at me with a mixture of awe and frustration. "Just had to jot something down, for later," I explained.

"Oh, yes!" she declared, as if a thousand flashbulbs had gone off directly in front of her face. "You are a W R I T E R."

She was clearly impressed with me, with us. Despite the fact that I wanted to flee from her like a bone running from a dog, it made me happy. Very happy.

I followed her through the breakfast room and into the kitchen, the sight of which made me audibly gasp—it was glorious, giving me the same triumphant feeling that I had experienced when Mary had turned into Northampton. Red countertops, dark-brown cabinets, harvest-gold appliances, a yellow porcelain sink and a half Jenn-Air grill with a butcher-block cover. Though the room wasn't big, Mom and Dad had somehow managed to shove an antique oak table into the middle of it, like it was the actual built-in kitchen island.

What really made the room pop was the gold linoleum flooring. The small, two-toned pattern ran wall-to-wall from the kitchen to the breakfast room and then, presumably, back into the laundry room and half bath. It was so repetitive and so, well, yellow, it almost made me dizzy. It was like the 1978 American suburbs' version of French toile.

Busy preparing something, Mom had her back to us. Once she figured out we weren't just passing through, she paused and turned. "Would you like something to drink, Amy?" she said. I got that she didn't like playing the hostess, I knew that, but she was trying.

"Well . . . what I'd really like," Little Amy blurted out, shuffling her feet like an Irish dancer, "is a Fresca."

"No!" Mom retorted. "Not YOU. Mrs. Daughters." Her voice changing to an almost genteel quality as she said my adult name.

"No, ma'am," I said, offering what might have seemed like undue respect given our similar ages. "I was going to offer my assistance here in the kitchen."

"Oh, no, that isn't necessary," she said, desperate to send me forth from the safe confines of her realm. "I've done most of the work now, the bird is in the oven, and, most everything else is as far along as it can be. You sit down and relax, everyone will be here soon."

Not wanting to go, but again wanting to run, I, as if by instinct, followed Mom's directions, pausing briefly to watch her go back to work. She seemed taller than I remembered but still just as determined.

I returned down the two steps into the family room and took my seat back in the rattan chair. Little Amy followed closely behind, careful to ensure I was not to be left alone, even for a moment. "You know," she squawked, "I have a bunch of stuffed animals . . . I have a spotted snake, a gray ape, a purple lion, a brown dog and my favorite, well, that's Charles . . ."

Mom's voice bellowed from the kitchen, apparently realizing that the freak that was her second child was off her chain. "Amy, go outside and help your dad and let Mrs. Daughters have a moment!"

I was relieved. She had been shut down. At least for now.

Not missing a beat, Little Me leapt up and smiled crazily and wide-eyed, putting her face way too close to mine, to the point that I could enjoy her questionable breath. She was leaving no doubt, to anyone, that she was a vicious mouth breather.

"See you in just a second!" she screeched, turning dramatically and literally skipping out of the room. Looking back to make sure I was still watching, she disappeared around the corner by the back door, with a flourish and yet another shriek of ecstasy.

She made me feel like I was going to throw up, laugh hysterically, and cry, all in the same moment. She was like a living, breathing stomach virus with a bowl cut.

Sitting back in the chair, I exhaled, looking around. I had spent so much time in this room, but had never, ever, thought about how it would look, or feel, as an adult . . . somebody from the other side. It was filled with colored glass, beams, macramé, and real houseplants, and screamed "1970s!" at the top of its raspy, smoke-filled lungs.

Looking through the French doors and out into the back-yard, I saw the massive back deck. It had three levels, numerous benches, and holes cut out for trees. For kids, it was ideal, stimulating imagination and encouraging physical play. Not that this lofty goal had been the purpose of its construction. No, it would be left to my generation to market a household item as a life-changing, educational experience. My parents had the deck built because it looked really cool, and they could sit on it, and put plants on it, and drink beer on it. Neither of them had ever had the slightest notion that it would ramp up our SAT scores or make us out-of-the-box thinkers or raise our earning potential.

They would have thought that was a load of crap.

Looking further afield, I noticed that the swimming pool had not yet been dug. I also spied the tree that would eventually flank the pool and hold the huge bug zapper that my parents would one day install.

I remembered the time, probably only a couple of years from now, around 1980, when Mom shocked herself with the purple-lighted zapper while blowing off the patio. It was the same day that Dad just so happened to be slightly intoxicated, or totally inebriated, and doing flips off of the diving board.

It was the middle of the afternoon, we were all there, and Dad's maroon and navy plaid terrycloth bathing suit came off after a rather stunning somersault. Mom was mad, really steamed. "Well, Sue, I'm naked as a jaybird!" Dad had exclaimed, paddling about like Esther Williams. Enraged, she got hostile with the leaf blower, flinging it around until she got her orange extension cord tangled up in the bug zapper. Somehow, the intertwined cords caused a current to travel from the zapper to the leaf blower and on to Mom. She had been, well, zapped. With Mom laid out on the pebble-grained patio like a tasered mosquito, a wet and barely covered Dad (remember his name is Dick), majestically leapt to her aid, leaning over her, dripping on her bouffant hair. "Sue! Sue! Are you all right?"

Chivalry was still alive and well in suburbia, but alas, on this day the (drunk) hero's concern would be met only with a flat *"Shut the hell up, Dick!"* from my mother, who rose from the prone position, mustering up enough strength to push him over.

Good times.

Back inside, there was a large TV set enclosed in faux wood cabinetry. It was huge, but a lot like the Ford LTD, it was all trunk and engine, or, in this case, all inlaid wood and fake drawer handles. Seriously, the cabinet itself had to be four feet across and over two feet tall. But the screen, the actual viewing surface, couldn't have measured more than twenty-five inches diagonally. It wasn't big enough to be legitimately considered suitable for group viewing, even in a bedroom.

Directly across from the fireplace was a striped couch and a large, ornate antique pedal organ that I remember my dad being very proud of. Mom was less impressed, even when Kim learned to pump out the theme to the *The Facts of Life* on it.

Between the chairs, where I sat, was a brown wicker lamp that looked like a mushroom, hung on a gold chain that stretched all the way up to the high ceiling. Behind my head, centered over each of the chairs, were two pieces of art (a term I use loosely) of a Mexican girl and boy, painted in fluorescent colors on a tan tweed background.

Across the room from me, next to the steps to the breakfast room, was the bar. It rose above the sunken room with a black countertop that would have been hard for anyone under five feet tall to reach. The interior had red tweed wallpaper, a stainless-steel sink and glass shelves stacked with flashy glassware. It was big enough to hold a couple of adults, but only for the purpose of bartending.

All in all, it was a grand space and could only be fully appreciated in real life.

On the edge of the fireplace, just in front of me, was the morning paper. That's something you wouldn't see in many houses owned by forty-somethings back in the future; no, that's what a Samsung tablet was for. Reaching over, I picked it up, immediately impressed with its weightiness. There must have been one hundred pages of ink in its two inches of girth. Ah, the *Houston Post*, back when it still had the *Chronicle* to compete with, back when newspapers were still keeping it real, or at least they were keeping it thick. It struck me that without news-only channels and the internet, this was the sole source of news in this house. That is, of course, with the exception of the evening news. We trusted those guys on the tube, because we had no choice. Maybe you couldn't count on the internet to be one hundred percent true, but at least you could double-check the facts and decide for yourself. Plus you could check your Facebook account at the same time and stalk people.

"Good Morning," the Post welcomed, "it's Thursday, November 23, 1978."

Doing a quick calculation, I realized, for the first time, that I had been hurled exactly thirty six years into the past. Thirty-six freaking years. If I had been one of those people, I would have said something like "*Wowzers!*" But since clearly I was not one of those people, I muttered under my breath where my mother couldn't hear (because she would have expected something a little stronger), "Holy crap!"

The Thanksgiving front-page headline read "Clements to Seek More Tax Relief, Initiate and Referendum Rights." Browsing the article, I halfway understood that Texas governor-elect Bill Clements—set to replace Dolph Briscoe in January—was advocating some sort of economic recovery. Wait a second, I wondered, who is the president? Obama had been the president this morning, but who was the president in November of 1978? Filing back through the basic history facts in the dark recesses of my mind, wedged somewhere between geography, algebra and that one class I took on fencing, I thought, "Well, Ford took over after Nixon resigned sometime in the '70s and then there was Carter, he came before Reagan, who came in 1980, or maybe 1981." So it must be Jimmy Carter, the Democratic peanut farmer from Georgia. Yes, this must be the national economic crisis highlighted in my memory by pictures of cars lined up at gas pumps. I had never actually seen any cars queued up, waiting for the limited supply of gasoline, but I had read about it and I had seen the photos. Really, the pictures were the only "fact" that had stuck around in my brain long enough to be called back up to consciousness.

Why hadn't we, here in Spring, Texas, seen those lines? And did we feel the financial crunch, suffer the effects of the inflation? I had no idea, and I saw no evidence of it here in this room stuffed with real plants, antiques, and treasures imported from Mexico.

I had lived in 1978, clearly I had, but could I really claim that I was a living, breathing part of the bigger world around me?

Flipping through, I was immediately struck by the ads. While you would expect lots of advertising with Black Friday and the Christmas season at hand, these were all in black-and-white, an artist's reproduction, rather than actual photographs of the goods.

The front page contained a sizeable example with a woman, wrapped in a fuzzy garment, who had an almost constipated look drawn on her face. It was for Joske's, a store I remembered, but didn't know if it was still in business. According to it, you could "Save one third off on soft Boulle coordinates."

Holy Toledo! Boulle! One third off! That was fabulous news! #whatisBoulle?

Continuing on, and wondering if the ink from the pages would stay permanently on my hands, I was shocked, and that was something given how my day was playing out, to find something called "Today's Prayer" on Page 27A.

What? Today's "prayer"? That meant that the *Houston Post*, think about it, the *HOUSTON POST*, sanctioned a direct line to the Heavens—and then published it, along with the weather forecast, the stock market report and the TV listings.

Did the Post employ a staff member to pen this "prayer"? I could still vaguely remember there being a "Religion" section in this same newspaper, or perhaps the Chronicle, but offering a city-wide devotion—that was another thing entirely.

"Dear Jesus Lord, God, help me to love my parents better, and my church and my world for our peace on earth. Amen."
—Pete Litcata, 2001 Hazard

SO, the Post printed the prayers of its readers. And not only did it allow a direct reference to Jesus, indirectly inferring that there was such a person, or being, or power—it printed the prayer's name and his address.

It was stunning. How much had we changed in thirty six years? This much.

I fished back into my blazer pocket and pulled out my notebook and pen. *"When did prayers stop being printed in newspapers?"* followed by *Look up Pete Litcata on Facebook."* And *"Is Joske's still in business? WTF is Boulle?"*

Dad and the kids tromped back inside. Mom's voice met them as soon as they hit the breakfast room. "Go on, and get out of here, I'm BUSY!" She added a quick "Happy Thanksgiving" at the end of the screech, suddenly remembering, I suppose, that she had a guest sitting in the next room.

I felt myself tense up. I think I would have been fine, even thrilled, if I could have been an invisible observer, not forced to interact with the other players in this production, or at least the one who was me.

Rick, Kim and Amy found seats near mine and discussed the impending arrival of their grandparents. Dad whisked through, enthusiastically stating that he was off for a quick shower. This was the kind of thing I remembered vividly, the clean-up always timed carefully so he could arrive back into the room, fresh as a daisy, AFTER the guests had arrived. This was much to my mother's horror and would ramp the stress level up one more critical notch.

Amazingly, as the kids chatted amongst themselves, no one made a move to turn the TV on. They talked about what they were going to play and when they could go back outside. More than anything, they talked about the approaching Christmas season.

"I wonder when the Sears Wish Book will get here . . ." Little Amy said wistfully, with a dreamy look in her Pekinese-like eyes.

"It's already here, A M Y!" Kim sung out, laughing heartily. "And I've already read it in the bathroom and marked what I want."

Little Amy looked disgusted, not by the fact that Kim was handling the Sears Catalog and toilet paper at the same time, but because she had not seen the said Book of Wishes.

"WHERE IS IT?" Amy yelled loudly enough to get the routine "AMY, SHUT UP!" from Mom in the kitchen.

Kim just laughed. "You'll never find it . . ."

This propelled Amy into physical action, fully prepared to fight for her right to look at the men's underwear section.

"Now, girls," Dad said, magically peeking around the door to the master bedroom. "Let's all get along. It's Thanksgiving and you two are sisters . . ."

Kim and Amy sneered at each other, but they stopped. Kim winked as Dad disappeared around the corner and Amy glared back at her sister, reminding her that asses could be kicked if necessary. Really, she should have pounced on Kim, but she didn't. I wasn't sure if I was thankful for that or not.

Kim, as would be her MO as an adult, did not look properly attired for outside play. She wore Jordache jeans tucked into a pair of long leatherette boots. Her shirt had a scoop neck and poufy sleeves, and her hair—well, that was perfectly, almost magically, feathered into wings. All in all, her personal grooming at twelve mirrored what it would look like in her way-off forties, immaculate.

I, on the other hand, looked somewhat disheveled, wearing an aqua striped, collared shirt that fit snugly. Then there was a marginally attractive turquoise Native American necklace. I probably thought it enhanced my status as a pretend warrior princess. My jeans were criminally tight, with crisscrossing multicolored ribbons embellished on the back pockets. Topped off with a pair of green-and-white Adidas tennis shoes, it was a look to be proud of, or not. My hair was surprisingly not unkempt only because its short length and bowl shape made it impossible to leave wholly untidy. Perhaps Mom knew what she was doing with my hair after all. Those frequent trips down to the "Sergeant Snips" hair salon now made perfect sense.

What really captured the essence of me at ten were my glasses. Brown-and-orange frames with enormous square lenses. Wavy arms led to gold metal hooks which attached the unit to my head. If this weren't enough, someone had paid extra money, actual dollars and cents, to have my initials, in gold foil wavy lettering, affixed to the bottom right of the right lens. Maybe that's why my eyes bulged so alarmingly. I was trying to read my initials from the back side of my lenses.

Kim and Rick explained that Dad had just upgraded the Pong game to Atari and maybe later we could play. "Great!" I said, "I've played Atari before, but not in a long, long time!" The kids looked back at me with a mix of wonder and admiration. Before they could ask how it had been *so long* since I played something that had just been introduced, we were interrupted by someone screeching "YOU HOOOOOOOO!"

Chapter Seven

THE WALKING DEAD

*I*t was my paternal grandparents, my dad's mom and dad. It was Grandma and Paw Paw.

Frozen to the seat of my rattan chair, I listened in shock. Everyone had said they were coming, but once the dead people starting showing up, my delusion was notched up to an entirely different level.

As they came down the steps into the sunken living room, I got up, unable, really, to take it all in. Then it hit me, the look on their faces; they looked enthusiastic and pleased, but they didn't know me. My grandparents, my own personal beloved old people, had no clue who I was.

What in the hell was I supposed to say?

Dashing out from the corner of the room, a freshly cleaned Dad gallantly introduced me. "This is Cousin Amy from Ohio!"

"Oh!" Grandma said as she came toward me. "It *is* a pleasure to meet you. Now," she continued while grabbing my hand, but not making me uncomfortable at all, "I am cousin Bee and I am so glad you are here, this is my husband, Gene."

As thrilled as I was to see them, the sight of my dead grandparents shook me to my core. Traveling back in time was one thing—seeing people I'd said goodbye to, forever, was another. I felt a cold sweat come over me, like when you're desperate to use the bathroom but can't. It was like that, only instead, it was my version of reality being spun violently out of control. I didn't need somebody to tell me what was going to happen next, life never allowed that, I needed somebody to explain why this was happening. How it could even happen in the first place.

I was going to need answers.

"Glad you are here!" Gene said. "OK, let's all have a beer. Kids!" he directed, "go out to the garage and get five beers and one small glass for your grandma!" As the three kids bustled off to serve one of the primary purposes of their birth, we all took a seat.

Bee and Gene must have been in their early 60s and looked healthy and robust. Hell, they were younger than my parents were back in my own time. Of all my memories of these two, none were like this. That is, with the exception of the fuzzy family photos. We were living in the photos. The dead people photos.

Paw Paw was wearing his traditional mustard-colored polyester jumpsuit. The cherry on the top was a bolo tie featuring a cow skull. Grandma looked lovely from her not-so-real blonde hair in an upsweep to her blue polyester suit and shiny gold shoes. Even though it was one hundred percent '70s, from top to bottom, she dazzled.

I felt myself go misty as I tried desperately not to stare at them. Being that they were a generation removed from my own, I had always known that they would die. When they did, the loss was metered by the fact that they had lived the "full lives" people were so apt to remind one another of at funerals. That didn't mean I didn't mourn them and miss them. Like a million other people, I regretted all the questions I wished I'd asked them. It wasn't tragic, but from a personal perspective it was monumental, one generation dying off leaving those who remained behind pondering the very meaning of life.

Seeing them now, I would have to fight the urge to weep openly, holding them dramatically to my breast, telling them that I was sorry I didn't appreciate their wisdom and guidance while they were still among us. I was in too big of a damn hurry, we were all in too big of a damn hurry.

It made me realize that I had messed up so many things. Not because I was an idiot, but because, just like everyone else, I was human. Life was about so much more than what it seemed like when we were actually doing it.

I supposed I would never stop missing Grandma. She had such a presence. At forty-six years old, I still found myself desperately wanting to update her on my life, filling her in on all that had happened since she died. No one knew any of these feelings here—it was just normal, regular life. Mom was trying to survive in the kitchen and everyone else was blissfully unaware that this was but a temporary scene, fleeting at best.

Grandma looked younger than I had ever remembered. Really, she had never aged drastically in my eyes, but seeing her in her mid60s, almost a decade younger than my own mother back in the present, put aging in a much different perspective.

"What time does the football start?" Paw Paw asked as he popped open beer number one, placed in a protective Styrofoam koozie.

"Let's see . . ." Dad said as he began to fumble with the large, clunky dial controls on the television set. "Hopefully the antenna will be up to it today!" he added optimistically, but no matter what he did the picture was awful, scratchy and grainy. Luckily no one other than me, from the land of the high definition flat screen 1080p television, seemed to notice or care.

That TV was crap. These people deserved better and they didn't even know it.

Grandma, sitting close to me on the couch, close enough that I could smell her familiar scent, Estée Lauder Youth Dew, began to question me about where I lived and about my family. The earnestness in her voice made me wish I could tell her about my current predicament but, as Mary had said, I knew my limits. There was no way I could tell Grandma, or anyone else, what was "really" going on, who I "really" was. It wasn't only that I was standing in a field of emotional landmines—how could I get anyone else to believe what was happening if I didn't even really believe it myself?

Crossing another item off my fantasy bucket list, I finally got to tell Grandma that I lived in Centerville, Ohio, the same town in which she had raised her own family in the late '40s, '50s and '60s. In real life, we—Willie and I and our oldest son Will—had moved home to Houston from England for less than two years when we added Matthew to our family—before magically being transferred to the Dayton, Ohio, area. Grandma had died just months before we found out about the move. I'd always felt like we missed out on talking about the irony of it. In my real life, I would take my children to the school where she had been the secretary. I drove by her house every day. The chances of us growing up in Houston and one day bringing up our boys in Centerville, Ohio, were a million to one, but it had happened.

Though I couldn't tell her who I was, I could tell her exactly where I lived, and she could say she remembered it. It wasn't as good as her knowing it was me, but it was close. And it was way better than the nothing I had started this trip with. I had always secretly wondered if she had gotten up there to Heaven and managed to arrange the relocation from Texas to Ohio. I obviously couldn't ask her that, because, well, she was really dead and I was really hallucinating.

"Tell me about your children," she said. She had known my oldest boy, Will, but died when I was pregnant with Matthew. As I was throwing up in the bathroom in her hospital room, she told everyone, "Amy and I are both feeling terrible." Only she was in the process of dying, while I was growing a new life, fertilizing it with moon pies and beef jerky. Life is ironic, and gassy.

Telling her about the things Will was doing in school, his aspirations for the future, and then introducing her to the character that is Matthew was nothing short of beautiful. I felt rare tears well up in my over-mascaraed eyes as I spoke of my children, her beloved great-grandchildren, one she would never know but would love just the same. Sensing my emotion, she reached over and grabbed my hand. "You miss your family on Thanksgiving, don't you?" she asked, looking into my eyes.

"Yes," I said. "Yes, I really do . . ."

She had always been my favorite person in the world, the one I respected and looked up to. This talk may not have been the reason for my time travel, but it provided comfort and closure that I didn't even know I needed. Before this meeting, the last time I had seen Grandma she was in the back of an ambulance, her feet flopping uncontrollably as she left the hospital for downtown Houston. That's when her journey would end for real, in the peaceful, unspoken sanctuary of a hospice. Now I had another picture to draw on, one she would have liked better. I preferred it as well.

As we continued to talk, Rick approached me with what could only be referred to as a legitimate dance move, handing me a beer can while completing a full lunge. He definitely had flair, part of his personality mirroring Little Amy's, but he exhibited a far better degree of self-control. "Thanks," I smiled, amused.

"You're so very welcome," he responded, shifting his head sideways, a sly, almost flirtatious look streaming across his face. I chuckled. This vote of confidence sharpened his look even further. He finished with a couple of quick but effective arm motions, returning to a state of cool before anyone even noticed.

He was hilarious.

I slid the can out of the protective holder and found a shiny, red-and-white Old Milwaukee. Wow, I had no idea that anyone would serve this kind of thing to a guest, on a major holiday. The can itself was shorter and wider than what I was accustomed to, but what it lacked in height it gained in sturdiness. Instead of aluminum, it felt like it was made of steel, including the top, which had a tab that had to be completely removed. I hadn't seen one of those in, well, I had no idea when the last time was, and I wasn't sure if I had ever opened a beer that way.

Popping the tab and then ripping it off, I took a huge sip of the full-bodied lager. I needed this nasty morning beer, I needed it in a way that's hard to describe. It was a lot like the pregnant girl with the moon pies, only it wasn't near as messy, or satisfying.

Putting the tab in my blazer pocket for safekeeping, I pulled out my notebook, jotting down, "*When was Atari introduced? When did pull tabs go away?*" and then, "*Buy a vintage Old Milwaukee can on eBay.*"

LITTLE Amy was thrilled with the arrival of new audience members, in a way that made the others' excitement look like amateur hour. She bounded from person to person with such glee, it seemed like she might violently crash into something at any moment. Her exuberance was borderline dangerous.

She reminded me, especially in the facial features, of my oldest son Will. Her actions reminded me more of my Matthew. The thought of me in them, or them in me, was alarming. It was almost as disturbing as when I looked at one of them and saw my in-laws. Nobody warned you that one day you'd look into the fresh face of your beautiful son, the same one who grew in your woman parts, and instead of yourself, or your people, you'd get a glimpse of your mother-in-law, or your husband's uncle.

So, in comparison, I guess seeing shades of Will and Matthew in the young me wasn't all that bad, unless we were talking about the young me that was dancing around like a wild freak, at ten. The same one with all those awkward, painful years ahead of her. They could have done worse for a mom, but surely they could have done better. It was just the kind of thought that made Milwaukee famous—for brewing this beer that I was going to finish in the next three seconds.

As I forced the last sip of the lager down, I could hear the back door open again. It must be my other grandparents, my mom's mom and dad. We called them Granny and Granddaddy. They lived in an apartment in the Bellaire section of Houston. One of the true highlights of our childhood was when Kim, Rick and I would go there for a visit.

The arrival of Granny and Granddaddy was met with an unexpected degree of casualness, on all fronts. The five people who lived in this house just didn't seem as excited as they had been when Grandma and Paw Paw had arrived. It's wasn't like it was blaringly obvious. It was subtler, like my breasts. Only I think that's called supple. If I had my iPhone, I could have looked that, and a bunch of other stuff, up.

"I'm Ruth MacCurdy, and this is my husband, Frank," my other grandmother explained, treating me like the stranger I had become. Ruth and I had been great friends when I was younger, from ten to twelve, or, right about now, I guessed. We talked on the phone several nights a week, discussing nighttime soaps like *Dallas* and *Dynasty*.

The greetings died down quickly, kicking off the small talk associated with adults that are forced together by circumstance. Funny, I had never seen this group from that perspective before now. I, in my pea-sized hyper brain, had assumed they were just as happy to be here as I was. But now, I could feel tension. Where before there had been lively conversation amongst the adults, now there was a great calming. It was almost like everyone was taking a collective breath, cautiously, before continuing. I shook my beer can, hoping one of the kids—maybe even the younger version of me—would help me visit Wisconsin again. I couldn't become a regular though. That might mean blowing this whole scene up, dramatically revealing an identity that didn't actually exist.

Dad made the shocking observation, shocking to me at least, that it was already the fifteenth anniversary of JFK's assassination in Dallas. I was totally mesmerized by the fact that I had lived in a time so close to events that seemed like they'd happened fifty years ago.

Granddaddy brought up the happy topic of "That crazy suicide pact in Jonestown, South America." I was fuzzy on the details, but I was sure they were referring to Jim Jones' "Kool-Aid" mass-suicide pact. I had seen a clip about it on the front page of the newspaper. It must have just happened because the headline was something about the bodies being airlifted out.

It reminded me of a song my sister listened to in the '80s. I think it was called "Guyana Punch." Was it sung by a local Houston group called The Judy's? I wasn't sure, but I was struck with the inappropriate and macabre nature of a song commemorating such an event, especially the jazzy number I was remembering.

AFTER her parents arrived, Mom had only sat down briefly and then returned to the kitchen. The kids ran in and out, mostly congregating in close proximity to the grandparents. It was easy to see that a special bond existed between them. Though I had always assumed this was due to the obvious grandparent/grandchild angle, I realized that they also all fell outside of the twenty-five to sixty age bracket. This meant that neither group—the kids or the elderlies—was considered a serious part of any legitimate decision-making. The kids were too young and naïve to add any value and the older people too out of touch. Even though I was still a certified forty-something, my precarious role as a time traveler made me realize that leaving either group out was a huge error in judgement.

I also noticed that not one member of the party had risen to offer Mom assistance with the daunting task of Thanksgiving dinner. Again, I had assumed that Mom would have had the help of the other grown women in the group. Did she do this all herself because she wanted to, or because she had to? Pulling the little notebook back out, I jotted down, *"Ask Mom about help with Thanksgiving dinner. This is ridiculous."* And *"Judy's—Guyana Punch???"*

Chapter Eight

BITCHES, BALLERS, AND OLIVE BRANCHES

*N*ot sure where the hell I fit into this picture, I rose and went, seemingly unnoticed, into the kitchen. I was hesitant, but justified the intrusion by convincing myself that Mom must need assistance.

"Can I help you, Sue?" I asked, trying to sound casual as I stood shuffling my rubber, leatherette heels on the linoleum.

"Oh no, I'm doing fine," she replied, dicing an onion on an unusual three-legged chopping board that was shaped like a birthday cake.

"Here, let me do that, I feel useless." Without a word, she moved across the room, not turning back to offer any instruction. "Thanks," I said, "I needed to get up."

"I understand," Mom said. "I prefer to be up and busy."

"Me too," I said, watching her as she shifted things around on the stove top.

She looked so different, so young and so steady. The aging she surely felt, today, at forty-something, wasn't near what it would become. I knew if she could hurl forward as I had hurled backward, she would be shocked at the sight of herself at seventy-five. All physical changes aside, she was the same Mom I had always known, busy, productive, and determined. For all her laid-back nature, the one that didn't care about material things, or what we were doing, or where we had gone, she had a striking undercurrent of intensity. It bubbled in a way I had never noticed before, at least at this age. The age when I apparently wasn't registering anything important.

Looking at her now, it was a lot like that feeling I got when I put a new prescription of contact lenses in for the first time, or like the first time I ever saw a college football game in high-def. I had seen it all before, only this time it was bolder, more vivid, with every detail standing out like a new discovery.

I felt an immediate closeness to this younger Sue, but I innately understood that there was no way she could return my misplaced sense of intimacy. I was an unwanted stranger in her house as opposed to a person whose life had begun at the end of her birth canal.

"What is your family doing for Thanksgiving?" Mom asked. "You have two children, don't you?"

"They are spending the holiday with close friends of ours in Ohio," I said. "I have two boys, one seventeen and the other eight. I'm sure they miss me but, really I'm rarely gone if ever." Mom nodded, but behind her casual look you could tell that this wasn't an arrangement that would have been acceptable in 1978, especially not in suburbia, where everyone stayed home. Come to think of it, there wasn't a mom on this block who worked outside of the home. How different that was from my suburban street in Ohio, where I was one of only two moms at home. In 1978, you would have been greeted with words like, "You work, really?" while in 2014 it would be more like, "You stay home, really?" What a difference those thirty-five years made for women in middle-class America. Was it their desires that had changed or, instead, was it expectations that had shifted? Either way, Mom and I were having very different experiences as mothers and wives, very different indeed.

"You write, don't you?" Mom asked, grasping at conversation straws. Without waiting for an answer, as if she had suddenly decided she was interested, she said, "I have always wanted to write but could never find the time." I knew that about her and remembered her orange Litton portable typewriter with the black-and-red ink ribbon. She had dreamed of becoming a Hollywood History writer, "Nostalgia," she had called it, especially interested in the stars and starlets who had passed away at a young age.

She was gifted with words, but unfortunately lived in a time where the typical housewife was not expected nor encouraged to express herself outside of her obvious duties. She wrote funny poems and could always be counted on for a humorous quip or biting comeback. People thought I was a good writer, but she had entertained far more words than I could have ever hoped to meet.

I couldn't tell her that in my opinion, the only difference between my part-time gig as a writer and her unfound aspirations was the year we were born. First, this established the expectation that she wouldn't have a side interest that generated income, and secondly, there was no internet to shrink the world and increase creative opportunities. Since I couldn't explain the effects of the World Wide Web on the role of women in society, I said the only thing I could. "Well, you should write, maybe when the kids are at school, even for just a little bit each day. It is a release for me, and it's not even about being good. Even if nobody reads it and you never get paid, it's a part of you and an accomplishment in itself."

Mom finally looked at me directly. "You know," she stated, "you're right, I need to try that. Try something."

After a long pause, she smiled genuinely, leaning against the red countertop. "Do you like the holidays?"

"I do," I responded. "I have happy memories of the holidays as a kid." Because apparently I was a truncated idiot completely oblivious to everything that was going on around me. "My immediate family is still close and even though we are all very different, we are lucky because we really do enjoy being together. You know, there is stress, it gets loud and people make unfortunate comments but, overall, it's all good."

"That's nice," Mom said. "Frankly, the holidays tend to stress me out." I couldn't believe she was opening up so quickly, but, then again, she had no female contemporary at most of these gatherings. She didn't have any sisters, and her brother, Frank, had died of cancer in his twenties. There was also a lack of cousins, or really any other extended family.

Dad had only one sibling, a sister, Aunt Susie, and as far as I could remember, at this time, the 1978 one, her family would have just moved into the Houston area. I didn't know why they weren't here today, but I guess they must have gone back to Ohio, from whence they came, for the holiday. So as of now, Thanksgiving 1978, it was just Mom, her mother—whom she had her own challenges with—and her mother-in-law, who was a great lady, but was just that, her mother-in-law. Then, of course, it was the husband and kids, the people that she needed to talk about, not with. Maybe she was happy just to have someone, anyone, to talk to on this, the national day of stress and giblets.

I tried to think of who her good friends would have been at this time, and honestly I couldn't think of anyone outside of our neighbors, a loose connection at best. I also couldn't remember her ever going out for a girl's night. That shocked me. Didn't everyone do that? Maybe she had lots of close friends, but I, once again, wasn't paying any attention to anyone but myself. Or, maybe she was so busy trying to survive everyday life, a marriage, and a family that there was little, if any, time for her.

Either way, Mom and I were having very similar experiences as mothers and wives, very similar indeed.

We definitely had our moments while I was growing up. We struggled with each other, especially through my teen years, well, I guess through all my years, including the ones that were going on right now. I guess that kind of stuff is typical of many mothers and daughters, no matter when they live in history. In fact, I knew that was true because I had plenty of friends with daughters. Conflict seemed almost inevitable.

As I got older, I had always assumed it was just that our personalities clashed, or that somehow my place in the family wasn't clear. Though I couldn't confirm it, I was always left with an overwhelming feeling that I wasn't her favorite, or even her number two. Sometimes I questioned if she even loved me, or liked me. Maybe I had made that up in my own mind, or maybe it was true, who knew.

Did things happen the way I remembered them? And what was the value of revisiting any of it? Did it really matter how we dealt with each other thirty years ago as long as we could still manage to be in the same room, happily, back in the future?

Mom had her fair share of baggage from her own childhood, stuff she couldn't completely rid herself of. Perhaps alcohol numbed her pain. I had always assumed that, but I also understood that alcohol seemed to amplify her emotions, both good and bad. I never knew any of that until I got older, until I moved away and had an opportunity to compare my life at home to my life not at home.

One of the benefits of being totally self-absorbed, or programmed to accept your circumstances as the way things should be, especially in upper middle-class America, is that you are, by nature, unaware of the unacceptable things going on right under your nose. Things had happened here, in this house, and I didn't identify it as worth questioning until I was gone. Perhaps it's also a mode of self-preservation—a subconscious choice not to feel everything as it's actually happening.

I had caught glimpses (as a young adult) at the harshness that could be suffered at the hands of my mom's mother, and though I began to understand life isn't always the way it appears on the surface, I never did a good job of connecting all the little emotional dots. It's something I still couldn't achieve at forty-six, so at ten it was bound to be a fruitless task. That is, if I ever even had a notion to think about anything like that.

Things get even trickier in a culture where the adults never talk about the difficult stuff. The result is that reality is draped in a thick fog. Did everything I thought I remembered really happen, or did I make it all up? Things that aren't discussed, over time, become almost surreal. The younger you are when it happens, the denser the fog.

Maybe we were a lot alike, Mom and I, or, maybe we were totally different. The process of becoming a mother had made me realize how wise she really was. Wise, and then ridiculous, and then old. It came in stages. I knew she hadn't always been right, I was damn sure of that, because I remembered some of it, a lot of it. And it was bad. But how was I so sure that I wasn't wrong?

And who held the keys to the real version of what happened if I didn't?

Rick and Kim dashed through the room toward the garage. Apparently it was time for everyone's next adult beverage.

"Amy," Mom said, "you should have the kids bring you another beer and sit down in the other room and relax. I'm almost done here." I tried to tell her how happy I was, well kind of, to stay in the kitchen, and she briefly relented, drawing out what felt like a very few precious moments, harrowing, meaningful, and empty.

Hell, we were both in our forties. We were both homemakers, we were both wives, we were both moms, we both had mothers-in-law. Everyone expected clean underwear and shiny toilets—we both probably thought that was crappy in a good kind of way. We were suddenly contemporaries. Yeah, there was the past, but there would always be the past, but here and now was worth trying to experience on its own merits. Even when here and now was the past.

"Let's go make ourselves social," Mom said, sighing as she

placed a dish towel back on the yellow sink. I smiled and agreed, following her out of the kitchen.

Finding our seats, I glanced at the TV long enough to realize that the Redskins were playing the Cowboys in Dallas. I looked for a score and realized that there would have been no such tally permanently affixed to the screen with sports updates scrolling endlessly beneath. This was pre-cable, pre-ESPN, pre-up-to-the-second information overload. Honestly, it was pre-historic. I wondered how these people dealt with not knowing what was REALLY going on.

"What's the score?" I asked, proud that I could offer up something audible to the entire group. Maybe I was blossoming into this role, maybe Mary was right—maybe it would be all right.

"It's the second quarter," Granddaddy answered with pleasure, "and Dallas is up thirteen to nothing."

Great, I thought, my team can't even win in the past. Just then, through the grainy reception, my spirits dropped even further as Roger Staubach flung a long pass to Drew Pearson, who scampered into the end zone for a fifty-three-yard Dallas touchdown. This followed by a Rafael Septien extra point made the score twenty to zip in the second quarter.

I never liked Rafael Septien.

The small Cowboys contingency, consisting of Granny and Granddaddy (who both grew up in Dallas) and my dad (who as the host was being hospitable, but couldn't, wouldn't root for Dallas in real earnest) were elated, while the Luv Ya Blue Houston Oilers fans, consisting of everyone else with exception of both versions of me, seethed with apathy.

Here's the deal—if you were from Dallas, you didn't root for a lowly Houston team, and if you were from Houston, you would never in a zillion years cheer for those snobby Dallas teams. Those folks thought they were the epitome of fashion, oil and banking. When in reality, what was going on up there was nothing more than a few half-decent-sized skyscrapers trimmed in green neon, a ridiculous glass ball on a stick, and a waft of cow patties from the Stockyards.

It's something that nobody seemed to remember—until the wind shifted.

I could really sink these Cowboys fans' ships if I told them that their precious "America's Team" was destined to experience a crushing loss to the Steelers (which both Texas fan bases hated) in the Super Bowl. At least there was that.

On the flip side, I could shock the Oilers' supporters by spinning a wild tale of turncoat-Houstonian Bud Adams yanking the team from H-town, leaving for Nashville, Tennessee, over a new stadium squabble. Suddenly, what we had once proudly heralded as the "Eighth Wonder of the World"—the Astrodome itself—wouldn't be good enough for the powder-blue-suited traitor. It would be a long wait, but these chosen football people, assembled here on this national day of thanks, were destined to become . . . Texans fans.

Drop the mic.

Mom slipped away back into the kitchen. While the guys continued to watch the game, I noticed that my paternal grandmother, Bee, was making continual, almost desperate attempts to engage my maternal grandmother, Ruth, in conversation. Despite her efforts, she couldn't manage to squeeze more than a few polite words.

"Did anyone read about that doctor from Houston involved in the mass suicide?" Granddaddy asked, during a commercial break, apparently intent on keeping it real.

"Yes!" Grandma said, moving to the edge of her seat, relieved that someone was willing to talk. "One of the survivors saw him mixing the poison into the juice before it was served."

"Good Lord!" Granny said.

"He graduated from Lamar High School," Granddaddy continued, "in River Oaks." He emphasized this part because, I guessed, a former student from the most exclusive neighborhood in Houston would be an unlikely candidate to use his hard-earned medical license to give hundreds of people an express lane to cult-driven suicide.

I hadn't known there was so close a personal connection to Houston.

"Dick," Granddaddy asked Dad. "Do you have yesterday's paper? It was in there."

Dad retreated to the kitchen briefly and then reappeared behind the cast-iron fence in the formal living room. He returned down the steps, while reading aloud, "The guy's name was Dr. Larry Schacht, he graduated from Lamar in 1968. His brother is Danny Schacht, who lives in Montrose."

"How in the world can that happen to someone with such a solid upbringing?" Granny asked.

"I suppose," Grandma stated with some level of caution, "money doesn't always equal decency."

"Hmmm . . ." Granny almost snorted. "But it doesn't equal criminal activity either."

She looked over to Grandma, as did everyone else brave enough to lift their eyes away from the burnt-orange rug. I guess Grandma had started it, but she wasn't going to let it go any further. That didn't surprise me, but even the hint of conflict certainly did.

I was sitting between my two grandmothers, people I had seen in the same room a hundred times, including at my graduation, my wedding and in the hospital room where I delivered our first son, their first great-grandchild. In all that time, I had never noticed conflict. They must have shielded us, the kids, from it.

As Grandma turned back to the game, the room fell silent.

I scanned everyone's faces quickly, almost manically, trying to figure out what I was supposed to look at. It was too much. Too freaking much. Feeling something touching my hand, I looked to my right to see Granny's thin, almost bony fingers.

"So," she asked carefully, with a sweet drawl apparently

reserved for strangers and grandchildren, "Sue tells me that you are a writer?"

"Yes, ma'am," I said with as much respect as I could muster. I knew that kind of stuff mattered to Ruth MacCurdy, plus I had to prove that I wasn't just another half-cocked Midwesterner. She had opinions about Northerners, Yankees—a viewpoint I had once shared, that is before I had moved away, back and then away again. There were good and bad people everywhere, in every city, every country, and even in this room—with a giant antique pedal organ, an instrument that my dad loved with all his heart, and my mom hated with every ounce of her soul. She would sell it for $125 in 1991. He would re-acquire the exact same model in 2013 for $1025.

"I mostly write about sports," I said, "but I also like to think of myself as an author of unpublished books."

"Oh," she said. "Sports . . . That's interesting . . ." Even though she obviously wasn't totally on board with skirt-wearers posting football stats, she didn't push it, instead shifting her body toward me in a way that made me feel wholly legit. "I write too!"

What? She wrote? Like me? That is where it had come from? I had always thought I was more like my "other" grandparents, the ones who seemed easier to connect with.

"Yes," she continued, settling back, but still maintaining a ladylike posture in her red pantsuit with wide white checks. "I wrote for the *Waco News-Tribune*."

"Really?" I asked. I had thought my deep connection with Granny had ceased when we both grew out of watching nighttime soaps. It had never seemed the same once I was a teenager. Then, well, there was the ugly incident after my wedding. Her neighbor and lifelong friend had graciously sent us a gift, and I had exceeded the three-month rule on sending a thank-you note. I could have done better, that's true, but she handled her disappointment aggressively.

It was one of those "lightbulb" moments. Mom had always hinted, not full-on described, that her mom could be a real pain in the ass. I had always seen her as my beloved grandmother, nothing more, nothing less. Being here, in 1978, and watching my ten-year-old cluelessness combined with the adults' "let's shield the kids from reality" stance made me understand how this worked. I guess in this case it was OK to sacrifice honesty for peace? Even if that was so, the peace was nothing more than a cover-up. It made what happened fifteen years from now, in 1993, even easier to understand.

Granny had called me at our apartment in the Woodlands. Without pausing for any niceties, she ripped me up one side and down the other. She called me an "embarrassment" and told me she couldn't believe that I had not taken the time to send a thank-you note when her friend had gone out of her way to send me such a nice gift. She told me she had always thought more of me, and would have never, in a million years, thought I would have done something like this.

Could I really be her granddaughter?

She didn't know, but she was sure she didn't want to see me, or speak to me, anytime soon. And I had better write the thank-you note, and any others still outstanding. Now.

I was devastated.

And this time I told people—my new husband Willie, my dad (who told my mom for me) and my sister, who had the decency never to really forgive Granny.

If nothing else, I had just been treated to the version of Ruth MacCurdy that Mom experienced through her entire life. Once the dust settled, and that took a while, I understood my mom, and some of the things she did, a little better. That said, it would never explain everything, because eventually, perhaps inevitably, things would spin totally out of control. Of course we never talked aloud about that. Never.

As for me, a couple of weeks after the incident I either (a) realized that I loved Granny and didn't want to spend the rest of her life with an ugly issue hanging over our heads, (b) thought it truly was my fault, and wanted to fix it or, (c) was inspired not by my own person, but by a higher power who better understood the long-term ramifications of the situation.

Regardless of why, I sent her a card. It said nothing more than "Thinking of You" or "Love You" or some crap like that. I don't really remember what the outside said, but I do remember the inside, because I wrote, "Granny, I love you no matter what. Love, Amy." Looking back on it now, in retrospect, it makes me feel like a total victim.

The truth is, I really should have written the thank-you note sooner after the wedding, and you know what? I should have done a bunch of other crap I should have done too, but that doesn't mean people, any people, much less your own grandmother, should call you up and tell you that you suck and they don't want to have anything to do with you anymore.

But, maybe that's what forgiveness isn't, it isn't so much about saying what the other person did was OK, but that you are releasing them from it for your sake. So you can move on. So you can have peace. So you can be a suburban wife and mother who is in her right mind at the Cub Scout banquet. And maybe, on the flip side, that's what we're all hoping other people will do after we've disappointed and hurt them. Because of all the things I didn't understand, my lack of perfection wasn't one of them.

ABOUT seven days after I mailed Granny the card, I got a reply, a small blue note card written in her shaky hand.

Dearest Amy,

Thank you so much for the sweet card. Hope I'm forgiven for being so horrible to you. There was no excuse for my behavior just because I didn't feel good.

You have always been so dear and thoughtful to Granddaddy and me. We do love you very much and there are no words great enough to express our feelings for you.

Our close friends the Loudens are celebrating their sixtieth wedding anniversary Sept. 29. Their two sons and grandchildren are honoring them with a reception and seated dinner at Ridgewood C.C. on the thirtieth — which is also my eightieth birthday. We are looking forward to it very much. We do so little. We celebrate our fifty-ninth on the twenty-ninth.

Hope this finds you and Willie OK. Take care and please know that we love you very much.

Granny

Until that moment, I hadn't realized that I would have never gotten Granny's letter, something I've saved in a box in my nightstand ever since, without first sending the card. Yes, I was, again, the spineless victim, the one who also sent a nice card to my attacker. But, without the olive branch there would have been no blue note addressed to "Mrs. William Daughters."

Was the attack justified and made welcome because of the heartfelt note? No, but all I could control was my response, which resulted in her finally telling me, on paper, that despite her actions, she loved me very much.

She was flawed, but so was I.

"What did you write about?" I asked her, desperately trying to keep my head above the water-line of reality.

"Well," she said, "I wrote a society column at another paper in Waco, but at the *Tribune* I was the fashion editor."

The fashion editor?

Really?

I knew she was fashionable, she always looked nice, but the FASHION EDITOR of an actual newspaper? That was totally, completely legit.

How could Kim, our resident expert on fashion, the same girl who wouldn't buy clothing in a store that didn't "smell" right, not know about this?

Why didn't Mom tell me about this? Why didn't anybody tell me anything? It was like that time that Mom and Dad told me, in like 2012, that those wild tomatoes that grew down by the pipe that crossed the creek deep in the woods behind our house, where we played when we were kids, grew only by virtue of people eating tomatoes and then passing the seeds, allowing the said fruit (or vegetable) to be born again near the sewage area where, you know, the seeds came back.

Why wouldn't you tell somebody that? Luckily we didn't eat them, but we could have. Good Lord, if I was the mom and knew that, I would have NEVER let my two boys down there by the said pipe, or, I would have gone down there and killed all those shit-maters myself.

Some stuff should be told.

"In January of 1966," Granny continued, unaware of my mental diversion to tomato-gate, "the *Tribune* sent me to New York City to meet with the director of the New York Couture Group and report back on the fashion scene. I stayed at the Hotel Astor and had a room looking out over the north part of Central Park."

Really? Seriously?

I pulled out my notebook as she continued, jotting down, "*Go to Newspapers.com: Search for Waco Tribune-Herald, Ruth MacCurdy, Fashion Editor, 1966*" and then, "*Google: Hotel Astor, Central Park, NY. Sewage tomatoes.*"

I couldn't help myself. I literally gushed, rather dramatically, as she continued with her story. She was overjoyed with my outpouring of awe. We were having a moment, an adult moment, and each party was thrilled in the company of the other.

Her feat was on par with my trip to the Orange Bowl press box to cover the Clemson-West Virginia game. It sounded like the outcome of her journey was less lopsided than mine, but both of us had experienced blockbuster, once-in-a-lifetime trips that nobody ever talked about.

My granny was a writer, and she was talented enough to have been sent to New York City on a fashion fact-finding mission.

Was I duly impressed?

Absolutely.

If I would have had the courage I wasn't born with, I would have gotten up and told the entire roomful of people I was sitting with, in 1978, just how impressive Granny's feat was.

But I didn't, and so, like a million other touch points in my life, the moment passed without action.

The conversation between Granny and me eventually faded into awkwardness. Now we were the ones who turned to the game, trying to seem interested in something we weren't, desperately wanting something more.

Maybe that was the meaning of life.

Chapter Nine

FUNK & WAGNALL'S

*U*nable to cope with the renewed silence, and my own inner monologue, I lamely excused myself and wandered off in search of something else that looked normal but wasn't. Winding back through the formal living room, I noticed the stained-glass windows that Dad had installed in the doors of the three tall built-in cabinets. I knew if I opened them, which I desperately wanted to do, I would find approximately three guns and then stacks of glass insulators—bell-shaped, thick-glass objects with internal threading. We had amassed the collection from the side of the railroad tracks when the phone and electricity lines had been modernized. Dad had loved to drive us three around, teaching us to carefully look out the back windows of his Oldsmobile for utility poles with missing insulators. When we signaled a find, he would pull his car slowly off the road and we would get out, combing the area for green or white glass treasures. Often, if a prize hung within reach off a leaning or damaged pole, he would put one of us on his shoulders and we would pluck it down. I wondered what happened not only to the insulators, but the actual memory of all the other little things I had forgotten to remember.

Climbing the stairs, I heard music, laughter and the distinct sound of a tambourine. It was at this point that I passed from being stunned and apprehensive to, if only temporarily, genuinely wanting to be involved in whatever was going on at the top of the harvest-gold stairs. I had never envisioned actually reliving my childhood in person, but if I would have, if it really was possible, I would have dialed up scenes of Kim and Rick and I playing together. They had always known what a freak I was and they never seemed to care, accepting me, literally, at face value. If they didn't, they certainly wouldn't verbalize it, as all we really had was each other. The alternative was a quiet closet.

But the merriment ended the minute my Sears Best shoe hit the top step. With the intrusion of a stranger, whatever they had been doing in the game room came to a screeching halt.

"Oh, I'm sorry," I said, not wanting to be forty-something. "What's going on?"

A trusting bond had not been formed and so, Kim, the obvious spokesperson, said, "We were just playing . . ."

"What were you playing?" Fumbling for the right words and not wanting to seem creepy, I said, "When I was a kid I had an older sister and a younger brother and we made up all kinds of crazy games." I emphasized the last bit. "It was the most fun I have ever had."

Apparently these naïve little suburbanites had been trained to automatically accept whatever an adult said as irrefutable, never debriefed on "Stranger Danger" or "Stop! Don't Touch Me There, This is my Special Square" because the young Weinlands politely let me roll on. "Yes . . . we did some hilarious things, no one else might have thought they were funny, but, we did. And you know what? I told myself I would never, ever forget what it was like to be a kid."

Even though it was true, every last word, it was also total crap. But it worked. Kim, Amy and Rick didn't really say anything, but they also didn't seem to mind when I sat down on the next half-flight of stairs up. They could never know that I was completely aware of the fact that these stairs—which had apparently shrunken down to where my big butt barely fit on them—were the "stands" for any type of performance that might be staged in this room. I knew this because I had once made that same stage shine.

"OK!" the youthful Amy screamed. "We call this the GONG SHOW and here is how we play it: Each of us comes up with an act and we do it for the other two. They are the judges, if they like it, they watch all of it and give it a score, if not they hit the tambourine—THE GONG—and we have to stop the show. Now," she continued as if this was the most important part, "we have two tambourines, one from Disneyland, it is blue and has a picture of Donald Duck on it, and you have to be careful with it because it's P A P E R. The second one is wood and is from M E X I C O." Good thing the bilingual Ms. Hyper talked slowly so I could manage to follow. Yes, I remembered this game, and if this had been Vegas, three-to-one odds were that I (in the form of ten-year-old Amy) would get gonged first. It was a sure thing.

"That's right," Kim followed up, walking toward me. "We'll give you the extra gong and use it only if you NEED to." I was given the Mexican gong, because apparently, I couldn't be trusted with the fragile one.

With this, the players went off to their respective areas to continue to prepare for their performances. Settling in my seat, I realized how rough and itchy the carpet was. I knew Mom and Dad would have selected a quality product when they did the interior of this house, but still, I was shocked at how abrasive it was. I tried not to wonder what would happen if somebody were to have actual sexual relations on this type of surface. It had to have happened, and would have resulted in serious burns. It made me think of that show *Sex Sent Me to the ER*. These were thoughts I had never had in this room, and as inappropriate as they probably were, it was hard to clean up my mind, even in the presence of the virtuous youths, especially the one I was.

My worlds were colliding.

In an attempt to get more comfortable, I reached down to

the bottom of the stairs and grabbed a bright paisley-print pillow, thinking I could put it between the hard step and my lower back. With the pillow in my hand I paused, realizing that the room had gone eerily silent, each of the three kids frozen, staring directly at me with a look of terror on their young faces.

"Noooo!" Kim screeched from the far-left corner.

"Put that *down!*" Amy chimed in.

"THAT'S THE PEE PILLOW! Rick added in high tones I didn't remember him being capable of.

A smile crept over my face. My God, it was the Pee Pillow. Instantly, I realized I couldn't smile, I couldn't even smirk—I couldn't know of the legend of the Pee Pillow. If I did, I would have lots of explaining to do and would likely have been thrown out of the house. Though that might have sounded inviting even thirty minutes ago, this was the part I wanted to see. I did not want to go now.

"What?" I said, trying to sound confused.

"It's the Pee Pillow!" Kim said, walking toward me.

"Yeah," Amy added, "we were playing musical chairs with the song on the record player and it skipped . . ."

"It WAS really funny," Kim cut in, defensively.

"Kim was sitting on that pillow . . ." Amy continued, pointing at the fluffy square I was still holding.

"Yeah, she was sitting on it all right," Rick added, snorting like his wife would do thirty-five years from now.

"And she laughed so hard, that, she . . ." Now Amy was also in hysterics, to the point that she couldn't continue.

"And, I peed on it," Kim said flatly, grabbing the pillow from me. "I peed on it, and it smells bad, and we never told Mom, because she would have been REALLY, REALLY, REALLY mad."

"Oh," I said, not sure how I was supposed to handle this stunning admission. "That's pretty funny, but I get it, I won't say a word."

Kim looked pleased with this, but Amy and Rick were too busy reliving the incident to care what I thought about it.

She, Kim, had always had a bladder, and even a bowel control issue. Really, Mom probably would have been OK with it if she had known it was Kim who was the pee-ster. Anyone else may well have gotten the wrath destined for someone bold enough to urinate on the housewares.

"OK," Kim said, "let's get on with the show."

In a dramatic flash befitting such an auspicious occasion, Little Amy flourished in front of the stairs and loudly announced, complete with over-the-top facial expressions and a certain amount of flailing, "WELCOME, TO THE THANKSGIVING 1978 GONG SHOW!"

I couldn't have been more pleased. I was ecstatic.

Rick was contestant number one, leaving Kim, as the contestant-in-waiting, with the other coveted tambourine. With Kim's help, Rick cued up a 33 1/3 rpm disc on the red-white-and-blue record player in the corner of the room. After the crackles and pops that occur when a needle meets vinyl, the familiar sounds of the *Star Wars* theme song filled the room with its dramatic, brassy tones.

Rick's act consisted of him running around the room while the song played, clutching to his breast—his man breast—a variety of small action figures as he darted from corner to corner. He switched figures on what seemed to be about a thirty-second interval, not unlike shift changes in hockey. R2D2, C3PO, Chewy, and Luke Skywalker all made appearances. The only thing better than his quasi-legit dance moves were his facial expressions, which were less hyper and disturbing than those of Little Amy's. What he did have was the gift of pure humor versus her knack for unadulterated bizarreness.

The best bit came when the music slowed down, a part of the song that seemed almost mystical, like maybe unicorns would crash out of the closet door and prance around. This was when he did some slow-mo stuff, winking at the audience while managing some almost inappropriate body contortions. If it had not been 1978, I would have sworn that it wasn't Rick but his youngest son, Finn, putting on the show.

As the end drew near, he threw his props and other random items in the air and then acted like he was shooting some invisible enemy with an imaginary laser.

Well done, Rick, well done.

Kim, Little Amy and I applauded as he bowed deeply. Luckily, and as expected, no gong was sounded in response to his performance.

I was next, or, Amy was next. Deep in my soul, I knew that this was going to be something to remember. My young hyper-self was nothing less than a robust performer. I expected a full-blown, overwhelming effort that would more than likely receive the dreaded tambourine gong.

It would be worth it. I was ready.

After several long moments, Amy emerged from one of the bedrooms that flanked the open game area. She was carrying a thin, hardcover book and was dressed in a bulky, ill-fitting outfit. "My show!" Amy declared loudly, as if we were in a concert hall. "Is brought to YOU by FUNK & WAGNALL'S animal encyclopedias!" Kim and Rick chuckled nominally, as if maybe they had heard this sponsor mentioned at an earlier date. She thought she was getting away with saying something funny and borderline profane. To her, and many others, it was the F-word of encyclopedias. But I knew that the young naïf didn't even know the word she thought she was referring to. This enhanced my appreciation, really.

After she discarded the book in a dramatic fashion, literally flinging it across the room, she started in on the main event. "I'm Sally from Sally's Pant Shop in Spring, Texas," she shouted, so excited she nearly couldn't go on. "And I'm here to introduce you to our new line of clothing." With this, she paraded around so everyone could see that she was wearing what I assumed to be one of Mom's old polyester knit blouses paired with blue polyester pants. They looked to be from the earlier '70s, that is, earlier than the ones I had magically been dropped into. Next, she screamed, panting loudly as if about to burst from sheer excitement, "And if you don't like these, then, there is another!" With this, she quickly took off the blue pants, revealing a noxious green-and-white plaid pair of pants. "AND, this!" she continued, yanking off the blouse to uncover a secondary shirt that might have matched the pants.

She repeated this one more time, exposing another complete outfit, and then flung about wildly screeching about how "it was three outfits in one." She was extremely pleased with her presentation. Young Rick, on the other hand, at the constant prodding of the gong-less Kim, reached for the Disney tambourine and readied it for the obvious and predestined shutdown. Reaching across time, decorum and reasonableness, I leaned down to the next step and gently put my forty-six-year-old hand on my eight-year-old brother's shoulder. He shuddered and looked up, probably shocked that I had touched him, but, displaying the respect to adults he had been trained to exhibit, he paused. "We should let her go," I whispered with Little Amy still banging on. "I think she needs the chance to finish." Rick looked at me with a puzzled expression, glanced over at Kim for backup, but followed my orders despite the fact that she was staring at me like I had three eyes.

The least I could do was help the poor girl out. This may have been the first (and last) time she was ever allowed to finish an act.

Thankfully, the ending was short and relatively painless. All it took were a few more flourishes, the introduction of a straw hat with a mound of colorful flowers on top of it, some exquisite facial expressions, and a near-disastrous run-in with the bumper pool table. It was the icing on top of what was a fine performance.

Rick and Kim laughed loudly, as did I, and as for Little Amy, she bowed as dramatically as she would have if she had just wrapped up four nights playing Maria in *West Side Story*.

OK, I was proud of the little freak. Suddenly, I made the connection that she would someday become the big freak, me. Shaking my head and exhaling, I made a mental note: *Let my boys dance around and be silly a little more when I get back to the future. It's in their blood. And don't walk away when they do it. Sit on the stairs and enjoy every painful, beautiful moment. Don't judge them for what, ultimately, you provided them.*

Kim was next, and like Rick, her act had music, "Summer Nights," from the *Grease* soundtrack. She did a decent job of lip synching the entire number, including both Olivia Newton-John's and John Travolta's parts. She knew every single word, nailing each "Tell me more, tell me more" and managed to play off the dramatic ending without looking like a total idiot. Her dance moves were definitely more legitimate, despite the fact that she felt the need to sing into what looked like a wood item that had been yanked off the top of her canopy bed. What she didn't do was oversell the act, something Amy definitely, and even Rick, couldn't claim.

Really, hers was the best overall act. But not in a million, zillion years would I admit that to her. Honestly, I was tempted to hit the Mexican tambourine squarely and get her off the stage, just because I could. I probably should have gonged her ass, but I didn't. I suppose it helped that I was forty-six freaking years old. I was clearly very mature, and despite Kim's training bra, which she strutted around in like she owned the Maiden-form factory, the whole battle of the boobs was going to end in my favor: Me with a C cup, and her in an A, sadly not much more cleavage than was on display here at America's favorite TV talent show.

As the game wrapped up, the three kids returned to the steps, side by side, laughing about the trio of performances. Though each individual thought theirs was the best, plenty of appreciation was passed around to the other players.

I moved up and back a couple of steps to give them space, in hopes that they would forget I was even there. It was amazing to me that the three of them could sit on one of the small stairs at the same time, Little Amy in the middle flanked by Kim and Rick on each side. What was also striking was the true affection they felt for one another. It was palpable, but nobody would have ever said anything about it. There was a lot of love there, but it wasn't going to be discussed, dissected and quantified. Maybe feelings were better that way, not so much repressed, but enjoyed silently rather than videoed and played back later.

Amy put each of her small, skinny arms around the necks of the other two, something I wouldn't have expected. "Well," she stated dramatically, her bowl cut jiggling in the air conditioning, "Funk and Wagnall's, friends . . . Funk and Wagnall's." Though it wasn't really that funny, Kim and Rick obliged with genuine laughs, not courtesy laughter, but the genuine "Ha Ha" stuff that makes 99.9 percent of everything better.

As quickly as the gorgeous moment came, it went, with Mom's voice calling upstairs for the kids to come down and get cleaned up for dinner. "Don't leave a mess up there!" Mom screamed.

But, alas, the three friends scurried down the stairs without picking up a single item. I happily admired the disaster they left in their wake. I didn't even think about how pissed I would have been if Will and Matthew had left a similar mess, on a holiday, with guests.

Long live the hypocrite who thinks she's perfect!

Chapter Ten

TRAILER TRASH

*B*ack down in the dining room, the pageant of food and awkwardness was in full swing. Mom had miraculously gotten enough chairs around the dining room table for everyone to sit quasi-comfortably. The large, antique hand-carved buffet was stuffed with food, as was the table itself, and a decorative, cast-iron cart.

What was the purpose of a metal-wheeled cart in a dining room? It would have looked hideous even outside, where it belonged—eventually rusting into the dust in the wind that people sometimes sang about. It was painted white, with huge back wheels and smaller front ones. I'm guessing it couldn't have moved twelve inches without leaving some sort of rust streak on the shag carpet. It made me think of a stupid picture of my sister, standing behind the controls of the cart, as if she was pushing it to some magical—yet totally delusional—garden party in her own head. It was Christmas Day, and she had some sort of horrible floral dress on, she was always a dresser-upper, complemented by a hand-knitted, or crocheted, shawl. Who did she think she was? Pretending to push a cart that wouldn't push, wearing that silly shawl, smiling with her head cocked just so. There wasn't even anything on the cart, which she wasn't really pushing out of the dining room. Seriously, it was a good thing I was so much more mature than she was . . .

Fully intoxicated by the holiday spirit (and/or spirits), Mom had lit the plethora of candles in both the crystal and brass candelabras on the buffet. She had really outdone herself: Turkey, ham, two types of potatoes, vegetables, stuffing, the ceremonial ridged (for your pleasure) cranberry sauce log, rolls, weird Jell-O salad, and pies. Granny had brought her southern dressing; Grandma had made turkey figures out of canned pear halves, cherries and other unusual but edible items. It was blatantly obvious that ten-year-old Amy, who was flailing dangerously near Kim's cart—which could result in the need for a tetanus booster—didn't fully appreciate the amount of work involved in this level of culinary achievement.

As everyone began to find a seat, I felt another wave of uneasiness come over me, feeling like a foreigner. It was a notion that was enhanced by the complete disconnect I felt between myself and what were supposed to be my people. Thankfully, the question of where in this emotional corn maze I was supposed to turn next was answered by Dad. "Here, Amy, sit on the end so you can see everyone." And so, I took the spot of honor at the head of the table under the large picture window looking out over the front yard.

As my butt neared the wicker seat of the chair, young Amy scampered across the room at full throttle, desperately attempting to claim one of the seats next to mine. Her efforts were thwarted by Mom, who strong-armed her and firmly directed her to the second chair from my left.

Directly to my right was Grandma Bee. Next to her sat her husband Gene (Paw Paw), Kimber and then Granddaddy Frank.

On my left sat Dad, then young Amy, then Rick and then Granny Ruth. Mom sat directly across from me at the far end of the table. Conveniently nearest the kitchen, where she could continue offering her delightful, yet totally free and wholly overlooked, services.

Looking around the room at the faces as everyone settled in, I was filled with an overwhelming wave of raw emotion . . . Here I was on Thanksgiving Day, in my parents' home, in my home, during my childhood, as an adult, nearing menopause. Ok—this really was a bunch of crap.

Dad looked down to the other end of the table and requested that Granddaddy say grace. We joined hands with one another, and in his rough, deep southern tone, always preceded by a clearing of the throat, my grandfather gave his customary offering of thanks as I held the hands of my dearly departed grandmother and my forty-something-year-old father. "Dear Lord, bless this food to the nourishment of our bodies and us to thy service. In Christ's name we pray. Amen."

Before Granddaddy even finished enunciating the first syllable of the final word, the other adults began to pass the food around the table. Wineglasses and serving spoons clanked. The holiday spirit temporarily rose up from the food and began to engulf the entire room. It was like the steam off the gravy boat had taken over our normally pessimistic, realistic and logical personas. The excitement of a simple meal together on a national day of thanks seemed to be what it should be.

Two bottles of wine came around the table, one red and the other white. I was passed the white option, a 1977 Blue Nun Liebfraumilch, which I knew was sweeter than the demure spirit of the blue-frocked Sisters depicted on the bottle. I couldn't go with that, even if I wasn't actually attending this event. Switching my attention to the red, I recognized the familiar "Paul Masson Cabernet Sauvignon" label. Since, at least the way I remembered it, Paul Masson would sell no wine before its time, I confidently poured a healthy serving into my silver-plated glass. Funny, I had only seen these glasses in the pictures my mom had taken of her fancy table settings in the '70s, but I had never drunk from the chalice of adulthood, that is until just now.

The conversation remained light as the meal went on. The kids seemed tantalized by Paw Paw's stories and mildly inappropriate jokes, but, again much to my surprise, my mom's parents seemed somewhat underwhelmed by their in-laws. The truth was, there was a striking difference between the two sides of my family. Ruth and Frank MacCurdy were Southerners. Growing up in a wealthy part of Dallas before the Depression, they had retained elements of a culture whose time had passed, especially by 2014 standards. Bee and Gene Weinland, on the other hand, were Midwesterners, Yankees by many Texans' calculations. They had both grown up in Indiana, marrying young and moving out west to Idaho before settling in the Dayton, Ohio, area. Their move south had been predicated by my dad's own move to Texas. They simply followed his lead. The result was what seemed to be a more open, down to earth approach to life, one not at all concerned—at least on the surface—with others' perceptions.

Even as a child I understood that the two couples were different, but those assumptions were based on where and how each couple lived, what toys they had in their extra room, what kind of Christmas and birthday gifts they sent, and what they cooked. I either couldn't, or didn't, get the more important dividing factors.

I wondered if the younger Amy really was as tuned-out as she seemed to be. Or perhaps I was judging her too harshly and she was absorbing the appropriate level for someone of her tender age.

When was it that I stopped being so self-absorbed? Was it a magical transformation that happened so covertly that it couldn't be traced by photograph or memory? Or, had I made the whole thing up in my own mind, never truly changing or improving, but only thinking I had because, at forty-six, no one was going to tell me the truth about myself anymore?

Before I could connect any more dots that didn't need connecting, Mom told the kids that they were excused. Dessert would be later. The three happily scurried off into the formal living area, back down the steps to the sunken family room and toward the master bedroom. Since I knew they weren't supposed to play in Mom and Dad's room, I assumed they were headed to what was supposedly an "office," located off the master suite. It was on the same level as the formal living room and therefore had two steps up into it. It contained a burnt-orange corduroy couch, a rolltop desk, a green-glass lamp that had been Grandma's and a huge bay window that looked out onto the front yard. Most importantly, it had two closets stacked with toys, board games and other treasures.

That left the adult me sitting in the dining room, primed to finally find out what happens at 24314 Creekview Drive on Thanksgiving after the kids leave the table on a quest to discover what's really inside of Stretch Armstrong, or, even better, what it would feel like to launch Evil Knievel off a hand-powered ramp and into your brother's or sister's personal parts.

Well, frankly, it's a disappointment—the post-dinner table activities as opposed to Evil Knievel's most provocative stunt—nothing more than forced adult conversation served up in the glow of alcoholic beverages.

Yes, Dick had laid down with Sue and now three couples, plus me, were sitting around a table wondering what they should say to each other and how freaking long an afternoon could last.

Not appreciating even a moment of silence, Bee began discussing her and Gene's travel plans for the following spring. They had a shiny Airstream trailer that they pulled from coast to coast behind their Chrysler sedan. When Gene retired as a civilian in the Air Force, they sold their home and stored all their possessions, and traveled across North America. Though this wasn't their gig now, in 1978, they still had a trailer, which they would own until they could no longer do what was physically required to travel in it.

Bee, and then Gene, who enthusiastically piped in when he was given even the slightest opportunity, detailed their plans including a "rally" that would be held by the Wally Byam Club (an association exclusively for Airstream owners), somewhere in Kentucky. On that hallowed ground, the WBCCI (Wally Byam Caravan Club International) would meet *en masse*, lining up millions of dollars' worth of travel trailers festooned with flags. All this while their owners, proudly wearing lanyards that signified their long service to the movement, mingled with one another. What service they provided, beyond drinking festive beverages underneath striped awnings, was a mystery.

This topic went on for a good thirty minutes with photos promised and occasional backtracking to reminisce about trailer parks of the past. Before this auspicious occasion, I would have never noticed that everyone, except for Bee, Gene and my father, looked as if they had lost the will to live about five minutes into the conversation.

"You know . . ." Bee stated in her trademark edgily emotional tone. "Our Airstream allows us to have wonderful adventures and meet wonderful folks from all over the country." Habitually playing with a mustard-colored linen napkin, she then went where no cautious person would have gone. Looking diagonally across the table, she asked Ruth if she and Frank had ever thought of purchasing a trailer and seeing the world on the hoof.

Ruth looked absolutely stricken at even the thought of living in something you could hook to the back of a vehicle. The only words she could manage through her obvious angst were, "No, really that wouldn't suit us."

If I were being honest, I'd have to say that Ruth's words were dripping with a condescending and snobbish tone. Neither Gene nor Bee seemed aware that their pitch was about as well received as a school librarian enthusiastically telling a group of fifth graders that "today kicks off National Poetry Week." This miscalculation was confirmed as Gene continued on, dangerously, "Yes, Frank, you could play golf at hundreds of different courses. And you could both meet lots of people who share similar interests, like bridge and good conversation."

Now it was Frank that looked stricken. Somebody evidently needed to be more candid, so why not leave it to Ruth to lop the head off the idea before it went any further? "Well, you have to understand . . . The social group we are members of would find trailer living to be a bit . . . well, rural and . . . it's safe to say, beneath us. Yes," she continued, "Our set"—the one with a country club membership—"is not necessarily the set that caravans in a mobile home . . . Really, we're not those kinds of people."

Alternatively, if you are from the aristocratic South—even if it is only in your own mind—play bridge, have a membership, have a uniformed African-American bartender hired for your high-brow social gatherings—in a duplex in Waco—you wouldn't be caught dead emptying your sewer hose at a KOA campground in West Virginia.

Never.

It would be akin to hanging your panties out on the clothesline in 2014.

The situation was a total shock to me as, again, I had never visited the world where undertones became overtones with this group. Ironically, Frank still worked as a car salesman, and while Ruth and he resided in a nice apartment, a rental, Gene was retired and had enough disposable income to both own a property and to travel at will. Add in the fact that Airstream trailers were pricey, meaning it's unlikely that Frank and Ruth could have even afforded to join the Wally Byam Club, and the entire situation was a paradox.

So, you've got the sophisticated set looking down their noses at the seemingly tawdry group who live a lifestyle that the former couple can't afford.

As Mom poured herself another glass of wine, Dad thankfully and mercifully brought the conversation to a close. "Well folks, I think we'll just agree to disagree on that," he said as Ruth leered across the table.

"Yes," Frank mumbled, "we won't agree on much."

And for the first and only time in my life, I saw Bee and Gene look transparently awkward.

"Well," Dad said, trying to redirect. "That sure was a good meal."

"Yes," Frank chimed in, patting his belly with delight. "It sure did hit the spot."

Before any additional compliments could fall magically from the sky, Ruth was quick to add, "Yes, it was very good, but I just don't understand why people use ridged cranberry jelly and rolls from a can . . ." Of course it was just an observation, not an insult, or so she thought. Mom sank even lower in her chair.

How does your own mom take a jab like that while sitting at the table after Thanksgiving dinner, the very meal that she slaved and stressed over, giving a little piece of her own soul away in the process? How the hell does that work?

"It's like having whipped cream from a plastic tub," Granny continued, clearly unaware of the container of Cool Whip thawing in the kitchen. "Or making gravy out of a packet . . ."

I couldn't be certain where Mom's gravy had come from, but I had no idea that she had ever taken this sort of verbal abuse after what was, in no uncertain terms, a fine meal, a fact confirmed by the rave reviews of the people with penises.

Looking over to her now deflated daughter, Granny added with a wry smile, "It really was good, Sue, you did a wonderful job. I'm just so glad we ate at the dining room table, it's just the right thing to do."

Now she was referring to that blasphemous occasion where we ate Thanksgiving dinner in the breakfast and family rooms, an incident that was no doubt fresh on my mom's mind when she defensively set up the dining room as fancy-dancy as she knew how. She probably had thought, somewhat pleased with herself, "Now she won't have ANYTHING to say about my meal."

It was no wonder why, thirty-five years later, she still flipped out about the holidays and really, gatherings of any size at all. She had never—in the opinion of the one person she needed validation from the most—pulled it off properly.

As much as Mom's world was obviously perfect, with the big

house, healthy family and wonderful husband, it could also be a load of crap.

"Looks like some of the neighborhood kids are outside," Dad said, looking almost wistfully out the front window. "I bet Rick and Amy will go out later."

"I wonder when she'll outgrow playing with all those boys," Granny Ruth asked, a legitimate question, I supposed. Of all the awkward things I could remember about my childhood, playing with the group of boys on our street wasn't one of them. They were the only other kids in the neighborhood, so it seemed natural, not deviant.

"She should do it as long as she wants to," Grandma Bee from the KOA remarked, almost daring Granny to respond.

"She's definitely a tomboy," Mom piped in, rather quietly.

"Well, it's good exercise as far as I'm concerned," Dad said.

"At some point she'll have to do something with that hair, and those clothes . . ." Granny said.

"Yes, she will, and she'll need to calm down, she makes people uncomfortable." Mom said, looking down at her lap.

What? I was only ten freaking years old. Give me some time to grow up before starting to label me as a fashion disaster. Was I already supposed to care about all that? Maybe that's why I struggled with it, because they told me I did, when I was still three years from being a teenager.

I was shocked. I suppose it was because of Granny's and my closeness at this age. But, I shouldn't have been, because that's how families work. There's the face you put on in person, and then the one you put on when you get to be "honest."

"Amy's a good kid, a sweet, intelligent girl . . ." Mom continued. "But she can also be a real challenge."

"Yes," Granny agreed. "She is a sweet girl, but she needs a lot of work on how she looks and acts."

"I agree," Mom said, looking down at her half-eaten plate of food. "I don't know what we'll do with her, we love her, we really do, but she's difficult to control, very difficult, and boyish, she doesn't care much about her personal appearance and she's, well, she's awkward. Difficult. Almost, well, odd. She's not right, not like . . ."

"Now, Sue," Dick interrupted. "She'll be just fine."

Good God, Mom could do without this nonsense. There was nothing worse than having some well-meaning family member attempt to tell you how messed up your kids were, like you didn't already know that. Sure, they were just trying to help, but why bring it up, here, in front of everyone.

On the other hand, how bad was I? Even if Granny was right, couldn't Mom have at least defended me? Really, other than her shocking admission that I was intelligent, she just threw me under the bus. She called me awkward, boyish and NOT RIGHT. I knew that was true, I could see it all for myself, but she didn't have to validate it. Out loud. As far as I ever knew, nothing got validated out loud here, at least nothing that actually meant something.

And another thing, I could have finished her sentence, the one that stopped with "not like . . ." I knew precisely who she was saying I was "not like."

It was as if everything I had been feeling and repressing and then feeling again, for forty-f-ing years, had been endorsed, certified, and proven in a single sentence. I was pissed. I was horrified. I was devastated.

Was this, this totally f-ed up conversation, the answer to a question I thought I didn't have? One of the questions that Mary had said I needed to answer, or ask? Is this why I was here? So I could almost die at this stupid table, with the stupid silver wine cups, with not enough alcohol in them?

F. F. F. F. F.

There were lots of layers to the dysfunction in this family. It wasn't as simple as one person being singled out. Everyone was at risk, which meant reactions weren't simple and logical. My mom was dealing with her own feelings of inadequacy with her mother, while at the same time she was trying to figure out what to do with me, her high-spirited, sometimes angry tomboy daughter who didn't fit in the suburban box. And so, three decades later Rick would marry Jen and she would try to get us to talk about our feelings.

I'm so freaking glad we didn't.

Ironically, though Kim and Rick fit in the box better as youngsters, they broke further out of it when they grew up. Maybe that's just the way it works; you either rebel sooner or later, but you always do.

Either way, was I seriously supposed to just sit here and take this crap? Not one person was defending Little Amy. Not Dad. Not Grandma. Nobody. I understood that this was a holiday table, which meant there was no way a fight would suddenly break out between the frank MacCurdys and the conflict-avoiding Weinlands, but couldn't anyone say anything in her defense? Even a single f-ing word?

On the outside, I calmly sipped my wine, while internally I fumed. It didn't matter that nobody knew who I really was, I should have busted the scene wide open. Screw this ridiculous space/time continuum limitation. Screw it.

"Now Amy," Grandma Bee said, "tell us about your family. I know you have two school-aged sons, but what about brothers and sisters, you have one of each, don't you?"

Looking down, and then back up, reeling from the words spoken out loud, I wondered how I was supposed to just drop what I was feeling and answer a perfectly reasonable question. But, I had been doing that my entire life. I was gifted at playing normal. It's just too bad there wasn't an AP class in high school for it. Clearing my throat, I fought the urge to answer in a dramatic tone, drawing off emotions that I couldn't own in this crazy f-ed up scenario. "Yes ma'am, I have an older sister and a younger brother."

"What do they do?" Granny asked.

"My sister is a flight attendant with United Airlines," I answered, hoping that United really was a company in 1978. My first instinct was to whip out my iPhone under the tablecloth and Google *When was United Airlines founded?* But, since I couldn't do that, I tried to act like I knew what I was talking about, also something I was quite accomplished at.

"A flight attendant?" Granny questioned, "What type of work is that?" You could tell by the tone of her voice that she was desperately hoping (so she could tell her bridge club on Monday) that my sister directed planes with flares, or had a job in the cockpit. Both would have been considered manly, like sports writing, given the time and place.

"Oh, I think you call it a stewardess," I answered, like I was from a foreign country. "She serves drinks and food, and is responsible for the safety of the passengers." I wanted to make sure that this specific group—Kimber's parents and grandparents—understood that the job she did in the future was important and well-paid.

"Well, you Yankees sure do have crazy words for things!" Granddaddy said.

"I've never heard that term either," Paw Paw chimed in, defending his Midwest roots.

"Oh," I said, backpedaling. "It must be a new term, used just within the airline industry. Yeah, Kim just referred to her job that way recently, maybe the last time we talked."

I carefully took my notebook out under the table and wrote, "*When was United founded? When did stewardesses start being called flight attendants? How much was a new Airstream trailer in 1978? When did Granddaddy finally retire? . . . Am I still not right?*"

"Oh, her name is *Kim?*" Mom asked while holding her poodle Cash like an infant. "That's so nice."

I could almost smell the artichoke dip.

"What about your brother?" Grandma asked, "What does he do?"

"Ri . . . I mean Greg buys properties—you know, houses,

duplexes, small apartment complexes—fixes them up and either sells them or rents them."

"That's interesting, a good business plan," Dad said.

"Yes," I said. "He's good with his hands and good with people, so it worked out to be a great thing for him."

"Do either of them have children?" Mom asked.

"Kim does not . . ." I replied, anticipating the excitement my next statement would bring. "My brother and his wife have five kids."

"Five?" Grandma said, looking impressed.

"Yes," I said, "five."

"How old are they?" Mom asked, a good question from someone who had a twelve-year-old, a ten-year old and an eight-year-old currently in her charge.

"Well, the oldest is nine and the youngest is three."

This armed Granny with a story to tell for many Mondays in the future. "You mean to tell me," she said with glee, "that your brother has five kids under the age of nine?"

"That's correct," I stated with satisfaction. "Of course, there's a set of twins thrown in there, but, that's right."

This group could have never known that these five little people were their own direct descendants. If they had, it would have certainly changed their reaction from shock to delight . . . well, at least in some cases.

I wished desperately that I could have taken a napkin and drawn out the family tree as it stood in the future. Everybody would have been overcome with joy.

But for now, before the grandchildren and great-grandchildren were even a twinkle in anyone's eye, they just wondered if Kim would be able to decide what she was going to wear on Monday morning. They wondered if Amy would ever grow out of her sports addiction and dial down the eye-bulge. And, they wondered if Rick would play football and take over Dad's business when he was grown.

They probably weren't wondering if we would have sex with some random people and provide them—collectively—with seven new family members.

"You know what I read in yesterday's paper?" Dad said, thankfully changing the subject. "Target stores will be open today from noon until seven p.m."

Everybody at the table gasped, including me, who had thought that Thanksgiving Day sales were part of my present and future, not my long-ago past.

"What?" Granny said. "How can they do that, who will even go?"

"And what about the employees' families?" Paw Paw added. "How will they celebrate Thanksgiving?"

"Are you sure?" I said, questioning Dad about something in 1978, something I knew nothing about.

"Yep," Dad said, "it was right there, in black-and-white ink."

"What kind of store is that?" Grandma asked. "I don't think I've ever heard of a Target?"

"I just know of one," Mom said. "It's on FM 1960."

"What's it like?" Grandma said, perhaps figuring it was better than sitting at the Thanksgiving table of doom.

"Well," Mom said, "I've only been in there a couple of times . . . But, it's like Kmart or Woolco, only more sterile."

"It's like a nicer, cleaner and higher-quality Walmart!" I blurted out before I stopped to think.

"A WHAT?" my mom said, looking at me like I had three heads.

"Oh, umm . . ." I answered, "I meant . . ." Hold it, was Walmart even a thing in 1978? How long had Target been around? What the hell was Woolco?

"Well," I said, trying once again to be legit, "I was referring to a local store."

"In Dayton?" Grandma said. "I never heard of it when we lived there, and we visited Susie in Dayton a couple of years ago and didn't see it then either . . ."

"No, it's not local to me . . ." I continued, working up a lie that couldn't be refuted in the land of no-Google. "It's local to my friend Kristi, who lives in Flint, Michigan."

What was true was that the eleven-year-old Kristi would have lived in Flint in 1978. What wasn't was the part about her shopping with her family at the world's only Walmart.

Pulling my notebook back out, I added, *"When did Walmart and Target start doing business? What is Woolco?"* and *"Ask Kristi where her family shopped in Flint."*

"God . . ." Granny said. "Flint, Michigan, that sounds awful!"

"I agree!" Mom added, with more than a single-serving of conviction in her voice. "That three months we spent in the north just about killed me."

What in the hell was she talking about?

"You spent time up North?" I asked, trying to sound casual.

"Yes," Mom said, rather dramatically, "Dick, Kim and I moved to Elyria, Ohio, in the summer of 1967 . . . it was the worst summer of my life."

"What were you there for?" I asked, shocked that I hadn't ever heard about this before.

"Well, *Dick* moved us up there for his job . . ." she stated, looking at Dad like he had signed them up for a harrowing, un-safe covered-wagon trip to Oregon Territory.

"Yes . . ." Dad said, not wanting to broach an already well-broached topic. "I was going to work in Cleveland for a year and then go to Purdue to get my master's."

"Your master's?" I said, impressed and surprised.

"Yes," Dad said with a resigned tone. "But it didn't work out, and we moved back here, and we had Amy."

As the topic got kicked around the table, I started doing the math in my head. If they had lived in Ohio in the summer of 1967 and I was born in April of 1968, there was every chance that I was conceived in the Midwest as opposed to the Tidelands Motel in Houston, within view of the Astrodome. That was the story I got one drunk evening in Galveston, my mom telling us more than she should have at the Holiday Inn Bar on the Seawall.

If I had been able to look at my iPhone, under the table, I would have pulled up a backward pregnancy calculator. Since I couldn't, I just went ahead and asked, out loud, in person, "So . . . you guys must have been pregnant with Amy before you moved back home?"

It was a conspicuous and personal question, I got that, but I wanted to know.

"Well," Dad said, "I'm not sure . . ."

"Either am I," Mom said, looking at me, perhaps wondering why I could possibly care. "It could have gone either way."

So, I woke up this morning, in 2014, a one hundred percent confirmed, native Texan, born and bred, but now, after this stunning revelation, in 19-freaking-78, I could have been bred in Ohio and born in Texas.

When Willie, the boys and I moved to Ohio in 2007, had I returned to not only the place of my father's boyhood, but also to the land of my own conception?

Had the sex that formed me happened in Elyria, Ohio?

Did I need to drive up to the majestic capitol building in Austin, dramatically climb the stairs beneath the Lone Star flag and turn in my cowboy boots, my spurs, my Stetson, my skinny jeans, my crossover SUV, my love for legitimate, certified Tex-Mex and my preference for hot, humid weather?

And then, gasp, should I turn north, way freaking north, to Columbus (the one in Ohio, not the one west of Houston on I-10) and park in front of the Ohio Statehouse, the topless one with a missing dome, in sight of the nautical flag, and be issued white Reebok tennis shoes, a "Life is Good" ball cap, Mom jeans, a Chevy Astro van, a love of "chili" spiced with cinnamon served in a "three-way" on top of spaghetti, and a preference for icy, sub-zero temperatures?

In other words, should I buy a necklace made of freaking poisonous buckeye nuts?

Who was I?

"Boy, Earl Campbell sure was something on Monday night, wasn't he?" Gene chimed in, not getting what a big deal it was that people had not been transparent on where the sex had happened in 1967. "Four touchdowns and 199 yards as a rookie!"

"And we beat Miami 35-30!" Dad added with glee.

All this was lost on me, the football aficionado who would have normally reveled in the fact that future hall of famer Earl Campbell was just a rookie running back for the Houston Oilers—despite the fact that he had gone, inappropriately, to the University of Texas, I had long loved his smash-mouth running style, like John Riggins with a different helmet on.

The sum total of the table talk—about my young self, the origins of my life and trailer parks—made me question how I fit into this family, both in 1978 and 2014. It was so big, well, it was bigger than football.

"Speaking of football . . ." Granddaddy added, chuckling at the other two adult males, finally finding something everyone could agree on. "Let's go see who is playing now."

Chapter Eleven

FEEL THE BURN

*A*fter the guys exited, Grandma, Granny, Mom and I stuck around to clear off the table. I couldn't help but think that in 2014 the men, especially the male host, would have been expected to help with the clean-up. It was good that Mom didn't know anything about that yet—that women's liberation would one day seep into the suburbs, along with cable television.

The Thanksgiving mess is apparently timeless, as is the awkwardness that goes along with in-laws, out-laws and kitchen clean-up. Mom was noticeably uncomfortable with not only me—the out-of-town stranger—helping, but also with the assistance of the two seniors. I got that, especially considering Granny's comments about the meal. Even though we were blowing that, and every other meaningful topic, off and apparently never speaking of it again, it definitely added to the tension.

Not much was said outside of Bee, who continued to talk aimlessly. I think this was both her way of coping and a strong, under-the-radar statement: "This is family and we're going to move on, no matter what happens."

As with Mom's meal, it was masterfully done and completely underappreciated.

We were about halfway through hand-washing the china when Dad came back through, headed to the garage to collect additional adult beverages. Amy and Rick followed him, asking if they could go outside. Mom agreed from the sink before Dad

could answer and reminded the pair to properly jacket themselves against the cool November air.

"I bet it is nice outside . . ." I said wistfully, as the back door
slammed behind them.

"Well," Bee pointed out, "I would imagine that it is much
warmer here than it is in Ohio right now."

"Yeah," I agreed, "it definitely is." I wished I could have
explained how passionate I was about this topic, the weather,
and how after growing up here (in this house) that I found winter in the Midwest nothing short of tragic.

"You should go outside and enjoy it, you'll have to go back
to the cold soon enough," Mom said. Even though I think she
genuinely meant that, she was also trying to get someone, anyone out of her space. If she could have pulled it off, everyone
would have been banished from the kitchen, never to return. I
suppose, and I had never thought about this before, that she
preferred doing all the work herself as opposed to sharing it
with people who made her feel self-conscious.

I tried to argue that I needed to help with the dishes, to do
my part as it were, but all three women urged me on, back through
the breakfast room and out the back door onto the driveway.

I agreed to go and it was easy.

All I felt was relief.

Stepping outside, I looked around and soaked in the quiet.
The beauty of dusk and the sweet smell of Texas comforted and
haunted me all at the same time, not unlike what had been, up
until today, only memories of my childhood.

Now that I was alone I could slowly walk around, absorbing
each bit of what before I had only viewed as a place to play, and
then a place to park my first car (and crash into my sister's second car), and then the place I left when I went away to college,
and then the place I totally forgot about.

The enormous concrete pad could have easily held four full-
sized vehicles. Again, everything seemed shrunken down, but

still, it was tantalizing. Attempting to take it all in was impossible. The overwhelming urge was to photograph it, to somehow make it, this time, something I could take with me. But could a picture really do that? Could a well-filtered, completely edited, hash-tagged and promptly shared image recreate an actual moment in time?

Just then, what looked like a shadow came around the sharp corner on the left side of the garage, where the long driveway stretched out into the street. It startled me. Backing away slowly, I saw a medium-sized dog, my childhood dog, running toward me, wagging his tail in excitement.

Oh my God, it was Cecil.

How in the world had I forgotten to go out and look for Cecil? It was the first thing I should have done when I got to 1978, but as usual, my most faithful companion was the one I thought of last. It was official, I sucked.

Leaning down, I petted the tan-and-white, short-haired mutt, "Hi boy, how are you?" Dropping to my knees, I felt tears streaming down my face, he was so small. "It's good to see you, boy—I've missed you so much."

Rubbing the familiar brown spot on his head, I couldn't help but tell him everything. "I've come back in time, boy, I'm a real woman now, I have hair on my private parts and everything . . . It's me, Amy, I'm all grown up." Cecil just wagged faithfully, with the same open-mouthed look that had always mimicked an actual smile. "You ought to meet my boys, Will and Matthew, they'd love you, boy. I told them all about you . . . they're such good boys, you'd be so proud of both of them . . . Mom and Dad, they said some stuff at the table, about me, about little me, I don't know what to think about it. I don't know why I'm here and if this is really happening. I'm not brave enough, boy, or strong enough to do this." Crap, I was telling the dog everything I wanted to say to the people in the house, the actual people.

"I was so sad when we had to put you to sleep, I was playing soccer and I just stood on the side of the field and cried, I couldn't stop. When we buried you down by the rope swing, we put a white-wire fence around your grave. Other than Paw Paw's funeral, it's the only time I've ever seen Dad cry. We all loved you so much, boy . . . we all love you so much right now." Really, I shouldn't have told him about his impending death. I didn't know what year it had happened, but it wouldn't be long in relative terms. For all I knew, he could understand everything I was saying. For all I knew, the only thing he couldn't do was talk back.

If there was one thing I had already learned from this experience, it was that I didn't know what was really going on . . . reality was crap. And that meant dogs might be able to understand human words.

"I've got another dog now, back at home, back in my real life," I continued, scratching his back. "His name is Sammy and he's almost as good as you, boy, but not quite." Cecil put his legs up on my knees as I continued to talk. He was the only one in 1978 who had figured out who I really was. Only the best dogs do that, you know, those once-in-a-lifetime dogs. They have an extraordinary sense of smell and they can be counted on to remember their people, even as they struggle with hallucinations and supposed time travel.

Tracing my steps back around the garage and down the driveway with Cecil following behind me, I could hear the kids playing in the street. The sun had set just enough to provide an almost heavenly glow, seemingly on cue to fit my nostalgic mood. Making my way silently down the drive, I strained to see what was going on—ah yes, it was the annual "after Thanksgiving dinner" football game.

Directly in front of our house was the intersection of two classic '70s suburban streets, Creekview Drive and Morningcrest Court. The two joined to form a giant T which the local band of kids—bonded by nothing more than geographical location— used for a wide variety of purposes, mostly sport related.

We were a similar-aged but male-dominated group, meaning athletic pursuits were on the schedule on most school afternoons and many a long, boring, hot summer day. Football, baseball and basketball were the regular games, but moments of genius, or desperation, drove us to get creative—like the time we made our own hockey sticks and created our own version of street hockey, sans any skates. It was a pursuit that inevitably ended poorly, especially given that we had never even watched a hockey game on TV. Seriously, this was the pre-NHL South. The best I can remember, it was a game that never really took off with us, mainly because some kid always ended up running home, bawling, because he/she had been wacked, unmercifully, by another kid with his/her homemade stick. Even though the aggressor always pleaded it was "an accident," it may have been a bridge too far to put wooden weapons in the hands of an over-competitive group of pre-teens on what was, really, a boring suburban street in the '70s.

Lucky for me, I was a tomboy who found sports more appealing than latch-hook rug or Shrinky Dink making. The other two young ladies on our block were my sister Kim and our caddy-corner neighbor Lynn, who participated in the sporting events until they grew out of it, much earlier than I did.

I can still recall the exact layout of our football field. When we were younger, we played in a large grass area that flanked Todd's house, situated directly across from us and to the left. But eventually, as we grew bigger and faster we moved the game into the actual street. Whoever had done construction in the area had left large drips of rocky concrete on the street surface, which served as landmarks for our games. We had it all down to a science. This shrub was home plate, that concrete dribble was first base, the end zone started with this crack in the street, and out of bounds was a complicated combination of curbage. These flimsy boundaries provided the gray area necessary to keep things interesting.

On this night, there was a relatively large group assembled, maybe four or five per side. The weather, by local standards, was cool and crisp. Growing up in Houston and loving street sports means that only rarely will you feel the sting of a cold football in your hands.

I recognized almost all of the athletes immediately: First, there was perennial team captain and the street's biggest and best athlete Greg (who I secretly thought was hot), the other Greg from further down the street (who my sister not so secretly thought was hot), Nick, Sean, Todd and then some guys from nearby streets. Rick and Little Amy were right in the middle of the activity. Kim and Lynn were pursuing other interests, indoors.

I had always wondered what Rick thought about me being one of the street "guys" for sporting endeavors. I guess it goes back to just being happy to have someone to play with. Who cares if your sister is really a girl?

I got as close to the game as I could, edging my way across the street to the stop sign in the corner of Todd's yard. Leaning back against the pole, trying to look casual, I was glad that at least Rick and Little Amy knew who I was, making me less of a candidate for the stranger-danger label. The game was well underway by the time I, the lone spectator, arrived. As far as I knew, I was the first-ever actual spectator, but, of course, that was before I knew that moms (and other nosey neighbor types) spent a great deal of time looking out the window. Ah yes, the crawling pace of suburban life made careful monitoring of the "goings on" of the neighborhood a well-played sport all its own. The lack of cable television, the internet, texting and free long distance would have made this even more pronounced. In 1978, I would imagine everyone quietly knew everyone else's business. I could totally get into that.

As the sun continued to slowly set, I knew the game would inevitably end soon, as natural light—and two dim streetlights we always threw stuff at—were the only illumination available. From the yelling, huffing, and puffing on the part of the red-faced participants, I deducted that the sporty Greg's squad (which included Rick and the young skinny Amy) were down by less than a touchdown to the Todd squad. As "our" group got possession of the football back from the opposing side, it was decided that this was the final drive of the game.

Sudden death.

The Greg team tried two plays that resulted in an incomplete pass and then Rick being hurled off the street on a running play for a gain of probably two yards. Two plays left to go for all the marbles. It was third down and I moved in closer.

The ball was "self-hiked" minus a center, and Greg went back to throw a bomb into the end zone nearest me. A kid I didn't recognize laid out Lynn Swann style but just missed it, the ball passing tantalizingly out of reach and onto the hood of a nearby car. As it bounced off what looked to be a white Camaro, I thought how pissed I would have been if it were my car. Really, what were these kids thinking?

Fourth down. Another "hut-hut" off the line of scrimmage and Greg was again looking downfield for an open receiver. Todd counted the obligatory six Mississippi and came after him.

He wasn't as big as Greg and was a full year younger but was quick and aggressive. Greg was forced to hurl the ball or be taken out, resulting in a short, desperate pass to the young and eager Amy, who was being loosely covered by a kid that I had just recognized. It was Brice, who lived near my cousins' house across the neighborhood on Fawnwood. He was tall, fast, and he knew it.

Miraculously, Amy snagged the ball at midfield, and as Brice turned to catch her she made an impressive juke and began to shoot down the field. Brice was fast, but Amy pulled her butt in and just took off . . . Holy crap, she was like a bullet out of a gun! She could play for Clemson! Luckily, I caught the look on her face when she sped past me and let me tell you, no sporting enthusiast wouldn't have been impressed with the determination in her eyes. She was a total badass. Now, this didn't make up for the fact that this was still the same little bowl-snipped-haired girl who brought awkwardness to an entirely new level, but she really did have some skills.

"GO AMY!" I heard the winded Rick yell from behind as she tucked that impressively petite rear in one more time, crossing into the end zone just beyond the lanky reach of Brice.

Hyper girl scores! Team Greg wins! Thanksgiving is saved!

Rick followed Amy into the end zone patting her on the back, all smiles. The defeated stood with hands on their hips, disappointed that they had been schooled by the tomboy. Greg just smiled casually, as the big man on the street he was too used to winning to make a big deal out of it.

It was all lost on the fresh-faced Amy, who didn't seem to care that she was a girl playing a boy's game or that she was a big dork. She had just outrun Brice for the winning score. The girl who would love football for a lifetime just had her actual on-field moment. I was glad she didn't see it for anything more than what it was, a great moment in sports.

Thank God she wasn't a hung-up, care what other people thought, uptight forty-something-year-old from the future.

Walking back toward "my" house enveloped by a hazy Houston dusk, I clapped my hands, pumped my fist, thoroughly satisfied with the little freak's performance.

This was who we were. Ass kickers. I could dig that. Totally.

Chapter Twelve

THE STREAKER

*B*y the time I came back inside, the adults were settled into the family room, comfortably perched on the rattan, spread out lazily on the couch, and in the case of my father, laid out in his usual place on the area rug, leaning against the hearth.

He had lain in that same position on what seemed like every night we lived in that house, propped up on a pillow, wearing a sky-blue jumpsuit, with a beer in his hand. Often times, we three kids would get our own pillows and lay our heads against him, lined up in a row, facing the TV. From there we watched all the classics: *Charlie and the Chocolate Factory*, *Tony Orlando and Dawn*, *The Flip Wilson Show*, *The Ten Commandments* and the *Peanuts* specials brought to you by Dolly Madison.

It made me hungry for a Zinger.

Rick and Amy—still red-faced—returned behind me, eager to have their pies dolloped with a helping of bastardized Cool Whip. I didn't know it yet, but as an adult, Thanksgiving pie was best served when you were slowly being pickled by the Chablis or Schlitz Malt Liquor Bull. Inasmuch as the kids saw the glow of Thanksgiving in the morning hours, only to be disappointed by the reality that was inevitably reached by sundown, adults dreaded the hours that would drag on, only to feel the glow, finally, in the night air.

And so pie was served.

"Pee Diddle Umpkin," Frank recited with a pie plate in his

thick hand, "Pee Diddle I . . . Pee Diddle Umpkin . . . Pumpkin Pie."

The TV buzzed and flicked as we watched *Mork & Mindy*, a horizontal line creeping up and down the screen, distorting the picture as it went. Though the show itself was almost criminally dated, Robin Williams was crazy good as were the commercials, which thankfully nobody flicked away from—because apparently, we were working without a remote control.

The common thread of the commercials was singing. Almost every ad had what sounded like a large throng of B-rate Broadway performers, belting out their cheesy lyrics with such gusto that I was afraid they might crash through the D-rate television screen. It reminded me a lot of that "Up with People" nonsense.

My favorite was a commercial for Camay soap. It featured the shadow of a man with a sexy voice, wearing a robe. He was attempting, apparently, to get a half-naked, blindfolded woman to smell a bar of soap—Camay wildflower—that had been inserted into a perfume bottle. Once she figures out what it is, the blindfold is removed and his hands, covered with soap, begin to lather her face. She enjoys the caressing, telling him, seductively, "Mmmm, that feels nice . . ." followed by, "Oh! Now I really smell the wildflowers." With that, his head finally gets into the frame and yes, he's good-looking, with reddish-blond hair and a matching mustache. He leans in close to her, temptingly, and replies, "To me it just smells wild."

It ended with the bar of Camay back in the perfume bottle, surrounded by fluorescent-colored carnations and daisies, like the kind of bouquet you'd see in front of a Stop and Go. It was difficult not to imagine the two people, now somewhere off set, wildly having soapy sex, shielded only by the huge bushel of baby's breath.

Pulling my handy notebook back out, I jotted down, "*When was Up with People? Brice: did he play college sports? YouTube: Camay*

Wildflowers," and, of course, "*Have someone spread soap on my face while I'm naked.*"

Granny and Granddaddy, who had to drive back into Houston proper, were the first to go. All rose to say goodbye, the children still more enthusiastic than the adults.

What would they discuss on the way home? Surely the bulk of the meal would have been well thought of, but then the customary post-holiday discussion of who said what and "I can't believe it" would have ensued.

In the driveway, I shook each of their hands. I wondered if this, again, would be the last time I saw Granny and Granddaddy alive.

Probably.

They felt no closeness to me, and therefore no warm hug parted us, no lonesome embrace marked the end of our brief meeting in time. A profound sadness haunted me, knowing that to them, I was just another "in law" who showed up randomly one year at their daughters' home. Yes, they could be difficult, even mean, but they were my people. They had loved me, been the people that grandparenthood makes you, and they were mine. Though I could have skipped the entire dining room scene, completely, it made me understand that they were nothing more than flawed people. Just like me.

This was a blow to my naïve memory, but it was somewhat comforting to a forty-something-year-old who had realized that perfection was an unrealistic and unhealthy aim, even for herself. Plus, they had shielded "us," at least the younger versions, from the inevitable undercurrents. As much as it was arguably beneficial, I understood it was ultimately love that drove them to it. And, even better, Granny was a writer, our pens surely flowed together, but still I couldn't help but hope that it was our only connection. If only we could pick the part of the DNA that each ancestor leaves us, it would make it much easier and cut down on blaming other people for our own faults.

Standing in the driveway with Little Amy nearby, I watched them pull away, Granddaddy in his felt fedora, pipe in hand, casually pulling what looked like a Buick Centurion out of the long driveway. Granny sat elegantly by his side, posture perfect, taking a long drag off her cigarette as she waved happily to her grandchildren.

I realized that life never really changes. It repeats itself over and over again, seeming new and astonishing to its short-term participants, the same people who feel like it's going on and on, forever.

ONCE we were all back in the family room, Kim, Rick and Amy drifted off again, eventually to take their baths and prepare for bed. It was only about seven-thirty but this was suburbia; things didn't go deep into the night. Dad brought in another round of beers as I continued to stare at the TV. *What's Happening* was on. As Dad settled back in his spot, the program broke to a commercial, a preview for ABC's Sunday Night Movie, something called *A Question of Love*.

"Shhhhhhh!" Mom shouted, even though nobody was talking. "I've heard about this, turn it up!"

Dad literally rolled almost Ninja-style toward the television, and from a covert position turned the volume knob until the audio was still scratchy but somewhat louder.

"*A Question of Love*," the deep-voiced announcer stated. "Based on factual events, the story of a child custody battle involving a gay parent, based on the actual court transcripts. Starring Gena Rowlands, Jane Alexander and Ned Beatty as attorney Dwayne Stabler."

The best I could tell, the movie was about two women, both mothers, who had moved in together under the auspices of post-divorce financial needs. It turns out the women are lesbians, something the main character admits to her teenage son when he asks her directly. The son tells his father and a custody battle ensues.

Apparently, it's based on a true story, only the names had been changed.

When the minute-plus commercial wrapped up, silence enveloped the room.

Mom, who seemed a thousand times more relaxed than before her parents went home started, "I can't believe there is a movie about this . . . two gay women fighting for custody of their children . . ."

"How can they have kids in their house?" Dad cut in, looking concerned. "Those kids might get the wrong idea about, well, how to be . . ."

"I agree," Mom said. "How can women be together, like that?"

Paw Paw was conspicuously silent, but Bee, not surprisingly, was not. "It's not right," she began, rearranging her beer glass on the table. "It's wrong . . . it's clearly wrong . . . there is absolutely no doubt about that . . . But the way that woman slapped her daughter . . ." she continued, looking out the dark French door windows, referring to a brief scene where the alleged lesbian's mom hits her in the face. "That . . . that wasn't right either . . ."

"It's wrong, homosexuality . . . at least I think it is, but . . ." she said, looking around the room at the rest of us. "Everyone deserves to be loved, especially by their own family."

It was hard to argue with her, and nobody did. It was no surprise that everyone in this room, in 1978, thought homosexuality was wrong, but it was shocking that any one person would be bold enough to defend the supposed "perpetrators" in the name of love.

Especially given that the person speaking was one of only two individuals from the Thanksgiving table that didn't regularly attend church. Yes, Grandma and Paw Paw didn't attend regular services, while the rest of us, including Granny and Granddaddy, did. How was it that the non-church goers could see the necessity of love above those who knew how to turn to Hymn 188, the one about love's redeeming work being done?

"Well," Mom cut in, "I can't believe they would put something like this on NETWORK TELEVISION. That show is on at eight o'clock on a Sunday night, on ABC. And what are they going to show these two ladies doing? Kissing each other? This is something for a movie, in a theatre, that's rated R, or X. Not something that some kid can just turn on and watch in their own living room . . . Some people don't watch what their kids are watching."

Dad and Paw Paw agreed with this, as did Bee. As for me, I was completely shocked that this kind of honest, challenging topic was being covered on national television in 1978. It seemed like something that was more suited for my time, 2014, when gay marriage was a hot-button topic, not now, in 1978, when the cloak of disguise was still apparently draped over the whole thing.

But, really, what in the hell did I know?

Sure, I had a decent education, a bachelor's degree and all. And we, the adult Willie and I, associated with an intelligent group. We all lived in nice neighborhoods, in nice homes, drove nice cars, and sent our kids to nice schools. We were respectable. We knew a lot of important crap.

Clearly, we did.

But, still, we were living in the bubble, in suburbia, behind the nice front doors with the decorative wreaths. We drove past the bad neighborhoods, but what did we know about what was really going on there, or any other place that didn't fit into our "box"?

We liked the box, the accepted rules of the game, because, well, if I were being honest, because the walls of the box, the sturdy top and bottom, make us feel safe. As for the rules, the clear lines in the undeniable sand, they make us the winner, always.

It justified, at least in our own minds, every single thing we did.

"What do you think, Amy?" Bee asked.

Good Lord, I wasn't sure how to answer this question. I had lived in 1978, and I was here now, but I was still the lady from 2014, the girl who had questions about how "wrong" this really was. I had come to believe that people didn't just wake up one day and say, "I'm going to be a homosexual!" Because, well, why would you choose a lifestyle that makes you a target for everyone from supposed Christ-followers to Communists to Neo-Nazis?

Why would millions of people do that by choice? And why would they hide it, sacrificing how they really felt to live a lie, just so they wouldn't be ridiculed?

And why was it perverted? Why did people, some people, think that it was down to something going wrong between conception and birth, a genetic mismatch or a chemical imbalance? Really, why was love between two people, not forced, not criminally instigated, considered deviant?

What about priorities? Why was homosexuality the one "sin" we couldn't forgive? You could come back from almost anything, with the other "good" people; cheating, divorce, abuse . . . but not sexual preference.

I didn't have all the answers, but I knew that if God was love and I shouldn't look for a splinter in another person's eye when there was a big Duraflame log in my own, I had no right, absolutely none, to accuse, much less hate, homosexuals.

If God really was love, then hating people, no matter how offensive they supposedly were, was absolutely not love. But how did I communicate that to this crowd? They loved people, I knew they did—they had loved me since I was a small child. It wasn't their fault that they were born in the 1910s and the 1930s . . . all they knew was 1978 America.

But, then, honestly, I understood that not even the passage of thirty-five years could guarantee that everybody in this room would see things differently. No, that might be left to my generation and the one to come next, the one that was already well underway in the future.

"Well," I said, slowly, hoping the alcohol would come in handy now, "I always believed that the longer I lived, the more I saw and the more of life I experienced, that I would gain valuable wisdom about how life works . . . But, in reality, as the years have passed, I have come to understand that I know less and understand fewer things." I paused, looked down at the floor and continued, "The one thing I do know, for sure, is that to love and to be loved is a natural right, not unlike the rights guaranteed in our own Constitution, like the freedom of speech, and the right to property and the right to pursue happiness . . . Because love is a part of happiness, maybe the biggest part of it. And who are we to define another person's happiness, especially if it's lived within the confines of the law? In this specific instance, I can't believe that gay people love and care about their kids any less than straight people. And I can't believe that they are wrong, and inherently sinful, just because of who they choose to love."

I stopped there, still looking down. Really, I was expecting to be attacked, not physically, not aggressively, but I did expect vehement disagreement.

Silence.

"I think that's an interesting argument," Dad finally said. "I'm not sure I agree with it, but I think you make a good point."

"I would have to think about it," Mom added. "But, love is important and I agree that you can't take it away from people."

"Really," Paw Paw stated, finally adding his two cents. "You can try to take love away, but it's impossible because you can't stop people from feeling. I'm not talking only about homosexuality," he continued, "but any kind of emotion people have is personal, individual, and untouchable."

"It's brave," Mom said, looking over at me in a way I had never seen before. "What you said, I'm glad you said it."

"It's complicated—" Grandma added, but then stopped, suddenly, as the kids began spilling down the stairs.

"That's the end of that," Dad said sternly, looking toward the kids. "No more." Again, I got what he was saying, but at some point, honest conversations like this one, with older children, couldn't hurt, especially if it was done in a loving way.

It's something I had been guilty of with my own children. It made sense, protecting them until they were ready. But I wondered, when was the right time to talk openly? Perhaps more importantly, were we really shielding them, or instead were we afraid of what they might say?

Looking around the room at Mom and Dad, Paw Paw, and Grandma, I understood that as much as I could accuse them of a bunch of things, I, once again, had been guilty of underestimating people. In this case, it was the ones I thought I knew the best. If you would have asked me how these people, my parents and grandparents, would have responded to the subject of homosexuality in 2014, much less 1978, I would have been totally, completely and one hundred percent wrong.

Where I assumed closed-minded negativity, instead I received well-thought-out open-mindedness.

Maybe they were just trying to be nice, avoiding conflict, a family trait that was probably honored pictorially on our coat of arms, but still, they hadn't looked angry. Instead, they had truly listened.

It was one of my worst personality traits, assuming the worst, underestimating everyone but myself. Could I ever improve? Would I ever change? How many times had I been the problem?

Perhaps the worst thing you can possibly be guilty of is assuming that the people you don't agree with also don't have a heart.

Pulling the notebook back out, I jotted down, "*1978 ABC movie about lesbian couple with custody battle. Was it a real story? Where was the case? What happened next?*" Pausing, I turned to a new page, writing in big block letters, "*STOP ASSUMING THINGS ABOUT PEOPLE. OTHER PEOPLE HAVE HEARTS TOO.*" Then I flipped again. "*Ask Mom and Dad about homosexuality, how they perceived it throughout their lives. What do they really think? What about love?*"

If only writing things on a to-do list could make them really happen.

The kids filtered back in their pajamas. You never saw a lot of "proper" pajamas anymore, back in 2014, but this group was well represented. Even at twelve and ten years old, Kim and Amy were wearing matching PJs, lightweight pink cotton gowns with cartoon chickens.

As for Rick, he wore a formal two-piece get-up, made of heavy starched cotton. The motif was some sort of exploding superhero, but what I remembered best about it, this same outfit, was one Christmas morning he wore it when my dad shot video with his eight-millimeter Bell & Howell camera. Based on the wear of the fabric, which looked almost new, it had to be this upcoming Yuletide when film history would be made. Though it was almost instantaneous, the sequence always got a good laugh because if you looked carefully, while Dad panned around the formal living room at the gifts and celebrants, he caught a glimpse of Rick's horse coming out of its barn door. To clarify, his snake was peeking out of its pot, or, his sausage was coming out of its bun.

Good times.

To avoid the looming threat of bedtime, the three kids began to plead with Dad to come up with some sort of game. Whether it was because he had come from the land of no TV, or due to the fact we only had three television channels, Dad was gifted at coming up with exciting competitions and diversions.

Nightly knowledge tests, high-impact hide-and-seek, full-scale bingo, art contests and other games requiring all the cunning and skill we could muster were a regular part of our childhoods.

Relenting, Dad set up a metal trash can from Mexico in the walkway that led to the master bedroom. It was the family-favorite "toss the tennis ball in the trash can." It consisted of Dad moving the can to different distances, offering varying degrees of difficulty, each of us in turn trying to sink the said tennis ball into the tall can. He always sweetened the pot in this game of daring-do and achieved his underlying goal of teaching us a life lesson by "betting" us more and more money as we sunk consecutive numbers of balls into the can.

Kim, as the oldest, was the most successful at the game. With every ball she managed to sink, Dad would up the ante. "OK, Kimber," he would say. "You've made three balls in a row now, if you make a fourth you will double your money, *BUT*, if you miss, you'll lose everything."

On the night of my delusional return, this night, Kim had gotten about five consecutive balls in the can, making the jackpot large enough to have all three kids, and me, giddy at the thought of such a big prize purse. Dad gave Kim the option of stopping at the total she had already "earned" or throwing one more ball. If she made it, she doubled her money. But, again, if she erred, it was all over.

Kim inevitably missed the last shot, badly, and lost all of her "investment" in a painful fashion. All told, she lost eight dollars in the game, eight dollars she never had to start with. But, Kim—with a flair for the dramatic—would no doubt amp up the level when she retold the story at a later date. Which I knew she would do.

As the contest continued, it became clear that Little Amy completely and totally sucked at "throw the tennis ball in the can." This probably came as no surprise to my dad, or my siblings, as I was horribly uncoordinated. Physical awkwardness combined with my hyperactive nature resulted in a poor showing in many such competitions. The only thing I really had going for me, a trait that is still a double-edged sword, is that I was and am over-competitive.

So, as Kim and Rick sank balls in the receptacle, Little Amy bombed out. The great thing about Dad was that he continued to encourage her, as he always had, even though it was clear that she was never going to go to the Olympics in "toss tennis balls in Mexican trash cans." Nope, Little Amy wasn't going to make the medal count in that event. Dad was going to have to wait until she polished her interpretative ribbon dancing skills for that to happen.

As good fortune would have it, finally, late in the evening (or 8:17 in the land of Dick and Sue), Amy made three consecutive balls into the can. Lining up for her fourth shot, she had some serious cash on the line. Though Dad issued all the stern warnings about gambling, bug-eyes was totally going for it. Oh yeah, she played it up, wiggling around and doing lunges in preparation for the biggest shot of her life.

It was the 1970s version of *Deal or No Deal* and she was all in: "*No Deal, Dick!*"

What happened next amazed and dazzled everyone, even my grandparents, even my mother who was sitting across the iron fence in the living room and even her poodle who she was holding in her arms.

Yes, Little Amy sunk the ball in, no bounce, no trick shots, nothing but pure, unfiltered air. The fuzzy fluorescent orb soared about ten feet and hit the inside of the can with the precise amount of spin necessary for a score.

Six dollars was in her pocket, Kim had lost, she had won and Rick, well, he would never even remember that it had ever happened.

Overwrought with pure glory, Amy did what any other ten-year-old girl would do. She took off every shred of her clothing, even her Hollie Hobbie underwear, and ran, pranced and flourished in the nude. Wait! I remembered this, this was an actual memory! I remember the streaking, the real streaking. As much as the football game was my one shining moment and badassery in a sport I would love forever, this, the naked run, represented actual participation in something I would spend the rest of my life talking crap about. Streaking.

I was an actual streaker.

As I watched, mesmerized, Little Amy continued, flinging herself unadorned from room to shining room as Dad tried, in vain, to regain control. "AMY, put your clothes back on!" He demanded, shaking his head. Honestly, I think I saw the hint of a smile behind his look of astonishment, a twinkle in his eye, as he watched the brilliant antics of someone he was biologically responsible for.

He had sexual relations, somewhere, maybe in Ohio, and this had happened.

As for the rest of the crowd, whether it was awe and admiration on the faces of my siblings, my grandparents, my mother and her poodle or just shock and terror, I couldn't be sure.

When Dad finally caught up with her, she was trying to scale the fireplace mantle. How mad could he really be? It was athletic genius and it was followed up with a magnificent display of enthusiasm and a salute to a fabric-free lifestyle.

"I am so sorry about that," Mom said to me from across the iron railing, her left hand resting on her left temple. "You didn't need to see that." As much as I thought what Little Amy had done was completely hilarious, and impressive as hell, I could also totally see how any mom would have been embarrassed for a stranger to witness it. I guess there really are two sides to every story.

Chapter Thirteen

ZIP UP YOUR BIBLES!

*N*ot surprisingly, Amy's gold-medal run ended the evening for the kids. Before they went, one of the adults had the genius idea of switching from foamy lager to full-on cocktails. Yes, after nine hours spent messing about with the light stuff, the bar was now open. After taking orders, Dad went up the two steps into the breakfast room, around the corner and then reappeared in the bar. Reemerging, he passed drinks to his parents and me and returned to his spot by the fireplace. Moments later, Mom returned from the formal living room and found herself drink-less. Quick to remedy this deficiency, she called for Amy, now fully clothed, to make her a scotch and water.

The request didn't shock me, because the memory of making drinks in the red tweed bar was vivid. As I got older it turned into a case of make one, drink some, make another, and drink more. That said, the forty-six-year-old mother in me was surprised. First, there was young Amy's age and then her deft handling of the drink-making process. She had plainly done this numerous times, scooping the ice from the maker with an odd familiarity, carefully measuring out the precise amount of Johnnie Walker Red, and then the water. As clear as it was that she had done it before, her enthusiasm was equally as obvious. Mom wasn't asking only because she needed somebody to fill her order, Amy liked doing the job. She liked it a lot.

But, this was a ten-year-old kid, she was in the fourth grade, freaking elementary school. It was different than fetching a beer or even pouring wine . . . it was legit bartending. The only thing she didn't do—and she would have given the opportunity—was to stick a cocktail sword through a couple of olives and fancy-cut a lime.

Most unsettling, was that Little Amy was quenching the thirst of someone whose desire for another drink would affect the equilibrium of the family collectively and its individual members. It wouldn't mean to, and maybe it really wouldn't be anybody's fault, but it certainly would throw things out of kilter.

It wasn't like it, the drinking, would lead to one single, life-altering dramatic moment when everything changed. Instead, it would lead to a long series of smaller dramatic moments that would grow huge in impact because nobody would ever address them. It wasn't so much that nobody ever discussed the drinking, but nobody ever discussed what happened because of it.

Watching my younger self mix a drink was a telling moment, it illustrated my confusing relationship with alcohol. I wasn't afraid of it, here or in the future, but I should have been. The connection and the impact were both lost on Little Amy. I wished that I hadn't seen it, or instead that it would have been just another harmless, meaningless trip down fairy-like memory lane, if there was such a thing.

With the drink safely delivered to mom, Amy sat on the fireplace hearth, swinging her legs excitedly, humming what sounded like a Christmas carol. "Kids," Mom said, scanning the room, "It's late, you three need to get to bed."

"Yes," Dad agreed, "Tell your grandparents and your cousin Mrs. Daughters good night and go on up."

Going around the room and kissing everyone, Little Amy paused longer with me, leaning in close, too close, but at least she had brushed her teeth this time. Loudly whispering, she asked, "Can you come and tuck me in?"

I agreed with a simple nod. I longed to do it, in a way that I still don't completely understand.

Perhaps her request was life's way of completing the delusion or fantasy with an exclamation point. Perhaps Little Amy could feel the direct connection between us—we were the same person, for the love of God. Or maybe she was just really needy . . . I got that. Instead, could it be that she wanted reassurance that her tennis-ball-inspired streak didn't offend? That last bit came to mind, I presume, because of all the times as an adult I had done something ridiculous one night—an inevitable consequence of a personality that gets carried away when people start laughing—only to wake up the next morning in a panic about what everyone thought. *Crap*, I would lay in bed and wonder, *I hope nobody was offended when I drank margaritas out of that crystal bowl with a huge velvet sombrero on*, or *why in the world did I think it was a good idea to reenact my own birth at Denny's?*

After the kids went up, I looked down into my bourbon and water—I had asked for a rum and diet, my go-to drink if a cocktail was required. Not only did they not have rum here, they didn't have a clue as to what diet anything was. In fact, this household seemed to be totally devoid of Coke products of any kind, or soda, or pop as they disturbingly like to say in southwest Ohio. Who in the hell would host Thanksgiving without a fridge pack of Diet Coke? I'll tell you who . . . people in the '70s who, while they don't have Diet Coke, have an outside refrigerator full of Schlitz, Old Milwaukee, and Coors, the freaking Banquet Beer.

I stopped to consider my trip upstairs to visit myself. People can generally be classified into two categories: Those who want to go back in time and those who would rather be launched into the future. I have always been passionately affiliated with the go-back people, not the forward thinkers. Hence my obsession with history, eBay, estate sales and my metal detector. Now I was faced with a situation that heretofore I would have only dreamed of . . . drooling at the thought of a visit to my childhood room. Yes, maybe this was all but a dream, and maybe I could have done without the layers and layers of adult drama I had previously known nothing about, but, this was getting good. Damn good.

Taking a generous slug of the bourbon—I briefly wondered how many alcohols I had mixed with turkey and dressing over the past several hours—I began to feel warm and fuzzy. I worried about the effect this relaxed state would have on Little Amy. I also didn't want to get sick in my parents' third-floor bathroom.

Who was I right now? Was I a forty-six-year-old mother of two—a person with maternal instincts—or merely a larger version of the little girl upstairs? And what in the world was I going to say to her? Then I thought of what Mary had said in the parking lot of the elementary school, "You can't mess this up, no matter what . . ."

With that in mind, I rose carefully and strode across the room, creating enough friction with my fibrous pantsuit to provide electricity to a mobile home park. Placing my drink on the black bar countertop, I hesitated, looking up to review the bottles lined up neatly, the padded brown vinyl ice bucket and the shimmering glassware. I wasn't going to stop drinking in the future, no, I wasn't, but I might think about it differently.

"I'm going up to say goodnight to Amy . . ." I said, semi-confidently.

The rest of the adults smiled as Grandma Bee emoted, "Looks like the two Amys are going to be friends, friends for life . . ." I had always sworn that Grandma had some sort of innate wisdom that allowed her to see things the rest of us couldn't. Yes, maybe she talked—with a sense of amazement that made no sense—about how the plastic patio chairs looked like real metal, but weren't. And OK, maybe she did make us stand away from our very first microwave oven so our personals wouldn't be radiated, zapping our fertile gardens. All that to one side, she may have been the most intuitive person I have ever met.

Making my way through the formal living room and up the second half-flight of steps, I paused in the game room, trying to determine which of the two bedrooms Amy was in. Luckily she had left her door open and I could see her busily moving about, preparing for my arrival. It was the room to the right of the bathroom, the only carpeted space in the entire house which didn't have harvest-gold shag. Instead, it was adorned in a light-green pile. The wallpaper and carpet were the only combination that had already been in place when Mom and Dad had purchased the house. The paper was green with huge white and pink flowers smeared all over it, screaming something inaudible, but disturbing. There was a built-in desk immediately to the right of the door, with bookshelves above it. Furniture dotted the room, all stuff that had been our great-grandmother's, green and hand-painted with flowers. The pieces were beautiful: a bed frame, a dressing table and an armoire. I seriously had never noticed how exquisite it all was, wasted in this messy room that I hadn't picked up in many days.

Little Amy was sitting on her bed, smiling wildly as I entered. "This is my room!" she stated with glee. No kidding, I thought, hoping Miss Obvious would have something more earth-shattering to add. As much as I wanted to do this, it was clear that she wasn't going to make it easy. "Let me show you my collections," she said with an almost pained expression. It was a plan she had probably concocted as soon as I had agreed to come up, or, in her heart of hearts, as soon as I had been thrown over the threshold of the front door.

She began with her collection of dice, a real treasure. She had dice from Las Vegas, miniature dice, and then dice she had swiped from the Yahtzee set and the Clue game. They were all different colors and sizes, proudly displayed in a glass, brass-trimmed, hand-etched case from, where the hell else, Mexico. It was, apparently, the Ikea of the 1970s.

"They are great," I said, secretly admiring this specific collection, as I wished I still had it. She sensed my appreciation, and though she should have been shocked that somebody else in the world, anybody, was interested in a collection of plastic dice, she seemed wholly satisfied.

She was so much so, it wouldn't have surprised me if she had laid back triumphantly in her bed, puffing a cigar. "Yes," she might add victoriously. "These are the finest dice known to mankind."

We moved on to a shoe box half-filled with dirty bottle caps, an album of used stamps, a paper lunch sack full of matchbooks—a safety hazard—and some proof sets of coins that Dad had started giving us every Christmas. Each collection was explained in laborious detail, with Little Amy wide-eyed, arms and hands waving wildly about. As her tone became higher-pitched —if that was even humanly possible—we entered her closet. The floor was covered with Barbie clothing, a Fisher Price castle, a half-cocked Super Perfection game and the fold-out stage for the *Donny and Marie* TV show. After nearly wiping out on an upside-down Simon game, I stopped to see her pull out what looked like a plastic locker with sports figures splashed all over it.

Now, here was a real treat, the baseball card collection. This must have been before I had the brilliant late-night idea of gluing a bunch of the cards inside of my closet walls—a move I had paid for dearly on a couple of different levels. Not only did I devalue the collection, incurring my own regret—I devalued the actual structure, incurring my Mom's wrath.

Plopping down on her bed to inspect the box, again Little Amy didn't seem amazed by my obvious enthusiasm. She was just happy, very happy. Guiding me through each subsection of the box, which had a badly placed sticker next to it detailing its contents in misspelled wording, she nearly peed her pants when she arrived at her (OK, our) favorite compartment . . . the coveted "uniformed catchers" collection.

Each of these twenty-five or so cards depicted, in gleaming

color, on not very glossy card stock, a catcher in his full pads. In most cases, the catcher appeared with facemask on and if not, it was held firmly in the non-gloved hand. This was a critical difference if you were going to properly sort the cards. In age, they dated from the '50s to the '70s. The biggest portion came from the 1978 Topps release that Rick and I had collected so faithfully just that year. These were exquisite. Yes, even though Little Amy was hard to digest as a full meal, she was a genius when it came to baseball cards.

She went on to explain how she sometimes stayed up late into the night sorting the cards according to a batter's RBI or a pitcher's ERA, in the appropriate ascending or descending order. I was immediately impressed not only that she understood what the acronyms meant, but that she was already mesmerized by statistical rankings. Oh, what I wouldn't do to show her the joys of sorting stats on an Excel spreadsheet. It would change her life. Literally.

As she returned the box to the back of the closet, I considered how it might have seemed odd to some, well, many, in sterile '70s suburbia where everyone had a carefully crafted, well-defined role to play, that a ten-year-old girl not only collected the cards, but that she so enthusiastically sorted them. I also wondered if my life, based on my interests alone, would have taken a different path if I had been born in say, 1998.

Little Amy was a dichotomy. On the one hand, there was the bright orange Malibu Barbie camper and the Sunshine Family treehouse complete with the creepy dad's facial hair, while on the other there was the Major League Baseball mini-pennant collection and a pile of old sports pages, with the betting line for each Houston Astros game carefully circled.

Yes, for every Barbie there was a corresponding figure from the Civil War battlefield set. And, for every Nancy Drew book, there was a copy of *Pro Football Digest*.

Who asked for what amongst the piles of items that were

thrown about the room and closet? Because at ten, she wasn't running out and buying this stuff on her own. Did she—or me —want both sets of things, or was one encouraged while the other was tolerated? Was the obvious diversity of the items celebrated or talked about quietly in the dark corners of the house? Was she the little girl they had always wanted, or was she the one they weren't sure what to do with?

And how did she feel about herself? Did she even have any thoughts like that, or was she just living in the moment, happy because she was totally unaware that there was a need for anything like that? Was there a need for anything like that?

How did they handle it when she drew pictures of army medals and worked hard to memorize each military rank and resulting insignia? Did they treat her differently? Did she feel different about herself? Who was she, and how was all this going to affect the me that we would become?

And why couldn't I remember the answer to any of these questions?

As she rifled around in the closet looking for another treasure to bedazzle me with, it hit me. I had two kids back at home. Did I treat them like who they were, or instead did I treat them like who I thought they were? Was it their reality or my expectations? And though setting a high bar for moral standards and building character were certainly good things, how much should my expectations have to do with who they became? When, if ever, do people find themselves if they've had somebody else tell them who they are for all of their formative years? And, which is better: finding yourself or taking somebody else's word for it?

And what business did I have questioning my own parents' intentions if I couldn't even be sure of my own?

Were these the questions that Mary said I would have?

As I was becoming completely convinced that I should have taken another shot of the noxious bourbon before coming upstairs, Amy burst out of the closet with a big Barbie head attached to a pink base. The almost sinister looking item, with strange fixated eyes, was the Barbie Beauty Center where aspiring hairstylists could work their magic. With a wild look in her eyes she said, "Look, I really messed this thing up!"

The Barbie head was all jacked-up indeed: The hair was sticking out at strange angles, goopy and frazzled. Some sort of permanent red color had been added to her lips and eyes, not in a good way, while other random features were drawn on her face with an ink pen. Barbie was wearing a collar that had been taken off of a stuffed animal, and the tray where her torso rested was filled with Hot Wheels, bobby pins, crayons, a Kazoo and a Chinese finger trap.

"I used my chemistry set to do her hair!" Amy said with an almost maniacal laugh. "I call it my secret super-duper magical hair potion . . ."

"That's AWESOME!" I gushed. "Did it foam up and smoke when you put it on her hair?"

Well, finally something had surprised her. She stopped cold and looked at me, stunned. "Yes, it did . . ." she said, with her eyes as big as checkers. "I thought it was going to blow up . . ."

"That's amazing!" I said. "I wish I could have seen it!"

Smilingly broadly, perhaps the biggest smile I'd ever seen, she said, "Me, too."

Suddenly, we could hear Mom yelling up, "Lights out up there!" Amy took the Barbie head and hurled it unceremoniously into her closet. Though this didn't bother me, if Will or Matthew had done something even remotely similar, I would have thrown a hissy fit.

Yes, it had just been confirmed, again, on my little field trip. I was and I am a hypocrite.

"Can you stay . . . until I turn out my lights?" Amy asked.

"Of course I can." I didn't want the moment to slip away to where it was headed, forever-land.

Climbing into bed, she swiped the wide variety of "other"

items off the top and tucked herself in the pale pink sheets and matching checkered bedspread. Leaning over to her bedside table, she pulled out two Bibles.

"I like to read the Bible every night before I go to bed," she said with a great deal of solemnity in her voice. I nodded as she carefully displayed the two books. I sat down on the edge of the mattress as she began to explain that she "liked the way the white Bible looked, but she couldn't understand it, so she read the green one every night instead."

"The white one I got for memorizing all the books of the Bible at church," she said. "It has my name on it in gold letters and a zipper around it with a cross on it. It's cool if you like to zip up your Bible like this," she said while zipping and unzipping the sacred scriptures repeatedly.

I didn't reply, so she continued, "The white one is a King James Bible," she said, using the same knowing tone as when she'd described the tambourines for the Gong Show, "and the green one is the Living Bible . . . it's hard to understand too, but I can read some of it."

Turning to the first page, she showed me a vividly colored picture depicting Jesus walking with two children. "I love this picture," she said with a far-off tone in her voice. "I like how Jesus looks like he really loves the kids. He looks so nice. I really like how he's holding the boy's hand and how he's got his hand on the girl's shoulder. It makes me feel good."

Turning another couple of pages, she came to a picture of a young shepherd boy sitting in a field at night, looking into the stars, with a lamb sitting next to him. "This is something I read almost every night," she said, pointing to the words on the accompanying page. "Can I read it to you?"

"Sure." I was sure she could hear the emotion in my voice.

Fumbling with some of the words and pronunciations, in her small voice, flat-faced Little Amy read to me:

Because the Lord is my shepherd, I have everything I need!

He lets me rest in the meadow grass and leads me beside the quiet streams. He restores my failing health. He helps me to do what honors him the most.

Even when walking through the dark valley of death I will not be afraid, for you are close beside me, guarding, guiding all the way.

You provide delicious food for me in the presence of my enemies. You have welcomed me as your guest; blessings overflow!

Your goodness and unfailing kindness shall be with me all of my life, and afterwards I will live with you forever in your home.

FOR a few long seconds after she'd finished, we sat in silence. I didn't know what to say. I knew that she read this passage on a regular basis, and I kind of remembered what it had meant, but I didn't know, after thirty-five years had passed, what in the world I could possibly say. I could have never imagined the opportunity to comment.

Looking away from me and then back into my eyes, she said, "You know, I really believe this, I believe in God. I think He holds my hand, like in the picture of the little girl, and that He's always here, even when things don't go right. Or when I mess stuff up. You know, I mess a lot of stuff up . . . But He's always here, He helps me mess stuff up less. He knows I want to be good."

I knew I had to say something, but what? I wasn't her parent. I wasn't some adult she looked up to. Hell, I wasn't even real.

She had it all figured out. She did mess stuff up. As hyper and entertaining as she was, she had a temper, she reacted poorly to things, and she could be a problem. Or, that's how I remembered it. That's what they said. But, though I had definitely seen the hyper stuff, I hadn't seen the angry side of her since I had, well, gotten here. But, that didn't make it not true. No, spending eight hours in someone's house didn't mean you got to see everything. No matter what you thought you knew.

She believed. She believed in God, and Jesus, and all the rest of it. It brought her comfort, and though I remembered the nightly readings, even at a young age, and the prayers, I had forgotten their impact, what they meant personally, before anyone else explained to me how it was supposed to work.

Little Amy didn't know a thing about the challenges of religion, the simplicity of grace combined with the absolute complicated nature of it. The double standards that mixed unconditional love with strict requirements, harsh judgment with hypocrisy and total inclusion with exclusivity. Feeling unloved not by God, but by God's people. Not being capable, myself, of loving all God's people. Judging. Being judged. All things brought on by the supposed advancement, promotion if you will, to mature adulthood.

In Amy's heart and soul there was no room for any of this. As idiotic, lost and naive as she seemed, and she was, her grasp of what was real was tremendous. If faith were real, she had it. Unsoiled, unspent belief formed in the face of real life, not some sort of milky white, childhood Fantasyland.

I wanted to hug her tight, perhaps causing some of her to seep into me and some of me to be transported into her. Inasmuch as we were wholly the same person, we weren't, because life had happened to me and she was still fresh from it. But, then again, life was happening to her too, only enough time had passed for me to forget most of it. Only the highs and lows of the memories of her time had stayed with me. All the details, even the important ones, the stuff I could use now, had been lived away.

Amazingly, she had sat quietly all this time awaiting my response. Maybe part of the delusion was that I got enough time to think things through while the experience was happening in real time. Or, instead, maybe I had thought it all through in less than a minute, who knew. The definition of what time was had been altered forever.

"You know, Amy," I said, fully aware that my words were destined to be inadequate, "I think you're right, I believe it all too, it's real, all of it. Sometimes I think of Him putting His hand on my shoulder, like you said, being there with me."

She nodded, seeming to look straight into my soul for some sort of guidance, some kind of answer.

"I mess things up too," I continued, treading carefully. "But sometimes, sometimes, we think we are messing things up worse than we really are. It's important to try and be better, always, but also not to blame ourselves for everything that happens in our life.

"Sometimes bad things happen, even to people who are trying really hard to be good, but, you are right, God is always with us, and will always love us. His love is bigger than anything. Even when things get hard. Even when things go wrong. 'Always' is a good word for it."

Smiling, she said, "I'm glad you believe too, it must be because we both are Amys."

"Maybe so," I said, trying to lighten the mood and not let on that I could only see this conversation through the perspective of thirty-five years of upcoming ups and downs. She saw only the hazy future, full of supposed promise, but in reality totally unaware of how it would play out or what growing up really meant.

She was safely there on the front end, and I was somewhat secure on the other side of forty, also unaware of my own future path. The only difference was I knew what was ahead of her. If I could only protect her, prepare her, hold her hand as she went. No matter what I did or said here, she would still have to live through a series of horribly painful events, culminating, or perhaps peaking, when she/we would drink way too much in college and slash her left wrist.

We didn't want to die, we wanted someone to acknowledge the pain we didn't even know we had. Then, the nineteen-year old version of us would have to call home from a pay phone, with our roommate standing behind us with a Bible in her hand, and explain to Mom what we'd done, using real words and being honest about what we thought we remembered when we were Little Amy. Then we'd have to convince Dad, who came alone, to let us stay in school . . . and then we'd have to face finding the empty bottles in the nightstand when we went home for Christmas.

How in the world was I supposed to get this little girl through that?

Holy Shit. Is this why Mary said I'd know what I couldn't say?

But helping Little Amy through what came next was as unreal as time travel itself. She would go, not alone, but not with her adult self to misinterpret and distort it. What she would have was the reassurance of that loving hand on her shoulder, the one that was there even though it couldn't be seen. It would be there—in high school, in college, and beyond, because it was still there, in 2014. Until just now I had forgotten that this is where it had all begun. In this room. Our needs had been met without us even knowing it. I'm not even sure we asked for it.

Little Amy returned the Bibles neatly to the bedside table, restoring order to the only orderly part of her room. I helped her pull her covers up and turned off the porcelain lamp, hand-painted with the delicate flowers we would not become. As I got up, she was still looking intently at me. I could barely make out her face in the dim glow of the Donald Duck nightlight. "Can I have a hug, Mrs. Daughters?"

"Only if you call me Amy," I said, leaning down to hug her.

Our embrace was long and meaningful, the kind of hug that should have ended sooner, but at least both parties were holding on for dear life rather than one person awkwardly wanting it to end. To be honest, I was probably the one more desperate for her little embrace than she was for mine.

Luckily, she couldn't see my teary eyes as I walked out of the dark room. "Goodnight Little Amy," I whispered as I went out.

"Goodnight Big Amy!" she said happily.

Standing in the doorway, I felt compelled to say just one more thing. "Hey Amy . . ." I said.

"Yes, Big Amy?" she said.

"Everything is going to work out really well, remember that, no matter what," I said, trying to sound as authoritative as possible.

"I promise, I'll remember," she replied, smiling broadly from under the covers.

I hoped both of us believed me.

Chapter Fourteen

THE HAPPIEST BITCH IN HERE

*B*ack downstairs, I was shocked to see that several other adults had joined my paternal grandparents and Mom and Dad for cocktails. Stupidly, I had assumed that Thanksgiving ended once we were tucked in our beds upstairs. Seriously, what was left to do? But, on the other hand, seriously, it was only nine o'clock at night and these people had a bar and a refrigerator full of nasty beer.

What immediately struck me, other than the stream of people coming in the front door, was how loud it was. How in the world were the three kids upstairs staying asleep with all this going on? Beyond that, why had we never known about the after-party? Or, had we just forgotten it, along with a million other hazy memories which had been filed away somewhere in our subconscious?

I suppose I had seen this group before, in the summer, wet and celebratory in ill-fitting and awkward swimwear, their hoo-hoos and dingle-dots bursting out. Both then and now they were drinking, talking, and enjoying the common ground of a mortgage, three kids, and life in suburbia. The same life that 85.3 percent of them once swore—in high school probably—they would never have. But, life got in the way, it just happened. They fell in love, got married, bought a car, and had married sex frequently enough for their mothers to cry hysterically when they found out they were pregnant. Then came the real work, the real joy, the real disappointment and the real love.

Yes, one day you're at the Fast and Cool dancing wildly in a cage. You're studying in the college library, your entire life and all the dreams you think you have are spread out ahead of you like an endless road. You have skinny thighs, you listen to the right music, you drive with nowhere to go, and you can eat McDonald's fries without worrying about that inner tube forming on your hips. Poochy stomachs and deformed belly buttons will never happen to you! That crap is for someone else.

Then, boom! The next thing you know, you're folding some guy's underwear, you're at the Chuck E. Cheese's—with eyes glazed over—trying to convince a four-year-old that he is not going to win the Angry Bird stuffed animal in the crane game, not even if you give him a hundred quarters.

From oh-so hot to oh-so tired in about four minutes. It's a whirlwind, it's the slowest process known to man, and it's over before you can even exhale.

I recognized some of the partygoers as parents of my childhood friends and others as owners of the neighboring homes. As Dad brought me another drink, I let myself slip into the crowd, starting up a conversation with a guy named Steve from the cul-de-sac. Before this, my interaction with him had been limited to a friendly wave when he came home from work in his Chevy Caprice Classic, or an awkward glance when we ran through his yard while he was mowing the lawn in his short-shorts.

He was mildly attractive, only this was somewhat hidden by the fact that he was wearing a powder-blue double-knit leisure suit with a wide-collared Lycra shirt. The shirt was unbuttoned enough to reveal a bushel of chest hair, in which rested two wide gold chains. The fact that he thought he was a player, and I was an unknown female in questionable attire, didn't really put me off. I knew the 2014 version of this guy, and frankly, the future was better looking and a little less obvious than the past. OK, a lot less obvious.

"What do you think of Texas?" he asked smoothly.

"Well, I could live here," I replied. "The weather is definitely better."

"Wait till the summer!" he warned, leaning down to wipe a pretend scuff off his crocodile boots. "Then you'll be careful what you ask for, you'll bake like a Yankee Pot Roast."

His wife, Joyce, joined us. She was pretty, very pretty, but by the way Steve leered around the room, he may or may not have totally appreciated that. And, perhaps she didn't appreciate how tight his pants were, maybe a full-size smaller than his actual dimensions. Seriously, these folks needed to reconsider what was becoming an epic failure in the battle of the bulge.

Joyce was wearing a dark-red double-knit pullover with a wide collar and matching polyester pants. The smock, I guessed that's what it was called, had two pockets, almost like something an art instructor would wear. It, the smock thing, was worn over a ribbed white turtleneck. The hemline of the pants was so long —almost dusting the ground—that that you could barely see shiny red shoes poking out. What really made her dazzle was a red-and-white plaid scarf that she had somehow managed to place on her head like a turban. Interestingly, it didn't cover all her hair. It was more like a ski cap with dark locks hanging out from each side. I'd never seen anything like it, in my life, outside of the Sears catalog.

Introducing me with a degree of intrigue, Steve told Joyce, "Amy's here on 'business'" almost like whatever "business" I was engaged in involved naked people, flashbulbs, and large containers of Vaseline.

Looking surprised, Joyce turned to me, and in an almost accusatory tone asked, "Really, you are traveling for work?"

"Well," I said somewhat cautiously, "It's not really 'work,' I'm just a writer and had to meet with an editor."

"Oh!" she said, somehow managing to add a splash of awe to what was otherwise a condescending tone. "How does your husband manage . . .? I mean, Steve would never be able to cope without me . . . Well"—she looked at her bridegroom —"how would he ever cook the meals, clean the house, take care of the kids, water the plants . . .?

"Do you have a live-in maid, or a nanny?" she asked, putting her hand dramatically to her chin so I could fully enjoy the red-and-white plastic bracelets she was wearing. Namely, how in the world could I pull that off, leaving poor Steve, and his chest hair comb, for seventy-two hours to fend for himself? A guy like this, with a degree in something weighty, and a big-time job with an attractive secretary, a Xerox machine, and socks that needed ironing. How could he possibly figure out to operate the oven and the mailbox door? It wasn't like I wasn't good enough to work, I think they were totally OK with that, it was more like my husband was above housework.

But you couldn't blame semi-sexy Steve or pretty Joyce. They were just living the way everyone else was. I wondered if Steve was happy being "THE guy" and if Joyce was happy being "the support role"? Maybe they were miserable, or perhaps they were both thrilled to bits with their choice to follow that long, gray line of people living the way everybody else had accepted as acceptable. It was the same line that would one day, not too long from now, be reestablished on Facebook for the whole world to monitor. Those who had a passion to follow the said blueprint for a "good life"—or who were successful at making it seem like they did—would be celebrated, "liked" or "shared." Those who didn't would be talked about offline, or shunned online. Exclusion by the lack of clicking in hearty agreement. Really, it wasn't any different than this. It wasn't any different than finding out that Steve secretly voted Democrat, or that Joyce was a lesbian who was in favor of abolishing the death penalty. In 1978, it would just take people longer to find out. In 1978, the front door to everyone's house was totally shut.

I also wondered, once stripped down to his briefs, if Steve—who suffered from a mild case of body hair—looked like Jim

Palmer from the Baltimore Orioles in those old Jockey underwear ads I used to ogle in *Sports Illustrated*. I'm not saying I wanted to see his kangaroo pouch, I'm just saying I wondered about it.

As Steve sauntered off to pursue more manly endeavors, Joyce introduced me to Patty and Lisa.

Though both ladies looked familiar to me, I immediately realized Patty was that neighbor who had always yapped about that ridiculous Loop De Loop salad at the Aviator's Grill at the Hooks Airport. OMG! That was her? She was a real person with a first name? It was almost like meeting a celebrity, like physically interacting with some memory you almost thought was made up.

Joyce's first order of business was to tell the other two women about my status as a working mother. I began to feel defensive, the same feeling I would have had in my own time as I tried to explain my dual roles as full-time mother and some-times writer.

"I write from home," I told the trio. "I still do all the house stuff, the laundry, the kids' activities, I just write when they are gone and, if I get behind, I write early in the morning or late at night." They seemed somewhat satisfied with that, but I couldn't be sure. It was the same scenario as me overplaying my writing work in 2014 and making sure everyone knew damn well how important and crucial it all was. They had to know it was a real job, not just a stay-at-home mom hobby.

Either way, my listening audience—in 1978 or 2014—could have nodded in hearty agreement, but that didn't mean they wouldn't be holed up in the half bath, a couple of drinks from now, talking about how they couldn't believe I worked, or didn't work, or was wearing that eye shadow, or had stared at Steve's southern hemisphere, or whatever. And the truth was, I could just as easily, given the right scenario, been the person leading the half bath witch-hunt, with another blameless victim totally un-aware in the next room. I could almost smell the scented candle.

Patty and Lisa were both eager talkers, and before I knew it I was happily submerged in conversation. It helped that I wasn't supposed to remember these people from my childhood and that the only thing that really separated us were the thirty-five years. Other than the whole time-travel angle, we were just four middle-aged women having a drink and talking. We covered everything from our kids' teachers to how we wished we could find a real way to lose weight. We were annoyed with our husbands about a myriad of things and we would have liked to take a vacation somewhere tropical.

"What I'm trying to use"—Patty was rocking a blue-and-white striped sweater worn over a tighter matching turtleneck, which reminded me of those costumes the Brady Bunch wore when they sang "Keep on Dancing" so they could pay for the engraving on their parents' anniversary platter—"are those Ayds Candies, you know, the ones that also have vitamins. You take them before you eat, with a cup of coffee, and then you don't want to eat as much. It's an appetite-suppression candy."

"Do they work?" Lisa asked, managing to speak despite wearing the largest bowed blouse I had ever seen in my life.

"Well," Patty replied, "I've already lost four pounds."

Though I remembered my mom taking those candy things, all I could think of now was what an unfortunate name for a product . . . seriously, "Ayds." That's just not right. And slurping it down with a cup of coffee? That sounded wrong on a bunch of different levels. Come to think of it, I couldn't ever remember people walking around with bottles of water in the '70s. How in the hell were these people staying hydrated?

The other thing that shocked and alarmed me was the number of people smoking. An actual haze blanketed nearly every square foot of both rooms. The many ashtrays, which had been standing ready, were already half-filled. Packs of Winstons, Camels, Kools, Kents, Pall Malls, and Vantages littered the flat surfaces of both rooms. While everyone puffed away, I wondered if all these people's stuff smelled like cigarette smoke: Their hair, their polyester clothing, their chest hair, their rattan furniture, their velour seats.

Mom made her way over to the group. She was noticeably relaxed, so much so that she almost seemed like a different person. Putting her arm around me, she asked, "Are you ladies getting to know Amy?"

"Yes," Patty responded as the others nodded. "So how was your Thanksgiving, Sue?" she asked.

"We almost had a fight break out at the end of dinner," Mom said.

"Oh, that's nothing," Joyce said, carefully turning her head as not to disturb her turban. "Steve's dad had too much to drink, got lost on his way to the bathroom, and peed in the pantry." This sent up shrieks from the pleased listeners. "He went right on the dog's Gaines-Burgers . . . Luckily they were individually wrapped."

"Did anyone see him doing it?" Lisa asked.

"Yes," Joyce said with a twinkle in her eye, "Steve's bitchy cousin Wendy walked in on him and screamed."

"Did she see IT?" Patty asked, verbalizing what we were all thinking.

"Oh yes she did!" Joyce said. "To soothe her nerves afterwards, she downed three crème de menthes and then proceeded to tell everyone exactly what it looked like." This sent us all into hysterics.

"Well, I don't have anything that good," Patty said. "But, my mother-in-law was constipated this morning, and she asked if I would help her with a suppository . . ."

This shocked everyone, even Joyce, who was still pretty damn sure she had won the round.

"Wow . . ." Lisa said, taking time to reposition the huge paisley bow protruding from her gray blazer-jacket. "Ours was really normal . . . makes me wish I had been at one of your houses."

"Oh, no, girl . . ." Joyce said. "You didn't have to clean up that pantry. Be so thankful."

"Has anyone read that book on the bestseller list . . .?" Lisa asked, changing the subject.

Before she could say anything else, Patty said, "You mean *The Thorn Birds*? The one by that Australian woman?"

Lisa tried to reply, but this time I cut in, completely forgetting where I was. "Isn't that a miniseries? I didn't know it was a book too?"

"What?" Mom said. "A miniseries? I haven't heard anything about that!"

"Yeah," I murmured, wishing I could Google *When did The Thorn Birds miniseries air?* and *Did an Australian woman write a book about it first?*

Trying to recover, I added, "Maybe I read they were going to make it into one."

"I guess it would be a good movie . . ." Patty said. "It's a beautiful story, one of the greatest romance novels of all time, it covers three generations of a family in Australia."

"Oh," I said stupidly, "I just thought it was about a hot priest who breaks his vows to sleep with a woman he's in love with . . . I didn't know it covered that many years."

Clearly, I was from 2014, a time where people watched the movie rather than read the book, or even knew there was a book.

"I was talking about *The Women's Room* by Marilyn French," Lisa said, annoyed.

"Oh, what's that one about?" Patty said.

"Well," Lisa said, with an air of confidence, "it's the most important book about feminism in history. It's about intelligent women in the 1950s who left their careers and aspirations to be married, eventually only to be left out in the cold by the time their husbands divorced them a couple of decades later."

"What?" Patty said. "That sounds awful and, well, interesting. Is it good?"

"I picked up a copy," Joyce cut in, "and, frankly, it's the most boring thing I've ever tried to read. I couldn't even get through the first chapter and on top of that, I had to hide it from Steve . . ."

"I found it fascinating," Lisa said, becoming defensive. "It's important for every woman to read."

"It's crap," Joyce said. "And who cares about all that feminism stuff? It's not right. Women are just fine where they are, at home." Glancing around the tight circle, her eyes fixed on me. "Well . . . I know what you are doing is different," she said. "But overall, we've got it pretty good."

"Maybe that's true," Lisa said coolly, placing her hands firmly on each side of her gray-and-red plaid skirt. "That is, until our husbands no longer want to be married to us and we have no way to support ourselves. That's what the book is about."

"Well, I never got to that part," Joyce said. "I do understand what an important issue that is, but all I got out of it was a bunch of inappropriate graffiti on some nasty bathroom stall wall. The main character had gone crazy and was pretending like whomever had written the words, on the stall, were having a conversation, with her. While all the time, she just sat there, fully clothed, on the actual toilet . . ."

"Perhaps you should reexamine it," Lisa said. "Did you know that in Louisiana, that's the state next to ours in case Steve didn't tell you, that there is still something called a 'Head and Master Law'?"

Silence. Yes, this was news to all of us, from all decades.

"It gives husbands complete legal control over the property of a married couple," she continued, pleased that she had finally gotten everyone's attention. "Just last month, the Supreme Court declined to review its decision to uphold the law . . ."

"That's scary . . ." Joyce blurted out, not allowing her to continue. "But that's L O U I S I A N A, lots of crazy Cajun stuff goes on over there, who knows what they're doing in those swamps!"

"The state line is less than two hours from where you are standing," Lisa said, riled up. "We know people from there— they are living under this law and have very few rights."

"Well," Joyce said, smirking, "then don't move there, and, if you already live there, move away."

"I need a drink," Lisa said, looking at Joyce like she was from another planet.

"I'll get you one, Lisa," Mom chimed in.

"She thinks she's so smart," Joyce remarked after Lisa was out of earshot. "Just because she went to Southern Methodist University suddenly she's a modern-day genius. I'll tell you what," she continued, snidely. "You don't need a degree in political science to separate the goddamn colors from the whites and add the goddamn Cheer into the washing machine." Patty looked stricken and backed away as Joyce continued to rant, "I went to the goddamn University of Houston for two years and that's just not good enough when you read all those important books and go to those goddamn meetings at the goddamn library.

"I'll tell you one goddamn thing," she nearly shouted, as Patty's drink began to quiver. "She's still got to come home, after the goddamn meeting about voting is over, and cook a goddamn tuna and noodle casserole, and have Wednesday-night sex with her husband and iron the goddamn sheets."

She spun around twice, almost magically, until she was directly facing Patty, who was unfortunately too timid to move away. Pointing her finger directly in Patty's face, Joyce slowly, methodically spoke, pure contempt oozing from every word. "I'll tell you ladies one thing, I may not be the smartest bitch at this party, but I'm the happiest."

Marching off, she had both hands on her turban, keeping it in place.

Silence.

Looking over at Patty, I nodded and said, "Ummm, wow, I'm sorry about that . . ." Before I could continue apologizing for something I had no control over, she smiled agreeably and thanked me, slowly backing away.

"I think I see my neighbor, Jean . . ." she said, her voice trailing off.

Looking around, I realized I didn't know anyone else in the room. Eager to distance myself from, well, everyone, I turned and went up the two steps into the breakfast room. Thankfully, it was empty. Leaning against the bookshelf, I reached down for my notebook. As I scanned the room to see if anyone was watching, I noticed a folded over piece of loose-leaf filler paper sticking out from between the cookbooks. I grabbed it, hoping no one was watching, and immediately recognized Mom's handwriting. It was one of her poems.

> *"Look to the East – Look to the West."*
> *North and South too – Which is the best?*
> *Catch a glimpse of little Nanny two shoes,*
> *Either way, you will not lose.*

What in the hell was she talking about?

> *His beautiful profile excels quite a bit,*
> *Any way you look at it, the baby is a hit.*
> *Look at that little snaggle tooth there,*
> *Sticking out just a tad under his nostril hair.*

> *Now usually he rests on the orange chair,*
> *Snuggled on his "A" blanket with care.*
> *He loves his "A" so it is easy to see,*
> *He speaks of her often as he itches his knee.*

> *Look at those little eye balls nestled just so,*
> *On each side of his crevice below.*
> *Take a gander at those ears of fluff,*
> *Crimped delicately into a perfect puff.*

Oh my Good Lord, she was writing about the dog. The poem was about the freaking dog.

What more can I say,
As I stare in wonder on this day
The beauty overwhelms me oh so much
And my heart feels a tender touch.

You can't make this stuff up.

Shoving the paper back onto the bookshelf, I pulled out my notebook and sloppily wrote, "*Look through old boxes for Mom's poems. Ask Rick and Kim. Have something published, or just printed, for Christmas. Ask Mom what was on my Christmas wish list. Find the Green Bible. When did water bottles become a thing?*" Turning the page, I added, "*When did* The Thorn Birds *become a miniseries? Read the novel. Look on Netflix. Look up* The Women's Room *on Amazon. Cliff Notes? Louisiana Head and Master Law, what is it? When did it go away?*" And, finally, "*Ask Mom for Patty, Joyce and Lisa's last names. Look up on Facebook.*"

Chapter Fifteen

IT HAPPENED IN THE CONSERVATORY . . .

Wandering back into the kitchen, I recognized the parents of one of the neighborhood gang. These people had always come across to me—as a youth—as the most upstanding of citizens. She was a tall, elegant lady from Mississippi and he was a balding oilman from the south of Houston.

I had spent a fair bit of time at their house growing up, and seeing them here, now, after throwing back a couple of cocktails, made what was already a surreal situation seem even more bizarre.

I was either going to have to stop drinking or limit my interaction to people who were strangers.

"Oh, you're the writer lady . . . the sports writer lady." Mrs. Crane said, somehow managing to look fabulous in her long plaid skirt that stretched from what seemed like her lower bra line to the linoleum. You couldn't tell where her top ended and her skirt began because of the green velvet vest she was wearing over a red turtleneck. Christmas had come early at the Crane's.

So, I'd been upgraded on the shock scale from writer to a sports writer. It was late enough and I had had enough to drink that my patience with the time-warp players was in quick decline. I wasn't going to justify my position again. If I did, it would likely just give them all something more to talk about.

In between heavy draws on her Salem—which should have, but didn't really subdue the sense of class she exuded—she introduced me to her husband. "This is Jim," she said in her thick southern accent, touching his shoulder. "He's an Oil Executive."

The way I remembered it, Jim was in oil, but the title of "executive" was somewhat diminished in my adult mind because of that one Saturday afternoon I had visited his office, with his younger daughter, a school friend. It consisted of only two rooms: his desk, a secretarial station with a lumbering Telex machine, and a couple of fake plants.

Jim stood a hulky six feet two and was dressed in a harvest-gold velour shirt. A zipper with a large circular pull stretched from about halfway between his nipples to his neck. If he had been wearing matching pants, he could have camouflaged himself on the living room carpet. The parts of his hair that remained were thick and bushy, as were his generous eyebrows. They were almost magical. Again, his man bulge was displayed proudly, leaving less room for the imagination of the lady folk. There was no doubt of who wore the pants in this relationship.

Jim and Toni seemed far less concerned with my employment status than others had. They just wanted to talk about how they were giving their sixteen-year-old son their Pontiac Grand Prix. "Yes, it's a cream-colored, two-tone 1974 model," Jim said proudly. "It's a fine automobile."

"Jim," Toni cautioned, "Little Jimmy MUST be careful if he's going to drive that car, it's so small."

If I was right, the 1974 Pontiac Grand Prix was about twenty-seven feet long, meaning little Jimmy—who, the way I remembered it, was at least six-foot-four—would have far less to fear than would the neighborhood trash cans, mailboxes, and fire hydrants.

"Oh God, *Toni*," Jim said, taking a lusty swig of his Lowenbrau. "That boy will be absolutely fine, he's almost a man now."

"Well, he may be big enough to be a man," Toni said, sipping on a glass of Black Tower wine, "but he still leaves ballpoint pens in his jeans pockets and he still needs help with his math homework."

Just then, another man joined us. "Hey, Jim!" he said, clapping Mr. C. on the back in a masculine fashion. "And, hello to you, Toni," he said, almost slyly, changing his demeanor to lean in and gently kiss her on the cheek. "I haven't seen you two in forever."

"Happy Thanksgiving, Wayne," Toni said.

"And, who do we have here?" he asked, taking me by the elbow. I wondered if all this touching was really necessary. It was almost like the men were supposed to pet the women, or were allowed to and nobody seemed to care. It was a subtle, unwritten amendment to the rules of engagement. It wasn't necessarily that I had a problem with men touching me, I just wanted to pick and choose the touchers and pass out bottles of hand sanitizer as necessary. These people knew nothing about ninety-nine percent antibacterial protection, liquid hand soap, or anything other than chunky bars of Lava and Dial. Oh yeah, and Camay, the naked wildflower-sex soap.

After being introduced to Wayne as the "professional girl," which made it sound like I might look wildly attractive in an extremely short skirt—I could totally go for that—he began rifling around in the front pocket of his red-and-white tartan pants. I think they were supposed to look like wool, but they were a double-knit fabric that was stretchy, itchy, and probably flammable. Up top he was wearing what I guessed was meant to be a fisherman's sweater, with knitted cable and diamond patterns.

Wayne was decent-looking despite the get-up and had what was perhaps the best head of hair in the room. And, he was trying to pull an oversized item out of his pants. Before you get the wrong idea, it was apparently an electronic item he was fishing out, which was shocking—at least to me—due to the severe lack of personal electronics at this party. In this specific wrinkle of time, every smartphone was canceled out by a pack of cigs. Finally managing to get the item out in the open, Wayne placed it directly in Jim's face, nearly scraping his generous-sized nose. "LOOK what I bought!"

"Is that a . . . .?" Jim asked, excitedly.

"YES IT IS!" Wayne shouted, before he could finish. "It's an Olympus Pearlcorder SD2, with the optional pop-in FM tuner."

"My God, I've never seen one of those up close!" Jim said, almost salivating, as if he were seeing an Apple watch for the first time.

"What does it do?" Toni asked, almost in a mystified state.

"Well," Wayne started, literally puffed up with pride, a move that freed more of his trapped chest hair. "First, it's a mini-cassette recorder, with a two-hour recording capability . . . AND—"

"Do you mean you can record two hours on that little, itty, bitty tape?" Toni cut in, southern accent on the full.

"Yes, ma'am," Wayne huffed, "it surely will . . . AND it has pop-in accessories, including extra speaker power and THIS little ol' FM tuner, which allows me to listen to music, and record it, wherever I am." To demonstrate, he snapped the small tuner in and out of the bottom of the device.

"And it's so compact!" Jim chimed in.

"Yes, sir, it is," Wayne continued. "The entire unit is not much bigger than a hand and a half!"

A crowd had started to gather, each asking to hold the device and each wanting a demonstration.

"Well, those are what we call 'voice actuators,'" Wayne explained to one mesmerized individual. "They prevent waste in recording by sensing when audible sounds begin and end."

All I could think, obviously, was how far technology still had to come. In 1978, Wayne was wowing a throng of upper-middle class professionals, and their spouses, with a device that would record two hours of audio and play FM radio stations through a tiny, scratchy speaker.

Thirty-five years from now, some guy would be standing in a similar slice of society—minus the flammable clothing—with his iPhone 6, which at a third of the size could literally answer any question known to humankind and record twenty-four hours of digital audio, or video, and play it, without a wire, through the neighbor's television or sound system.

Finally, somebody was brave enough to ask the most important question of all. "If you don't mind telling us, Wayne," a guy dressed like the cowboy from the Village People asked, "how much did you pay for that little gem?"

"Well, I'm not going to lie to you fellas," Wayne guffawed, pulling up his pants, embarrassed, but not cheesy, but, well, yes, totally cheesy. "I bought the base unit for about two hundred and forty bucks at Skylark Camera, and then shelled out a few more clams for the accessories."

"Dang . . ." the Village People Cowboy said. "That sure is a lot of money, but that little thang sure is purty."

"Well folks," Wayne explained, "when you get right down to it, this technology business, well, it's a pretty neat little deal."

Seriously? Two hundred and forty dollars, that was like eight-hundred bucks, or two iPhones, in 2014 money. Of course, I couldn't be sure, because I didn't have Siri to look it up for me. Pulling out my notebook, I scribbled, *Find out the value of 1978 money today. EBay: Olympus Pearlcorder WTF.*

As I placed the notebook back in my blazer pocket, I noticed a woman watching my every movement, transfixed as if I had just rolled a joint. "I'm a writer," I said, putting my face very near hers, so she'd have no doubt that I was a vicious mouth breather. "I write about college football, men's college football. And, I left my husband at home in Ohio, alone, with my kids, and three toilets."

She walked away, quickly, heading straight toward the half bath.

As the crowd around Wayne began to die down, I was left standing in the haze, alone, at a time of night later than I would have ever imagined, in this time, in this place. I needed a breath of fresh air. Weaving through the crowd, I let myself out the back door to the driveway.

Venturing out past a couple huddled in the shadows underneath the basketball goal, I turned the corner to the long brick wall on the side of the garage that followed the driveway out to the street. This is where I used to throw a tennis ball or kick a soccer ball, trying to set a record for the most consecutive catches or stops. Why was it my kids never practiced like that, just for the sake of doing it?

I had always assumed that it was technology that separated us, me and my kids' experiences, but perhaps it was personality and circumstances. Catching me by surprise, a heavyset man rounded the corner from the back of the house. He looked equally shocked but decidedly more pleased with his discovery than I was with mine.

"I was wondering where you went . . ." he said, not so softly. "I noticed you inside, but haven't met you yet." He was a big guy. I knew precisely where he lived and who his family was.

Dressed in a tan turtleneck that displayed his man boobs in an unattractive way, he moved closer until I could see the beads of sweat on his forehead. Despite his obvious drunkenness, his swarthiness, and his desire to break my personal space barrier, I felt no real fear from the man we used to refer to as Professor Plum. It was an apt name for the stout, balding man with a streak of Grecian Formula running through his wispy hair. He was no Colonel Mustard . . . hell, he couldn't have even pulled off Mr. Green. Though I didn't get the feeling I should run for my life, I did feel the need to find a polite way back inside, so I moved to my right, which was closer to the wooded side the driveway.

Sensing my desire to flee, he lunged forward, using his size-able torso to corral me back toward the side of the garage. In a heartbeat, I realized that something had gone terribly wrong. He shoved me against the bricks, bracing each of his fat arms on either side of me with his thick hands on the wall.

I was in trouble. I was in really big trouble.

He was bigger than me, and despite my sturdy, handsome size, he had trapped me. I could smell his perspiration and feel his heavy, labored breath. His thick, sweaty lips came close to mine and he slurred, in an eerie, sick whisper, "I've never had a girl from Iowa . . . but I want you."

My attempts to wiggle away, moving side-to-side between his arms, only sharpened his resolve. As he pressed against me, I could feel what little manhood lurked beneath his Sansabelt slacks. It didn't seem like much, but I didn't want it. Purring softly, or more like drunk grumbling, something about how he was "going to give me an early Christmas present, something I'd never forget," he put his open mouth on the side of my neck, his tongue wandering wildly. He whispered obscenities in my ear, words intended to arouse one of the two of us.

No matter how hard I fought him, the sheer girth of him meant that I would lose. He weighed enough to ruin both my life here and the one in the future. This had happened to me before, most recently about ten years from now, in college, but it was nowhere near as sinister. I had known that drunk guy, and he had ultimately let me win the fight, leaving me in the empty parking lot of an apartment complex.

Bringing his left arm down from the wall to unbutton and unzip his pants, the Professor crushed me against the brick wall. The pressure was so great that I had difficulty breathing. With his cat out of the bag, he latched on to my shoulders and shoved me toward the shrubs around the front of the garage.

As he threw me down to the mulch, my polyester pants sliding through the brown pine needles, he made a series of costly errors. His center of gravity, the same heftiness that allowed him to trap me and get me to the ground in the first place, combined with his inebriation, caused him to lose his balance. Next, his most vulnerable body part was fully exposed and in plain sight.

Acting on adrenaline, fear, and sheer panic, I raised my left leg and bashed his exposed man parts with the bottom of my strappy heeled sandal. Initially he was stunned, staring down at me with a dumb look on his fat face. The fact that he was already wobbling meant that my second counterattack, more violent and accurate than the first, took him totally out.

Across the driveway he went, stumbling, grabbing his privates in his thick hands. Moaning, he continued backward into the dense tree line, stopping only when he slammed against the translucent greenhouse. With his hands still covering his man tool, he slid down the ridged wall, finally landing with a thud. Slumped over, groaning, he began to vomit.

If I could have imagined this scene beforehand, in horror, I'd have pictured myself telling him off as he sat pathetically, bereft of any type of manhood or humanhood. Strong words that he'd never forget, delivered forcefully, preventing him from attacking another member of womankind.

But, in reality, the altered one, I didn't stalk off like the rape-stopper I was; no, I was no badass, I was lucky. I was fortunate to have gotten out of the situation and I was scared to death. Not relieved, not victorious, and not self-congratulatory. I was in shock.

My dog, apparently, was not. I'm not sure where he came from, but Cecil emerged from the darkness, sauntered over to the aggressor, now laid on his side in front of the greenhouse, lifted his leg and peed on Plum's wide butt.

Looking on at the scene in shock, my dog urinating on my would-be rapist, I tried to fix the visible, outward damage as I walked hurriedly across the driveway. Gone were the couple I had seen before, leaving nothing but the single light fixture to guide me back to relative safety.

I had thought I would be safe here, in the sanctity of my own home.

Once inside, I turned instinctually left and then right, entering the half bath. Shutting the door and locking it, I sat down on the toilet and began to shake. I couldn't tell anyone this, I couldn't accuse this guy, I wasn't even from here and who would I tell, anyway? Who would be my advocate? My parents, my new friends, my siblings, my younger self, upstairs dreaming of the World Series? That was the way I had always handled things. It was the way of our people, not to tell anybody the bad stuff. Not to talk about it, ever. To shelf it, box it, close it up and forget about it. In our world, or at least mine, discussing it and actually dealing with it only made it worse, more real. No, I wouldn't tell anybody about this. It wasn't even one of Mary's imagined questions. It had already been answered.

And, the truth was, there was every chance that none of this was real. And that included Professor Plum, in the front yard, with the pink lead pipe.

Standing up, wavering, I did a half-ass job of putting myself back together. I was dangerously losing sight of my mission. Onward was the only way through this, the only way to get to tomorrow, the only way anybody ever got through anything. I rushed back out of the bathroom, fleeing, I suppose, myself.

The crowd looked to be dying down. I milled aimlessly around the breakfast room. Sitting on the antique wooden trolley bench, I was surprised to see Dad come up the steps from the family room.

"Well, cousin," he said, "I hope you are having a good time!" Really, he was the last person I needed to see right now, or maybe he was just the person I needed to see. I could tell that he sensed that something was wrong. "You OK?" he said, looking almost puzzled.

If anything would make me cry right now, something I rarely did, almost never in front of another human being, it was his young face, full of confused concern. It wasn't the angst he would have shown if he knew who I was, but the compassion was still there.

"Let me get you a drink," he said, trying to fix things. He

swung back through the western doors to the bar and swung back out almost as quickly, drink in hand. I wasn't sure what he had concocted, but I took a healthy, medicinal gulp of it, trustingly, almost like when he used to give me a shot of white-chalky Kaopectate for a bad stomach.

"Thanks, Dad," I said, stopping myself halfway through the last word. "No . . . um . . . I'm sorry, I mean, thanks, Dick." Luckily, he'd had enough to drink that he either didn't catch what I said or was operating on the same "don't ask, don't tell" MO that I was.

"You're welcome," he responded, plopping down next to me. "So, we're cousins," he said, with almost a wistful tone in his voice, "and you live in Centerville, Ohio." Continuing on without waiting for a response. "You know, I loved growing up in Centerville. Things seemed so simple then . . ."

"It's still a great place to live, it's bigger now though, but my boys like it too," I responded.

"Yes," he said, "I think our three kids have a wonderful place to grow up, here, in Spring, in Northampton, but I don't know . . . you know, what's the best.

"I wonder how they will turn out," he continued, looking at me. "Do you wonder that?" Dad was opening up more than I thought he would have, but I was family and that meant everything. And, now that I thought about it, he did tend to become cheesier when drinking. More introspective, open and willing to share his feelings.

"Yeah, I wonder that too, with mine," I said, the most truthful I had been during this entire bizarre trip. "Who they will be, what kind of adults they will turn into, what jobs they will do . . . Will they be able to take care of themselves and did we do the right things for them?"

"Exactly." With an almost comical fist pump on the cast-iron bench arm. "I wonder," he said, "about all this," Motioning around the room, sweeping his arm toward the fake banana plant, the red countertops, the harvest-gold appliances and the mustard-colored linoleum floor. "We have so much, so much more than my parents had. That's what we want for our kids, we want more than we had, but is that good, or bad?

"Is simple better, or not?" he wondered aloud.

"Those are the same questions we have," I responded, not able to tell him that in my world, in 2014, what he thought was over the top now had gone berserk, materialism overload, everything wanted RIGHT NOW and so delivered.

"You're lucky to be raising your kids in Centerville," he continued, as if the picturesque, serene memories of his own childhood had caused the town to freeze in time, remaining ever the same. Maybe that's what we all did to a certain extent, romanticizing our own childhoods, blurring reality until we were completely convinced that nothing could have been better. The result was inevitable—a strong conviction that "kids today" had it all wrong. "Back in my day . . ." was something that all of us were destined to say, no matter how much we insisted that we would never participate in such illogical, nostalgic banter.

"My kids are the most important thing in the world to me," Dad continued. "And to Sue. We love them more than anything. I'd do anything for them, but I want to be careful not to do too much. I never really believed there was a God until I saw our first born, Kimber." He said, on the verge of what looked like actual tears. "Then I realized that miracles can and really do happen."

As much as I was touched to the core by what he said, this was the guy who I'd only see cry twice, ever, so, I was equally shocked. He had just explained the underlying reason Kim reigned supreme in the home of Dick and Sue. He had just cracked the mystery of the chip and dip and solved Nancy Drew's secret of the hidden emotional agenda.

Holy crap! He'd just explained the freaking meaning of life. Apparently, and if I was reading this correctly, Mom and Dad had been so bedazzled by the sight of Kimber coming out of

Mom's young womb that they literally were knocked out of their senses. It was, of course, done in love, in overwhelming, ecstatic, life-changing and disastrous love.

I could cancel the appointment with my therapist next week. I could call my best friend and tell her I didn't need to talk about it anymore. I could stop taking that medicine that softened my stool. OK, scratch that, I wasn't taking stool softener right now, but if I was, I could have canceled it.

It was a whole new world.

Just then, as if on cue to thwart my one shining moment, the remaining partygoers burst into the breakfast room, equipped with a box, a bottle of Johnnie Walker Red, and a few decks of cards.

"OK, everybody!" Mom announced in a high-pitched, excited voice. "Now it's time to play a little game we like to call Tripoley!"

Mom was animated and unsteady. From the small, shallow box she pulled a dark-green vinyl mat and ceremoniously un-furled it onto the table. It had a center circle labeled in a simple white font "POT." I remembered that we three kids found that almost as funny as one of the outer sections, one of eight which surrounded the center circle, labeled "KITTY." Though we never understood the object of the game—or other adult board games like Facts in Five or Probe (did you need a plastic glove to play that?)—it didn't stop us from getting all the pieces out of the box and playing with them.

Poker chips and fresh glasses of scotch were distributed. "Here we go!" one of the men said. I had learned to play Tripo-ley as an adult, on a board that was made out of hard plastic, with a series of dishes or trays where the lines on the mat had been. The best I remembered, it was a cross between poker and rummy, but at this point in the evening I was groggy enough that I had no idea what was going on.

Or, perhaps the participants were zapped enough that the rules didn't really apply.

Though they had asked Dad and I if we wanted to join in, we both refused. Dad liked poker, but that was about it. That is, unless it was a special family gathering complete with the seven grandkids he didn't know that he had. Mom said that Dad pretended to like games—especially card games—when they were dating, but then miraculously became less enthusiastic after the knot was officially tied. Apparently, card games didn't seem near as fun, or necessary, after the marriage license was signed and everyone's clothes finally came off.

Even though I was old enough to have been involved in, and the leader of, a number of adult-content conversations, the dialogue here, at this Tripoley game, was shocking. Maybe it was because I was at least four drinks under the 1978 limit. Maybe it was because I was standing in my childhood breakfast room. Or, maybe it was because I was in direct view of my second-place soccer trophy.

Mr. Anderson, the man with a green Camaro who liked to edge his lawn shirtless, began to explain why his wife claimed to be "very happy" living here in Northampton. "I'll tell you what keeps Evelyn happy!" he exclaimed, with a brand of suburban masculinity that accentuated his faux-suede western jacket. "It's a regular serving of the Golden Sausage!"

If revealing the pet name of his man part wasn't enough, he backed up from the table, flung his arms aloft and gyrated, making his western fringe fly. The scene was enhanced by his tight western pant, held up by a rainbow-colored, Camaro Z28 belt buckle. It was as stunning as it was dangerous, a drunk man thrusting his man business with a lit cigarette in one hand and a full tumbler of scotch in the other, flicking ashes and sloshing hard liquor in equal doses.

"You know it, baby!" Evelyn screeched back, exuding as much sexuality as a board game, the smoky haze, and her flight-attendant-like scarf would allow.

The room filled with laughter as the others offered their

own semi-lewd comments about Mr. Anderson—the neighbor-hood love machine, wife pleaser and the holder of the permit for the safe operation of the bronzed appendage.

Things just went downhill from there, some players visibly staggering as others began to nod their heads downwards, eyes heavy.

"Hey," one of the last ladies standing asked, "Does anyone know what time it is?"

"I do!" Mom answered, fumbling toward the desk. Picking up the receiver on the phone, she dialed quickly.

Was she calling somebody, on the telephone, to ask what time it was? It was the middle of the freaking the night. Who did that?

"It's 1:14 in the morning," Mom reported, phone still in hand. "And fifty-one degrees outside."

Oh my Lord, she had just called the automated time and temperature number. Seriously? That was beautiful. I hoped to hell I could remember that.

The party finally started to wind down. As hearty as the welcome had been when they arrived, the farewell was, well, it was emotional. It was the long, drunk goodbye complete with assorted sloppy claims like, "I love you so much," "You are the best neighbors we've ever had," "You are my best friend in the world," and "Let's do this again EVERY Thursday night, only next time we'll have it at my house and hire a Mariachi band!"

It was all the kind of stuff that everyone would regret say-ing in the morning, if they could remember saying it at all. How many people were wholeheartedly scheduling coffees, trips to the sunny shores of Galveston or mall outings that they never intended to really go on? And, which of these polyester-clad drinkers had promised to watch the Watsons' kids when they went to New Orleans in February?

They would regret that, and wonder how they could get out of it, but at least it wouldn't be on Facebook.

"Thanks for talking to me about that bitch," one lady told Mom, "You saved my life, Sue, you f-ing saved it."

"That's what friends are for," Mom said, relishing in the joy that only being needed can bring. As the long embrace continued, the lady rested her huge head of hair on Mom's shoulder, her makeup leaving an ugly mark on the orange polyester. The streak would remain long after the memory of the night itself drifted away into drunk slumber.

Dad, usually the unemotional rock, was not equally emotional, but for him, it was a scene.

"Come again, friend," he said to Steve. "You're one hell of a guy, and, well, I like you," he said, almost as if he was addressing his long-lost brother.

As the last few neighbors exited, I began to panic, realizing that while everyone else was going home to the respite of their spousal beds, I was staying here. Of course I was staying here—where the hell else was I going? It was 1:30 a.m., in 1978. This was my parents' house, and I was ten years old and asleep upstairs. There was no escaping this. Some of us were more inebriated than others, some of us had memories that hadn't happened yet, some of us knew too much, had baggage, had kids back in the future. And a husband who would have told her to go directly to bed.

And then there were three. That's when I realized I hadn't said goodbye to my paternal grandparents. I hadn't even seen them leave. When did they go? God, I loved them. But, that said, maybe it was better that I just got to say hello again and left out the final, repeated goodbye. Maybe that's the memory I was supposed to be left with. I could have never said goodbye properly anyway.

As Dad started turning off lights, he half-slurred, "Sue, it's time to go to bed."

She evidently wasn't ready to call it an evening. "How about one more drink?" she said, looking at me. "Kind of a, well, nightcap?"

"No ma'am," I responded, trying to escape. "I'm good, I better get to bed. You know, I'm still tired from the travel . . ." My voice tapered off as she caught up with me in the family room.

"You know what, Amy?" Mom said, grabbing my hand in a way-too-familiar fashion. "You are loved here. You are loved." Tears welled up in her eyes as she continued, "Everyone is loved here. We're so happy. We're so happy that you are here. You made tonight *so* special."

I knew she meant what she was saying, but she didn't. She didn't want me there, but she did. She didn't like me, but she did. She didn't love everybody, but oh my God, she really did. It was complicated. Life was complicated. She wasn't the only person in the world with layers; she was just the only one who also gave birth to me. That apparently gave me the right to be harder on her than anyone else in the whole world. But she had rights too. Hers were in the here and now, mine were in the then and later. Both of us could abuse them, screw them up, and with any luck, we'd love each other anyway.

"I love being here," I said, desperately, because I needed the moment to end. "I love your family. You have great kids."

"Oh God," she said dramatically, like the next breath could be her last, "I love them so much, I love Dick too, even though he bugs the living crap out of me. I love that damn man so much."

"You did a great job with Thanksgiving," I thought to say. "I think people forget about the mom, I think that happens a lot."

That struck her with the gravity that I had hoped it wouldn't. Yes, I wanted her to feel good, but no, I didn't want to hold her in my arms. Rocking forward, she grabbed both my shoulders. She was unsteady, so I stood firm. She wasn't the only drunk one in the room, she was just the drunkest. That was an important point really, because it wasn't like I was better than her, or above her. I had just stopped before she did.

Dropping her head, she emotionally whispered, loudly, if that's possible, "Thank you . . . you have NO idea how much I needed to hear that."

I knew we weren't going to talk about her mother dogging her at the Thanksgiving table, any more than I would tell her about my own mom's comments or Professor Plum's short rope.

It all made a lot of sense.

Dad poked his head back out of the little hall leading to the master bedroom. "Sue, time for bed. We should let Amy go to bed too."

"Yes," she said. "Yes, it's time." She hugged me with all the force a small-framed suburban wife and mother can muster at almost two o'clock in the morning on the Friday after Thanksgiving. "Good night, friend," she said slurring, staggering back to her room. "I love you, girl. I'm glad you were here today. You are good for Little Amy. She needs people to love her."

As she disappeared around the corner, I stood quietly alone in the family room. As the door to Mom and Dad's love chamber closed loudly, the only light remaining drifted down from the stairs. It was dark and I was groggy, but I found my way easily. Running my hand down the long cast-iron fence, I heard the motion detector click, sensing my presence. As a teenager I had learned to jump the beam and move around undetected. As an adult, I couldn't get off the radar of this place, no matter what I did.

Chapter Sixteen

EMOTIONAL DIARRHEA

Stumbling into the third-floor closet, I tried to hold it all in until I could get the door shut behind me. It was almost like trying to get to a toilet before dramatically hurling. I fell to the harsh, gold carpet and sobbed uncontrollably.

What was I even crying for? Why had I been sent here? It made no damn sense.

I realized how wrong I was, how right I was, and how memories are nothing more than aged perceptions.

I was right about my mom and I was wrong about her too. It hurt almost inexplicably to witness actual events that validated my feelings. I had always thought that I had made half that stuff up, playing the victim with no real evidence to validate what was deep inside. But seeing the way she treated Little Amy and spoke about her—even in front of a stranger, who she would have made her best effort at normalizing for—was cold, hard validation. These were actual facts, not feelings. It was shocking and disturbing, only because it meant that all the other memories—the ones not on display in this crack-induced voyage through time—were true.

It was, in equal doses, healing and freeing.

I hadn't made it all up in my head. It wasn't all my fault. I had hurt myself, and I was responsible for that, but there was a reason for it. And that reason had nothing to do with a personality defect.

On the other hand, and it was a big hand to be sure, Mom

was a product of the swirl of crap that had been the life that led her to her adult one. She was the daughter of oppressive people who, while they loved her, expected perfection, or their precise version of it. Yes, she had it good, in a big house in a beautiful suburban neighborhood. She had a loving, decent, hardworking husband. She had respectable parents who showed up, sober, to family functions. She had friends who liked her. She had beautiful, healthy children. But, as happy as she was, and she really was, somehow she wasn't fulfilled, or complete. There was something missing because she didn't like herself. She didn't completely accept who she was. For this, she was normal. But she was still my mother, and she either didn't like me or love me. Either way, something in me triggered something in her.

I didn't and couldn't understand how the one hand affected the other. There was no way to figure that out. Regardless, I was seeing Mom in a different light, an experience that was both very good and very bad. It was progress, I guessed.

Yes, it was all freaking marvelous with one huge exception. In no way would Little Amy comprehend all of this so she could be better equipped to handle life as it was. First off, I couldn't tell her. I was just a stranger, here on a one-time basis for twenty-four very short hours. Even if we could get closer, if I could gain her trust and get her to calm down long enough to listen to me, she wouldn't understand. She couldn't get it not because she wasn't smart, but because she was too young and she thought this situation was "normal." In fact, she would think that for the next thirty years.

Even though that was true, it was her take on what was happening now that would shape her future emotional foundation. It would be as big a part of who she thought she was as being born a native Houstonian, becoming a Texas Tech alumna, a wife and a mother. Naïve ten-year-olds shouldn't be given the responsibility to remember important emotional stuff. Without any premeditation, they are destined to mess it up, and then their forty-something-year-old future selves mess it up even further.

My natural reaction to this wild set of revelations was to call somebody, text somebody. I was a girl who needed to talk, and I needed to talk to another girl. This was something that needed to be laid out on the table delicately, carefully dissected, put back together again and then reopened fifteen minutes after it was declared solved. This is what lady friends are for, the essence of their absolute necessity in the life of, well, a lady.

So, I could sneak down to the game room, where one of only three phones in this house was, but who the hell was I going to call?

My best friend at the time, Catherine, was ten years old, across the neighborhood in bed and totally unacquainted with the adult me. Sure, I could call her, at two-thirty in the morning, half-drunk and forty-six years old, sobbing hysterically, and her parents, Edna and George, would have me arrested. My best friend in the future, Julia, lived in England. Sure, she was twenty years old in 1978, but she had absolutely no clue who I was, plus I was pretty damn sure my parents didn't have an internet phone line, meaning there would be no magically free international calls offered to desperate time travelers. Then there was my other bestie, Mary Barr. I didn't know where the hell she lived in 1978, but she was only eight years old. If I could have found her, she would have believed me. Really, Julia, Mary Barr, Willie, Will and Matthew were the only ones who would have ever believed this. Or at least they would have said that they did so I wouldn't think I was crazy. But they weren't here. No one knew me here. Crap, I didn't even know myself.

I kept going back to young Amy—primed to be different, not a clue about fashion, rough around the edges, wound tight and uncomfortably unique. Yeah, she was funny, creative and spirited, but she was destined for a run of awkward, painful years. She would struggle because of a lethal combination of who she was mixed with her situation in this house. Though it wasn't anywhere near what other children faced, it was real. That and the perceived perfection of suburbia and middle-class financial security made it more sinister because it would never be recognized, discussed or validated. "Come on, you had it so good growing up. You lived in a beautiful home and had beautiful things. So your mom drank a little too much and yelled at you, pushed you and made you feel bad. Suck it up, there are a lot worse things in the world."

Maybe there are a lot worse things in the world. But, maybe there aren't. Who established the meter for "good" and "bad," and who set the priorities for what constitutes a "good childhood" or a "good life"?

Having a swimming pool in your backyard is fun, going to Disneyland on vacation is awesome, but feeling truly loved and accepted is better than both. You will never see a television commercial in America that reflects that theme. Or, at least not one that won't end by trying to get you to buy fabric softener, or a Hallmark card, or sour cream.

Nobody would explain any of that to Little Amy. In fact nobody would ever talk about what was going on, what was really going on. Why would they? Everything seemed to be going so well, I got that about my own adult life, and frankly the thought of the perceived goodness scared the life out of me.

And the best part? She had no clue. I wanted her to have a damn clue. I wanted her to suddenly "get it." I wanted her to see the bigger picture. She needed to change herself. To be like everyone else, just so she didn't have to spend the next nine years being convinced that she wasn't good enough. Or, maybe I just didn't want to see her doing it. God, I was glad I wasn't transported into 1984 or 1985 when things were even more intensely weird and painful. That would have been the era of perms, braces, lots of acne and fake attempts at wearing ruffles and shoulder pads. God help us.

Maybe that was it. Maybe I was still so uncomfortable with my past self that I couldn't see that the Little Amy was nothing more than a victim of the Big Amy. Oh crap . . . what did that even mean?

"Oh, Mom and her drinking . . . Oh, I'm the least favorite . . . Woe is me, the mistreated middle child . . ." Even though it was true, really true, truer than I had ever thought, and way more justifiable all at the same time, maybe the bigger truth was that I was an awkward child. An awkward, graceless, uncoordinated, angry girl who was difficult to love; mostly by herself, mostly by her adult self.

Was she unlovable because of the freak she was, or, instead, was she a freak because she wasn't loved?

Did she throw herself down the stairs in the middle of the night, just to see if anyone would come and check on her, because there really was something wrong with her, something dysfunctional, or as a reaction to what was going on under the surface in this house? That actually happened, I was there. Did they ever discuss it, because they never talked about it with me? Were they worried? Or did they, like certain people who hallucinated, drank a lot, and almost got raped, just act like it never happened? How deep did this all go and what parts was I not remembering?

Was it any coincidence that the crap that only Jack Daniels could manage to squeeze out was the same messed-up stuff that Johnnie Walker had initially put in? Why was it that only after drinking almost half a bottle of Jack did I finally tell someone—my college roommate—a bunch of the real stuff that had happened to me? The sick irony was, I couldn't remember what I told her that night any more than my Mom could remember everything she'd done.

In both instances, it was a choice. She chose the scotch and I chose the bourbon.

Wiping my eyes on the leg of a polyester pantsuit hanging

over my head, I realized that the really screwed up part of this whole business was that everyone was going to forget about all this shit. Yeah, there would be pictures of the actual events, and sharp flashes of memory, because they were real, but still, everyone would forget. Because that was the thing to do. It wasn't on purpose, it was human. And who wanted to go through life with all those memories in their head anyway? Maybe the luckiest people were those who couldn't remember.

Eventually, thankfully, I lay in the fetal position on the floor and passed out, slobber moistening the gold-shag surface. Sometime before dawn I awoke, opened the door to the closet and crawled over to the bed. It was quiet and I felt sick. I began to question myself, almost completely subconsciously. *Why did I let myself drink so much? Idiot. Why did I cry like that and fall asleep in the closet? Idiot. Why did I go outside at the party? Total Idiot.*

It was all my fault, but at least I didn't drunk-post on Facebook or text a bunch of people. At least there was that. As I drifted off, I thought about how lucky people were, thirty years ago, not to have the internet.

Chapter Seventeen

SMOKED ANKLES

Of all the things I had ever been at 24314 Creekview Drive, hungover wasn't one of them. But, like any other day, tomorrow finally caught up with me.

Stretching out on the non-Tempur-Pedic mattress, not equipped with a down topper or even a fluffy mattress pad, I turned bleary eyed to the bedside table where a white clock sat. Rubbing my eyes, I zeroed in on the black and white numbers: 7:07. Staring, I heard a low buzz and then watched as the entire unit heaved. The last number suddenly flipped, turning the "seven" magically into an "eight." 7:08. Cool.

Sitting up slowly, propping myself on the smallish pillows draped in dusty pink, I watched the sun begin to break behind the tall loblolly pines. Yes, loblolly pines. I had read that somewhere, and boy, wasn't it coming in handy now? The scene would have been even more beautiful, breathtaking really, if my head wasn't pounding and I wasn't still pretending I was in 1978. I had to admit, if I had dreamed this up, I had done one hell of a job.

Finally willing myself to get up, I made my way to the bathroom and took a long, hard look in the mirror—it wasn't pretty. Tear-smeared mascara mixed with blue eye shadow steaked across my face. I had tried the old half-drunk, soap-and-water routine in the wee hours of the night, but that didn't even get half of what had been slapped on twenty-four hours ago.

Rifling through my cosmetic case, I pulled out the blue tub

of Noxzema. Pulling back my massive, wild hair with what looked like a tennis sweatband, I slathered the thick cream on my face. Turning on the faucet, I realized, too late, that apparently the water pressure was weak during time travel. This stuff was going to be in my pores for the next thirty years. It was like trying to scrape peanut butter off a tortilla, only I didn't have a spatula.

Finally rubbing off the last bit with an abrasive maroon-and-pink textured towel, I jumped in the shower, which had the same feeble water pressure as the sink. I was impressed with my naked self, though. Yes, if I was going to be delusional at least I was going to look freaking amazing in the all-nude. Maybe people ate better in 1978, despite the Crisco, butter, fat and oil. Maybe they dined out less, ate fewer snacks and had less access to access.

Afraid of what the "Supermax" styling device might mean for my already jacked-up hair, I used the provided shower cap and enjoyed a decent shower minus a hit off the bottle of Body on Tap. I began to wonder how in the hell I could create the same look I had arrived with yesterday. The best approach, I calculated, was to double the normal amount of every item in the case. It was a recipe for a potent cocktail: Half a can of Miss Breck, six dollops of Cover Girl Clean Makeup, twelve puffs of Coty Airspun Powder, seven strokes of Maybelline Ultra Frost blue eye shadow, seventeen dashes of Coty Nature's Blush, three fingerfuls of Yardley Pot o'Gloss Super Tinted Lip Gloss and eleven tip-touches of Charlie perfume.

Next, I swished the golden Listerine and filled a small Dixie cup from the dispenser on the wall with water and downed four Bufferin. Checking my look in the mirror, I teased my hair, re-sprayed it with Miss B and then topped the entire package off with a slather of the Kissing Potion lip gloss. Though it definitely wasn't good, it wasn't too bad either.

Returning to the bedroom, I looked through the suitcase for

something to wear. First, I pulled out a pointy-cup bra with several extra straps. I think it was supposed to be sexy, but to me it was just confusing and borderline dangerous. Next I found a jade-green nylon pantsuit. Slipping it on, I admired the drawstring neckline, the generous elastic waistband with a tie belt and the flared pants. The best part was that there were no snaps on my crotch. My crotch had been set free.

It was a breezy look. Very breezy. I opted not to tuck the flowing top into the pants—there seemed to be an option—and then completed the look by tying the cord on both the blouse and the pants. I guessed I could pull these in case of emergency and all my clothes would suddenly come off. This could be helpful if I caught on fire, a definite possibility given the silk-like Qiana nylon fabric advertised on the tag, apparently not a natural fiber.

Dipping back into the case, I pulled out golden-heeled t-strap sandals, the least offensive item I'd discovered thus far and something that could almost be stylish back in 2014. Almost. Balled up in the toe of each shoe was something altogether different, a pair of knee highs. The shade was smoky, giving my foot and lower leg an almost charred effect. I think I could've gotten away with parking in a handicapped spot with these on— that is, if there were handicapped parking spots in 1978.

Wait! Where is that notebook? I bolted across the room to the far window where my brown blazer was flung across a powder-blue wicker chair painted the same color as the walls. If not for the pink paisley cushion you wouldn't have even known it was there. I wondered if it too had been peed on. Digging into one of the pockets, I was relieved to find the notebook and pen.

Turning to the next open page I wrote, *"When did handicapped parking spots start? What is Qiana? Isn't it an ancient grain? Do they still make it? Can you still buy knee highs? Can you put Dippity-do on dry hair?"*

Flipping back, I realized my most recent entry was from last night, after everyone had freaked out about that guy's miniature tape recorder. Sitting down carefully on the chair, I didn't want to ruin my breezy look, I wrote, "*Facebook: Professor Plum and Mr. Golden Sausage. Can you still call for the time and date?*" Then I skipped a few lines and scribbled, "*SHOULD I STOP DRINKING?*"

Closing the notebook, I sat back in the chair and reflected just long enough to know this wasn't the time, or the place, to rethink or overthink anything. To be fair, there may never be a right time. But if I was a betting woman, and I wasn't, and I was, this would all spill out late one evening on Julia's couch. I would have told myself, on the twelve-hour plane ride across the Atlantic, that I wasn't going to tell her, and then later one night, when all the talking was done, and I was going to bed, because it was midnight, I would "just mention it" . . . for two hours. She would listen patiently and dissect each bit of it with me, carefully and methodically and yes, the best part is it would be done lovingly.

I should send her a card, or a million bucks, or my left arm.

Back in the case, I found the jewelry that was apparently meant to compliment my wrinkle-free extravaganza, a jade green and gold necklace and bracelet.

I looked as if I was ready to whip up a Swanson's Hungry-Man Salisbury Steak TV dinner, rush off to a sale at Kmart or be ready for date night down at the Steak and Ale. It was a look that transcended the time of day, the time of year and the time of the month. This flexibility worked well for me, because I had no idea where the final eight hours of my delusion would lead me.

Chapter Eighteen

MR. AND MRS. COFFEE

Descending the stairs, I stopped briefly on the second floor. The mess from yesterday's epic Gong Show performance was still scattered across the room. Tambourines lay silent on the bumper pool table, polyester outfits flung across the old couch, the record player, lid up, still plugged-in on the far wall.

I took a moment to look out the window facing the front of the house. The November sun was now blasting through every crevice of the neighborhood, a fresh dew still blanketing every visible surface. As much as everything on this journey had seemed draped in a surreal haze, this, nature, was spot on.

It was then I noticed the rattan roll-up shade, hanging solidly at the top of the antique window frame. It had threads of green, gold and brown woven in among flexible wooden slats. The construction was illogical. Even when fully unfurled, there would have been numerous gaps for the light to peek through. Despite how fashionable it looked, it would never achieve its functional intent of keeping sun out of the room. I guessed it was all about being pleasing to the eye rather than providing actual coverage. It was a lot like the macramé tube top I had seen in my suitcase, only the glaring sun wouldn't be near as offensive as my boobs oozing out of the elastic.

Down the next half-flight of stairs and then another, I landed back in the entryway and walked through the dining room into the kitchen. Mom was stationed at the stove, her back turned to me. As I came across the room, she managed a weak, "Good morning."

Dad was sitting directly in front of her at the breakfast room table with the *Houston Post* spread out in front of him. "Well good morning, cousin!" he said. "Let me get you a cup of coffee!" He literally leapt out of his chair, past Mom and toward the Mr. Coffee machine on the red countertop next to the harvest-gold refrigerator.

Opening one of the dark-wood cabinets, he pulled out a floral mug and filled it with the nectar of what looked to be, according to the open can sitting nearby, Sanka. He didn't ask if I wanted cream or sugar, but instead brought the cup directly to me, presenting it like the Jewel of the Nile.

"Thanks very much," I said.

Behind him, Mom had turned from the stove and was glaring directly into his back. "No, Dick," she almost whispered, but didn't, "I don't need anything. I'm fine . . ." Turning back to the pan, she worked the eggs over almost violently. As I followed Dad back through to the breakfast room, I was smart enough not to ask Mom if she needed my help. First, she didn't really want my help to start with, I got that, and had this been my kitchen, I would have felt the same way. Secondly, she would have been even more pissed than she already was if someone spoke to her directly. And that would have been the case even if I was just trying to be courteous.

This was a time for silence. Well, almost.

"He's never, in fourteen damn years of marriage, made coffee for anybody . . ." I could hear her mumble from behind me. It was a departure from her earlier guardedness. She was either more comfortable with me being in the house, or she had stopped caring what I thought. "He may have made it for his parents, but never for me, or anyone else. Fool. Fool. Fool. I married a fool."

Though it was awkward, standing next to my beaming dad

while in front of my pissed-off mom, all of us magically the same age, all of us in man-made fabrics—I got where she was coming from. Men act differently in front of "other" people than they do in front of the "regular" crowd. They do stuff, by virtue of having a penis, I guess, that can surprise you, or enrage you, or make you so happy you don't think you can even go on. It's a good thing that people with a vagina are so consistent, so much so that the regulars in one's life can count on them as a beacon of light—providing an even, metered and calming presence, never wavering from one situation to the next. Yeah, men sucked. Totally.

I could see Kim and Rick from around the corner in the laundry room. She was "teaching" him how to spell with colorful magnetic letters attached to the front of the washing machine. Kim was authoritative, mesmerizing a dutiful Rick as he sat cross-legged, wearing a white plastic helmet with green plastic goggles. She banged on about which letters were vowels and that one day he'd be able to spell complex words like "cheese" and "marker." She explained that this, his future in academia, would have been easier to illustrate had she been provided with more than one plastic letter *E* in her teaching kit. She was a genius.

Amy, who was apparently beyond Kim's educational reach, was talking to herself on the back porch. Sitting on one of the many benches, she was having a pretend conversation that required a certain amount of physical activity. Every once in a while, she would jump up and make a hand or leg flourish. As far as I could tell, she couldn't even manage to respect imaginary people's personal space, getting all up in their business even in pretend. Finally, after literally dashing around the entire deck three or four times, like a chicken wing had been attached to a string and she was trying to catch it, she rushed down the steps closest to the driveway. Thankfully, she was temporarily out of sight. I had no words.

Did she think that nobody was watching and was simply

letting her imagination run wild? I could have lived with that. Or, instead, I wondered if she had seen Dad and me watching through the French doors in the breakfast room and amped up her performance accordingly, making it seem "natural" even though it wasn't. The thought alarmed me, and fascinated me, and if I was going to be honest—which I wouldn't in public but apparently would in a book I wanted everyone to read—I knew it said a lot about who I was. It was who I was.

Breakfast was ready. Dad did his part to get the kids re-assembled as Mom delivered the food to the table. She was wearing what can only be called a coat of many colors, harkening either a Bible story or a Dolly Parton song. It was a zip-up velour housecoat or robe, richly adorned with jewel tones running in a dramatic north-to-south pattern. Each color was separated by a black divider, adding boldness to morning time.

Dad had on a maroon-and-blue velour robe, covering what I knew were the shorty button-up, collared pajamas he always wore. As far as I knew, he still wore the exact same outfit back in the future. I will say—in complete confidence—that his legs were far different than the ones he sported in 2014. He had manly legs here, young manly legs. They were impressive and attractive. Funny how I had never noticed that my dad was an attractive guy, a man that other people, girl people, would have thought was handsome.

Much to my surprise and delight—begging the question of why I kept being surprised and delighted by what was only normal, everyday stuff—everybody sat down in their traditional places around the family table. This was the site of virtually every meal, the highlight being the dinners we shared almost every evening after Dad got home from work. My little family in the future rarely ate at the table. We tried to, but we couldn't seem to all be on the same page timing-wise, and when we did, we usually gathered in front of the television. I knew this was probably a huge parental error, but in all honesty, it was me who liked eating in front of the TV more than my husband or even our boys did.

The table was antique, dark oak, with lion's feet. Overhead was a giant ceiling fan that most certainly didn't come from the Home Depot, Lowe's or Wayfair.com. No, this rare beauty had been yanked out of an old bank somewhere and had huge gum-drop-shaped shade that was decorated with strands of iridescent glass pearls. The tan wallpaper had baskets brimming with fruits of the harvest and bouquets of fall flowers.

Facing the back porch, the left wall was reserved for the family trophy case, a heavy piece with glass shelves and brass, cage-like accents. This tribute to family excellence sat directly across the room from a built-in desk featuring a gleaming, yellow push-button phone, hardwired into the wall. Above the desk were built-in bookshelves with everything from popsicle-stick picture frames to a small glass Coke bottle covered in eggshells sprayed with gold paint. That *objet d'art* was my creation. I knew if I flipped it over, careful not to disturb the questionably sanitary egg flakes, I would find my crudely written name on the bottom. I had made it in the second grade.

I remembered how, when I brought it home, Mom had said she was so proud of it. I had carefully wrapped it in a paper towel and put it in my blue-plaid satchel, riding my bike home with special care. I had beamed with pride as Mom admired it, saying all the right things, placing it in a prominent place on the shelf. It was impossible not to connect with both my mom's place in this memory and that of the little girl I had once been, and figuratively and actually—in this impossible scheme—still was. I understood the pride and often unsaid deep love and appreciation felt on both sides of the equation. Why was it that I couldn't stay permanently connected to that part of the story, the warm, yummy part? I definitely was hooked in to the good stuff sometimes, while at other times I absolutely was not. Was it even a choice?

We always sat in the same places: Dad at the head of the table, facing the doors to the deck; Rick and Mom to his right, in front of the desk; Kim directly across from him, facing the kitchen; and then I—in my truncated form—to his left, in front of the trophies.

Since the table was oval, the only available spot for the adult me was next to my former self, Little Amy. As expected, she was nothing short of ecstatic with the seating arrangements. I'm not going to lie, at this point I didn't mind sitting next to her, as I had begun to notice that she may have been—despite the hyperness and bug eyes—the one of the five I felt the most comfortable with.

Bowing our heads, we chanted together, "God is good, God is great, let us thank Him for our food." I didn't know if anyone had picked up on how well I remembered that part of the ritual, but if they did, they probably just assumed that this was the prayer that all of suburbia repeated before launching into their peas garnished with cubes of cheddar cheese or hamburger patties smothered in cream of mushroom soup.

The dinner plates mirrored the wallpaper in a way I hadn't noticed heretofore—browns, greens and golds used in yet another flowery harvest theme. The glasses, juice-sized and being used for their actual purpose, were gold and decorated, again, with flowers and vines. And what did we stay hydrated with the day after Thanksgiving, secretly hungover, desperately needing to push the liquids? TANG, of course.

Though the food was plentiful, there wasn't enough to go around for seconds, which struck me as odd, because portion sizes where I came from dictated enough for, at minimum, one more heaping helping. Perhaps this was why my thighs seemed less flabby, and my middle less generous and tire-like.

Looking around the table while lifting forkfuls of the hard-scrambled eggs—Mom didn't make fluffy eggs like her mother, Granny, did—I watched as Dad tried to direct the conversation to mature topics. "Now, kids," he said, "can each of you tell us something interesting that's happening at school?"

"Well," Amy said with a twinkle in her eye, "somebody had an accident, in their blue-plastic chair, when we were watching a filmstrip about the nine planets . . . and it leaked all over the floor!"

"Amy!" Dad said. "That's not an appropriate topic for the table."

Despite his rebuff, the story had its intended effect on Kim and Rick, who were now giggling while they pretended like they were eating their toast. This pleased Amy greatly; she was literally shaking with delight.

This was precisely the kind of mealtime shenanigans I remembered. Dad normally appreciated our ridiculous behavior, or at least put up with it, but this, the family meal, was different. It was sacred ground, used, apparently, for maturity training. But he was dealing with some characters here, people who would grow into forty-something-year-olds who would still laugh, out loud, when someone said tallywacker, or God forbid, penis.

Dad's technique to shut down what was escalating into a frenzy was fascinating—he simply relegated control of the floor to Kim, knowing that we would all listen to her, each for our own reasons, or pay the price. This pleased the younger version of her as much, or more, than last night's touchdown run had delighted both versions of me.

After Kim regaled us with her knowledge on the subject of cursive writing and the TV show *Eight is Enough*, the conversation turned to what we might do during the remaining hours of my visit. In my mom's mind I'm sure it was a matter of, "Holy crap, what are we going to do with this freaking lady for the next eight hours?" While to my dad it would be more like, "Oh crap, we only have eight hours remaining with her . . . "

"Why don't we take cousin Amy to the brand-new Greenspoint Mall," Dad said.

"The MALL!" Kim screeched. "We can go to the MALL?"

Though this was part of Kim's dream sequence, I knew that the mall, especially the day after Thanksgiving, even in 1978, wasn't Mom's idea of a wonderful day out. I assumed she agreed simply because it meant we didn't have to sit here and look at each other for the rest of the day. She had a point, really.

With a plan in place, everyone was sent forth to drape themselves in their finery, that is except for Mom, because somebody had to clean all this mess up. Since I was already decked out in my man-made fabrics, I stayed behind to help. The good news was, her angst toward me, the guest, had seemed to dissipate. We had semi-bonded last night, at least the parts that people could or would want to remember.

I cleared the table as she cleaned up the kitchen. Once I had all the soiled surfaces wiped down, I crossed back into the kitchen where she was leaning casually against the countertop. "What are your people in Ohio doing today?" she asked.

"Well," I answered carefully, not wanting to come across like it wasn't a big deal that I was gone for a holiday, because it was. "They will likely hang out at the house, watch TV and maybe put the Christmas tree up."

"Put the tree up?" Mom said. "Good Lord, it's not even December!"

I hadn't thought about how we would have waited until well into December to even start talking about trees in this house, in this decade, in this millennium. In fact, I couldn't ever remember putting a tree up before the middle of December.

"Umm, yeah," I said. "Sometimes we get things started early up there."

"Good God, I guess so!" she said, looking down at the linoleum and then backup. "So, did you have a good time last night?"

"Yes!" I said, half lying and half being truthful, an approach I was familiar with. "You have some wonderful friends around here."

"Yeah, they're OK . . ." her voice trailed off. "I just hope they all had a good time, you know, and that everything was . . . well-received."

I totally got what she was saying, in a way that almost shocked me. It's not just that I understood where she was coming from. I had come, and would continue to come, from that same place. For me, and her too apparently, questions like "How do you think it went?" were only the tip of the iceberg. What wasn't said, the real thick stuff that was nearly impossible to melt, were things like *Do you think I made a fool of myself? Could people tell I was drunk?* And *Was I even good enough to be at my own party?*

We were more alike than I had thought, deep down where people didn't compare notes. It was comforting and terrifying all in the same breath.

"No, no," I said, trying to sound confident and authoritative, for both our sakes. "It was great and I think everyone had a wonderful time!"

"You are so brave," she said. "Walking into a strange place with people you don't know and flitting around talking to everyone like old friends. I wish I could do that."

"The drinks definitely help," I said.

"You remind me just a little bit of our Amy," she continued, more thoughtfully than I ever would have given her credit for. "Not completely, or anything specific, but it's like something is there. Maybe it's a distant relative thing, something genetic."

"Hmmmmm . . ." was all I could manage in response, because really what in the hell was I supposed to say to that? Should I dramatically flail myself in her direction? Cornering her between the harvest-gold sink and refrigerator, whispering into her ear, "Mom, it's me, AMY! Amy the Flute. I've come from the future, I've come from 2014, I'm married and I have two kids. Mom! Look, here, I can prove it, on my knee, it's that scar I got when I ran through the plate glass door at New Waverly. Oh crap, wait, that hasn't happened yet . . ."

"I hope our Amy will be like that someday," she continued,

looking away to the back of the sink, where a window should have been. "Confident, sure, and fun to be around. I hope she's very happy, like you."

Again, I could say nothing. What was I supposed to say? And again, I was as disturbed as much I was comforted. She truly loved Little Amy. It was written on every inch of her face and dripped from every word that came out of her mouth. But, she didn't like her, or she did. Layers. More freaking layers. Questions. More freaking questions. I couldn't freaking believe it, Mary had been right.

Then, abruptly, as if she sensed the need for this bizarre, but wonderful, but death-defying, but ever-so-simple conversation to end, she headed toward the breakfast room. "I'm going to get ready to go," she said as she went down the two steps into the sunken family room. "Dick will want to get out of here before the traffic piles up."

Heading back upstairs to give the appearance that I cared about my '70s appearance, I focused, again, on not registering anything that was happening emotionally. Because it wasn't real, it couldn't be real. Suddenly, Little Amy burst out of a closet at the back right of the second-floor game room.

"Hey!" she sputtered, breathlessly, her eyes bulging like a shih tzu's. "Come and see my office!" Her office? I had totally forgotten about her/my/our "office" located conveniently just steps away from the bumper pool table.

Following her into the closet, which had previously seemed huge, Amy motioned toward a chair located in front of her "desk" for me to sit in. She went around to the other side and sat down in a yellow executive's chair, a discarded reject from Dad's office in town. Surrounding her on all sides were a bank of TV tray tables containing a wide variety of office supplies: an old goose-neck lamp, a metal file holder, a flip-style Rolodex, a faux-wood pencil holder and a bunch of "signs" scratched out on spiral notebook paper.

"So," I said, "what kind of operation do you run here?"

"Well," Little Amy replied, with weird excitement, "I do several things here at this location—I have a photography business, I find money, and I take bets on Major League Baseball games."

"What do you call your business?" I asked, already knowing the embarrassing answer.

"Well, I mostly go by 'The Betting Machine' but sometimes it's called 'The Amy Weinland Co.' *Co.*," she explained, pleased with her technical command of business-school abbreviations, "stands for *company*. That's very official."

"Wow!" I said, wanting to make her feel legit and important. It was the least I could do while I was in town. "How do you generate funds, well, you know, how do you make money?"

"Oh, I know what funds are," she said confidently. "That's what we deal with here. The first way we make *the* funds is we look for money under couch cushions, under the washer and dryer and in drawers." This was the loose-change angle.

"Then," she said with a twinkle in her eye, "we take bets against the line on Houston Astros games." She motioned to a messy stack of folded sports pages behind her. "I put the money here," she said, pointing to a plastic orange replica of the Houston Astrodome with the top crudely cut out. "And pay out the winnings based on the score in the paper every morning."

"How many customers do you have?" I asked, knowing Dad was the only one who faithfully visited, putting pennies on each game.

"We stay really busy, especially on the weekends."

"Oh," I said. "It sounds like a great business plan."

"Yes," she said, becoming quite pleased with herself again. Leaning back in her chair until she almost tipped over, she crossed her legs dramatically and continued, "We do pretty well here . . . yes we do."

"How about the photography business?" I asked, relishing

the operational overview I was receiving. "How does that work?"

"Well," she said, with grim seriousness, "that's just getting started. I am interviewing people to be my assistant and I'll make my decision soon."

"Who are your applicants?" I asked, again knowing the answer before she replied.

"Well, Kim and Rick have both talked to me, you know, here in the office. Kim even wrote me a letter about the job, on Mom's orange typewriter. See . . ." she continued, pulling the important document out of a file on her foldable desk and shoving it under my nose.

DEAR AMY,

HAVE YOU DECIDED IF I CAN BE YOUR SECRETARY? PLEASE CONTACT ME IMEDIATELY WHEN YOUR DECISION IS MADE. PLEASE NOTE THAT I WILL CONSIDER A PAY. THINK ABOUT THIS IS YOU WILL. IF YOU DO NEED ME SEND ME A LIST OF THE THINGS YOU WILL EXPECT ME TO DO ALSO INCLUDE THE BUSSINESS YOU WILL BE GOING INTO. PLEASE TRY TO WRITE ME BACK TONIGHT IF POSSIBLE.

SINCERELY,

KIM WEINLAND

"That's a good letter," I said, trying to speak with the gravity she/I would have expected when discussing such weighty business matters. "Will you hire her?"

"No," she said, "I think I'll go with Rick, because he's the only one with a camera, and it's a photography business. Also"—apparently she had deliberated on this decision for more than twenty seconds—"he's better at finding change in the couches. Kim doesn't like doing it, says it isn't worth it."

"Will Kim be upset?" I asked, not so much caring about Kim's feelings but instead wanting to know if little me cared.

"Probably," she replied. "When she gets mad she'll get Rick to start another business with her in the downstairs coat closet."

That was the better of the two locations, really. It was right by the front door, but the big drawback was Mom made you clean it up more often because everybody could see what you were doing.

"Last time she opened 'K & R Crafts,'" Little Amy continued. "They made stuff, but mostly they just had a big cardboard sign with their name on it that they carried around the house." Looking thoughtfully into the distance, bug-eyed, she dramatically flourished her hand across the sky. "It will never last though . . . They don't really care about having an office."

What they did care about, clearly, was not being a total freak.

"Well," I said, rising from my folding chair, "I had better go up and get ready and you better get changed into whatever you need to wear."

"Wait!" she said. "I need to put you in my new electronic directory." It was a proud moment for her, adding an adult friend to a battery-operated Rolodex that held the names of her Camp Olympia friends, her grandparents, her siblings, her BFF Catherine and her Aunt Susie and Uncle Chris.

"What's your LAST name?" she asked, stressing the "last" in case I didn't understand how address filing worked.

"Daughters," I said slowly, enunciating, knowing she was a crappy speller.

She looked up with huge smile and pressed the *D* button on the device, the wheel quickly turning to the appropriate part of the directory. Reaching inside, she carefully removed one of the small plastic cards, which was affixed with a sticker.

"OK," she said, "Amy Daughters, what's your information?"

It suddenly occurred to me that she couldn't get a hold of

me at home, in 2014, no matter what I said. Should I give her my actual address and phone number, and just hope she never tried to use it, or should I make some stuff up? I thought about what Mary said, that I couldn't mess it up, *no matter what.* With that in mind, I gave her my actual details, the home phone number, the address and then, in a total lapse, I said, "Do you want my email and my cell number too?"

"What?" she screeched, looking up from her messy writing. "DO I WANT YOUR WHAT?"

"Oh, my bad," I muttered, trying to figure out what to say. "That's work stuff, things people need for my writing."

"Oh," she said thoughtfully. "Maybe we should get those things here at my work."

"You will someday," I said, with a certain level of confidence.

She genuinely appreciated this, it made her seem quite legit. Which she certainly was, at least in her own head. And that's all that really matters, not just when you're ten, but when you're forty-five.

As she finished her scrawling, I thought about how unfortunate it was that she couldn't contact me back in the future. What if she needed me after I went back? If she needed help, or somebody to talk to, I wouldn't be there.

"I wish I could meet your kids, my other cousins," she said, breaking the silence. "I bet they are nice."

"Yes, me too," I said, holding back the tears that wanted to well up but weren't welcome. "They would love you." Looking around the room I continued, "They would love your office . . . This place is amazing. You've done a good job. Keep up the good work!"

Again, she was supremely satisfied. I was glad about that. Maybe it would all work out the same, like Mary said, no matter what I did, but it felt damn good, amazingly good, to make her feel good about herself. The only feeling I could compare it to was watching the pride come over my own boys, in sheets, when they received a heartfelt compliment.

Those types of things seemed so small, taking a moment to say something positive, but maybe they were bigger than buying a trampoline or even booking a fancy hotel room with a pool.

Maybe that's the meaning of life, along with Kim getting the chips and dip because she was the first one to erupt out of Mom's lady parts.

Reaching down, over the tray table, I shook hands with Amy. This pleased her so much that she dramatically pulled an old brown briefcase out from under her desk, opened it, and inserted Kim's letter.

Changing the combination lock to keep the highly critical documents safe, she followed me out of the small closet. "I'll need to look over Kim's letter one more time before I decide."

She made me smile, especially when I didn't think she would.

Chapter Nineteen

FIRST BLOOD

Realizing that there was nothing more I could do to be any breezier, I went back down stairs, discovering Rick in the living room. He was sitting almost formally, as if he was about to have his portrait painted, on one of the two gold velour armchairs. "Is anyone else ready?" I asked.

"No, I'm the only one," he said, politely.

He was dressed in powder-blue denim jeans and a long-sleeved western shirt with blue-bandana accents. Sitting down in the chair next to him, with the massive brass birdcage between us—the one Dad had purchased, while boozy in Reynoso, Mexico—I lamely asked, "So, how's school?"

"It's OK," he said. "I get to ride my bike every morning now, with Amy, because I'm in the second grade."

"Wow," I said. "Is it a long ride?"

"Yes," he responded, "but we go together every day, unless one of us is running a temperature or it's below forty degrees outside." He had a clear understanding of the rules of biking to school in Northampton.

"Sometimes Amy goes really fast, but she never leaves me behind." That made me happy. Rick and I had always been close, had always had our serious talks, even when we were younger. I wasn't sure if that had started up yet, the deep conversations, but at least Little Amy put someone, anyone, first.

"What kind of stuff do you like other than school?" I said, trying to steer away from the same questions adults always ask kids, especially if they don't know them well. It was ironic in this case, because here was the little boy I had grown up with, the kid I had spent endless afternoons with, but from an adult perspective I realized I didn't know much about the younger him.

In the future, in 2014, Rick was a combination of this little boy, loving and hilarious, gifted with insanely accurate comedic timing, and a full-fledged adult—serious and almost brooding. I had never thought about it before, but that's exactly what I was seeing here, the same thing—the funny ha-ha guy who winked at adults he didn't even know and then the controlled, almost overly-adult child—sitting maturely on the formal chair.

I had always thought that was the grown-up adult him, carefully playing both sides of his personality when suitable and necessary. Apparently, this had been going on for way longer.

So the adult Rick wasn't a new guy, he was the same guy. Only, he had replaced Mom's Sears-Best fashions with his own cool, vintage look. At least there was that transformation to appreciate.

"I like Star Wars, and baseball, and playing outside, and you know . . . all kinds of stuff. We just got a new playhouse in the woods. It's two stories and has a real front door and a ladder to the upstairs!"

"Oh, that sounds cool," I said, having forgotten about the playhouse our parents surprised us with. It was a generous gift, one given for no particular reason. They had built up momentum by saying that they had something "important" to discuss. Retreating to their room, but eyeing us a little too closely, they shut the door and proceeded to talk as loudly as possible, tempting us to stand outside the door and eavesdrop.

Their plan worked perfectly.

"I DON'T KNOW IF WE SHOULD TELL THE KIDS, SUE!" Dad said loudly enough for the neighbors to hear.

"YES, DICK," Mom said, with that tone of voice she reserved for when she was supposed to be keeping a secret. "IT IS SUCH A BIG S U R P R I S E."

This went on and on until we almost wet our pants. The way I remember it, they extended the anticipation even further by bringing out a giant coloring book and telling us that it was the "big surprise." I remember being at least quasi-impressed with it, but after the adults went back inside the room for more yelling, Kim informed us that there had to be something more. She could see it in their eyes.

Perhaps she did know something that the rest of us didn't.

Eventually, they must have told us about the playhouse, but I don't think it came that day. I think we had to wait for it to arrive and then to be erected. It, not the erection but the waiting game, made me think about how Amazon Prime has changed everyone's expectations as much as the internet itself. Think about it this way, let's go back in time, to 1978 or 1958 or 1988 and tell somebody that they could order something, anything that Kmart or Walgreens or any other retailer carried, or didn't carry, from the comfort of their rattan chair on a Sunday night, and it would be delivered to their own front door, guaranteed, by Wednesday.

Need *Blubber* by Judy Blume? Bam. It's there. How about a set of electric curlers? Bam. Delivered. The complete Cagney and Lacy series on DVD or VHS or Betamax? Bam. Thirty percent off the list price and free shipping. Hell, you could probably even order a playhouse, a wooden one, and it would be there and erected—you guessed it, on Wednesday.

Dad had the playhouse set up deep in the woods. I'm not going to lie to you, it was badass. It was accessed either by a narrow path that went up the fence line—past the burn pile—or straight through the thick trees and brush.

"What do you play down there . . . in the woods?" I asked Rick, as he gave me a sly grin and pulled a comb out of his back pocket, slicking back his bowl cut like we were at a '50s diner.

"Well, our new game," he said, "is pine cone wars. We fill the upstairs deck of the house with pine cones and then one person climbs up. The other two people stay on the ground," he explained, "and they try to hit the person upstairs with the pine cones while that person throws theirs at the people below."

I could picture the set-up perfectly even though I hadn't seen it in thirty-plus years. As far as I knew, no pictures existed of it.

"That sounds awesome!" I said.

"Do you want to go see it?" he asked hesitantly.

"Sure!" I responded, "I would love that!"

He got up and leaned over the iron railing. "Mom! he yelled. "I'm going outside with Mrs . . . this lady!"

"OK," Mom answered back from her bedroom. "Don't be long, we're leaving soon!"

As we paused to go out, Rick fumbling with the knob, I glanced into the utility room, seeing the washer, dryer and freezer (with a key lock, so nobody would steal our pork chops). Shockingly, I saw no dirty clothes, no clean clothes, and really nothing, other than the magnetic letters Kim had used in her instructional session before breakfast. Where was the laundry? I knew Mom hadn't done any yesterday, because I hadn't seen it, or at least I didn't think I had. If that were the case, she was at least one full day behind in doing laundry for five people. Where was it? In fact, I couldn't remember Mom doing laundry at all when I was here the first time, when I really was ten years old. WTF?

Putting my best Nancy Drew sleuthing skills to work, as I continued to follow Rick outside, I knew that if Mom was anything like me, all the laundry, clean and dirty, was hiding somewhere until the guests, those from yesterday and the one still lingering today, had left. It was likely pocketed all over the place, out of sight, but never out of mind. Next, I realized, again, for the zillionth time, that in my youth I had not done a good job of absorbing what was actually taking place. Come on, if you told me that one of my boys, thirty years from now, wouldn't remember me doing loads and loads, and yes, loads, of laundry, I would be shocked, and offended and bedazzled. Absolutely bedazzled that they didn't recognize, and validate, and issue an official commendation from the government that I, me, their mother, was the reason they wore sparkling clean briefs, every single day.

Surely Will and Matthew were better than me. It was my only hope for righting the wrongs of my misspent, unfocused youth. I pulled the notebook out of my pocket, still walking, and jotted, "*Tell Mom, thanks for doing my laundry. Add, 'I do laundry because I love you so much' to the agenda for the next family meeting.*" And "*I SUCK!*"

Walking to the far corner of the parking pad at the bottom of the driveway, Rick turned back, looking me quickly up and down. "You think you ought to go out in the woods in your nice clothes?"

Good point really.

"Yes," I said in an authoritative tone, "I'll be fine . . . very careful."

"OK then . . ." he said. "Follow me!"

We stepped down to the trail that ran along the fence line, wooded on both sides with branches, weeds and bushes. Given that it was late November, the underbrush wasn't as thick as it would have been in August, but there was still plenty to grapple with. The journey was shorter than I remembered, much shorter, but the feeling was so familiar that it jolted every one of my senses. I stopped briefly, only long enough so he wouldn't notice, and literally sucked the air into my chest. God, how was I going to remember all this? I had screwed it up the first time, so how was I at fifty or sixty or even seventy going to be able to correctly recall this? Just this moment, that's all I wanted. No, scratch that, I wanted all the good moments, all of them. I wanted my brain, or my memory storage, to have those delivered first, making me into the person I could be, the person I should have been all along. I pulled out the notebook again. "*Where are memories stored? Can we control what we remember and how and when we recall it?"* Crap. I should have listened more in school. I should have found out how all this worked before I got started. You always hear about how "babies don't come with an instructional manual," a statement that assumes that the parents are the ones operating the new gizmo they'd had sexual relations to produce. Maybe the baby should have the manual, and read it, from Day One, or before he or she starts using all the parts. Then they will know how to be whole when they are forty-five or fifty-seven, and everything is really good, but messy, but great, but confusing.

"You coming?" I heard Rick shout from up ahead. I hurried on, toward the only reality I could find at the moment. Coming to a small clearing, I approached the glimmering cedar playhouse. The sun shone through the top of the trees in an almost heavenly way, the new, unfinished wood gleaming like bronze. It was beyond beautiful.

As towering as the playhouse seemed during my first trip through 1978, it was tiny this time around, only a foot or two taller than me. Rick stepped up onto the little porch, unhinged the front door and went inside. "Come on in!" he shouted, peering out from the window. Crouching almost completely over, I managed to squeeze through the door and into the small space. Inside were two windows with plastic panes and a small picnic table.

"Welcome!" Rick said, waving his hand around.

"Wow," I said, hunched over like the Big Butt of Notre Dame. "It smells wonderful, like fresh cut timber."

Exiting, with me following, struggling to get back out, Rick went around to the left side of the house, to a short ladder that stretched from the ground to the upper floor. "I'll go up," he said, "but you better stay here, you probably might not be able to do it."

"No!" I barked as if he had told me I couldn't finish my big beer. "I can manage, I want to go up."

"OK," he said. "Go on up then, little lady." I could remember him referring to people like that, when we were kids, but didn't get how out-of-place it would have sounded to a stranger. Despite that, it was funny and I loved it.

I mounted the tiny ladder with my heeled sandals and slowly crept up the few rungs. It wasn't very far up, which was definitely a good thing, but when I got to the top I realized that the entry to the second floor was a small, square hole cut into the railing where people—kids or extremely small people—crawled through.

Looking down at Rick, who was smiling in a knowing fashion that made him look like Kim, I knew I had to get myself in there. I had to do whatever it took.

Squeezing myself through the hole would only result in a tragedy that would involve my petite—well OK, even if it wasn't technically petite—upper body making it through the opening, while my value-sized butt and thighs got stuck on the other side. This option would result in the rest of the family trooping dramatically down the pathway, following an alarmed little Rick to view the spectacle at the new playhouse. Then Dad would try awkwardly to assist me through, one way or another, while the rest of the Weinlands stood and watched in utter disbelief.

Mom would be on the phone with somebody, maybe Lisa or Joyce, later tonight after I'd left, saying, "You won't believe it, she tried to climb up the ladder and she got stuck, right there in the woods. What was she thinking? She could have broken something, or fallen on little Rick. Who does she think she is? And she made the biggest mess out of my third-floor toilet . . . and who will clean it up? Dick? NO! I will . . ."

Since going through the hole was obviously out, I did the only other thing I could, other than slink down the ladder in utter defeat, making little Mr. Bowl Cut positively right. Since we couldn't have that, I braced my hands on the railing, swung my right leg over and hoped for the best.

Unfortunately, it wasn't as big of a drop as I had anticipated and my leg buckled, sending my knee crashing dramatically into the rough wood floor and my backside up into the air. Grabbing the railing I steadied myself, pulled the other leg over and stood up, looking like a freaking jade-green giant standing on top of a regular-sized house.

"I did it!" I said, totally overzealously, my hands over my head in victory. "Now throw me up some pine cones and we'll have a little battle!"

Rick looked up at me with a genuine smile on his face. "OK!" he sang. "Here we go." After he'd thrown about twenty pine cones up, soft tosses, he retreated back to the trees and screamed, "GO!"

The only way I could take cover was to get behind the railing, which was only about four feet tall, so I fell flat on my stomach and waited for the barrage that I knew would come. Rick laughed as he launched cone after cone in my direction. I was getting pelted. It was a good thing he was so young, otherwise I could have gotten hurt. His throws were accurate, just not overly hard.

When he stopped, I peeked down and saw him collecting more ammo. Sensing my opportunity, I popped up on my knees and peppered him with three good hits. Screaming, he darted off into the woods, delighted that I had such skill despite my perfectly proportioned features. It was the same kind of thing he would think when he saw me in 2014.

As he ran around between the trees, I continued my attack, never noticing that he was filling his arms and moving in closer. Suddenly, he whizzed in front of the playhouse and made a brilliant shot on a straight line. Though I tried to spin around and avoid it, I was a second too late and the cone grazed the side of my head. Reaching up, I felt the slightest evidence of moisture on my cheek. First blood. It was just like Rambo. "Great shot!" I shouted from the prone position, where I had returned quickly enough to make the entire house shudder dangerously.

The game went on for about ten more minutes when we finally called a truce, realizing it was probably time to go inside. Lumbering carefully over the railing, I gingerly made my way back down the ladder and landed with a small—well, OK, large thud. Rick was waiting for me, carefully sizing me up. We were both grinning.

"Thanks!" I said. "That was great! Just wish it could have lasted longer."

"What happened to your face?" he asked, somewhat alarmed. "You're bleeding!"

"Oh," I said, laughing, "that's from that great shot you launched when you ran in front of the playhouse. You sure did get me."

"I sure did!" he said, without a hint of apology in his voice.

"You better tuck your shirt back in," I advised as we hurried up the path.

"Yeah, and you better brush yourself off," he said.

I was covered in pine needles, pine cone parts and a light fairy dusting of dirt. It felt amazing, right down to my smoke-colored knee highs.

"Yeah, right," I said, "I'll zip into the little bathroom when we get back inside."

Following Rick down the path, I joined him at the edge of the driveway where, again, he waited for me. "I loved that SO much!" I said, fighting the urge to either emotionally embrace him or tell him who I really was.

"Yeah." He smiled back, before I could do anything stupid. "I've never played with a big lady before."

Walking toward the house, I looked down at him and smiled. His facial expression was similar to what I had seen yesterday and, again, he was winking and churning his arms up and down. For a second time, I saw the striking resemblance to his youngest son, Finn. It was almost like we were walking, my nephew and I, on just another ordinary, normal day back in regular life.

Maybe the past does repeat itself, over and over again. Maybe we do go back in time, only not all at once, but instead, in little bits. Only we don't notice, because we're too busy to see it, or too obsessed with other important stuff. We can talk about it and get all philosophical, but changing it seems almost impossible. Unfortunately, ADT doesn't sell a security system to keep human nature from busting in and messing everything up.

Chapter Twenty

U TOTEM

I headed for the half bath while Rick went on into the breakfast room. Shutting the door behind me, I looked in the mirror and realized that my hair had also been compromised. Repairing as much of the damage as I could, I swabbed my oozing wound and began the tedious work of removing all the debris from the greedy pantsuit fabric. I wondered if the scratch on my face would still be there when I went back, back to the time I was supposed to be living in.

Suddenly, I thought about the last time I had stood in this bathroom. I had just been sexually accosted by P. Plum. Though it had happened only hours earlier, it seemed like a year ago. That was the good thing about not talking about it. It made it go away quicker.

Were there really upsides to acting like something had really happened? Sure, you could "deal with it," but what does that even mean? Do you talk about it at great length, looping around endlessly like the baggage carousel at the airport, until you realize you've started back at the same point over and over again, still lacking a solution? And what good does it do, really, to be reminded that you can't fix something, make it un-happen or even understand why it happened? Isn't that worse than just leaving it? That despite the fact that it crackles under the surface, waiting to explode, disguised as an overreaction to some other, unrelated issue?

How do you draw that fine line between talking about

something enough to understand that yes, it happened, and yes, it was bad, and yes, it affected me; and the realization that talking about it makes it even worse?

Coming back out and around the corner I was met by Kim, who looked dazzling in her 1970s finery, stylish jeans, again tucked into her long, leatherette boots. This time she topped it off with what looked like a men's tuxedo shirt with puffy sleeves and a little tie around the neck. It was ruffly and cute, and she knew it.

"Rick said you guys had fun," she said confidently.

"Yes, it was good!" I replied. "You should have been there!"

"I don't play such childish games anymore," she said, sounding almost like Marsha from the *Brady Bunch* during the episode when she believed she was having a torrid affair with the family dentist.

Before we could continue, Mom and Dad entered the room, Mom wearing an objectionable lavender pantsuit while Dad was in another pair of snug pants and a blue sport shirt with a penguin on it. Everything was tighter on Dad than it was on Mom.

"Where's Amy?" Dad asked, counting heads.

"I'm coming!" Little Amy screamed from the bottom of the stairs, rushing in through the dining room like the Freak Express. As she came to a sudden and violent stop, I nearly gasped. First, there were her jeans, which were (1) entirely too small, hugging tightly everything that shouldn't have been hugged tightly, and (2) a good two to three inches too short in length. Think high waters meet camel toe.

Up top was the worst part of all—a maroon, short-sleeved Texas A&M t-shirt with a huge A&M logo plastered across the front. The rest of the shirt was pockmarked with other Aggie symbols, everything from the profile of a half-cocked sergeant with the strap on his hat tucked up underneath his overstretched lower lip, to a series of cartoon thumbs. To seal the deal, squelching all question as to who owned the noxious frock, the back had "AMY" spelled out in bold, white block letters.

Holy crap.

Thrusting both arms straight in front of her, she stuck her thumbs up with a motion that looked like she was flinging out switchblade knives. After a painful pause for effect, Little Amy looked me straight in the eye and said, "Gig 'Em, Aggies!"

It was the most shocking and devastating moment in both my lives, the one here and the one back in 2014. This couldn't be happening, it was not real. There was no such thing as time travel or magical carpet rides to a far-off Whole New World. I was a proud graduate of THE Texas Tech University, a devout Red Raider football fan, a certified non-Aggie. I laughed at the sight of the long, brown leather boots worn by the A&M Corps. I walked on the un-walkable grass on the Aggie's College Station campus. I thought male cheerleaders in white Dickie jumpsuits were categorically ridiculous.

In the future, I had told my children they could attend the college of their choice with one big exception: Texas A&M. It was a directive they likely wouldn't ever have to worry about heeding, because thankfully our SAT scores were too low.

Who had taken this small, impressionable child down to the t-shirt shop in Tomball, Texas, and allowed her to pick this combination from among the large files of iron-on decals? Surely there were Houston Cougars logos, Holly Hobbie silhouettes, Donny and Marie doo-dads . . . Anything, even a Dallas Cowboys themed tank top, was better than this.

It was irresponsible, it was disgusting, it was—

"Amy," Mom said. "Go upstairs and change into something appropriate for the mall and quit showing off."

Good Lord, my mom had football-fashion sense after all. We were on the same page, finally. Only, wait, didn't she hate the Longhorns? What was going on?

Amy looked devastated.

"Listen to your mother," Dad added.

As she sulked off through the kitchen, Kim's voice followed

her. "Hey stupid, you have to dress up to go to the mall, it's a very fancy place." Rick found this funny, because, well, it was.

So—it wasn't about the A&M shirt being indecent—even though it certainly was. Instead, it didn't meet the standards for a day out at the mall. Amy had put it on to impress me, an idea that went horribly wrong on all counts.

After Amy left, Mom followed behind her. I remained behind with Dad, Kim, and Rick. Sensing a moment to bedazzle me, Kim asked me if I would like to see the family's Avon bottle collection. As if I could have said no, or even wanted to refuse, I followed her to the bookshelves in the breakfast room.

"See," she pointed out, with an air of dignified intelligence. "We have lots of them."

Continuing, she motioned with fanfare but no undue drama. "First, we have lots of cars. There is a golden antique car, a green car with a plastic top and a blue car that's newer, but still old."

Pulling down the blue car, which looked like a 1960s-model sedan, she showed me how the trunk could be removed to reveal a bottle opening with a screw-on cap, safeguarding precious ounces of a rare, manly scented fragrance—Wild Country Cologne.

Next, she pointed out a blue swordfish, an old-fashioned shiny gold telephone, a brown pipe that stood on its bowl, a stagecoach with a bronze suitcase packed on the back end and a Liberty Bell. All in all, there must have been fifty pieces.

"Wow, that's amazing . . . Can I hold one of them?" I asked, still reeling from Amy's crime against college football.

Kim climbed the desk chair and reached up on the second shelf for a brown chess-piece decanter. Just then, Dad walked through the room, advising, "Careful, Kimber, those will be worth a lot of money some day!" *Good call, you'll want to make sure you can cash in on the one dollar a piece Mom will get for those in a 1987 garage sale.*

As Kim came down from putting the bottle away, Mom

reappeared with a much-less-exuberant Amy following slowly behind her. Mom looked almost out of breath, but managed a chirpy, "Well, we're ready to go!"

Amy had changed into a sweater and powder-blue slacks. Though she definitely looked more suitably dressed—a colorful sweater with a cat perched in front of a sunlit window—she had lost the bulge in her eyes and the hyperness in her step. I was almost positive I knew what had happened when she went upstairs, but, then again, I couldn't be sure because I wasn't physically up there. Flashes of memory, impossible to verify or dismiss, made me almost sure that Mom's message had been delivered physically. But, old memories and a strong intuition weren't enough to be absolutely sure. Was I really supposed to just let it happen, whatever had happened, or should I try to defend her? Defend us? Defend me? What was I supposed to say, *Excuse me, I feel like whatever just happened, well, I think it's not right. And it should stop. Now.* And then what was I supposed to do, without a car, without a cell phone, without any phone numbers? Whisk Little Me away from my home and family, protectively, because I, some random freaking person nobody really knew, didn't like what was going on?

This, my implausible and impossible role as the time traveler, meant that I had zero options. I was captive and powerless. It was something I had in common with the younger version of myself.

Were these the questions Mary had mentioned? The ones that I knew I couldn't ask?

Looking over at Little Amy, our eyes locked briefly. She didn't smile but gazed almost intensely, as if I knew every-thing—what was happening, what had happened upstairs, what was going to happen. Who she was, who I was—who everyone was. It was as impossible as my supposed trek back in time. It was the moment that we connected, but didn't. It defined every-one, only it never actually happened.

We exited out the back door, drawn to Dad's mint-green Oldsmobile Delta 88 four-door like flies to an uncovered tub of pimento cheese in July. I held back as the family got in, again waiting to see where everyone else sat before presumptively taking my seat. Having a non-family member in the car was something I could never remember happening.

Mom motioned for Rick to sit up front between her and Dad while Kim and Amy piled in the back. The only seat left, my place, was behind Mom. Given that Kim was the biggest, she sat behind Dad, leaving Little Amy to sit between us.

The car was in excellent condition, not a surprise as Dad kept a clean car and replaced it every couple of years, a necessary business expense for an engineer/salesman. Though it wasn't as enormous as the Ford Mary and I had taken from the airport, the Oldsmobile was roomy, but not roomy enough to prevent Little Amy from scooting closer to me in tiny movements until we were thigh to thigh, her staring at me wildly. Her characteristic energy was returning in bucketfuls.

Managing an uninspired smile, I was reminded of how it annoyed me, back in the future, when my boys got wound up. For instance, my younger son's entrance into the Palm Sunday service at church last year, which made me cringe. He had broken his palm leaf in half and went down the aisle of the sanctuary in an almost dance-like fashion. I wore a similar, underwhelming smile that day, until I realized that given the same scenario, I would have palm-danced too. Thinking of this, I managed to unconvincingly pat Amy on the back, placing my hand on her shoulder. As much as this wasn't my thing, it was hers.

Dad backed the car out of the driveway and I was treated, once again, to a slow stroll through glorious Northampton. What struck me immediately on this, the morning after Thanksgiving, was how many people were outside. Since it was Houston, where winter rarely visited for long, there were a handful of suburbanites out on the lawn, raking, sweeping or even hosing down a car, but more telling was the number of youths. Kids on bikes, kids in yards, kids walking on the street, kids sitting together on the curb. There were no sidewalks, no parks, no community play sets, just kids doing stuff, outside.

As much as things had stayed the same from this life to the one I lived in the future, *this* thing had changed. The lack of 115 cable channels, Netflix, DVRs, the internet, smartphones and mini tablets meant that staying inside didn't have a lot of upsides, unless you wanted your parents to notice you were there and subsequently give you some sort of ridiculous job to do to "help out" around the house.

That's not to say that we—the children of 1978—were any more intelligent or driven than our counterparts in 2014. No, it just meant that we were tanner, leaner and smellier and had to communicate face-to-face.

Exiting the neighborhood, Little Amy made a big deal out of showing me the armrest that came down between the two back seats—a nice upholstered feature that was generously sized. Jumping onto it, she collided with Kim, who rolled her eyes, sitting maturely in her seat, cross-legged like a proper sixth grader.

As Amy continued bouncing around, Dad yelled back, "Amy. This is a car, not a toy."

Then it hit me. She was moving freely about the car. We all were. Not only was no one seat-belted in the family sedan, there wasn't even an option to buckle up in the backseat. They either weren't included by the manufacturer, they had been removed, or they were tucked down in the seats. I did notice that the front seat had shoulder straps on both sides, but they were left hanging in pristine condition. This meant that my little brother was free to sit on my mom's lap—which he was—only a few precious inches from the huge windshield that separated us from the road.

My parents weren't irresponsible, they were mere victims of

their own time—playing their parts, only to be frowned upon by the wise and knowing people of my time. Yeah, my mom had thrown back a couple of beers the night of my actual birth. That seemed so wrong now.

It made me wonder what my kids' generation would think of the hours we spent on Facebook, ignoring our own families. How would they perceive an era that prided itself on being "green" only to buy huge-ass Suburbans, five-bedroom houses with media rooms and mailboxes stuffed full of meaningless circular ads that went immediately into the trash, not the recycling?

It was equally ironic, despite the growing warnings, that they, the 1978 adults, didn't think nicotine was a big deal. Then, of course, we, the 2014 version, couldn't stop ourselves from checking our phones while driving . . . no matter how many shocking, graphic commercials we looked away from on the TV.

Eventually it would catch up with both groups, it always did. And then some smart-ass twenty-year-old would be there to point it out.

Out of the subdivision, we began making our way to Interstate 45. Passing the Texaco station, I looked up at its vintage hexagon sign with the company name in bold-black letters, outlined in a wide red stripe. I admired the '70s design of the building and the clean, professional look of the operation. Outside were racks of tires and stacks of Havoline Supreme Motor Oil. There was still a full-service lane—no option to pay at the pump —and rolling mechanical numbers that tracked the gallons and dollars. Gas was sixty-five cents a gallon. I could have filled up my minivan for $11.70, that is, if I could've found a way to drive it back in time. People here would think a 2005 Honda Odyssey was all that. They wouldn't care that we hadn't opted for the automatic side doors; here I wouldn't be shunned in the parent pick-up line; no, I'd be the bomb because my door COULD slide open. It was so much better than having your eight-year-old kid, in 1978, try to grapple with the 400-pound car door on a Buick Park Avenue.

I pulled out my notebook and scribbled, with Little Amy's eyes bulging from over my shoulder, "*When was the sliding van door introduced?*" and "*Are there still full-service gas stations?*"

Next door to the Texaco was the U Totem, a convenience store that carried everything from beer to pantyhose to candy. The sign spelled out the now-insensitive name of the store vertically, complete with a Native American totem pole to the right of the letters. It would eventually become a Circle K and is now, as of 2014, the highly touted "EZ4U Food Store."

Next was a huge open field, and, much to my surprise, the almost-forgotten Northampton Stables, an amenity that had been offered since the neighborhood was built. I didn't know when this edifice would be razed and its equine tenants shipped off to another location, but I knew it had to be soon. Eventually, houses and streets would rise from the ashes of the stables, bringing people who would never know they were living their everyday lives on the sacred ground of our evaporating memories. My BFF Catherine and I had walked through the quiet fields and meadows many times, playing on the old fence lines and climbing among the branches of the massive hardwood trees. Once we had found out the dastardly adults' plan of reclaiming the tract for suburban sprawl, we would exclaim, dramatically, "This is God's country, it shouldn't be touched!"

We probably sang the lyrics to that song *Wildfire*, where the girl comes down from Yellow Mountain calling for her horse. I wondered if Yellow Mountain was near Yellow River, where the mystical I.P. Freely lived. Either way, the girl in the song died looking for her horse, I think. At the very least, I knew the lyrics were tragic. We cried about them the way young girls do, in the same way they get freaked out when they play that awful slumber party game "lighter than a feather, stiffer than a board." That's the one where a group of girls circle the participant chosen to play the "dead" person. Each putting two fingers from each hand under the "deceased," who is lying flat on her back. The group chants "lighter than a feather, stiffer than a board," and if everything goes as planned, the "dead" girl magically rises, levitating above the other girls' fingers. It was the same concept that made the Ouija board both creepy and infamous.

I pulled out my notebook. "*Wildfire song, who sang it? Download it on iTunes.*" Then I added, "*Lighter-than-a-feather, stiffer-than-a-board game. What was that all about? Google it.*" And "*Pictures of the Stables—ask the I Grew up in Northampton Facebook page if anyone has any?*"

Next up was the iconic Dave's Express Store on the corner of Root Road and Gosling, the anchor of what was an early example of the strip mall. According to the white plumes of smoke in the air, BBQ was cooking in the pits behind the building.

Other than that, there wasn't much to see. The lack of any sort of business—other than Booger Red's salvage yard and the M&M Food Market on Spring Stuebner—was because FM 2920 (the main artery from where we lived to Interstate 45) hadn't even been built yet. It also explained why the folks at M&M's were, like their counterparts at Dave's, cooking BBQ behind their store—the total lack of fast-food restaurants in the area. There was no place to stop and grab a quick, on-the-go lunch. These little all-in-one stops were it. It made me understand that I grew up in a rural setting. I hadn't appreciated that, the isolation, but could now see how my parents would have. That is, until they needed something.

Even I-45 seemed simpler. Separating the narrow northbound and southbound lanes, only two of each, was a steel guardrail with a chain-metal screen or fence, not a concrete barrier with trash piled up against it. Rather than rumble strips, the shoulders were dotted intermittently with raised reflective strips that I greeted, oddly, as some sort of fond, far-off memory.

Though I caught a glimpse of the Allied Bank, Krause's

Pharmacy, and Minimax on the east side of the interstate, the other 500 businesses normally visible from I-45 weren't there. Instead, there were acres of farmland, fields of cows and thick rows of pine trees. No water parks, cheap furniture stores and half-burnt-down motels. No Walmarts, no used-car dealerships and no abandoned antique malls with U-Haul trailers lined up in the overgrown parking lots. It was an entirely different Spring, Texas, one that would be unrecognizable to its many residents of the future, and to the 125 cars destined to be lined up at the yet-to-come Chick-Fil-A.

Passing Spring proper, but before reaching the FM 1960 exit, I was treated to the most glorious site of all, something I had completely forgotten to remember. It was the Goodyear Blimp Base. The enormous hangar, positioned on the back right of an expansive, well-manicured green field, was painted mustard yellow and white with massive blue letters spelling out "GOODYEAR." The complex was huge, with a massive amount of frontage, maybe thirty acres in all. A smoky glass viewing area, shaped like two hands folded in prayer, topped the sunken visitors center. The entirety of the tract was bordered by a bright-green chain link fence, enhancing the look of the sprawling, lush lawn.

Luckily, and much to my immense delight, in front of the hangar was the mother ship itself, the America, the blimp . . . our blimp. Held to the ground with an enormous yellow pyramid structure, which attached to the blimp's front-facing red nipple, it was captivating, shiny and silver against the bright green field and blue sky. Its four fins were red, white and blue.

You can't imagine what growing up with the Goodyear Blimp in the '70s was like, unless you had. Our neighborhood was only a moment's flight from the hangar, meaning that on long, hot summer days, the blimp's crew would often fly slowly over our street, waving and sending messages on the rolling display on the side of the magnificent silver bird. "Have a Nice

Day," the blimp would tell us, or, "Go Astros!" or "Happy Birthday America!" or "Quit Hitting Your Sister."

The low buzz of the engines would signal its arrival, calling us to run from wherever we were—inside or out—to look up in the sky, waving wildly. The rest of the country saw it on TV. We were literally friends with it—it belonged to us. We knew that the pilot lived nearby, and almost everybody claimed a family member that had been aboard for a magical flight.

For all that suburban life in far north Houston wasn't, the Goodyear Blimp was something special.

The delicious incident passed too quickly. And, again, like a bunch of other stuff, I was faced with the reality that I would never see it again. Never. Our blimp base—along with my own childhood—were both torn down in the early '90s. Both ultimately relocated to Ohio. I had forgotten how much I had missed both, that is until I smoked crack and went back in time.

Chapter Twenty-One

DON'T LIGHT A MATCH

*A*fter exiting Greens Road and turning under the overpass, we entered into the Foley's parking lot. I could hardly believe that this was the same Greenspoint Mall I had driven past last summer. To say it was clean, sparkly and glorious would have been a major understatement—it was only a couple of years old and lived up to its billing as one of the finest, if not the finest, retail center in the country. Houstonians have short memories, as do Americans at large, which made a fresh look at the young Greenspoint Mall—referred to as "Gunspoint" in the future—as mind-blowing as walking into one of the new casinos in Las Vegas, awed by a seven-story crystal chandelier with a multi-level bar inside.

We parked relatively close, especially given that this was the day after Thanksgiving. Yes, there were lots of people and cars, but nowhere near the hysteria that would overtake Black Friday in the new millennium, an auspicious event that actually started on Thursday morning, prior to any nonsense about being thankful for what we already had.

We entered via the east entrance to Foley's, headlined by a smoky glass, paneled awning with lighting that gave off a subtle disco effect. Passing through the double set of doors and into the store was like literally being transported to a magical new world, only this fantastic realm was laced with unmistakable déjà vu undertones. I had been here before, but never like this, with hair on my hoo-hoo. Pausing just inside the entrance, Dad cautioned us to stay together while Mom warned the group that touching anything was a punishable offense. Before I could even exhale the fragrant retail air, the kids lined up behind the parents, and with me in the rear, away we went.

On sensory overload and desperate to stop every couple of steps and absorb everything I was seeing, I attempted to take mental pictures. If I had a smartphone, even a first-generation iPhone, I would have been taking photos uncontrollably. It was better than being in the best museum in the world, only I couldn't stop and look at the displays. It was like I was at the Pro Football Hall of Fame with people who considered sports absurd. I got that, I understood it, but it was killing me. Softly. Since in reality I was still an adult, I suppose I could have signaled ahead to Dad and told him that I would catch up later, giving me an opportunity to put on a cashmere beret and twirl around in the couples' Western Wear section, but that wasn't going to happen. Somehow, I was scared to do anything but follow. I was still that unsure girl from the South, who would never, ever want to inconvenience the rest of the group, or the rest of the world for that matter. That—other people not getting what I perceived they wanted because of me—would be worse than me not getting what I wanted. It was true even if I didn't really know what anyone really wanted—myself included.

Crap, I really was screwed up.

The walls were done in a deep bronzy-orange color, with chrome accents and a dizzying array of lighting. Most of it was big naked bulbs with hardly any room between them, the kind of thing you would have seen in a bathroom in the early '80s, stuff you would want to rip out in the future.

We had come in through one of the women's fashion departments, snaking our way through dozens of snap-posed mannequins modeling everything from gaucho pants paired with something called a "hooded blouson" (perhaps the son of a regular blouse), to polyester coordinates with shiny-gold translucent belts and geometric jewelry. One displayed high-waisted, baby-blue corduroy "jeans" with gold stretchy belts AND glittering-gold cowboy boots. The ensemble was made complete with a matching crewneck sweater and wide-collared shirt.

Though the list of fashion atrocities compounded as we walked on, what really struck me was the number of man-made fabrics, each offered not as an offensive, low-rent alternative to the real thing, but instead as a marvel worth paying extra for. Missing were organic cotton, natural bamboo, Alpaca fleece and boiled wool. In their stead were a list of vile textiles that were worlds away from being sustainably sourced, ethically made or even ten-percent organic. Qiana nylon, acrylic knit, velour, double knit, lustrous-cotton velveteen, satin of acetate—which was, based on price, a step up from satin of polyester—Dacron, Fortrel (wasn't that a programming language they taught in business school?), brushed/flocked rayon, Kodel, Orlon, Trevira, Lurex, Super Suede and my personal favorite, rayon chiffon.

If that weren't enough, these unnatural, chemically spawned materials were further treated to become even more useful, and perhaps more dangerous. These magical processes earned the garments additional honors like Wonderfeel, Superwash, Perma-Prest, Flame-Resistant and Easy-Care.

Among the few natural products that I could find, only in passing, were a sweater made from angora rabbit hair and what was advertised as a "natural" fur-collared coat featuring, of all things, opossum. So, while yes, these were sourced from nature, in this case that meant slaughtering and skinning furry friends—not necessarily a practice well thought of back in 2014.

I pulled out my notebook and quickly jotted down, "*Man-made fabrics, what's still available? Have things really gotten greener or has marketing and advertising changed?*" Also, "*Were skin irritations more prevalent in the '70s?*"

Passing through the shoe department, we entered the main

arcade of the store. It was glorious, a two-story courtyard with dark-wood paneling, disco lighting and long, orange and red banners that mirrored the walls we had seen earlier. Two escalators stretched from the main floor to the second level, which featured a wraparound glass balcony with chrome railing.

Then there were the Christmas decorations. On the one hand, they were shiny and oddly colored (again, it was all about oranges and yellows), but on the flip side, there weren't quite enough of them. The wow factor of late '70s design was balanced by a different approach to quantity.

Passing through the jewelry department, perfume and makeup counters, we were in sight of the mall proper. As we approached the edge of the world, where Foley's met the great beyond, it was obvious that we needed a plan. Mom looked pensive. Sure, we were at the mall, safe from having to talk directly, for too long, but what in the world was next?

"Do you have anything you want to see or shop for specifically, Amy?" Dad asked. "Greenspoint is an incredible shopping mall, it has everything."

"Yes," I responded, peering down the passageway leading away from Foley's. It was a seduction of the senses. The sounds of gentle fountains and waterfalls enticed my ears. Long lines of Ficus trees, draped and then draped again with lights called hither my eyes. As for my nose, it was treated to a scintillating mix of tobacco, chlorine and Brut cologne.

"Well . . . What I'd like to do, as a thank you and because I never get to see these guys . . ." I continued while placing my hand on Kim's shoulder, "is to buy each of the kids something . . . something they've picked out here at the mall." Not only would this give me a chance to repay Dick and Sue's kindness, it would give me an opportunity to have a precious few moments alone with each of the younger versions of my people. While I hadn't digested even half of the events shoved down my throat in the last twenty hours, I could feel the end coming.

Selling the plan to my parents wasn't as easy. "These kids have everything they need," Dad rightly asserted.

"That's just too much!" Mom chimed in.

"Well," I said, "it's the least I can do, after all, you put me up on Thanksgiving. Gave me a place to stay, a family to celebrate with . . . Plus, when in the world will I get another chance to buy my little cousins a Christmas present, in person, in the greatest mall in America?"

"Well, I suppose," Dad said, looking down at the three kids, a firm hand on Little Amy's shoulder as she did her usual squirm routine. "I guess it would be OK . . . as long as you stick to a reasonable amount . . ." He wasn't going to define the number, the reasonable one—that would be taking it too far, that would be getting too personal. I got that, and I would have handled it the same way but would have still felt awkward no matter what amount of money was ultimately spent. This knowledge basically gave me *carte blanche*.

"Great!" I said, glancing down at the kids, who looked shocked. This was 1978, not 2014 when expectations were way higher. These poor people didn't even know what Costco was. My parents had been beyond generous to us materially speaking, but never, ever had I remembered an event like this, in a mall where everyone dressed up like it was the traditional service on Sunday morning, the one with lots of old people and actual hymnals.

"If it's OK," I continued, not sure of the correct approach, "I could take Kim first, then Rick, and leave Amy for last."

Little Amy wasn't happy with this, but Kim, on the other hand, was thrilled.

What Little Me didn't know was that I was trying to do her a service by leaving her until last, until I could see what I could get away with spending on the others. But, as she would continue to do for the long haul, much to her own disservice, she assumed that she was getting the total shaft. I ignored that, as did Dad and Mom, but her siblings basked in Amy's perceived predicament.

"Should we say we'll meet back here in thirty minutes?" I asked. "And then give each kid the same amount of time, moving the meeting point if we need to?"

"Sounds fine. And again," Dad said, "be reasonable."

"As for you kids," he said, "your cousin Amy is being extremely generous, so let's not take advantage of her, and ask for something ridiculous." Mom nodded her head in agreement.

"Don't worry, Dad," Kim said, with a twinkle in her eye. "We know how to act. Don't we, Amy?" She gave Little Amy a gentle yet bombastic shoulder shove, whispering something in her ear.

"Yes," Amy agreed, wiggling with delight. "We understand."

"Well, Kimber," I almost sang, using her full name on purpose, because I could and she couldn't stop me. "Let's go!"

Chapter Twenty-Two

THE BEST NINE BUCKS I EVER SPENT

*A*s the rest of the family turned into the mall—with Amy desperately being pushed onward, as if in a forced march —I looked down at Kim. "So, what are you interested in getting? Think of something you really, really want."

It reminded me of shopping with Rick's kids in the future, the possibilities were endless—we couldn't be stopped, not by parents or decorum. It was the essence of the aunt-niece/ nephew relationship.

"Well . . ." Kim said, testing the waters before jumping in. "Could we look at say, maybe, well the accessories at Foley's?" I had thought she would ask for shoes, like YoYo's, or at least vinyl boots, so I wasn't sure what she was after. "Accessories" was such a broad category. But I had to give her credit for starting off on the right foot, vaguely.

"What is it you want?" I asked. "Don't worry, I'll tell you if I think we shouldn't."

"Well," she said, "everyone at school is wearing those stick-pins . . . you know . . ."

"Oh!" I said, remembering the gold lapel pins that were the epitome of 1970s fashion. "Yes, oh, I've seen those, aren't they beautiful?"

"Yes!" Kim almost gushed. "I have always, always, always, always wanted one."

"Great!" I said. "Let's go have a look! Should we try Foley's or a jewelry store?"

I knew she would know the answer to that, she would have known it before I ever concocted the "let's buy everyone a gift" idea. Inasmuch as seeing the Goodyear Blimp was in my dream sequence, the procurement of gold stickpins was in hers. It pretty much summed up who we were now and in the future.

The thing about Kim was, at all ages, she was generous. One far-off day, but sooner than she could ever imagine, she'd pick one niece or nephew, or a combination of them, and take them out for hours, buying them as many "specials" as she could afford. This made me want to treat her, if I could, in advance of her treating the small people of our collective futures.

"We could look at Sweeny's, it's there," she said, pointing down the corridor leading away from Foley's, an area dominated by a huge sculpture, like something you'd see at an upscale city park. "Or," she continued in earnest, her finger resting on her lips, as if we were deciding where to house our elderly parents, "we could go to Miss Bojangles or, we could just go back into Foley's. Really, lots of stores have them, even Sears, but, you know, Sears . . ." her voice trailed off, cautiously, hinting at the slightly down-market nature of a serious jewelry purchase at Sears and Roebuck. I had to give it to Kim, she was retail savvy and way ahead of her time. Sears was still in fashion in this decade, a fine retailer with a huge catalog following, but that didn't stop this young fashionista from detecting a waft of future wrongness.

This was the same Kim who would refuse to go into stores to look at clothing because the smell was off. The same Kim who didn't feel as if the Weiner's department store in Spring, Texas, was quite up to her high standards. I guess Kim was already who she was, and who she would always be. It was just the lack of a car, and a paycheck, and some distance and time that separated the 1978 version and the woman I knew and loved, and was still jealous of, in the future.

"Well . . . which place do YOU recommend?"

She was as pleased with this statement as Little Amy had been with my visit to her office, in a closet.

"I think Foley's is our best option . . ." she said, looking back to the jewelry section behind us.

"OK, let's do it!" I said, almost a little too enthusiastically.

Turning around, we retreated from the Ficus tree forest and back into the wood-paneled Mecca. Working our way around the chrome display cases, shimmering in the disco light, we finally located the stickpins. The selection was generous: traditional pins, bar pins and even golden safety pins adorned with everything from butterflies to keys. They were all displayed in a burnt-orange, deep-pile carpet, deeper than anything you would have seen in any other period in history. It was amazing how the jewelry didn't get lost in the carpet. Instead it almost floated on top of it, like it was levitating.

"Which one do you like?" I asked. "They have hearts, apples, owls, love knots, doves, stars, the word 'love' spelled out and roses . . . Oh look," I said, motioning toward the right end of the case. "They have birthstones, which is yours?"

"Mine is the garnet . . . or ruby," she said. "Amy's is the diamond, for April." Her voice trailed off wistfully. "But she doesn't care about that, even though she's got the best one . . ."

"Would you like one with *your* birthstone?" I asked, thinking she would go for that for sure.

"I do like that . . ." she said. "But what I really want is one with my initial."

Scanning the display, we found the monograms, but we didn't see a *K*. Looking around, I wondered if there was a salesperson we could ask. It was crowded, but eventually I caught the eye of one of the two women working the section.

"Excuse me," I asked, trying to play my best adult for Kim, who was suitably impressed with how I could handle such important business matters. "Do you carry a stickpin with the letter *K*?"

The woman—dressed to kill in what looked like a curtain fashioned into a green sateen dress—kneeled down to the drawers below the display and began rummaging around. Eventually she re-emerged with three boxes. "We have three choices in the *K* monogram," she said.

Now that she was directly in front of us, I noticed that she was wearing four thick gold chains. Each hung lower than the one before, from a choker all the way to a breast-length rope—the effect added dazzle to her shimmery lips, sparkly green eyelids and platinum blonde Dorothy Hamill haircut.

Kim was as mesmerized as I was—this woman was everything Kim wanted to be, and would become, and everything I wanted to be, but knew I would fall way short of.

Opening the three boxes, Debra, as per her aquamarine Foley's name tag, presented us our options. "First," she said, "we have a gold-tone monogram, it's five dollars." This pin had a smallish *K* only about an inch and a half long from the bottom of the pin to the top of the initial. "It's popular with younger girls.

"Next," she continued, "we have the 'gold-filled' twelve-karat stickpin, it's six dollars and ninety-nine cents." This option was about two inches long in total, offering not only higher-grade materials, but a bigger *K*.

"Finally," she said, presenting the remaining box, covered in mustard-colored velour, "we have our finest option, a full fourteen-karat stickpin, its nine dollars." This, Foley's finest, had a block-lettered *K* that was a full half inch high on its own and fatter than the other choices. It was noticeably superior.

"What do you think?" shiny Debra asked.

"Well, what do you think, Kim?" I asked, already knowing which one I would purchase.

"Umm . . . well, we should probably go with number one or number two," she said. "They are the best price . . . "

"But which one do you like best?" I asked, "Which would you pick if you didn't know the price?"

"Well . . ." she said, pausing to look at me, at Debra and at the pins. "I like the third one, the finest option, but that's just too much."

"We'll take it!" I said as I pushed the nine-dollar box toward Debra.

Looking down at Kim, I was pleased to see her beaming up at me. "Are you sure? Mom and Dad will . . ."

"No, this is my treat." I said, "And I'm happy to do it!"

Kim was enamored with me, something that pleased me so much that I almost yanked the jaunty scarf off the neck of the patron next to me. I wanted to wave it about in a celebratory fan dance. I had no idea it would feel like this.

"How will you be paying for this?" Debra asked, as she turned to put the two unwanted boxes away. "With your Foley's charge card?"

"No, no . . ." I said almost calmly, dipping into my huge purse, realizing that I had no idea how I would pay for this or anything else. *Crap,* I thought, panicking, but keeping it real for Kim's sake. *How was I going to pay for anything? I hadn't even packed this freaking purse?* Fishing out my wallet, I was relieved to find a healthy stash of folded cash, a checkbook, and three credit cards. One was a gold-and-white Texaco card, another from the well-heeled Diners' Club and the last, thank God, was a really old MasterCard. Hopefully, that would do the trick. Again, whomever had hallucinated this had done a damn good job of covering the details.

Debra took the card from me and moved to the center of the octagon counter. Even though there was plenty of crowd noise, I could hear her violently whacking the credit-card machine back and forth. I wondered how much money I had just spent. Pulling out my handy notebook, I jotted down *"Nine dollars in 1978 money today, how much did the stickpin really cost me?"*

Re-emerging with the form—purple and distressed from being swiped within an inch of its life—I noticed that Debra had filled out the financial particulars by hand, in blue ballpoint ink. I was amazed at how much extra work, and muscle power, each transaction would have taken. I took her pen and signed the form, pressing hard to ensure it went through all the copies.

"Thank you," Debra said, as she retreated back into her chambers, reappearing almost simultaneously with a Foley's gift bag. Handing the bag to Kim and the receipt to me, she said, "Merry Christmas and come again!"

"Merry Christmas!" we replied, in unison, looking at each other and giggling. Hell, I didn't even approve of giggling, but I was enjoying bonding with the young Kim so much I didn't care. I seriously, totally and completely wished the forty-eight-year-old Kimber could be here too. Maybe she would be as uncomfortable with her little self as I was with mine. But maybe, just maybe, she too would find something out along the way, something she didn't already know, or something she had forgotten that she knew. And then maybe, just maybe, we would drink six glasses of wine together and try to forget it all over again.

Walking back toward the mall, I looked at my watch, which was so small I could barely read the numbers. "We've still got about five minutes," I told Kim, who was suddenly looking at me with even more awe.

"Can I see your watch?" she asked.

"Sure," I said, throwing back my wide Qiana sleeve.

"Oh my God!" she said, freaking out. "YOU HAVE A DIGITAL WATCH!"

"Oh yeah . . . I do . . ." I said unenthusiastically, looking down at my Phasar 2000 watch, complete with a golden mesh bracelet.

"CAN IT LIGHT UP?" Kim asked, enthusiasm bordering on hysteria.

"Well, yes . . ." I fumbled with the two buttons on the right side of the small face. "Yes, it does."

Cupping my right hand around the watch, I drew Kim in

and activated the light using the tiny button. All it did was dimly light the crystal display, nothing more than four black numbers, separated by a colon, against a gray background.

"I have never seen somebody actually wearing one of THOSE!" Kim continued, impressed with the watch regardless of the fact that it wasn't attractive nor was it made out of anything near a precious metal. I supposed that the face, at least the part surrounding the numbers, would have been considered stylish at the time, browns and golds smeared together in a shiny, brushed look.

"Paw Paw . . . I mean my grandfather," Kim stated, careful to sound as grown up as I obviously was, "has a gold digital watch with red numbers, but I've never seen one like *that*, in person."

"Oh, yeah . . ." I said, like it was no big deal. "It was a gift from my husband, for our anniversary." I totally made that up, but Kim was duly impressed, so I continued, "He got it for me at Macy's . . ."

"Macy's!" she said. "That's only in NEW YORK CITY!" Apparently, this was before Macy's had cheapened its name by buying a regional mall anchor in virtually every zip code, including the same Foley's we were standing in right now . . . crap, now I was going to have to act like he had bought the watch in New York.

"Yes," I said casually. "He was there on business."

"Wow . . ." she said, mesmerized by the ballers Willie and I were in the future. "Have you ever been there?"

"I went once, a couple of years ago," I said, telling the truth this time. "We met some colleagues from England there."

"ENGLAND!" she screeched. "You know people from ENGLAND?" Little did she know she would be going to England in just a couple of years, with Dad and Little Amy, on a business trip.

"Yes, well, we lived there for a few years.

"YOU LIVED IN ENGLAND, YOU NEVER SAID THAT!"

"Yeah, we did . . ." I said, again being completely truthful, and realizing that our future was exciting even in the past. I liked that, I really did.

Before we could continue, Dick and Sue approached us at the meeting point.

"How did it go?" Dad asked.

"Oh gosh, Dad," Kim literally gushed. "It was wonderful . . . and cousin Amy, well she's just the best, most generous, most glamorous person I've ever met . . . and to think WE'RE RELATED TO HER!"

It was perhaps the greatest single moment of my entire life. The most wonderful thing anyone had ever said to me, or about me, the biggest compliment and the highest praise. And to think, all it cost me was a stickpin, a cheap-ass digital watch, and a wild, probably made-up, trip back in time.

"Well," I said, laughing with more than a hint of self-superiority, trying to act like this wasn't the pinnacle of my very existence, or, just being breezy in my breezy emerald-green fabrics. "Rick, it's your turn."

"Be careful with my little Snake," Mom cautioned, putting her hand softly on little Rick's head.

"I will, don't worry, Sue," I said, once again getting where she was coming from, as a mom and everything. It's just the kind of thing I would have said if some stranger cousin was taking my little Matthew off for thirty minutes in the mall—that is, if I would have even let that happen. The very thought of it conjures up a vision of myself in Ficus-camo, stalking the shoppers.

If I had to make a list of all the many things I liked about myself the most, my rock-solid, concrete sanity would be at the very top.

I took Rick's little hand. "Where to?"

Rick pointed down the corridor leading away from Foley's. Looking back at the rest of the family, I could see Kim proudly displaying her stickpin. I couldn't hear what she was saying over the sound of the fountains, but I didn't need to. It was the best nine bucks I had ever spent.

Little Amy, on the other hand, looked to almost be writhing in pain from not being the next in line. She wiggled and stared back at Rick and me, totally missing out on the impact that I/ we had had on Kimber. We were rolling this thing, deep, and she didn't even notice, instead choosing to take her bug eyes off the prize.

Rick cautiously led me to a sign in the next courtyard. It was near a huge fountain, a whopper, with a café next to it and over it, the upper part accessible by a set of stairs. Yellow-and-white umbrellas rose up from among the tables, giving it the air of a French sidewalk café rather than what it was in reality, a site located about three-hundred yards from Interstate 45. It was so pleasant that I felt myself wanting to sit down and order something. Couples and families sat at the small tables, enjoying a cup of coffee, a meal, or even what looked like a cocktail. Just the thought of alcohol made my stomach turn and my mouth salivate at the same time.

Everyone was well dressed, manicured and polished. Why wasn't the future like this, shiny and acceptable? Where were the pajama pants, the piercings, the tats, the tits?

Was the idyllic scene even real, all these people lunching properly, or nothing more than a shiny veneer? Or, instead, was it labeled "perfect" because it left out about eighty-seven percent of society? And what did it say about me that I found this exclusivity an attractive feature?

Yanking on my hand, pulling me back into reality, Rick pointed at the sign. "Here it is!" Though he was short on words, he was still big on facial expressions, again pulling that almost flirtatious smile.

MEET DARTH VADER AND CHEWBACCA IN THE TOY DEPT. AT MONTGOMERY WARD FROM 11:00 A.M. – 12:00 NOON ON FRIDAY, NOVEMBER 24.

Checking my digital watch, the same one that added to my obvious sophistication, I saw that it was mere moments before the appointed hour. "We're just in time!" I said. "Let's go!"

Rick's eyes filled with wild excitement as he looked up at me, cocking his head and giving a humorous wink. It was the same thing young Finn had done when he wanted an extra Starburst last Christmas. Oh the circle of life.

Now I had to find Montgomery Ward . . . Wards, who in the hell ever went there? I asked Rick if he knew which way we should go. He answered with a shrug. Crap. If Kim had still been with me, we would have already been halfway there. I loved people who just required me to follow along, happily.

Scanning each of the three passageways leading away from the courtyard, I vaguely remembered that Wards was back down by the movie theatre. Whirling around, I pulled little Rick in that direction, passing Coach House Gifts and Wicks 'N' Sticks. Whizzing by the red-carpeted General Cinema, I quickly glanced at the marquee to see what was showing. National Lampoon's *Animal House* (R), *Midnight Express* (R), Walt Disney's *Escape to Witch Mountain* (G)/*Return to Witch Mountain* (G), *Comes a Horseman* (R) and *Boys from Brazil* (R).

Though I totally remembered *Animal House* and the *Witch Mountain* films, I didn't know anything about the *Express*, *Horseman* or *Brazil*. Wasn't it hilarious that the *Witch Mountain* people were now on the *Real Housewives of Beverly Hills*? And where in the hell were the PG films? At this theatre it was either full-on frontal nudity or young over-actors preparing themselves for a future in reality television, where mascara runs down your face while you're drunk in a limo. Maybe that's where the PG comes in, later.

Pulling out my notebook while continuing, only more slowly so I could make sure Rick remained at my side, I scribbled, "*When did the PG rating begin? What is Midnight Express, Comes a Horseman and Boys from Brazil? Check Netflix.*"

In front of Wards, we encountered what had to be the finest fountain in a Greenspoint Mall blessed with water features. Not only did it look good, the water spraying in this masterpiece filled pipes and made music. People were lined up around it, as if it was the Pied Piper. It was attractive and well-engineered, but these overdressed suburbanites were crowded in, three rows deep, staring at it like it was freaking YouTube, which they didn't even know they were missing. Come on, folks, it's a fountain, A F O U N T A I N, move along.

Though it was clear that Wards was not up to the modern, cutting-edge interior-design standard set by the Foley brothers, it wasn't bad. To me, it had much more of a true '70s feel, kind of like a super version of Kmart. Plus it was clean and brand new.

The amount of stuff piled up, neatly, in Wards was mesmerizing. Following the signs to the toy department took us through the sporting goods, an area decorated with pine shingles, giving it an earthy yet flammable feel. I wouldn't have been surprised if a duck flew overhead, a trout flopped and splashed in the distance or a chain-smoking shopper caught one of the shingled posts on fire.

What outdid Foley's, and the rest of the mall for that matter, were the Christmas decorations. They weren't necessarily better, or more numerous, but they screamed '70s with lots of tinsel, plastic and weirdness. I liked it. I liked it a lot. Think giant illuminated plastic candles and nativity sets, fold-out paper bells, creepy Santa heads circled by foil-backed lights and reindeer fashioned out of colored popcorn.

Finally in the Toy Department, we joined the crowd around a runway. It was wooden and oddly yellow. It stood at about three and a half feet tall and had exposed lightbulbs running up and down its entire length on both sides, glowing so furiously you could almost hear the glare. These were a burn hazard, capable of charring the flesh of any client who dared to brush against one. Where in the hell was OSHA?

This was where we would "meet" Mr. Vader and his hairy friend. Settling into a couple of chairs, we waited. Looking down at Rick I went with the obvious "Are you excited?" To which he produced a huge grin and another thumbs-up.

The seats filled in around us, as did the standing room, before a male employee eventually emerged from the back room and onto the runway, making it shake in a way that made me question, again, whether anyone had inspected it from a safety standpoint.

"Boys and girls!" he said excitedly, utilizing a small microphone that looked as if it had been ripped out of a nearby cassette-tape recorder. "I hope you are ready for our very special Christmas visitors.

"Boys and girls," he repeated, his voice a weird mixture of cheesiness and manliness, like a Disney character who also sold used cars. "On behalf of THE toy department at Montgomery Ward, I am happy to introduce you to some very special guests . . . Here they are, boys and girls, from a long time ago, in a galaxy far, far away . . . Darth Vader and Chewbacca!"

From out of the swinging doors a pair of shadowy figures emerged. Darth Vader was first, looking almost genuine and believable in his black garb. The crowd oohed and ahhed over him, clapping enthusiastically. Though the people were impressed, and why shouldn't they be, most every youngster was looking past Vader to Chewbacca, who was waiting in the wings.

As he emerged, on cue with another dramatic announcement from the master of ceremonies, the crowd roared, most of the kids on their feet. While there was no doubting that this figure was the Chewbacca who had been so promised, because who else would he be, his costume was almost laughable by new-millennium standards. Though his plastic head was problematic, what had really gone wrong was the hair, or fur. Instead of mirroring the long, almost stringy all-over hair of the character in the film, the mall version was covered in short, matted stuff that looked more like carpet fuzz. It was a lot like the hair on a doll after ten years in the back corner of a girl's closet.

So while Chewbacca looked friendly and jaunty as he sauntered down the runway and waved at his fans, anything resembling authenticity wasn't happening. But this didn't diminish the crowd's enthusiasm.

After about five minutes more of showmanship, the employee directed the crowd's attention to the other side of the department, where an enormous Star Wars display just so happened to be. "If you'll head this way, folks," he instructed, "Darth Vader and Chewy will be happy to sign an autograph, no purchase required."

Rick grabbed my hand, looking up. "Let's go!"

Somehow, maybe because I nearly knocked fifteen people down, we managed to get past the throng and found ourselves at the beginning of the haphazard line. When it became our turn, Rick edged up hesitantly to Darth Vader, who was the first character stationed at the long bank of tables. It was obvious he was nervous, so I did what I would have done with my own two boys, placing my hand on his shoulder and speaking for him.

"This young man would like your autograph, Darth . . . um, Mr. Vader."

Rick liked that, and smiled. "Yes, I would like one, please."

"What's your name?" Darth grunted, between heavy, laborious breaths from the depths of his heavy resin mask.

"Rick," he said. The character swung his marker at lightning speed across a black-and-white eight by ten of the real Darth Vader, or at least a realer version. Apparently it didn't matter what Rick's actual name was because all I could make out was an *R*, *D* and *V* in the autograph. That was understandable, being that this Darth Vader was burdened with a huge pair of what looked like vinyl combat gloves.

"Thank you very much," Rick said, almost as if he were ten years older than his actual age. Darth Vader nodded, adding some sort of official hand salute.

Sliding down to the other end of the table, Rick said, "Hi, Chewy!" Chewbacca cocked his head humorously, grunted, and then shook his hand. Rick absolutely loved it. I marveled at how we can make believe something is the best thing we've ever seen, even when it's clearly not. Maybe the happiest people are those who don't grow out of that.

Chewy had a better grip on his pen and was careful to get Rick's name correct.

"To my good friend Rick. Love, Chewy"

I realized that we needed a photo of this auspicious occasion. Instinctually, I dipped into my purse. I may not have been able to apply seven filters and post this on Instagram, but surely I could take a picture of it . . . Where was my phone?

Crap.

This would have to be yet another memory that we just remembered in our heads.

Moving on, we stepped toward the *Star Wars* toy display, impressive not so much for the number of items on sale, but because they weren't wrapped in five layers of hard plastic. Everything, all of it, could have been opened standing right here, without the help of any tools.

I knew that Rick already had the R2-D2 and C-3PO action figures, a fact I picked up from the *Gong Show* act yesterday, so I pointed to a small set that included Darth Vader and two Stormtroopers. "How about this?" I asked.

"Oh, yes!" he said, taking the set out of my hand. "THIS is what I want." Examining the package, I found the small price tag, $4.88. That was only half of what I'd spent on Kimber. Even though he'd never know the difference, I felt like I should keep things as even as possible, another lesson from Dick and Sue, who had always made a big effort to be fair when spending money. It was one aspect of life that could be kept even.

Looking around, I saw the Land Speeder, a brown vehicle I vaguely remembered hovering around in an early *Star Wars* movie. It was $4.76. "How about this for everyone to ride in?" I asked.

"Really?" he responded. "I can have that too?"

"Sure!" I said.

"Great!" he said, grabbing the second package and heading toward the packed register. "Let's GO!"

This time I was much more comfortable with the check-out process, whipping out my card and not groping around for a place to self-swipe.

Looking at my watch, I realized that it was past time to meet Dick and Sue. I was hoping Mom wouldn't overreact, though I wouldn't blame her if she did, I got that, totally. Grabbing Rick by the hand, we hurried out of Wards, past the singing fountain, still surrounded by eager onlookers, and back toward the first courtyard. There they were, just behind another fountain, this one with a frog spitting water at mosaic tiles. Mexico had met Italy, and nobody had won.

"It was so cool!" Rick told the rest of the family. "We MET Darth Vader and Chewbacca IN PERSON!"

"IT'S MY TURN!" Amy screeched, busting through our joined hands as if this was an impromptu game of Red Rover. She didn't care about what Rick or anyone else had gotten. This was all about her. "Red Rover, Red Rover, let freaky selfish hyper girl come over."

"Amy!" Mom scolded. "Calm down, give Mrs. Daughters a chance to catch her breath. My God, you need to control yourself . . . Dick, she's out of control again . . . "

Dad put his hand on Amy's shoulder. "Sue," he said firmly, but calmly, "she's fine."

I desperately wanted this moment to end. I couldn't handle the obvious conflict between Mom and Dad regarding how to handle Little Amy, who was, without a doubt, difficult to control. It was precisely what he, Dad, had eluded to in our recent conversation, the one back in 2014 that had so affected me. "I tried to protect you . . ." were his words. Now here it was, in black and white, on display for validation. Only now, I was seeing my part in it too.

Maybe this was one of the questions I didn't have, the ones that Mary said needed answers.

But this, just like real life, was moving too quickly for me to ask or answer anything.

"Are you ready to go?" Little Amy asked.

"Yes," I said, wondering if there was any way to get her to the see bigger picture.

"Where should we meet this time, Dick?" I asked.

"Well, there is a kids' play area by the Food Court," he said.

"Great," I said, putting my hand on Little Amy's head. "You ready?"

"Now, Amy," Sue cut in, "YOU KNOW HOW TO ACT, DON'T YOU?"

"Yes!" Amy screamed, unconvincingly, "I will be SO GOOD!"

"Just CALM DOWN and LISTEN," Mom continued, "MRS. DAUGHTERS IS BEING VERY KIND AND SHE DOESN'T NEED ANY TROUBLE."

"She's OK, Sue," Dad interjected again.

Mom didn't look convinced.

Chapter Twenty-Three

FISCAL PACKAGE

*W*ell, it's just US now!" Little Amy said as we began to walk away.

"What do you want to do?" I asked, feeling half-scared and half-intrigued. Maybe that's how I felt about my adult self too, half-delighted and half-alarmed. Half-ashamed and half-proud. Therapy, I needed therapy.

"Well, I'd LOVE to go look around Oshman's Sporting Goods," she said.

"OK . . ." I said.

"But first, can we just walk through Hickory Farms?" she added with an air of desperation.

"*Hickory Farms?*" I asked, wondering what the hell she was thinking.

"Yes . . ." she said, almost dreamily, pointing to a barn-like façade about seventy-five yards down the corridor toward the Food Court. "It's right there and did you know it's a lot like my favorite catalog, The Swiss Colony? Only it's different, and you know what? I've always really, really, really wanted to go there. But, guess what, I've never been?"

"Sure . . ." I said. I wasn't at all surprised that she was different, but I was alarmed at how different. Beyond that, it was her willingness to put it out there. Come on, you can like summer sausage and cheese that doesn't require refrigeration, but why admit it to a stranger?

She was confident about being a freak. I hadn't expected

that. Really, I had thought she/I/we were freaks who had long operated a complex cover-up scheme, the masterminds of a hoax that made us look normal—well, almost—to the outside world. But, or so it would seem, that was the MO of the forty-six-year-old me, because the younger version of the voice inside my head was confident. She had confidence. It was more shocking than my parents' party last night and a bigger surprise than finding out I really was, by far, Mom's least favorite.

Perhaps we are all born with confidence, but life robs us of it. Maybe we're all pretending we still have it, some of us more than others, while secretly dying inside day by day. Have we replaced it, our confidence, with unfounded smugness, hiding behind our bank accounts, expensive purses and riding lawn mowers?

We want better, for ourselves, for our children, but we don't know how to fix it. Because we aren't even aware that it's broke.

Hand in hand we walked slowly toward Hickory Freaking Farms, in a mall full of what had to be the best retail shops in what was the fourth-largest city in the nation. It's what she had picked. It's what I had picked. *Oh God . . .*

The store itself was way better than I had imagined, a huge improvement over the holiday kiosk you still saw set up in malls during the holidays of the future. It was a little like a dumbed-down Cracker Barrel gift shop. What it lacked in Yankee Candles and weird old-lady sweaters, it made up for with poufy table skirts and stacks of canned nuts.

Mini-Me was thrilled as we sampled cheese balls garnished with shiny cherries, the famous beef stick, "cheddar" out of a brown crock, something exotic called "Sesami Stix" and a generous slice of a delicacy labeled "smoked cheese bar." Pausing at the rear of the store, I watched as Little Amy literally salivated over the display of holiday gift boxes brimming with meat logs, cheese bars, miniature mustards, dessert loaves and imported petit fours. Each was lined with a healthy serving of fake Easter grass and hard candies wrapped to look like, I guessed, foil strawberries.

I really shouldn't have, but only because I knew how she operated and what it would mean to her, I reached up and grabbed the biggest gift box I saw. It was something called "The Big Round Up." Without turning back, I hauled it to the register. Following right behind, she literally squawked, "Wait up! You're buying that? Who is it for? Your family back home in Ohio? My mom and dad? The lady friend who dropped you off? Your husband? Your postal carrier? You know . . ." She stopped, putting her hand on her hip in an almost Kim-like fashion. "That will make a FINE gift!"

I didn't turn around as I shelled out the $9.99 for the three-pound box of happiness. She continued on, not being able to cope with the fact I was making an actual purchase at the ONLY fake red barn in this mall. "Oh it is nice, especially that beef stick summer sausage . . ." she cooed. "Oh, it will be delicious . . . Whoever gets that is LUCKY!"

The clerk, wearing a red vest and a black Colonel Sanders tie, put the box—which looked like a Duraflame log—inside a red bag and handed it to me, smiling over the faux butcher-block counter. "Don't forget your complimentary holiday gift . . . free with every purchase!" he said, handing me a booklet called *Cheese Chatter—A Fine Cookbook*. I think the alternate title was something like *Twenty-Three Ways to Not Have a Normal Bowel Movement for Two Weeks*.

Amy followed me out of the store, past the Hickory Farms Christmas tree and past a ginormous wheel of "Citation Swiss," still talking, still wondering. Once back into the mall, I finally stopped, looked down at her and smiled. "Do you know who this is for?"

"No," she replied, solemnly turning her head to-and-fro, not understanding that I, well we, were about to alter the entire course of her life. Mary had said nothing in the future would change as a result of anything I did on this supposed journey, but if Little Amy remembered receiving this box of goodness, it could change the future. Yes, the actual receipt of fake meats and cheeses could mean she got something—a categorically ridiculous something—that she had always wished for. Something that in the future she would never admit to even wanting. If she got the beef stick, now, at age ten, would it mean that she wouldn't push herself quite so hard later, trying to be something more, trying desperately to please every person she ever met?

I didn't know whether that was a good thing or not, tinkering with the delicate wiring of what was to become my adult personality. I may not have always liked myself, but the reality of who I was, and wasn't, might be better than an unknown, untested alternative.

So, I would do this while trusting Mary that it would change nothing between 1978 and 2014. And, I would make a mental note, not a written one, because that would be keeping it too real, that this could be one of the questions that Mary very unwisely said I freaking had.

"YOU!" I said, with a degree of satisfaction I couldn't explain.

She gasped, and staggered back as if someone had punched her right in the gut. "ME?" she uttered, barely managing to spit the word out.

"Yes, YOU," placing the hefty bag squarely in her small hands, causing her to shift her weight.

"You mean this is for ME, it's all for M E? The Hickory Farms BIG ROUND-UP pack is for *ME*?"

"That's right, Merry Christmas, Amy!" I smiled. "Now, where is Oshman's?"

"*Where is Oshman's?*" she gasped, enunciating every word with eyes on full bulge. "You mean we're still going to OSHMAN'S SPORTING GOODS even though I am holding a BEEF STICK SUMMER SAUSAGE?"

Oh my God, she was a freak, standing there by a fully lit Ficus tree, within hearing distance of eight different man-made fountains and a kiosk of hand-blown crystal animals, the same ones you couldn't get in 2014 unless you went to a truck stop with showers.

"Let's just call it an 'Amy bonus' since we share the same name." I said, still smiling, because I couldn't help it. If I couldn't appreciate her, who would? And if I, of all people, couldn't love her, who in the hell would?

With Little Amy grappling with the red bag in the same way I had struggled with my luggage yesterday, we headed back to the café courtyard and into Oshman's, Houston's finest sports retailer.

It was stacked to the gills with merchandise. So much so it was hard to gauge the décor, other than the wood shingling that copycatted what was going on over in Wards. Only this time around, there was more wood, but you couldn't see it as well. Maybe it wasn't so much that the '70s had less "stuff" on sale, maybe it was just crammed into a smaller space.

Walking down the main path that zigzagged through the store, we looked at a dizzying array of shoes, balls, camping equipment and a bigger-than-necessary display of bumper pool tables. The deal of the day, or what everyone was gawking at, was an octagon-shaped table that could be a red-felt bumper pool table, a poker table, or, a regular dining set. It was advertised as a 3 in 1, a term that reminded me of how chili restaurants in Ohio—the same places that dare to mix cinnamon and nutmeg into their meat—offer their products in "three way" or "four way" variations. Look, I understand they mean you can have your "chili" with spaghetti noodles (yes, I just freaking said that) and cheddar cheese and sour cream, or not. But, what most everyone else in the country is thinking, when they see it on the menu, is that it comes served not on a bed of noodles, but on an actual bed with two, or three, nude people.

242

And where I'm from, that just ain't right.

Before I could take anything else in, Little Amy gasped and pointed at a display to our right. There, stacked in two separate pyramids, were NFL locker bags and jersey and helmet sets.

"OH MY GOD!" she screamed, bug-eyed and arms in full flail. "I have ALWAYS wanted one of THOSE!"

Pointing in the general direction of well, everything, it was difficult to figure out specifically what she was so excited about. I got that she was way into NFL football—this is the same girl who would save up her allowance to subscribe to the *Pro Football Digest*—but which of these items had she "ALWAYS" wanted?

"What have you always wanted?" I asked, trying to decide if I should be enthusiastic or scared.

"ALL OF IT!" she stated dramatically, gasping like the oxygen level had suddenly dropped in the store.

"Oh . . ." I said, walking toward the jersey/helmet sets. "Which team do you like?" I knew exactly what she was going to say, but I couldn't let on to that, because frankly her choice was unusual given we were in South Texas, where she had lived for the entirety of her short life.

"Oh, I love the Washington Redskins!" she said, again confident despite the fact we were likely to be within earshot of at least a couple of Dallas Cowboy fans. "But," she continued, still in the full throes of drama, "they probably don't carry that here . . ." Her voice trailed off like nothing in life could have been more disappointing than the shocking statement she had just made.

"Well, I could ask . . ." I looked around for somebody who worked in the store.

"Oh, could you?" Little Me said, in a tone that both delighted me and made me want to throw myself in front of the truck that had delivered the bumper pool tables. "That would be so fabulous."

Suddenly she sounded like a thirty-two-year-old woman

from Vermont, but her marginally impressive grasp on the English language couldn't hide the fact that she was a prepubescent girl asking for a football uniform as a gift, when she could have anything in the entire mall. And, beyond that little anomaly, she had almost fainted upon receiving a processed meat log.

Again, and this time with feeling . . . Oh God.

It didn't surprise me one bit. How well did I know this kid? But, seriously, who was she? WHO WAS SHE? How was she ever going to survive what was coming? Her life wasn't necessarily going to be worthy of a Childhood of Famous Americans book, or one of those Dear America diaries, but it was going to be a life. And that meant all the twists, turns and painful moments that are destined for any living, breathing thing.

I couldn't help her. And she couldn't help me. We were just going to have to trust God that this would all work out, despite our obvious combined shortcomings.

I waved down a salesperson wearing gray sport slacks and a snug white shirt with a wide collar, the orange Oshman's logo emblazoned over his eastward-facing nipple. He looked like he might be on the coaching staff for the Miami Dolphins, with thick black hair, a mustache and an attractively bulky body.

"Yes, my lady, how can I help you?" he asked, as if we were standing just outside the drawbridge of the local medieval castle.

"Uh, yeah," I started, not sure if I wanted to ask him my question or date him and his caterpillar mustache. "We were wondering if you had any of these NFL items, the bag or the helmet set, for the Redskins . . . The Washington Redskins?"

"Well, miss," he said. "That is an unusual request, indeed it is. Now," he continued, "are we looking for a Christmas gift for a special little boy who lives at some great distance from us, because we can ship directly."

Good Lord, these people needed a good internet connection. Back in my day there would be absolutely no reason, ever, and I mean ever, even with a hefty discount, to make the arduous trek down to the mall, on the Friday after Thanksgiving, to mail order some stuff to be shipped to another state. This was precisely why eBay and Amazon were created. More things to be thankful for.

"No!" Amy the Younger cut in, marching right between me and Mr. Gallant. "It's for me, for today, I'm a BIG Redskins fan."

"Oh," the salesman said, pausing to scan Amy's bowl cut and cat frock. "Well, isn't that something?"

While his voice wasn't dripping with condemnation, it was easy to detect just the slightest change in his tone. Suddenly, I felt myself becoming defensive, for her, for us. She could be confident about her fanhood all she wanted to, but I wasn't going to take any crap from this guy, even if it wasn't actually happening. Even if I was the only one who noticed there was anything to be offended by.

"Yes," I said as firmly as I could, putting my hand on my hip in a decidedly Kim-like fashion. "She's a big fan, she's a prodigy, really. She can run like a deer, catch a ball in full stride and she's got a real head for statistics . . . And she, well she . . ." I said, unable to stop myself. "Plays championship-caliber soccer."

I may have been overstating things a little, OK, I was flat out making stuff up, but, at the very least, I was going to speak up for her/myself/us and most of all, me. I wouldn't be here tomorrow, or for the 13,140 days that separated the age of ten from forty-six, but I was here today. And even if I only had the guts to defend us in front of a total stranger, I had the kid's back.

I had my own back.

Little Amy looked at me as I worked up a suitably direct glare for Mr. Handsome, her eyes glowing in what I perceived was pure awe. Though I'm one hundred percent sure she didn't really get what was going on, she got it.

"So, what's the deal . . . do you have anything?" I asked him, now completely uninterested in him except for the purpose of getting what WE wanted.

"Well . . ." he said, still dashing, but not quite the same guy he had been forty-five seconds before. "You won't believe this, but the supplier sent one of each for every team in the NFL, just in case. And, we still have one bag and one uniform set for the Redskins. Would you like me to show yourself and the young, um, lady, the sets, or— "

I cut him off before he could continue. "No, we'll take both."

"Well, ma'am," he said. "The helmets and jerseys are technically sold separately, the jersey is $7.99, the helmet is $9.99, and the bag, well, that's $7.89, so . . ."

"We'll take all three," I barked. "Wrap them up please." I made a big deal of looking for his employee name tag and added, "James."

"Yes, my lady," he said less enthusiastically, but proving that while chivalry hadn't been completely vanquished, we were moving further from the castle gates. "Follow me, please."

I didn't even look down at Amy. I just grabbed her hand and followed Jim's tight ass—and I'm not referring to his fiscal conservatism—to the register.

"Are you sure, Big Amy?" she asked, almost shyly now.

"Yeah, I got this . . . We got this," I replied.

She was thrilled. I was riled. And as for James, he was either perplexed or totally unaffected as he handed Little Amy the Oshman's sack containing everything she had ever wanted, only she wasn't afraid to ask for it.

For all I knew, I was the only one of the three us of who thought James was judging Little Amy because she loved football and wanted to wear a helmet and jersey and store them in a vinyl locker bag with plastic handles and fake stitching. She looked so happy, he looked so hot, and I was ready to punch somebody, or lay on the floor in the fetal position and sob, or do both, at the same time.

Little Amy had spent hours looking at the NFL page in the

Sears Catalog, the Holiday Wish Book, dreaming of having these items, falling in love with the freaking Redskins' logo and uniform. I knew that, and I was happy to comply.

But, I was still not at one with her wanting them. What did it mean that she was OK with it, but I wasn't? After all, she had to live with that, not me, right? I knew too much to spend time with her. And she knew just enough. Maybe that's why we were meant to stay in the parts of our lives that we were supposed to be in. Maybe that's why time travel isn't possible.

Mary and her damn questions.

LOOKING at my watch, I realized that despite hitting two stores, we still had a couple of moments left before we had to meet up with Mom and Dad. "You thirsty?" I said.

"Yeah," she said. To be honest, I could have really used a Starbucks, or any kind of caffeinated coffee drink, but that wasn't happening here, any more than I was going to be able to look up the meaning of life on my iPhone.

And so, we settled for an Orange Julius.

"I've never been here before, Big Amy," she said, looking up at me.

"I know . . ." I said. My response didn't seem to faze her. Did she know what was going on? Clearly, no. What concerned me even more was that she seemed oblivious to everything that was going on. She was so trusting, dangerously so.

I ordered two smalls, totally unsure of what an Orange Julius really was. The mall had become busier since we had arrived. The only place I could find for us to sit, even though we only had a few precious minutes remaining, was outside of the Children's Place store. It was a shop that was still alive back in the real world, that is, minus the yellow neon sign and the red entrance.

As Little Amy stared out into the crowd, I pulled out my

little notebook. "*Orange Julius . . . What the hell is it? Buy somebody, or myself, a Hickory Farms giftset this Christmas—what can I get for $9.99? Find a place to show Will and Matt how to play bumper pool.*" And finally, "*Should I write down some questions about my life and try to answer them?*" Pausing for a moment, I added, "*HELL NO!*"

We made quite a picture, the two of us, sitting in the glossy red circle cut-out, sipping our Orange Julii and saying nothing. We both liked to say nothing and we both liked other people who were OK with saying nothing. We liked pretending that special moments didn't faze us, but inside absorbing every emotion, delighting in each one. The reflection of the lights on the red gloss and the shiny mall floor made our drinks glow. I wondered if her heart was doing the same thing mine was.

Chapter Twenty-Four

DIAL 411 FOR INFORMATION

We found Dick and Sue sitting on a bench in the Children's Court, located on the outskirts of the food court, called "the Patio." Kim and Rick were somewhere in the play area, a plastic maze consisting of interconnected red-and-yellow cubes stacked randomly on a black-rubber floor. Missing from the scene were automatic dispensers of hand sanitizer, height-restriction signs and really any sort of rules.

Little Amy ran over to Mom and Dad, detailing our retail adventures. I hadn't thought of it, but it was good that Kim and Rick couldn't see the huge haul of items I had bought for Amy. I had spent about four times as much on her, a fact that made me feel extremely uncomfortable once I realized it.

Dick just smiled as he looked down at the goods, but Sue, while she wouldn't confront me, surely understood the level of inequality I had achieved. I worked hard not to care about either—my complicity or her reaction to it—but I knew that wasn't going to happen.

"Amy," Dad said, "if you want to play, you had better go now, it's getting busy and we can't stay here all day. Cousin Amy has to be back by this afternoon for her ride into town."

"Yes," Mom agreed. "We'll need to get her back."

Little Amy plopped down her bags and started toward the nearest cube. "Amy," I said, following behind her. She stopped, looking perplexed. Guiding her closer to the play area, but further away from our parents, I whispered carefully, "Hey look . . .

Don't say too much about all that stuff I bought you. Umm, you know, you got a little more than the other two, but there is no reason to rub it in." Looking up, a sly smile came over her face, an expression that made her look like I'd just given her—and only her—the launch code for the nuclear missiles on our submarine.

"It will make me look bad," I continued, trying to make her understand that it was more about protecting me than not hurting their feelings. I understood that she, and everyone else with siblings, would wholly appreciate any edge she could gain over Kim and Rick. "Let's just say I got you some stuff that was on sale—and that you're sharing the Hickory Farms box, even if you're not."

"OK. Yeah," she said, still looking like we were about to engage in some sort of espionage. "I got it, I understand . . . I surely do . . ." As she turned to go, she patted me on the back firmly, as if we had just sold some unsuspecting yahoo a used car with no air conditioning.

Who knew what she would say, later, after I'd gone and the three kids were alone, upstairs, lowering stuffed animals down the stairs in laundry baskets with jump ropes.

Turning back toward Mom and Dad, I knew I had created an awkward situation. And then I had made it worse by trying to tell the younger version of myself how to handle it. Little Amy may not remember this specific instance in thirty years, but it combined with the 1,000 other times people would instruct her on how to interpret things, or maneuver through issues, would shape who she was.

It made me think of Will and Matthew and the millions of words I had spoken to them or for them since they were ripped from my nether regions. The everyday, never-ending nature of talking covers up the fact that every word means something, especially as a parent. The words themselves, the tone of voice, and most importantly, the perception of the recipient.

Even if I got that and understood the vastness of the potential impact—the big "lightbulb" moment in front of the Children's Play Center, where one hundred kids frolicked in itchy polyester shirts and Toughskins jeans—it was wholly improbable that I would act on it. Maybe once or twice I would slow down and think about what I was saying to my kids, to my husband, to my friends, to my family . . . carefully considering how it sounded, what it meant and the effect it would have, both in the long and short term. But, eventually, and probably very quickly, my own human nature—the same force I blamed everyone else for letting go out of control—would take over, and I would run my mouth nonstop, talking at more than listening to, and making all the same mistakes that I accused everyone else of.

LOOKING past my young parents, sitting quietly and staring blankly, I scanned the retail vista. Brother's Pizza, the Taco Spot, Baskin Robbins, the Original Cookie Co. and Famous Ramous Pretzel Shoppe. I was having a moment, a hungry moment. I wondered who Famous Ramous was and if Wyatt's Cafeteria—that dark and smoky wondrous haven between here and the movie theatre—was still open for business.

"Well, folks," I stated as I approached Mom and Dad. "This sure has been a lot of fun."

"Yes it has, Amy!" Dad said, as Mom looked on. "It's close to one o'clock, I bet you are getting hungry."

"Well, honestly," I said, "you just read my mind! I am hungry!"

Mom joined the conversation. "Yes, the kids will be starving any minute, desperate to eat." Without me in tow, the family would have dashed off to Dairy Queen in Spring or Charlie's Hamburgers, if that was even open yet. Either way, it wouldn't be fancy, but it would be a big event simply because eating out, anywhere, was a big exception to the normal rule.

"I'll round the kids up," Dad said, rising slowly from the bench, because, well, we were all hungover at the mall, even though we weren't going to talk about it. "And you ladies, you can discuss where to eat."

Mom and I watched as Dad walked over to the play center. "Thanks for buying the kids such generous gifts," Mom said as I sat down in Dad's seat.

"You're welcome," I said, happy for the silence to be broken, but not really. "I enjoyed doing it."

"Look," Mom said, finally turning to me, "I know you feel a connection to Amy, and I think that's really nice. She craves attention, she can be difficult . . ." She stopped, looking down at her shoes. "You treating her like she's special is exactly what she needs."

I didn't reply because I had no idea what to say. She was right about the craving attention part, but I wasn't as sure now about the difficult label. Before this trip, I would have bought into it all being my fault, my own personality fueling this perceived difficultness. But now, after being here, I wasn't at all sure if Amy's status as a "handful" was completely her—or our—fault. I would need to think about it more, obviously, but I couldn't help feeling that in a lot of ways, she was just reacting to how she was being treated. That isn't to say she wasn't responsible for her own actions, because she was, but that they were driven by something deeper. What didn't help was my role as a visitor, meaning I was seeing a watered-down version of "reality." It was all muted—Mom's bias and Little Amy's challenges—for my benefit. Sue was nicer and the younger version of me was better behaved. Something was definitely there, something that before this I had been convinced was a figment of my own imagination.

Either way, I couldn't believe that she would say such revealing things, out loud, to a person who was virtually a stranger. But, on the other hand, of course she would. She was a mom, and a woman, and I was another woman, and a mom too. She needed to talk as much as I did and wanted the conversation to be with another female, just as I did in the wee hours of last night. And, really, she had no idea who she was talking to, and I had no idea who she was either. The only 411 she had on me was what she had been told and what she had seen since I walked into her house, basically unannounced on the second-biggest holiday of the year. As for me, I only had the scattered memories of forty-six years. They weren't woven in any particular pattern, and though I guess I had no control over how they were wrapped around my brain, they were the foundation of my emotional response to her and everything else.

"You know, Kim and Rick are special kids too . . ." she continued. "And Kim does a really great job of being a big sister to both of them. She's such a special girl."

"I agree," I said, knowing she was one hundred percent correct, but still nonetheless bedazzled that she felt the need to point that out. In case there was any doubt: Kim was exceptional. We all got that. But, that said, Sue Weinland was these people's mother, and she didn't want anyone left out. And, as much as I had always felt like I had gotten the shaft with her, and Dad had overcompensated for it, maybe she felt like Kim got the shaft, and she was overcompensating for it. So, all those people who thought I had an over-serving of Dad's support might see Mom's clear fascination with Kim as nothing more than a natural response to the situation as it was.

Maybe both these themes—Amy shafted, Kim shafted and Rick as the only owner of an actual shaft—were all running together at the same time, and depending on who you were, you probably only saw one side of the story. Little Amy would grow up feeling like it was all about Kim, little Kim would grow up thinking it was all about Amy, and Rick wouldn't see any of it, instead wondering why everyone was dredging up the past, unnecessarily.

Maybe these were the questions Mary was talking about.

Looking over at Mom, I thought about what I could possibly say. "You have good kids," I said, my voice trailing off. "I know they will all turn out good."

Mom glanced back over and smiled. "Thanks, we just have to survive this part."

"Yeah," I said, "I totally get that, but I think it's going to go way faster than we think."

"But," she responded, "it will feel like it's taking forever."

"Yep . . ." I said. "You are one hundred-percent right about that."

Dad returned with the kids, his hands on Kim's and Amy's heads as Rick bounced over and hugged Mom. "Did you girls decide where we should eat?" he asked.

"You mean we're eating lunch OUT?" Amy screeched.

"TODAY! AT THE MALL?" Kim said, with her hand on her hip.

"With Darth Vader and the Stormtroopers!" Rick added, winking, holding his Montgomery Ward bag high in the air.

"Well," Dad looked down at Mom. "I think the mall is getting a little crowded, what do you think, Sue?"

"Absolutely," she said, scanning the area. "I am ready to get out of here, this place is crazy."

"Your mom is right, let's get back in the car and decide. Here we go, kids!" he said as he turned, putting his hand on Mom's shoulder. "And you too, Momma Bird." It was cute the way he said it, loving and sarcastic at the same time.

Winding back through the mall, which was now packed with overdressed shoppers, I followed the family of five. Looking back to me lagging behind, Little Amy left the group and joined me as Mom watched, making sure she wasn't running off to the brick façade of Casual Corner. I shifted the Hickory Farms box to my other arm and reached down to grab her hand.

For the moment, Little Amy and I had everything we needed, and had ever wanted, right here. I had always wanted to go back in time, maybe not to this situation specifically, but backward nonetheless. As for Little Amy, she had always wanted that football helmet and the beef stick. We had both wanted to feel loved, mostly by ourselves.

Chapter Twenty-Five

THE GOOD STUFF

E xiting the dark paneling and orange hues of Foley's, the bright Houston sun blinded us as we searched for the family Oldsmobile. It was a lot like coming out of the womb, only this time I remembered it.

"Well, kids," Dad said as we got back into the car, which was amazingly toasty given it was late November. "Your mom and I have discussed it . . . And we've decided, we're going to have a big treat and take cousin Amy to BONANZA!"

This sent the backseat into absolute hysterics. It was as if they'd been told they were going to Six Flags or Disneyland or even the Red Lobster. This—the thought of burger patties smoked on a pit, a full-fledged salad bar and a dimly lit dessert buffet—was apparently the best news they had heard in years.

And, OK, if I was going to be honest, I'd admit that I too— the well-heeled connoisseur from the future—was equally excited about a trip to the Bonanza Sirloin Pit. It was yet another memory that would, after this, never be the same, transformed into the double-edged recollection of two completely different people. Only they shared one body. Mine.

North on I-45, the sense of excitement was palpable, so much so it lessened the blow of the classic roadside scenery whizzing by, sites that would be relegated, once again, to mere photos before the sun rose on the morrow.

Dad pushed the horizontal, silver buttons on the car radio until a scratchy but familiar melody began to waft from the speakers. It began with what sounded like a small Casio synthe-sizer being pounded on by fat fingers. "Cryin' on my pillow . . ." a male voice sang.

Though I couldn't remember the title, or the artist, it's a song I had heard before but not in a long, long time. Kim and Amy sang along, Dad did his rhythmic whistle, Rick flailed about in his seat and Mom gazed out the window at the passing scenery. As the chorus neared I suddenly remembered, BOOM, it was UNDERCOVER ANGEL. Oh my Lord, this was that sweet, old-fashioned midnight fantasy.

I loved this song, I loved singing this song, and I could defi-nitely dance to it. As I began to rock my shoulders to the beat, I looked ahead and saw little Rick dramatically repeating the cho-rus, "I've never had a dream that made sweet love to me."

Hold the phone! Wait a second! It hit me. OMG! We were all, in unison, singing about a wet dream, a guy's freaking wet dream. Apparently, there were no song ratings here in the land of eight-track tapes and AM radio. While this, the undercover naughty business, wasn't worthy of an "Explicit" rating, it needed some sort of warning, because the truth was, my eight-year-old little brother, sandwiched between my parents, was lyrically commemorating something well, something we weren't supposed to talk about, either in 1978 or 2014.

Unsheathing my notebook I scribbled, *"UNDERCOVER ANGEL. Artist? Year? Download on iTunes. When did song ratings begin?"* Then I added, *"Download lots of music from the '70s."* And, *"Find Andy Gibb poster."*

Pulling off the interstate in Spring, we stone-cold grooved our way into the Bonanza parking lot, just a short walk from the Rattan Mart, Graham's Menswear and Weiner's department store. Speed ahead thirty years, and a Goodwill occupies Wein-er's old space, the Graham family now sells liquor rather than three-piece suits, and instead of rattan furniture, suburbanites can purchase Geico Insurance at the same location. As for the

Bonanza itself—a building that on this fine day sparkled with a bright-red roof—it would become the El Palenque Mexican Restaurant.

Exiting the car we walked past an orange Honda Civic that was the size of a golf cart and then a two-tone beige Dodge Maxi Wagon that was the size of my first apartment. Reaching the double doors to the restaurant, we were welcomed by the dim lighting suitable for a fine steakhouse. Through a second set of doors, the lights dimmed further, so much so we had to grope our way down a long, wooden corral to find the ordering station.

There we were met by a short-haired young woman wearing a brown-and-orange plaid shirt and a matching brown apron, with straps that made it look like she was wearing overalls.

"Welcome to Bonanza!" she said, almost over-convincingly.

"Well, thank you," Dad said. "Glad to be here."

"What can I get you today?" Lizette said, her name embroidered on the brown western tie she wore loosely around her neck. She looked a lot like a grown-up Brownie scout, only better, I guess, because adults in scout uniforms never, ever look quite right.

"Well," Dad looked at Mom, "we'll have three chopped steak dinners, two rib eye steak dinners and . . ." He paused to look back at me. "Whatever our cousin here, from *Centerville, Ohio*, wants."

That made Mom wince. "Dick, why in the hell does *Lizette* need to know where Amy is from?" Looking back at me, she smiled. "Just ignore him, and order whatever you want."

Though the possibilities were endless, well, kind of, I went for the rib eye dinner as well, a real value at $1.99. It included a well-charred steak, a baked potato, Texas Toast and a trip to the new all-you-can-eat salad bar.

After putting table-tent numbers on our trays, Lizette sent us down the long, stainless steel road that would ultimately end at the cashier. This was where the real fun started. First up, we had to decide on what to drink. The cold choices—because there was also copious amounts of coffee available—were basically water, iced tea and lemonade. Though Coke products were offered, those were behind the bar and not in high demand. The other thing that surprised me was the size of the drinks, eight to ten ounces at the most, made of actual glass, and pre-filled. I wondered about refills. Where were the sixty- four-ounce mediums that you could refresh on your way out the door? Everyone in the family grabbed a water, Kim helping Rick with his. I opted for the same thing.

Next up were the desserts, laid out on three stainless-steel shelves. There was chocolate pudding in tall parfait glasses with whipped cream, a rainbow of Jell-O cubes and then the cakes and pies—all playing the naughty temptress under the fluorescent lights. Looking longingly at the display and back at Mom and Dad, the kids hesitated, hoping for a miracle. Dad couldn't resist, seemingly overcome with the collective moment we were sharing. "OK, kids," he said. "Take your pick!"

"Really?" Kim questioned both him and Mom, her eyes nearing bulge-status. "We really can?" "Yes, Kim, pick whatever you want," Mom said.

While Kim and Rick chose their desserts quickly, Amy took forever, fingering almost every plate until she decided on the cherry pie. "Oh, I love cherry pie," she whispered to me, "even more than chocolate cake." I understood.

Lurking in the smoke behind the drinks and desserts was the grill, or pit, where a couple of guys were slaving over a ton of thin steaks and chopped-beef patties. There was no chicken, salmon or tilapia ready to be placed on these jumping flames, and when I say "flames" think actual fire, lots and lots of fire. So much so, it made me think somebody had been assigned underneath the grill with a can of Gulf Lighter Fluid, squirting it every couple of moments for effect.

The smell was captivating as the smoke swirled through the darkness, up through the fake brick walls and into the exhaust fan far over our heads. Maybe that's also where all the real memories went.

The cashier rang Dad up as he reached for his wallet. "Wait!" I said from the back of the line. "I'll get this, Dick!"

"No you won't!" he said, grinning as he counted out the bills. "This is our treat." The total was a whopping $14.04, a hell of a bargain, even if the rib eye didn't quite live up to Morton's or Ruth Chris' standards.

As we carried our trays out into the dark dining room, a collection of vinyl booths and wooden tables, we passed the new salad bar. "Oh, look at it, Rick," Amy said, almost losing her tray. "It's beautiful . . ."

"Wow . . ." Rick said. "It's so big, and look at all the ice between the stuff."

"OK, kids," Mom said. "Let's put our trays down before we do the salad bar." Following Mom and Dad, we got our food situated in a booth and then reassembled to attack the vegetables.

"Look at this, kids," Dad said, waving his hand over the bar. "It's all-you-can-eat, so load up on the good stuff."

Looking it over, I couldn't believe the shock-and-awe the family felt over such a small display. These folks had never been treated to the Golden Corral or really even the salad bar at Wendy's. All Bonanza's wonder bar had to offer was the largest single vat of iceberg lettuce I'd ever seen, proudly displayed as if it was the purest organic arugula available to mankind, along with some containers of cherry tomatoes, sliced onions, carrot strips, cucumbers, sliced radishes and some suspicious-looking croutons.

Where were the pasta salads? The hummus? The blue cheese chunks? The grilled chicken strips? The cherry peppers? The six kinds of olives? The avocadoes? The heirloom tomatoes and the self-serve ice-cream machine?

What was the big damn deal?

Not wanting to be the buzzkiller to this underexposed group, I whizzed my tray down the bar, filling my small plate gleefully with the "good stuff," taking a few extra tomatoes just so I could feel like Dad got his money's worth. Wait—this cost under two dollars . . . .

As underwhelming as the actual salad selection was, the dressing offering was even more dubious: Italian, Green Goddess, Catalina, Roquefort and extra-creamy, extra-chunky Thousand Island. Ranch, Balsamic and Cabernet Vinaigrette were not welcome here. Ginger-Sesame, Chipotle Ranch and Creamy Caesar had no place at this bar! Knowing from Granny that Roquefort had something to do with blue cheese, I flung some of that on top and moved on. Wait! Here was something with redeemable qualities, yes, it was a food-service-sized container of Betty Crocker's Bac-Os . . . Yes, I believed that the bacon-like flavor would enhance my salad. And so it did.

The joy around the table struck me as somewhat profound. It made it obvious that this family didn't go out often, especially for a daytime meal, but when they did, oh the pleasure they took. Did it make them better than my people, in my time? We ate out as casually as we did in and would have never, ever been able to achieve the levels of sheer joy these five did when presented with what was in fact a thin-meated meal. Or instead, did it make them—and us—simply products of our own times, really no different than the family from 1855 who didn't even know what a restaurant was?

The other thing that stood out—other than the number of diners who were vigorously slurping seemingly bottomless cups of coffee—was the lack of entertainment that Bonanza offered up with its $1.99 rib eye. Where were the TVs blaring the news and sports? Where were the online trivia games or Keno or lotto screens plastered across the room? Where were the table-side video screens with games to keep youngsters amused? Or, at the very least, what about a few cranes by the bathroom to shuffle off to when the fidgeting inevitably began? In fact, I scanned the room and realized that not one child was playing with a phone or tablet. Instead, they were just sitting there.

Think about it—one hundred percent of the kids in a restaurant were just sitting there.

It was more shocking than the huge-haired lady sitting two tables away from us, wearing a *Little House on the Prairie* inspired dress, taking a drag off her Virginia Slims menthol cigarette in between each and every bite of her loaded baked potato.

With nothing to distract us, we did the only thing we could do—eat and talk. Little Amy had a lot to say, with Dad alternatively listening and trying to steer the conversation.

"This one time at school . . ." she said, with a gleam in her eye. "Theresa got a Fudgesicle and she dipped it in her ketchup. And then . . . SHE ATE IT." Even though everyone chuckled at the story, Amy wanted more of a reaction, so she continued, this time looking directly at Rick. "And then, Tensie told her to stop, but Theresa dipped it again and then opened up the top of her chocolate milk carton and dipped it in there too!" Rick found this humorous and laughed accordingly.

"Amy?" Mom asked. "Do you play with your food at school?"

"No," she responded, as if this was suddenly the presidential debate and it was her turn at the podium, her answer requiring forethought and serious consideration. "But I do play with my school at home, and sometimes I'm eating food while I do it." Laughing hysterically, she tried to explain that she had a Fisher Price schoolhouse that she played with, and that sometimes she ate her snack or dessert at the same time.

As funny as Rick thought this was, and even Kim was smirking, Mom wasn't amused. I got that. Amy was being obnoxious just for the sake of it. On one hand, I was impressed with her hilarity, and on the other I could see where Mom could have been over it. Totally.

"OK, kids," Dad interjected. "Let's all talk about something more serious. I'm going to go around the table," he continued, in his Mike Brady style, complete with robotic hand motions, "and each of us is going to say what we are thankful for . . . Now, we didn't get to that yesterday, but we'll do it today, since our cousin Amy is here with us."

The truth was, we didn't do it yesterday because, to my knowledge, we'd never done it before or since.

Dad looked across the booth at Kim. "Now Kim, since you are the oldest, you can go first." Before this, I had never realized that Kim might have gotten pissed off about the whole "since you're the oldest" approach. I always thought of it more like "She *gets to* because she's the oldest," rather than "She *has* to because she came out first."

Anyway, she was first. "Well," Kim said with an edge of drama. "I'm thankful for my family, for my parents, my grand-parents, my brother, and yes, even my sister." Everyone oohed and aahed over this emotional display, spurring Kim onward and upward. "I'm also thankful for my friends, Melanie, Juli, and my science fair project that won first prize."

Even though the mere thought of Kim's blue-and-gold sci-ence fair trophy brought the family into what was almost a state of applause, it was crap. I knew it was crap, little Kim knew it was crap, young Dad knew it was crap, and Mom knew it was crap—only nobody would admit it, even if somebody started to bang their Bonanza steak knife against the table.

"Oh," I asked, knowing damn well what the answer would be, "what was your science fair project about?"

"Well," she said, "I AM in the sixth grade . . ."—she was always eager to play the *look at me, I'm the freaking oldest, with a preteen bra and everything*—"and so I created a series of pulleys that demonstrated that by using simple objects, in this case a rope and a wheel, less force is required to move large items. Re-ally . . ." she continued with a hint of superiority that only I caught on to, "It's all about force and leverage."

If this had been 2014, I would have accused of her of looking it up on her iPhone, but since we were still in a Google-free zone, I let her off the hook. Clearly, my dad, the engineer, was not only an excellent designer and manufacturer of pulleys, he was also a badass teacher and life coach.

"Yes!" Little Amy said with loads of unexpected enthusiasm. "The pulleys were black and red, and there were three of them, and they were on a board, and she won first prize, a real TROPHY!"

Now hold on just a damn second, who in the hell did Little Amy think she was? She wasn't supposed to, we weren't supposed to—I wasn't supposed to support Kim on her little delusional induction into the Junior High School Science Fair Hall of Fame. We, every one of us with the exception of Rick, who didn't know what was going on, knew that Dad had made that thing. He was so proud of it that it sat in the attic for ten years, until Mom finally tossed it out when he went on that golf thing in Oklahoma.

"We were all SO proud of Kim's trophy . . ." young Amy continued, plainly meaning every word as Kim looked on, satisfied and pleased with the sisterly support. I had no choice but to look at the younger version of myself and wonder. Who knew that I had once been less eager to set things straight, to be right rather than righteous? Who knew that I was proud of her not because I understood what she did, or what she didn't do, but just because she was my freaking sister? And her accomplishment was our accomplishment, because after all, we were family. That was true no matter how you sliced it, diced it or discussed it in therapy.

For all her screwed-up qualities, Little Amy had humbled me, and reminded me I could still be something I wasn't, something I had been before, before I started compulsively comparing myself with everyone else.

Next was Mom's turn. Predictably, she told my dad she

didn't have an answer, but to get back with her once everyone else had gone. "Now, Sue," Dad said firmly.

"DICK . . ." she retorted. This helped him to settle on Rick as his next contestant.

"I'm thankful for Star Wars, and the Battlestar Galactica, and our dog Cecil," he continued, "who saved Amy from being bitten by a snake. His head was swollen and the doctor said he was going to die, but he didn't."

I had forgotten about that story, about Cecil biting the water moccasin in the garage, just as it raised its head to attack while I unwittingly had half my body in the refrigerator, one hand on a can of Old Milwaukee. It was the same sort of protective instinct he displayed just last night, urinating on the drunk would-be rapist.

"I'm thankful for Cash," Rick continued, referring to the overpriced poodle with a blue-turquoise encrusted collar that Mom had named *Carlos Andre Sir Henri*. We had always told people that story, the one about how much the dog had cost and his ludicrous acronym name, with such pride. Now I knew that behind the polite nods and agreeable looks that they must have thought we were nuts. It had only taken me thirty years to figure it out. Good thing I had passed the point that I even cared.

"And I'm thankful for my Doggy," he continued. OK, that was cute. He was referring to the little stuffed animal he slept with every night. On this day, that Doggy was everything to him. Speed ahead thirty years from now and I wondered if he even remembered it. His memory retention was different than mine.

Now it was Little Amy's turn. I still hadn't come to terms with her, but she did add excitement to any and all proceedings. Apparently, or so it would seem, everyone else understood that undeniable fact too, some parties looking on with anticipation, and others—the ones who had engaged in the sexual shenanigans associated with her very existence—with anxious fear. She was like the bowl-cut version of E.F. Hutton.

"Well, friends . . ." she emoted, almost slobbering with excitement now that she had the floor. "I'm thankful for many things . . . I'm thankful for the Washington Redskins, my new helmet, my castle playset—complete with moat—my books about George Washington, Francis Marion the Swamp Fox, Sam Houston and Abraham Lincoln." Leaning back and crossing her legs dramatically, she continued, "I'm thankful for my mom, and my dad, my brother and sister, the Northampton Elementary Colts, my best friend Catherine, Camp Olympia, the Shamrocks, all soccer balls all over the world, archery, Christmas and that one time I was a star on the stage . . .

"Yes friends, I'm thankful for the Second Grade Play, a performance that lives on in our hearts and minds, when I was a leaping part of history in a red-velvet costume, lined with actual gold, shouting 'Wassail, Wassail,' as the crowd roared! I had white tights on, and no shoes. And—do you know what? I was a star, a real star, a delight, a total delight. I was in the newspaper, I was on the front page—"

"Amy . . ." Dad cut in. "Those are all wonderful things, but it's time to wrap it up."

"I am thankful!" she said, ignoring him, her hands flailed out to her sides. "For the Houston Astros, for uniformed catchers everywhere, for stewed tomatoes, for lemon pepper, for gentle love and Chantilly Lace, and a pretty face, and a ponytail, hanging down. I AM THANKFUL!"

"AMY!" Mom nearly shouted. "THAT'S ENOUGH!"

But, for Amy, apparently, it was not.

"I am thankful," she almost whispered, but didn't. "For thankful feelings . . . in my pantaloons . . . "

Though this final declaration, delivered in full bug-eye, pleased the younger set, the parents weren't feeling it. I got that. It was funny, but it wasn't. If she had been my kid, and she reminded me of one of them, I would have shut her down, talked to her about the appropriate use of her own super power—humor—sent her to her room and then laughed hysterically. I may have even taken her cherry pie hostage.

Silence.

"Sue?" Dad asked, carefully. "Do you have something you'd like to add?"

"Yes, Dick . . ." Mom replied. "I'd like to add that I am thankful for everyone at this table."

"Anything else . . . ?" Dad asked, as if he was setting the stage for a dramatic ending.

"No, Dick, T h a t. I s. A l l . . ." she said, more slowly than he had asked.

Silence.

This is why we loved the silence. It was awkward, but sometimes, or every single time, it was better than the alternative.

Undaunted, Dad turned to me. "Well, how about you, cousin Amy?"

Chewing on the gristle of my rib eye, I knew I desperately did not want to pontificate on my thankfulness, especially given my current state of time travel, but there was no way I was going to let Dad the Younger down. It was a common theme in my life, in the lives of my siblings. As much as I couldn't successfully operate a flat iron, or a regular iron, or a seven-iron, I couldn't stop myself from pleasing Dad. And blaming Mom. Crap, I was screwed up. We were all screwed up. Everybody was screwed up. There was no such thing as the "new normal" because "normal" is a pipe dream.

The hope of it, the fantasy of it being anchored in reality, was precisely what would-be cult leaders used to suck people into dangerous lifestyles, promising a prize that was, after all, unobtainable.

You can't get to normal, 'cause it don't exist.

Cancel my Facebook account! I didn't care about normal anymore, or showing anyone what my version of it was. I was into this screwed-up mess, because, after all, it was our screwed-up mess, it was my screwed-up mess. And if I had to put money on it, ours was better than anyone else's. Gene and Bee's and Frank and Ruth's had been, Dick and Sue's was, and Amy and Willie's would be. And Rick and Jen, yeah, them too.

"Well, I'm thankful for everyone at this table, and for my family back home in Ohio. Not for who I want them to be, but instead, just for who they are, right now. We may not be perfect, or even close to it," I continued, "but I am thankful for us!

"Even when it's messy!" I said, banging the red, smoky candle holder on the booth. "Even when it doesn't seem like it's going to work out. Even when it doesn't make any damn sense. Even when the bank account shrinks, and my thighs are big, and he doesn't call me when he's out of town, and I'm supposed to act happy, but I'm not. Even when I can't see my way out of something, and I'm sick of remembering the bad parts. Even when I'm afraid I am the bad parts. Even when I can't stop eating the Funyons, or drinking the red wine, but I know I should. Even when Texas Tech loses to the Aggies, and my kids lie, and my iPhone loses service. Even when I'm bloated, and feel ugly, and can't stop thinking what I do is meaningless. Even when my toilets are disgusting, even when I start thinking time travel is real and even when I'm not thankful, even then, I'm freaking, completely, one hundred percent, for-real T H A N K F U L."

I said it all with a vengeance, staring out over the fake wagon wheels, or maybe they were real. Pausing, I looked around the table into a bank of wide eyes, well, those that weren't looking at the floor, or their feet, or at the cell phones they didn't yet own. Collecting myself, well, kind of, my voice softened, my tone changed. I meant this part, and probably all of it. "I am thankful, most of all for love, but also for all of you and this trip, and for everything."

Silence.

It was obvious that no one had expected my tirade, not in a million years. Crap, I hadn't even expected it. I barely knew these people, but I did, but they didn't know that. I had said things that were impossible. I had crossed several uncross-able lines. But, I was lucky, I had a get-out-of-jail-free card with this group because to them, denial, or De Nile, or the Nile, really wasn't just another river in Egypt. Instead, it was the sacred code we lived by. It was the law. If we acted like it never happened, maybe it never did. Who knew, but, for right now, I was thankful for that too.

More silence.

"Well," Dad stated, finally. "Thanks for that, Amy, it was, well . . . inspirational. That leaves me."

Yes sir, I could count on him as much as he could rely on me.

"I'm thankful for your mother, for each of you kids, who I'm proud of, and that our cousin Amy from Centerville, Ohio, came to spend Thanksgiving with us. I'm thankful for this country, and freedom, and the Second Amendment, and even though I don't like Dan Pastorini, I'm thankful for the 8-4 Houston Oilers. I'm thankful for my own parents, my job, and a really fine steak for lunch."

"OK, Dick," Mom cut in. "That's enough . . . Let's finish our food and get out of here."

Chapter Twenty-Six

MENSTRUATION WITHOUT
REPRESENTATION

$\mathcal{R}$etracing our steps, we headed briefly north on the I-45
feeder road, turned west on Spring Stuebner, past St.
Edward's Catholic Church and past the brand-new Dove Meadows subdivision. Rick was sleepy, leaning into Mom's lap in the
front seat, almost purring like a cat. Dad, eyes forward, was tap-
ping his fingers on the steering wheel to the tune on the radio,
now reduced to a reasonable volume. Kim was across the backseat from me, quietly admiring her stickpin, which she had taken
carefully out of its box.

As for Little Amy, she had climbed up on the shelf behind
the backseat. Though it was unsafe, in a car traveling fifty-five
miles per hour on a bumpy, rural road with almost zero shoulder,
it was an accepted, known practice, as no one made a move to stop
her. She had her football helmet on, of course, strapped completely and tightened to a game-ready standard. Lying on her
side, she had managed to line up the ear hole on the right side of
the helmet with the car speaker. Listening, smiling and bug-eyed,
she quietly sang along, "Sky rockets in flight. Afternoon delight."

It was another inappropriate song, this time sung word-for-
word by the ten-year-old version of myself. I was fully geared up
for a pretend NFL game and singing about daytime sex.

Good Lord. I wondered if our parents were as stressed
about "appropriateness" as we were back in the future. Seriously,
while Harry Potter's supposed demonic connection and Miley

Cyrus' swing-ride were intriguing in terms of their long-term effects, these folks, here in 1978, were singing about SEXUAL RELATIONS openly. And, in this case, "Everything's a little clearer in the light of day." Think about it, "EVERYTHING IS CLEARER." Hello! They are talking about naked sex parts, being clearer, in the daytime, when you can't turn the lights off and hide them. On the one hand, it was disturbing. Where was the filter? On the other, it was reassuring—I had turned out "fine," clearly a relative term, and knew all the sex words to all the sex songs, as a small child.

Returning to Northampton, I was overwhelmed again with its palpable beauty. As captivated as I was, I felt sad and empty. It was all so fleeting, destined to fade away just like my grand-parents—both gone in a flash, forever.

Maybe that's what social media is about, a fruitless attempt to recreate something special, a feeling, an emotion. If that weren't enough, we seem to collectively believe that the moment can only be validated by sharing it with others. In reality, we aren't recreating anything, because we can't. Soliciting one hundred likes doesn't make it any realer, in your heart.

Turning into the driveway, I wondered what was next. Looking at my watch I realized that it wasn't long until Mary was supposed to return. Would she really come back? Once out of the hot car and through the back door, I had that sneaking feeling I sometimes get. OK, I get it once a month. Retreating quickly back upstairs, I darted to the bathroom and disrobed. Crap. I had been correct. I had started my period. I had always hated it when my "time" coincided with vacation, and this was worse . . . unplanned time travel, when I didn't even remember packing my bags in the first place.

I went back out to my suitcase. This may well have been the most ridiculous sequence of events in my entire life, thus far, but I knew myself well enough to know, regardless of the time or place, I would have come prepared for my period. I was always prepared—like a Menstrual Scout—with a small package of the necessities. Just in case.

Rifling through my bag, I found the emergency supplies, packed neatly in a small box rather than a Ziploc bag. Reviewing its contents, I was not so much shocked as wholly disappointed to find what looked like a set of straps and three or four bulky pads. Clearly, whoever packed this had not yet tapped into the cutting-edge technology of beltless feminine napkins.

I was mystified by this. I was convinced that most of the world had moved on to sticker-pads. Regardless of why, this package of underwhelming protection would have to suffice until I returned to my own time. Just to be sure, I looked in my purse, emptying the entire contents on the bed. Next I moved on to the train case, and finally, my satchel. Surely I had some belt-free business, or an ancient, awkward-shaped, non-plastic tampon somewhere.

No.

With desperation creeping in, I took the small box of horrors into the bathroom and searched through the cupboards. Nothing in the three brown cabinets under the sink, nothing in the towel cabinets over the wooden, built-in hamper, and yes, nothing in the hamper itself.

Crap.

I would never, in a million years, ask Mom if she had anything. No—this was something, both now and then, that I would have asked Kimber. Let's see, she was twelve years old now. When did she start? I couldn't be sure, but to the best of my knowledge it hadn't happened yet. Her first period was a dramatic, memorable instance. We were in the Bahamas, on vacation in July, near her birthday, and she "started." All I really remember was her gasping and exclaiming that it was "her worst birthday EVER!" Rick and I were thrown out of the hotel room, into the lush tropical surroundings, Rick dancing around yelling, "She got her period, and I don't even know what it is!" I was laughing hysterically. Obviously.

I could also remember when Kim received "the talk" at school that covered periods, lady flowers and such, only because she flaunted her newfound knowledge. Then she received "the box" in the mail. I wondered where the box factory was and who worked there and, then, when it went out of business. When did young American girls stop receiving that special post-fifth-grade "talk" parcel? Or were they still receiving it? Because what did I know, I had two boys.

The one thing I was absolutely sure of, the scrap of undeniable truth I could conjure up after thirty-six hours in la-la land, was that I knew nothing.

Absolutely nothing.

Mom's approach to "the talk," "the box," and "blossoming" was apparently less than direct, because I could still remember finding the box, Kim's box, unopened and slightly damp on my dad's workbench in the back corner of the garage. Presumably, it had been there a while.

Not knowing what it was, I opened it, probably carefully gouging its contents free with a screwdriver. Inside was a sanitary belt, the first and only one I'd ever seen, that is, before now. Back then, I had shoved the contents back into the box and placed it back on the workbench. I never mentioned it to anyone and as far as I knew, it was never discussed.

Was it just me or was this a central theme in my upbringing?

Though even two days ago this would have been a major thinking point for me, now it seemed so ordinary. First, I got it, I was here, back in time, and this is how we were surviving. It, the silence, was basically a genetic gift. Next, having learned as an adult that we aren't all as unique as we think we are, I understood that we couldn't be that different from the millions of other families that lived in suburbia, with workbenches in garages, with musty boxes of outdated sanitary products. We weren't the only ones who didn't discuss things.

Back to the task at hand, my immediate need for absorbency,

I examined the belt. It was rose-colored and elastic. Hanging from the front and back of the main part were two smaller straps. Each had a fastener on the end that looked like a pink monster.

The pads, or I guess napkins in this case, were huge . . . gigantic. What was interesting, and confusing, and disgusting, was that the pads didn't have any obvious way of being attached to the belt-like item. Instead of any plastic connectors that paired with the metal monsters on the straps, the pad had loads of extra "fabric" at each end. The only thing that made any sense was to tie off the pad end on each of the monsters, a connection that looked dubious at best.

That was the moment I needed the Menstrual Scout handbook, or, at the very least, my son's Cub Scout handbook, to tie the proper knot. This was as important a knot as I'd make in my adult life, to keep this entire farce connected. Anything less would mean an embarrassing leak onto my breeziness. And again, I was on the road, meaning there wasn't much backup in the way of extra clothing.

I needed to completely disrobe from the waist down. It was a lot like a visit to the ob-gyn—without the awkward silence or perhaps the oversharing that happens when you stare at the ceiling while a stranger has his or her hand up your hoo-hah. Why did I sometimes say "thank you" while she was doing whatever it was she did down there? Totally ludicrous. Then, on top of all of that, I got a bill in the mail.

In both cases, it would be a relief to clean up, put your clothing back on and rush out to your car, blocking it all out—acting like it never even happened. Again, it was an awful lot like real life.

After pulling the belt up to my midsection, where I guessed I would tighten it once I got it all rigged up, I realized that I wasn't going to be able to tie the pad, or napkin if you will, onto the back connector without help. Then it struck me, oh the irony of standing in the blue bathroom on the third floor of my childhood home, with the plaid wallpaper and the linoleum floor, the same place where just a few short years from now my big sister Kim would show me how a tampon worked. In fact, she had basically done that first application for me.

Maybe I should call downstairs and get her up here, at twelve, to work this out for me, in the same bathroom. You know what? She probably would and could do it. God bless her and her perfect hair and small thighs. Who in the hell did she think she was?

Removing the belt, I could tell that it was not going to be easy to keep the apparatus in one place or untangled, mainly because I couldn't even keep it straight during the act of simply taking it off and putting it back on. I tied the end of the pad to what I thought was the back of the belt. Next was putting it on again. Everything had to be positioned correctly so I could attach the front of the napkin to the belt. Good Lord, those adhesive pads, those whispers from the heavens! I hadn't really ever appreciated them before, but now they seemed more crucial than the Wi-Fi signal staying steady during my Netflix marathon. Better than that was tampons, any kind of tampons. Surely those, even in 1978, would be better than this crap.

It was crap.

Putting my clothes back on, I came back out into the bedroom and looked over at the flip-clock. 4:32 p.m. Damn, I was going to have to get my stuff together and get downstairs.

It was almost time.

Placing my things carefully back in the bags, I thought of Little Amy. There was so much she needed to know, but, as Mary had suggested, there were limits to what I could say or do. I knew now that my involvement, the one with lots of hindsight, would screw things up. I knew things she didn't need to know—like why I would always wear a wide watch band on my left wrist to cover the embarrassing self-inflicted scar that never went away—and she knew things I should have already forgotten. But still, I had to do something. My instinct was to leave her a note, some sort of inspirational written message. I had always liked that kind of thing.

Over time, Little Amy would likely lose anything I gave her on paper, not entirely a bad thing given this wasn't supposed to be a lucid memory, but at least she could have the words for a while, giving her an opportunity to consider them later, when this had all died down. When she was alone again.

I knew I couldn't change anything, but that didn't mean I wouldn't try.

Frantically, I thought about all my favorite sayings, quotes and adages, but had a difficult time coming up with anything useable. I thought of that Theodore Roosevelt quote I had always liked, the one about how it was better to do something daring and fail than to never try at all. But, there were two clear issues with this. First, and though she would think a quote from a president was heavy stuff, what in the hell did being daring have to do with surviving the next ten years? She was only nine years from hitting rock bottom, and she wouldn't even know why or how she had gotten there. What I desperately wanted her to know was that she, or we, were going to be OK. I didn't want her to be afraid, even if she wasn't. Beyond the problem of content, the TR quote wouldn't work because I couldn't remember the exact wording, and sans my iPhone or laptop, I couldn't look it up.

Then it hit me—whatever meaningful words I shared would have to come from my own mind. No smartphone meant that I was going to have to be smart without Google. It was a sobering thought, and if I had had more time to consider the implications, I would have realized that true intelligence has little to do with the speed of your internet connection.

My next thought was a Bible verse. I could probably come closer to hacking Scripture than American history, and it would be more apt, but I still couldn't think of something that precisely fit my needs. Plus, I couldn't be absolutely sure of quoting chapter and verse, which would make me seem less than legit if she wanted to look it up later, and I knew she would. I could have raced down to her room, hoping she was being a freakazoid somewhere else in the house, and copied something from the green Children's Living Bible, but there was no time for that. The same issues applied to a covert mission down to the formal living room bookcases, which held the brown-and-black leather set of World Book Encyclopedias.

What could I possibly say anyway? Really, there were no great words that were going to gently guide her until she hit the magic age of twenty or twenty-five, when things would even out and she would begin to discover that she actually was well and fully OK. Perhaps the note was nothing more than a futile idea, designed more to make me feel better in 2014, than for her to grapple with in 1978. For all I knew, she didn't consider what she was doing as grappling, or struggling. She was just living and this was the only life she knew. All my misplaced words could do was to paint a complicated forty-five-year-old picture of what to her was a simple ten-year-old paint-by-number. I would think my canvas was a masterpiece. She would look at it and never be able to sleep again.

With that in mind, I got up and finished my packing.

Stacking my bags neatly outside the door, I turned around and looked into the bedroom, a place that had been buried in my memory for years and was now starkly presented in front of me for one last time. If I could have imagined this sequence from the safety of my living room couch, I could have come up with hundreds of meaningful feelings and thoughts. Now that it was real, I had no idea what to think or how to feel.

Starting down the stairs I stopped. I just couldn't shake the feeling that I had to leave the younger me with something more than a Hickory Farms gift set and some above-average NFL items. It was the same sense of overwhelming commitment I had felt coming up the sidewalk yesterday. I didn't know what to do, but I had to do something.

I would do something.

I returned to the shaky wooden chair in front of the desk. Looking through the drawers, I couldn't find anything to write on. Though I had the little notebook tucked away in one of my big pockets, that hardly seemed suitable. I sat back and sighed, scanning the rest of the room. I was running out of time. I'd have to settle for tearing a piece of paper out of the notebook. Staring at the blank page, I wondered how, in my own words, I could possibly sum up everything I wanted to say. How can you adequately express the way you want somebody as important as your own child self to approach the rest of her life? That is until they catch up to the part where you are living, only by then, you'll already be gone.

And then it hit me. I knew what to say. I knew what to tell Little Amy so she could survive the years that separated us, not just so she could get through it, but so that she could be truly whole. It wasn't my own words I'd use, they were somebody else's. What they lacked in prestige—this guy wasn't a president, prophet or poet—they made up for in actual meaning.

Just last year, my oldest son Will had filled out an application to work at Camp Olympia, the same place my husband and I had met, the font of many of my closest friendships and the place that our boys had also happily attended. He had been adamant about completing the forms himself, yet another sign that he wished to be independent from us, a frightening and delightful prospect all in the same breath.

He had told me there was a question on the form that asked him to sum up his approach to life. I had given him specific advice on how to answer it, what I viewed as one of the trickier questions. As a sometimes writer and a once camp counselor, this was something I could really help him with. With me guiding the process, he couldn't miss.

Ultimately, he had completed the application without my final approval, and I could only hope that what he had said—either word for word or in the spirit of—was basically what I had told him to say. Had he not asked me to mail the application for him, I never would have known how it turned out.

Did I read it? Absolutely.

It was a solid job, but not without a few grammatical and spelling errors. That said, I totally respected that this was his deal and resisted the overwhelming urge to "fix it" for him. Scanning all the way to the end, I came across "the" question, the one about his approach to life. The first thing I noticed was that he had only used two of the five lines provided. This immediately alarmed me, as (1). I was afraid he had given a half-ass answer and (2). The brevity was proof positive that he had not utilized my rambling pontification on the meaning of life.

Before I could completely overreact, my disappointment and alarm were squelched by reading the simple words he had scribbled. From them, I experienced one of those life-changing moments when you realize not only that your kid is going to be just fine, you also find out that he was better off not taking your advice. Will was, for real, one hundred percent certified better off doing it on his own. Without me.

The moment was humbling, disturbing and pride-filled all at the same time.

And so, now, in this impossible, crack-induced situation, I knew what to say to my ten-year-old self, because my sixteen-year-old son had told me, without actually telling me.

Little Amy,

Meeting you was the best part of this Thanksgiving. If you are ever wondering what to do, or are having a difficult time with something, here are what I think are the two most important things to remember in life:

(1). No matter what the question (ANYTHING), <u>LOVE</u> *is always the answer.*

(2). There isn't anything in the world that <u>LOVE</u> *can't fix.*

I hope to see you again soon!

Love always,
Big Amy

Smiling, I folded the note and placed it carefully in the hidden pocket of my flowing emerald pants. Before putting the notebook and pen back in, I turned to the next empty page and jotted down, *"Tell Will he's a genius. Listen to what he says. Really listen!"*

Standing up, I knew in my heart of hearts I wouldn't heed my own advice. Yes, here was yet another earth-shattering, ah-ha moment that would eventually slip out of consciousness. And this kind of thing didn't just happen in time travel. I got glimpses of the much-bigger picture all the time, in normal, regular, everyday, boring life.

Was I an emotional simpleton, or just another individual so human she believes she's an exception to every rule?

Still holding the notebook open, I added, *"When did belts and pads go away? Was I supposed to tie the pad off? Fifth-grade box? When did that stop? Did it stop? Go on YouTube and watch the 'talk' film? Could I write an article about the box and the talk? Talk to friends about their experiences."*

Chapter Twenty-Seven

WIDE OPEN SPACES

*C*oming back down the stairs, I was greeted by the sight of the three kids dancing. They had wacked the Bing Crosby *Merry Christmas* eight-track tape into the Lloyd's stereo.

Putting my luggage by the front door, I darted through the performers—careful not to injure myself or anyone else—and sat down on the edge of the gold velour couch. I had never appreciated how cushy and fancy it was. The last time I had seen it was, well, I really don't know—but it didn't look, or feel, like this. It was soft and supple—like my breasts—deep gold and brown intertwined with a *fleur de lis* pattern and long enough for five adults to sit on. It could have been quasi-on trend in the future, if it could have held its condition.

Oh God! If we could all, like this couch, have held our condition until 2014.

I realized how clean the room was. And I don't mean it was just picked-up, or tidied. It was clean, as in no dust, dirt or grime. Mom had put on a complete Thanksgiving yesterday, and then opened her house up to God knows how many people last night, people who had, to varying degrees, been liquored up and were subsequently not so careful with the décor. This begged the question, how in the world did she have it this clean by the next evening? Especially given that she made a cooked breakfast, spent a couple of hours at the mall and then went to the Bonanza Sirloin Pit. The younger me wouldn't have even noticed the transformation, much less been called on to help with it. To us,

Dad included, it was like a magical clean fairy had sparkled down from the clouds and successfully conquered what must have been a nasty mess. It reminded me of the little wooden sign I had noticed in the breakfast room this morning, which stated, in Old English font, "God Bless This Mess." Indeed.

The reality was more like Mom up at six-thirty, hungover, tired, and groggy, but determined to have her place of business, her home, in good order at the start of yet another workday. It was as much commendable and laudable as it was OCD and psychotic. Either way, I totally got it. So much so that I wanted to stick my head in the brass birdcage and hurl, and cry, and dance along to holiday tunes, all at the same time.

Bing and the Andrews sisters crooned about what Christmas was like in far-off Ireland as the kids acted out the lyrics. Little Kim and Rick shook hands heartily and bowed as Amy flung about, fake laughing in the background like she had done shots of George Dickel.

As the track clicked to the next song, a non-fluid event that nearly caused the entire tape deck to hurl itself from the shelf, I realized I would never see this again. I could literally never, ever go back. I could remember it all I wanted to, but as far as physically returning, that was totally off the table. If the house ever went up for sale, say in thirty years, I could schedule a showing and thereby engineer an actual physical return, filling the same space again. I could even bring the same people, these people, back with me. But no matter what any of us did, this moment could not, would not be repeated. And as precious as it was to me, right now, as golden as it seemed, for reals, it meant nothing to the others. It was as normal as any other day.

But it wasn't.

Time marched on regardless of anything. Once a moment had passed, it was over. Once a life had ended, it was gone. In a culture that was confident enough to be smug, it didn't know what really happened when life ceased, and, it couldn't stop time.

My BFF in England, Miss Julia, said that managing life was about putting stuff into boxes, taking out the stuff you could deal with, needed to deal with, or wanted to deal with, as you were able. Other things were left locked tightly in other boxes, only removed when absolutely necessary or simply because the time had come to unpack or declutter.

I was going to need a big box for this crap—with a lid, and a strap and a lock on it. Miss Julia and I would take turns watching the box, and would endlessly discuss what to do and what not to do with it. There was comfort in knowing that somebody else really cared about my boxes. Maybe being friends is all about boxes—the best ones are gifted at record storage management. Or, at memory storage management. Or, at deftly uncorking bottles of Pinot Grigio.

As five o'clock neared, Mom and Dad shuffled into the room, joining me on the couch. Dad looked slightly deflated, while Mom seemed somewhat recharged. She would be relieved to be back in her routine, just like I would be in 2014 when my in-laws waved, backing slowly out of our driveway in Ohio. It was a relief that bordered on ecstasy, an intoxicating cocktail of "Job well done!" and "Whew, that mess is OVER." I got that, so why did I choose to take it so personally? She got that, so why did she have to be so obvious about it?

We were both so right, we were both so wrong.

Between another loud click, we collectively heard a car honking.

Though this marked the end of what was probably the most monumental event of my life, outside of birthing my large-headed children and marrying my hairy husband, there was no pomp and circumstance to mark my farewell. As far as these people—my people—knew, I was just another guest leaving their house after a short, unmemorable stay. Yes, guests were rare here, but so were lucid memories. So, this moment, like a million others procreated here at 24314 Creekview Drive, was destined to be forgotten, or barely remembered, or intensely analyzed—depending on who was doing the thinking.

Dad grabbed my bags and followed me as I crossed back over the threshold of no return. He had no idea that I was the future, wielding an unstoppable power that meant nothing. Looking back at the interior of the house, my house, our house, I was mixed with a toxic combination of raw emotion. I wanted to leave, I wanted to stay, I didn't believe it was real, I had no doubt it was real.

Wanting to pause, I knew I couldn't. They were waiting, life was waiting and Mary was waiting. Kim, Little Amy and Rick were waiting. Willie, Will, and Matthew were waiting. Belt-free absorbency with wings was waiting.

Back out into the Houston sun, I looked out at Mary, smiling and waving happily, just as she had yesterday. Turning back to my hosts, I made an effort to execute the proper goodbyes. Just the sort of thing that Dick and Sue Weinland would have expected of me, gracious, thankful, and warm. This was what they taught me, this was who I was, who we were.

I shook Dad's hand, finally able to look directly into his bright, young eyes, and thanked him for his hospitality. "It was a pleasure," he said, with a genuine quality that was hard not to love. "Bring your family with you next time," he said, sincerely.

"I will," I said, also fully intending to deliver on my promise.

Next up was Mom, who I had learned so much about during my jaunt across time. "Thanks so much, Sue," I said, hugging her lightly, but trying not to mimic the inebriated farewells bid just last night. "I'll never forget it," I said, meaning it to a degree that even I couldn't understand yet.

"Me neither," she responded, feeling the love, well sort of, but not understanding the gravity of the moment. Clearly, she was glad to see me go, and finally, at long freaking last, I was OK with that. Or, I would tell Julia that I was, and she would understand that I really wasn't, but that I was trying to be.

Next was Kim, who hugged me warmly, thanking me again for the stickpin. I wanted to tell her I wasn't really jealous of her and was OK with her hair being better and her thighs being skinnier. I wanted to thank her for a million things, like supporting me and having my back no matter what, and for always telling me the truth, but that would have been ridiculous. She was twelve and I was forty-six, but she was still more mature than me. Who in the hell did she think she was?

Instead, I patted her warmly on the head, almost in a condescending way. I enjoyed that immensely. I told her that meeting her was a delight, a real delight. I think she knew where I was coming from.

Turning to Rick, I put my hand on his shoulder and thanked him for the pine-cone battle. Smiling genuinely, he put both thumbs up, and said "Aaaay, it's OK, lady." Laughing, I told him I'd see him soon.

He just winked and reeled off an impressive dance move, controlled yet hilarious. He would never remember this meeting. As far as he was concerned, it, like about sixty-three percent of his childhood, had never happened.

Finally, I looked down at Little Amy. Eyes bulging, arms flailing, she looked up at me with a mix of excitement and distress. "I really like you, Big Amy."

"I really like you too, you were the best thing about this trip," I said, unsure of exactly how I was supposed to leave it with her. I knew I'd see her again, like every single day, but I'd never see her like this again. It made me both ecstatic and devastated. Shoving the note I'd written upstairs into her little hand, I crouched down until I was at eye level with her bowl cut. Putting a hand on each of her skinny shoulders, I looked directly into her eyes, working up the most meaningful approach I could muster in knee highs and sandals. "Remember, Amy, everything is going to work out so well. Your life is going to be amazing."

Not caring what Dick, Sue, Kim or Rick thought, I embraced Little Amy. Holding on tighter than I should have, for me, for her, for us, I whispered in her ear, "YOU are going to be OK." Maybe somebody else, perhaps somebody from the future, a well-meaning friend, should have jumped out of the azalea bushes and whispered the same thing in my ear, while hugging me very tightly, but not too tightly, but very tightly.

Finally pulling back, she looked into my eyes and softly said, "Thank you, Big Amy."

Standing up, I allowed myself one final look at the younger version of me—freaky-deaky, weird, small, and wonderful. She was who I had been, I was who she would become. I was OK with that.

Somewhere the seventy-year Older Amy was watching all this, bawling hysterically. She knew that despite all our well-meaning attempts, it would still be messy, and beautiful. I hoped she was reassured by that. I hoped her thighs were smaller and that she hadn't cut her hair short. I hoped she traveled. I hoped she had a small motorhome called the Mobile Command Unit. I hoped she had found actual valuables with her metal detector. I hoped she and Willie still played golf. I hoped she still went fishing with Kim and Rick. I hoped she still talked to our boys every day. I hoped she was going to talk to Julia and Mary Barr soon. Very soon. Very freaking soon.

"Thanks again," I said to my family, as underwhelmingly as I had said hello initially. "I'll be seeing you."

Walking away, slowly, down the pebbled path, I looked back as they waved me on.

They had no idea that it was a monumental day in my life, in our lives. They had no idea that sometimes when normal, mundane, everyday life is happening that the world is being altered, turned on its axis, and changed forever.

Somewhere below the surface, below what we think we see, is real life.

Chapter Twenty-Eight

TOMATO CATSUP

*A*s I neared the drop-off point at the end of walk, Mary got out, came around and unlocked the trunk. There were no words as we loaded my suitcase, trolley case, and satchel into the gigantic trunk, its massiveness swallowing them up.

Rounding the car until I was at the passenger door, I looked back at the five Weinlands. From top to bottom, they waved eagerly, Little Amy dancing around like she needed to pee. Mary slid in behind the wheel and reached across the front seat, somehow managing to open the heavy door. "It's time, Amy," she said softly, but with that same undeniable confidence that compelled me to take those gigantic leaps of yesterday. "You can't stop it, you have to go now."

Getting back into the car, I rolled down the window, almost disjointing my wrist with the hand crank, and waved one last time as Mary turned the car around at the base of Morningcrest Court. As we drove away, I looked at the fleeting image of my young family for the last time as they disbanded and scattered inside their unique front door. The story of the Weinland family wouldn't end there, with Mary and me driving away in a silver Ford LTD. Though this part of the tale had ended for me, the forty-six-year-old me, they would go forth, grow pubic hair, have acne, graduate, get apartments, have apartment sex, get an electric knife sharpener as a wedding shower gift and eventually add to our collective family tree.

As Mary traced our way down Creekview, I struggled to

hold my emotions together. I didn't cry in front of other people. It was a rule. Beginning to shake, I wondered what a flood of tears would do to the velour seats. I wondered if I knew Mary well enough to break down. I wondered if I could fit my head into the accessories bucket that sat on the floor hump between our two seats, a feature that was anchored with vinyl maroon sandbags.

I was so raw, so confused, that I couldn't enjoy the final precious moments of our subdivision in its prime. We passed the esplanades, Kristi Beauchamp's white house, the clubhouse, the tennis courts, and the fire station. All were within actual physical reach, but I was emotionally disabled, rendered powerless to enjoy the fruits of the past. Where in the hell was my iPhone? If I had that, I could have made a video; that is if there was enough memory available. But I didn't have time to delete photos now, I was having a freaking moment over here.

Mary guided the car out of Northampton's shiny, white brick gates one last time, taking one right turn followed immediately by another, back into the elementary school parking lot, the same place where she had given me my bizarre marching orders yesterday morning. Pulling into a parking spot in clear view of the army of gray bike racks, she said nothing. As I began to lose it, sputtering like a Ford Pinto, she scooted across the massive front seat.

There were no words as I sobbed uncontrollably. I didn't have to explain it to her, because she was the only one who would ever know—or believe—that this, the wrinkle in time, had really happened.

Reaching into the massive glove box, she pulled out a box of tissues. I guess that sort of thing would have been packed into the time-travel transfer vehicle ahead of time. It was sensible. Handing me the box, she watched compassionately as I blew my nose and tried to do damage control, mascara running in thick clumps down my face. I looked just like the drunk girl in the limo on TV who used to star in the *Witch Mountain* movies. Ironically, even after this, and all that was yet to come, I would still think I was better than her, the aging actress who was the same age as me, because I may not have ever been a film star, but at least I had all my crap together.

We sat there for a few long, meaningful moments, her comforting me, not with words but unfathomable care and compassion. Gentle pats, light hand touching and just the right dose of cheesiness. It was powerful. It was ridiculous. It was totally stupid. It was completely beautiful. Most of all, it was silence. But this was a different kind of peace, because this time around we weren't saying anything because we didn't need to, not because we were afraid to. There was, after all, a big difference. As I began to pull myself together, she eventually, again with perfect timing, made the long journey back to her own seat, putting the huge armrests back down into place, where they would stay, forever.

Though I didn't really want to talk about everything that had just happened, I really did.

"Why? . . . *Why?*" were the only words I could manage to squeeze out, muttered between trying to dab my eyes in the little mirror lodged in the huge windshield visor. It was the only other thing in the car that was bigger than the maxi pad I was wearing.

"Because every life, no matter how seemingly ordinary, no matter how seemingly insignificant, is a unique story, worth telling and retelling. Worth mattering." She paused. "A story, or a life, doesn't have to be exciting, or extraordinary, or exceptional, to be significant and profound."

She apparently had been put in charge of this event because of our previous relationship, the one with clear boundaries— because I respected the hell out of her, and because she looked good in polyester. She was also incredibly wise.

More than anything, Mary was safe. I trusted her even though I didn't really know her. I had enough of a history with her to know that she possessed all those things I would need in somebody if I was going to let them know everything.

But given her place in my real world—the wife of my husband's boss—we would never, ever actually be that close. It wasn't going to happen. This made her the perfect person to engineer my supposed time travel.

I knew my "stuff" wasn't that shocking, or horrible, or wonderful. But it was mine and for some reason, I felt compelled to protect it and was terrified of sharing it.

That made Mary safe.

Perhaps that's what I looked for in relationships. Perhaps that's one of those freaking questions she said I needed to answer, or ask, but I knew I absolutely didn't have.

It all made sense now.

Reaching into the backseat, she fumbled around in what sounded like a hollow box, eventually pulling out two pink cans. "Here!" she said, breaking the somber mood. "Drink this, it will make you feel better."

It was TAB, the diet soda, a pink can that screamed not once, but twice, in an Astro-inspired, yellow-and-white font SUGAR FREE! SUGAR FREE! I popped the top—which again came completely off—and took a long, deep drink. It was horrible, the nastiest single calorie I'd ever not enjoyed. It was so bad that I shouldn't have continued, but like a hungry Texas girl stranded at a Cincinnati chili restaurant, I consumed out of need, not out of desire.

As Mary sipped her Tab, I thought of the notebook, still in my breezy pocket. Holding it up, I asked, "Can I keep this, just this?"

"No," she responded firmly, but not without feeling. "Those notes will be transferred to your iPhone . . . So, well, you can find them there . . . You know, later."

"Oh . . ." I said, looking achingly at the notebook. It was like somebody saying that they were taking away, forevermore, my old, worn copy of *The Raven* by Marquis James, my all-time favorite book. "Not to worry," they'd reassure me, with a condescending tone. "The contents of your old, dated book will be copied onto your Kindle, where it will remain safely, f o r e v e r."

But the Kindle, which could fritz out and never work again, also wouldn't have the coffee stain on the back cover, or the writing on the first page from the previous owner, or the pictures and antique maps in the middle.

I felt the same way about my little notebook, with Old Milwaukee splashed on page two, mint lip gloss on page eleven, and drunk scrawl on page ten. Later, when I returned to reality, I could pull it back out, at my desk, next to my laptop, and read it. It would make me feel I went back again, or if nothing else, I'd remember the entire episode with greater clarity, just by looking at the actual pages and seeing my own handwriting. I wasn't sure what I'd actually do with it, back in the future, but I knew I needed it.

Scanning my observations on the yellow, lined pages of the iPhone's notes app, using my finger to scroll, could never achieve that.

I could feel myself falling apart all over again. Of all the stuff I was going to be forced to give up again, right now, forever, I just couldn't bear giving up my words—they were my own freaking words.

"Well," she said, getting that this was a sticking point, "I'll see what I can do."

"You mean it?" I said, like she was a parent who could pull off whatever impossible magical boloney I believed she could.

"Yes," she said. "It will cost me, but I think we can work that out."

Smiling, she returned to her position behind the wheel, put the car into gear and reversed out of the parking spot. Turning right out of the school's lot, slowly, almost lumbering along, we began retracing our steps to the airport, through the seemingly everyday landscape of dense pine forests and open pasture. Reaching down, Mary turned on the radio. Like before, I was sure I knew this song. Yes, it was etched somewhere on a forgotten corner of my soul. The female voice became more dramatic with each note, suddenly joined by a loud, shrill, overbearing flutist. Though my lips remained pursed tightly, my heart sang quietly along.

It was Debby Boone's smash hit "You Light up my Life." It was like a supernatural salve, oozing out of the plastic burl wood speakers, filling the emotional crevices gaping open in my time-weary heart.

It was my story, it was everyone's story. Mary, her Michigan accent shining through, was singing almost vociferously now, as if on cue, but I couldn't join in. I would never join in.

But really, honestly, did I even know who I was? And if anyone could change it, or redefine it—the person that was me—wasn't it, well . . . .me? Could I, after this, this supposed journey of answering questions I didn't even have, finally drop the solo act and sing a duet? Sing about the truth and celebrate it, both the good and the bad? Could living in the land of honesty, where I was truthful with myself and everyone else, save me? Could it save us all? Could love really fix anything?

Switching off my brain, and relying completely on my heart, I snorted, coughed and joined Mary in song. It was as if we were destined for this moment of musical solidarity. Her, the chosen caretaker of my yellow brick road through time, and me, her reluctant follower, needing to feel comfort and understanding, but from a distance. Needing to feel not alone. Needing to bond on velour seats. But, also desperate to be seen as infinitely resilient, incapable of joining souls over something that had never even happened.

My days were being lit up, and as for my nights, yes, they were filled with love.

West on Root Road, a hard left onto Dowdell, left onto FM

2920, right on Stuebner Airline and finally, at long freaking last, right into the David Wayne Hooks Memorial Airport parking lot.

I didn't want to go back, but I did. I knew I had to get out of here, but I wanted desperately to turn around and retrace every beautiful, painful step.

It couldn't be wrong, especially when it felt so damn right.

With visions of Debby Boone looking out a window and singing to the endless ocean, I fantasized about candles, and a lighthouse, and a boat, steered by Tennille's Captain, and Isaac from the Love Boat, and maybe that guy who used to swirl around in the toilet bowl in a little yacht. No, hold on, cancel that, the Ty D Bol guy wouldn't be right. This was a job for the Gorton's Fisherman—manly, bearded, in a protective yellow slicker and a blue woolen scarf. Sexy in a Grizzly Adams kind of way. Like the Brawny Paper Towel guy, but instead of swinging an axe in the dense forest of disposable napkins, my hero was out bravely dropping his nets for hand-dipped fillets.

I would dip the bounty of his harvest in catsup. Tomato catsup. Because that's how we rolled here. In 1978.

Chapter Twenty-Nine

I'VE GOT A GOLDEN TICKET

What kind of car does your dad drive?" Mary asked, as we sat waiting in the parking lot of the West Houston Airport. It's where we had agreed to meet my dad in the first place, before our flight, and lives got temporarily diverted to David Wayne Hooks Airport, home of the Aviator's Grill.

Just then, Dad's white Toyota Highlander pulled in. I watched as Kim and Rick, who looked like shiny aliens, got out of the car. Kim was wearing skinny jeans, high heels and a beautiful, colorful blouse. Her oversized hoop earrings, rose-gold watch and platinum-blond hair created what almost looked like a haze around her entire body. Rick wore a straw fedora, a brown t-shirt, jeans, and his regular waxed mustache and goatee. My friends had always said he was hot. I never got that, which seemed a terribly appropriate and decent way to feel.

They appeared to be almost magical, standing there, all grown up, realer than they had ever seemed before, but also like a mirage. I knew now that they were transparent, destined to change as the time that hadn't yet, but inevitably would, march by. I had always known that I loved them, but I hadn't ever fully grasped just what their long-term presence had meant. I suppose I had taken for granted that they would be around, thirty years later, assuming that normal would continue on being itself, normal. And I had never made the connection that they, at whatever age, were the living link to my past, to our past.

Looking at Mary, I didn't know what to say. "Ummm . . . I'm not sure . . ." I started.

She grabbed my hand from across the landscape of the much smaller car. The act of physical touch didn't seem so foreign now. "You don't need to say anything, Amy, I understand."

"There is so much I should thank you for . . ." I said, desperately wanting to bridge the gap between what had happened over the past forty-eight hours and the fact that I was now teetering on the perimeter of my regularly scheduled life.

"No," she said firmly, "I did what I was supposed to do. I wasn't chosen for this assignment, I wanted it. I suppose I needed it too. I'm glad it was you that I got to take back home."

What could she possibly mean by that? She had wanted to do it? I hadn't considered her having a choice. Did she log on to some website, like WTF.com, and scroll through time-travel job postings, see mine, obviously posted by somebody other than me, and think, "YES! I'll do THAT." She hardly knew me as much as I hardly knew her. And as far as her "needing" it, my trip backward, as much as I did, that seemed unbelievable.

First, this was all about me, right?

Life was all about me, especially my life.

Beyond that, what did she see in me? What had she seen all these years, other than a heavily buzzed underling at the cheese platter at the Christmas party?

I had no clue. No freaking clue. And, if I was a betting person, I'd never ask her. Never in a million years. That's why this "relationship"—our connection—worked for me.

Is it why it worked for her too?

Unhooking her seat belt, she smiled, perhaps the most meaningful look anyone had ever given me, in a flash, full of everything I needed to see. "Well," she continued, "I guess I'll see you at the Christmas party next month."

"Ah, yes . . ." I said, hurled back into reality. "Yes, I'll definitely see you then."

That was it, it was over. We were back to normal. She was going to act like it was normal. I was as thankful for that as I had been for anything in my life. Well, that and the fact that I could feel the self-adhesive absorbency securely in place in my Old Navy skinny jeans.

The only thing that worried me, the annoying little thought that was trying to unsettle how settled I felt, was what would happen if, next month at the Christmas party, after three glasses of Cabernet or Malbec or Riesling or Carlo Rossi Moscato Sangria . . . I tried to take normal back from Mary?

Fear of fears, what if she continued playing her normal card only to have me come out of the ladies' room sobbing, needing only momentarily, blurrily, to play the keep-it-real card, a move that would require her to discuss "it," all of it, in front of the ice sculpture, the well-lit carving station and the huge, boiled shrimps?

What then?

Getting out of the car, I met Mary around the back as she raised the rear door of her Lexus SUV, smaller than the LTD we had been in earlier, but at a more reasonable height. As we took my bags out— a backpack and rolling suitcase—I heard Dad's voice behind us.

"Well, hello there!" he said. "Welcome back to Texas!"

He looked ancient, shrunken, wrinkly, and as white as a sheet. He wore a blue golf shirt with colorful horizontal stripes, tucked into a belted pair of Wranglers. When he turned to help with my bags I could see that his butt had magically flattened— a pancake replacing what had once been hot crossed buns. Yes, friend, my father, my dear dad, was suffering from a serious case of the Gone-Asses.

The thirty-odd years that had passed since I saw him last, just a couple of hours ago, had been good to him, but still, they had been.

"Hi there, neighbor!" Rick said, offering up his routine half-embrace.

"Sister of mine! It's good to see you!" Kim chimed in, providing a fuller hug. "You ready for Death Camp Thanksgiving Eve?" she continued, referring both to today's meetings and back to the 'arrangements' conference Dad had put on the year before.

I was speechless, but I don't think they noticed.

I looked at my siblings again closely as they joked around and introduced themselves to Mary, who Dad was regaling with tales of his recent photography safari to Africa. She was no doubt deeply thrilled that he got his 2,500 photos down to a "tight" 271. If I looked ever-so carefully, I could see their younger counterparts, the ones on the "other side" of that magical wall, but it was just a glimpse, glowing stronger today because of our recent reunion in the past. I knew that soon, very soon, time would, once again, fade the memory of their youthful countenances. All that would remain were the adult forms, the ones that existed in this version of reality. It was tragic, and beautiful, and disturbing.

"Well, kids," Dad said, looking down at his Fitbit. "We had better make a move to our meeting."

"Yes," Kim said. "We've got important death business to attend to."

I gave Mary a final hug, awkward but meaningful, resisting the urge to make it seem like the big deal that it was. I didn't need to do that, because she understood. Maybe the best thing in life is when somebody "gets it," even one person. For me, it's even better when they get it and don't want to talk about, unless of course, I do.

Maybe that's what being a good friend is, knowing when and when not to get it and knowing when and when not to talk about it. Crap. I needed a package of thank-you notes and a dozen Bic pens. This time, it would be good if I actually sent the letters.

Loading up in Dad's car, we all simultaneously put our seat

belts on. Rick got in the front, just like the old days, and Kim and I shared the back. Driving away from the airport, I felt tears welling up in my eyes. It was over, my magical journey of hallucination had ended. Looking out the window, I watched as West Houston, busy, crazy Houston, passed by in a blur. Strip malls, nail bars, abandoned Walmarts that were now Goodwill stores and dialysis centers dotted the sides of the road.

I had gone misty, small tears sputtering out of my eyes. I couldn't help it. I felt almost stuck between the two times, the one I had left behind again, forever, and this one. The same people were in both, I had experienced it all with them, but they didn't understand it. They would never understand it. Either because it never happened or because it actually did, but only to me. It meant that I had no one to discuss it with, nobody to re-live each detail with. It meant that it wasn't a memory at all, or at least it felt that way. Like it never happened. Perhaps that's what makes certain things unreal. It's not about whether something really happens or not, it's about whether it can be shared.

Glancing back over at Kim, I was met by a wide-eyed stare. "Are you CRYING?" She laughed. "What are you CRYING about?"

"I'm not crying . . ." I retorted, "I'm just tired . . . and my contacts are bothering me . . ."

"Amy's crying back here," Kim blurted out. "This whole thing, this flying on little private planes and the talk of arrangements . . . it's too much for her!"

Rick looked back and smiled. There was no way he could have known what was going on, but his compassionate demeanor made me think it was more than just a smile. He was just being nice. That was his deal, that and having the penis. And I was clearly just being the Great Erroneous Assumer. That was my deal—that and thinking I was hilarious.

"Well, kids," Dad said, almost like we were back at the Greenspoint Mall play center, "we'll go straight to the Fidelity office, and then to lunch, and then home to see your mother."

Looking back down, I noticed a book sitting in the seat between Kim and me. "Is this yours . . . you're reading *The Thorn Birds*?" I asked, picking up the weighty volume.

"Yes," she said. "It was a book before it was a miniseries."

"Oh," I said, clearing my throat. "Yes . . . I know that one . . . It's a beautiful story, one of the greatest romance novels of all time, it covers three generations of a family in Australia."

"Hmm," she said. "I just started reading it. I thought it was about a hot priest who gives up his priesthood to sleep with a woman."

"Yeah, that too," I said.

Silence.

Eventually we were back on I-45 North, basically retracing our steps from earlier, thirty years earlier. The differences were stark. The road was a couple of lanes wider, the fence-like barriers between the north and southbound lanes were replaced with concrete bunkers and the lights were taller and fewer. The cars were smaller, but also taller, with smoother, less boxy lines, and they moved faster. Everything moved faster.

Was everyone in a bigger hurry or were their cars just capable of doing more? Was it technology or personality that had changed, or had one coerced the other over the edge? Or maybe my perception was the only thing that had changed?

Coming past the beltway, we passed by Greenspoint, still standing, but only a shadow of its former self on the east side of the freeway. Though I certainly wasn't surprised by the decay, I had a much better gauge for the level of decline. Seeing it in its prime made me realize not only how far it had fallen, but what a waste it was. Though you could argue that the deterioration in the general area precipitated its fall from grace, what if it had been kept up? What if money had been pumped into it, enough to give premier retailers no choice but to stay? Was it inevitable or reversible, and at the end of the day, did it even matter? Who would care when they eventually tore it down, only to build another shopping center atop its ashes?

Gone also was the Goodyear Blimp base. In its place were a Home Depot, a Sprint store and a Lowe's Home Improvement Center. It was the kind of set-up you could find in virtually any city in the country, but underneath it, hidden by parking pads and lookalike structures, was a part of aviation history. I wondered if anyone else remembered.

Reaching down, I patted my brown leather jacket pockets. It was impossible that my notebook would really be there. It wasn't like a vacation where I could and would bring stuff home, souvenirs and photos, intended to help me remember my trip. Perhaps it had all been downloaded onto my iPhone, a device that didn't seem near as critical now. If fact, I hadn't even checked it since we landed. It didn't seem as necessary.

That was as shocking as almost anything that had happened in the last forty-eight hours.

At the very least, I would have Dad stop at Walgreens and I would buy a notebook, similar in size and color, and try to rewrite my observations based on either the phone version of my notes or my sketchy memory. It would have to be done quickly, as I knew the longer I spent here in glistening Future Land, the quicker it would fade.

Putting my hand in my left pocket, I found nothing. Slowly inserting my opposite hand in the other pocket, I felt myself morphing into little Charlie from the Chocolate Factory, slowly taking the wrapper off a Wonka Bar to see if I, little ole' me, had been the one-in-a-million winner of a Golden Ticket.

If it really was in there, *my* version of the priceless coupon, I would dance with my four grandparents, who were dead today but alive three hours ago, emerging from the huge, two-sided bed they all shared in our living room. I WANT AN OOMPA LOOPA NOW, DADDY!

The pocket wasn't big, so as soon as just the tips of my fingers were in I felt something. The smooth curls of the spiral top. I almost couldn't believe it. I worked hard not to gasp, but didn't succeed, sucking in air loudly enough for Kim to give me a bug-eyed look which crazily mirrored Little Amy's face from the past.

Trying not to be quite so obvious, I slowly pulled it out.

I was elated, flabbergasted and amazed.

It was the notebook. My freaking notebook.

It was all there, my notes, my precious scribblings. Crap. Either all that crap had happened, really happened, or when I was hallucinating I had the forethought, or delusionary capabilities, or gifts, to write notes along the way. I was gifted, or not. The test scores said not so much. This damn notebook said absolutely.

Fishing back into the pocket, I pulled out a pen. Only this time rather than an orange Bic ballpoint, it was a Uniball Vision Needle rollerball, an upgrade. There was small white sticker on the cap. It looked like it had been printed on a label machine. "YOU ARE WELCOME ☺" it read, almost chirping at me.

Thanks, Mary. Then it hit me, what she had said, when she agreed that I could have my imaginary notebook back. She had said that it would "cost" her. Good Lord. What had it cost her? Did she have to pay something for my bubbling joy? And which did I want more, the notebook, my notebook, or for it not to cost her anything? If I could only know the price, then I could decide what I wanted.

Opening the notebook to the next blank page, I uncapped the pen and happily scribbled, "*GOODYEAR BLIMP BASE. Is anything left? Go on Google Earth and look at aerial maps. Drive around old site and take pictures.*"

"You guys remember the Goodyear Blimp base?" I said.

"Yeah, why?" Kimber said.

"I was just wondering if anything is left from when it was here," I said.

"I remember that!" Rick added.

"Yes," Dad said, "it was a big deal. It didn't come to the area until after we moved out here in 1969. One of the pilots lived in Northampton," he continued. "And once, I'm not sure where it was, maybe while I was playing tennis, he asked a couple of us to go up with him."

"On an actual flight?" I said.

"Yes," he said. "The guy had a certain number of training hours he had to complete, so he took us with him."

"What was it like?" Kim said.

"Well," he said, "it was a lot like that balloon trip I took in Africa."

"Did you go far?" Rick said.

"Yes, I think, well, I think it was about an hour and we covered the entire area."

"What was the inside like?" I said.

"It was a lot like you'd see on a ferry, like crossing the English Channel," he said. "You know, theatre-type seating and lots of windows."

"I never knew that . . . That you went up," Rick said.

Kim and I both agreed by nodding. It made me wonder about all the other things we still didn't know about the lives we'd supposedly lived and the important people we'd supposedly lived them with.

Passing by the site of the former Bonanza, now the El Palenque Mexican Restaurant, I was shocked to see what looked to be a six-lane highway being built east-to-west, directly north of Spring Stubener, the little farm road we'd traveled to the mall on in 1978.

"WHAT'S THAT?" I said.

"That's the Grand Parkway," Dad said.

I had heard of that, a plan for the next in a series of outer loops for the ever-expanding fourth-largest city in the country. First 610, next Beltway 8 and the Sam Houston Tollway, now the Grand Parkway.

"Where does it go from here?" I asked as we passed beyond it. Looking to the west, I knew that out there somewhere, in the near distance, were the quiet rural confines of Northampton. It had already been linked to the massive Woodlands development to the north, but this, this road, could mean something totally different. It could mean Northampton was accessible by freeway.

Crap. That was like science freaking fiction.

"Well," Dad said, "it's supposed to cut in just behind Klein Oak and Hildcbrandt."

He was referring to the two schools—the high school and middle school—I had attended. Even more astonishing was that these two edifices were located just across the street— Root Road—to be precise, from Northampton Elementary and yes, Northampton subdivision proper.

"I've heard," Rick said, "that they are already building an overpass over Gosling . . . Just across the street from Dave's Express."

"Really! Seriously?" I said.

"Yes," Kim said, "it's near where my friend Tommy grew up."

I knew exactly where they meant, but I was having a hard time digesting it. It was almost like I'd sped ahead into the future after just visiting the past. Like the end of that first *Back to the Future* movie. It was too much. And I didn't have a flux capacitor.

My childhood, our childhood, really was well and truly over.

Northampton as we knew it was gone and moving even further into an unrecognizable future. Why in the hell hadn't I been allowed to video it in its prime? I couldn't tell anybody about what I'd seen during my journey. I would sound like a crackpot. But a video, sharing a video would have allowed everyone to see what I saw.

Pulling the notebook back out again, I jotted, "*NORTHAMP-TON – Does anyone have an old video? Look through Mom and Dad's old eight-millimeter movies. Post in the Northampton Facebook page. Look online.*" Then I added, "*GRAND PARKWAY. WTF? Get maps, plans drive the route to Northampton. What does this mean?*"

Looking up, I watched as the south part of the Woodlands began to zoom by.

The Woodlands itself—now a booming city in its own right with over 100,000 residents spread over forty-five square miles —didn't open up officially until 1974. My first memory of there even being something called "The Woodlands" was Dad driving us to see a sculpture that had been erected at I-45 and the Woodlands Parkway. It was brown, or rust colored, and modern, featuring a weaving of ribbon-like objects. I had Googled it once, way after the fact, and found out that it had been one of two original art sculptures installed for the grand opening. All I remember is Dad lining the three of us up in front of the towering edifice and telling us to consider the "craftsmanship" and "creativity" it required.

Really, and even though I didn't get what he was trying to do then, I should thank him for it now. As should my children, who I had recently lined up in front of an old Toll House on the National Road in Addison, Pennsylvania, dramatically imploring them to step back into history with me, to a magical land where you had to pay somebody, who sauntered out of their own house and hand-lifted a wooden gate, to take a public roadway.

As we exited the freeway, I strained across the car to see a glimpse of the statue, now partially blocked by four lanes of traffic. It looked like it might be impossible to stop and stand quietly in front of it now, reflecting on its meaning. Instead, residents of the new millennium would have to settle for driving by at forty-five miles per hour, forced to bullet-point their innermost connections to the art and artist.

"Remember that statue . . . over there." I pointed across the lanes after we'd already passed it by. "You know, Dad . . . the one you made us go look at."

"What statue?" he asked.

"The brown one that was all wavy, it was just as The Woodlands opened and you took our picture in front of it," I said.

"Vaguely," he said.

"I think you're making that up, Amy," Kim stated.

"Yeah," Rick added. "There goes her memory again."

"That actually happened!" I said, annoyed that these hooligans would question my grasp on the past. How could they not remember that? Surely there was a picture somewhere?

Pulling out my notebook and then my iPhone, I scribbled down, *"Find picture in front of Woodlands statue."* Then I pulled up the internet on my phone and Googled "Woodlands statue" and scrolled through the images until I found it. Saving it, I went back into photos, selected it and texted to Dad, Kim, and Rick.

"I just sent you all a picture of it," I stated, smugly. Then it hit me. I had just found a picture of something that nobody could remember, an obscure item, in under fifteen seconds. That Wayne guy from last night might think THAT was a "pretty neat little deal."

That is, if he was still alive.

OK, so I was glad I had the phone back, and Google, and, yes, Facebook, which I had also just checked. Seventy-three freaking likes on the picture I had posted before I left Dayton. The same one where I superimposed my face on the Statue of Liberty. Seventy-three likes, it wasn't great, but we were going places. We surely were.

Chapter Thirty

THE FITTEST RED BIRD EVER

*W*e continued down the Woodlands Parkway until we reached Six Pines, taking a right toward the mall area. Crossing a bridge, we turned right on Lake Robbins and then took an immediate right into the Fidelity parking lot. Approaching the entrance to the building, we were stopped by an elderly man dressed in khaki pants and a blue blazer. "Are you a Northampton Family?" he asked.

"Yes," my dad answered. "We are . . . Or, we were."

"I thought I recognized you, we still live on Bayonne, I'm Ray Frontain," the man said.

"And, I'm Dick Weinland," Dad said, introducing himself and then each of us.

Though by sight alone he was unrecognizable to me, his name was unmistakable. He was my childhood friend Elaine's father. She and I had been through all of school together, from kindergarten to graduation. I remembered her from our senior prom, an event that was now hazy in retrospect. I could only recall little glimpses: going to the mall (Greenspoint, again) with Kim to have my makeup done at the Clinique counter, getting my shoes dyed to match my dress, feeling awkward and ridiculous in my huge pink taffeta gown complete with sleeves the size of my head. The darkness and elegance of the Greenspoint Wyndham ballroom, the well-lit Ficus trees and the white lattice partitions covered in fake ivy. The real highlight, or lowlight, came prior to the festivities when my "date" and I, Eric (a junior from my chemistry class), went to the Glass Menagerie restaurant to eat. This was a super fancy-dancy place in an older part of the Woodlands. I was following Eric as he descended the long, steep stairway into the restaurant when I stumbled and fell down the last ten steps. Though I didn't injure myself or any of the other diners, including my date, it was impressive.

The reason I remembered Elaine more clearly than the actual event, even now in the Fidelity parking lot twenty-eight years later, was because of a snapshot I had kept in an album. She was wearing a gorgeous yellow gown while sitting on the lap of our mutual friend Tom. Perhaps that's where we draw many of our memories from, photos of actual events that we don't really remember.

Unlike what the overeager younger version of myself would have done, I waited to fill everyone in on how I knew Elaine until after the discussion between Dad and Mr. Frontain died down. A week ago, I wouldn't have realized how far I had come from being the hyperactive experience I once was. But even though I had matured and improved, I also realized that she, the younger version of me, had qualities that I had suppressed, wrongly assuming that every bit of the naïve version of us was discardable. Seeing her, all of her, made me understand that it simply wasn't true. There was as much goodness in her as I thought there was in me. Maybe there was more.

I hoped she was proud of me.

"I was friends with your daughter, Elaine," I finally said.

He told us that Elaine was in New York City, with her two little girls, her husband and a job as an executive in television. I knew that because of Facebook but acted like it was all news to me. It made me realize that, for the supposed evils of social media, there was something inherently good about it.

Social media was kind of like suburbia. Both got a lot of bad press, perhaps rightfully so, because both made things look shiny, landscaped, and perfect on the surface. Though this insinuates that something terrible lurks behind the shiny wrapper, most of the time reality is more a mixture of both the good and the bad.

Regardless, "real" life isn't fairly depicted on social media, nor is it on display on the neat suburban streets with their rows of tightly locked doors. In both cases, we only see what people decide to show us. On the flip side, we only show people what we want them to see. Think about it, when was the last time you saw a post on Facebook that was hauntingly one hundred percent authentic? *My husband is a dick, he's mean and drinks too much,* or *My kid has an F in chemistry, sucks at all sports and refuses to flush the freaking toilet,* or *I don't like myself right now and I am really hurt.*

Along the same lines, how many household fights do you see spill out onto the streets in places like McKinney, Texas, Anaheim Hills, California, or Centerville, Ohio? Sure, you might hear some shouting, but nobody really knows what's going on in there, behind the locked door.

And the ultimate question, what we really need to ask ourselves is—does it really matter? What if you knew that somebody else was hurt, or what if you told the world that you needed help?

What if I went on social media and told people I had lingering issues with my mom. That I had memories but mostly feelings that before this, I couldn't verify? What if I posted about how I was worried about my son, who was trying to discover his own identity while I was smothering him?

At least in my case, I would feel like every "I'm praying for you" and "I've got your back" comment posted in response would be matched by a dubious smirk and a text message to a mutual friend followed by a discussion, at Panera Bread, between other friends who couldn't believe I'd post that kind of personal information.

But really, that's me just assuming the worst in everybody again, including my supposed "friends."

What's the point of authentic living?

Perhaps it comes down to giving the rest the world the satisfaction, and unfathomable reassurance, that they aren't the only ones living a screwed-up, beautiful, horrible, amazing real life.

Maybe these were the questions Mary was talking about. The ones I obviously did not have.

The second-floor meeting with the attorney and financial advisor brought me fully back to the land of adulthood, where I not only wondered what all the words meant, even though I nodded along dutifully to everything that was said, but also wondered if Willie and I would ever reach this level of readiness.

As the meeting wrapped up, Dad and the financial lady—a stunning thirty-something-year-old who reminded me of the 1978 stickpin clerk from Foley's—went out to make copies. The big difference was, as similarly shiny as the two women were, the 2014 version was also pulling in 175K and driving an Audi. That left the three of us sitting there, like adolescents in adult clothing, waiting for our father to come back and tell us what to do next. We really were adults, in real life, just not here, at Dad's meeting.

Pulling the notebook back out, I quickly wrote, "*What did women sales clerks make in 1978? How much money is that in 2014 dollars? What is the average amount women made then vs. now? Is there another mall planned for north of Houston? Send Elaine a message on Facebook. What would I do if I saw someone in trouble online? Would I seriously do ANYTHING?*" and "*Would Little Amy be proud of me?*"

It was quiet, presumably because we were all trying to absorb this glimpse into our shared future, when all these plans would be in action, when Mom and Dad were really gone. We all knew what was going to happen. It was a history book that had already been written. It was just a matter of the when and where, and then the how. Spending a couple of bizarre hours with my dead grandparents had made me realize that. As slow as this was all going, as slow as this meeting was, it was all furiously ticking toward a predictable ending. Dick and Sue were going to die, and we were going to deal with their money. We, the three kids, were going to handle this really big crap. Maybe that's when we'd really become adults, when we dealt with the crap. The death crap.

And maybe as important as it was to get the financial part right, it was even more crucial to get all the emotional dots connected. Only there were no "Death Camp" weekends, no important business meetings, no folders and calculators provided to somehow, someway, connect memory with reality, or some form of it that would make us look back and only smile. Because what was the point, really, of looking back if you couldn't feel good about it?

We couldn't control what had happened in the past, even something as simple as the car ride over to this meeting, but we could definitely decide how to react to it. No matter what had happened. Did it really control us, or were we just letting it?

Who had the key to that door and who was really in charge of all of that crap?

Looking over at Kim and Rick, who were both reviewing their phones for any important updates, I wondered how weird it would seem if I attempted to ask a philosophical question. Though I couldn't tell them that I had just hallucinated myself into our shared pasts, I could still ask questions. It was tricky with this group, not so much the asking, but the timing of the question itself to garner actual thoughtful responses. We were still a weird mixture of immaturity and adultness, of silliness and wisdom. What had fostered our three-way relationship (don't get any ideas, we mostly kept our clothing on), and kept both sides of the equation fresh, were the annual "brother-sister" trips we took every summer when I was in Texas for my boys' terms at Camp Olympia. We picked a different location each year and spent two nights playing cards, talking crap, being mildly obnoxious and basically just being together. We had accomplished everything from serious discussions on religion, relationships, and Mom and Dad's sex life to having our photos taken at J.C. Penney wearing rubber animal heads. Most trips involved a visit to a local Goodwill, or other thrift store, where we chose outfits for a photo shoot or evening event.

These brief trips had essentially canceled out the longstanding rule that we weren't supposed to talk about our feelings. Each year we talked more frankly, and even though we hadn't quite reached the point where we could talk about everything, we were getting there.

Clearing my throat to get their attention, I asked the question that had been ricocheting around in my head since my second flight, the one that brought me back to the land of the internet. "Do you ever think about what it was like when we were kids? Do you ever think about what you remember and what you don't?"

"What?" Kim asked. "What do you mean?"

"Well . . ." I continued. "Do you ever think about being a kid and wonder why we remember certain parts but not others?"

"For me," Rick said, "it's when I see something, like an old picture, or like that time you guys bought me my old drum set for Christmas, then a memory comes back. Other than that, I don't think about it much."

"I remember a lot of things," Kim said, looking off into the distance through the huge picture window. "It was perfect, the way I remember it . . . We were so happy, we had the perfect childhood."

"Why do we each remember different things?" I asked. "Like you guys are always saying I made half the stuff up that I remember, but what if I just remember more of the details because of my personality?"

"I do remember that you were a freak," Kim said, laughing. We all agreed with that, it was true.

"Memory is a powerful thing, but we don't really have any control over it," I continued.

"We do choose what we focus on," Rick said. "You can't control the memory coming to mind, but you can decide whether it stays there."

"Hmmm . . ." I said, "You might be right about that. But sometimes it's hard to kick stuff out, maybe because it needs to be dealt with, or maybe because we just get used to it being there. Maybe it's our identity."

"Or maybe," Kim cut in, "maybe we just think it is. Maybe we can, if we work really hard, flush that stuff out, the stuff that we don't want and maybe, just maybe, who we really are is behind it."

"I guess the only way to do that," I said, "is to consciously choose not to focus on the stuff you want out. You can't just say 'BE GONE' and it goes. You have to actively choose not to let yourself think about it. To focus your mind and heart on other things."

Silence.

"If you do that, are you also saying that everything that happened is OK?" I asked. "That everyone who ever did anything to cause any of your bad stuff is off the hook? Is it denial, acting like nothing ever happened?"

"I don't think so," Kim said. "I think it just means you're taking the power back from whoever hurt you and from whatever happened. Maybe it's forgiveness . . ."

"Or maybe," I said, "it's forgiveness and forgetness. Moving on simply because it's the only thing left to do."

"I hope people forgive and forget some of the crap I've done," Kim said.

"You are so right," I said. "Me too."

"That's brave stuff," Rick added. "It takes courage, and something much bigger, like love."

Silence.

But this time I think we were all just thinking, not avoiding.

"Why do each of us have such different memories?" I continued, not ready to drop it. "We all grew up in the same house, with the same people. And it affected us so differently."

Silence.

"What is reality?" I continued, taking advantage of the fact they were still acting like they were listening. "If all of our perceptions are different, who decides what really happened? And does it really matter anyway?"

"Well," Kim said, "I guess we're lucky we did it together, because that way we can talk about it."

"Or maybe . . ." Rick said. "Maybe we've all got different takes on it because reality is nothing more than what we want to be, what we need to be, for a single moment."

"Wow," Kim pondered, "I'm not even sure what that means."

"Me either!" Rick laughed. "We should stay hydrated!"

"Yeah!" I cut in. "We need a round of beers. That's sensible."

"My doctor said to push the liquids!" he said. It was one of our running gags – making the consumption of alcoholic beverages seem medically necessary. It didn't mean we were actually going to grab a six-pack on the way out. It just meant we were going to stop being philosophical.

Dad and Ms. Finance returned to the room with a set of papers for each of us. Dutifully, we placed them in our Death Camp briefcases like Dad had told us to. We were lucky on a bunch of levels, but him having us prepared for what was inevitable was major.

"Zip up your zippers, ladies," Rick instructed. "And keep your satchels close."

"Yes!" Kim agreed. "Those complimentary calculators are going to come in handy when the time comes!"

We could laugh about it, but we were as ready as people were going to be. Everybody's parents died, but this was a big deal to us. Even if we were just another family among billions, we mattered, we mattered to us, and that was enough. It was like Mary said, every life mattered—it wasn't insignificant just because nobody ever made a movie about it or put it in *People* magazine. It mattered because it was ours.

Back down the cubicle-lined hallway and into the elevator, we were noisy, all talking at the same time and cracking bad joke after bad joke. I guess we were all relieved that this part of the day was over, the part with the meeting where we signed papers just in case Dad went nuts and tried to spend all his money growing grapevines for wine in his backyard, or raising flamingos, or whatever.

It was his damn money, but still, he shouldn't go out and do something ridiculous with it.

"S e x u a l R e l a t i o n s," Rick said, slowly and clearly as Dad struggled to hear or understand what we were all laughing about. "Kim had the s e x u a l r e l a t i o n s with him down at the barn."

He was referring to a pretend liaison between Kim and a guy we all knew, someone who she wasn't really going to do anything with, especially not in a metal barn that was falling down. We liked to make stuff up like that, either to annoy Dad or make our lives sound more exciting in case somebody in the lobby of Fidelity Investments was listening in.

"Kids . . ." Dad said, shaking his head. "Get in the car, we're going to lunch at the Chick-Fil-A . . ."

"Well, I 'spect she gone and done it, Daddy," I added.

"I 'spect she has . . ." Rick said almost woefully, putting his boot up on the back bumper of the Highlander.

"I 'spect I did . . ." Kim added. "I 'spect I gone and dishonored Daddy and our whole family with those sexual shenanigans. Well, friends," she continued, almost tripping over her own feet, "I'm not sure how to tell you this, but, well, my womb . . ." she gasped, "my womb is a barren desert, in which his seed could find no purchase."

I had to admit, that was funny, damn funny, and remember

funny wasn't necessarily Kim's gig, it was mine. She was pretty and knew what to wear under white Capri pants and how to get into a small boat with wedges on. I was hilarious, freaking hilarious. Though it had never seemed enough, the funny business, it was my deal. That didn't mean she didn't have her moments of comedic genius, she really did—like the time she wore her red rubber cardinal head late one night in San Antonio, lowering herself into the pool while perched on the handicap lift, screaming "I'm doing it, I'm doing it . . ." It took about four agonizing minutes for the chair to reach the water, but she worked it the whole painful way. It was hilarious, grade-A amusing and to top that off, she was wearing a bikini. At forty-five years old she had done it in a bikini, and looked fabulous. She was the best-figured middle-aged red bird any of us had ever seen.

Who in the hell did she think she was?

LOOKING down at my spicy Chick-Fil-A sandwich, waffle fries, and huge Diet Coke, I wasn't so concerned with calorie counts, ethical approaches to food service or even the past—I was hungry. The last time I had eaten was at Bonanza, and though that was really two days ahead of now, it was at least seven hours ago in stomach time. Time travel was a lot like flying to and from Europe—days were lost, meals were repeated and people needed to poop.

Looking over at Dad, I wondered if he even remembered the meal at Bonanza, the day after Thanksgiving, when the cousin from Ohio banged on the faux-wood booth with a red candle globe, in the shadow of a dimly lit wagon wheel, emotionally stating what she was thankful for.

Or did that even really happen?

I looked at him, gnawing on his sandwich like the old man that he had suddenly become, examining it closely in between each bite. What was he looking for? And, more to the point, what did he know? Could he really be responsible for all my memories, specifically the way *I* remembered them?

I decided not to ask, for now.

Because today, not only did I know what I remembered as the ten year-old me, but I knew what I had seen as the forty-six-year-old me.

For now, I had all the validation I would ever need. Anything else might mess it up even more.

I wondered if that was also true for the parts of my life that I didn't go back into time to see? Even those that were too horrible to share? Maybe I didn't need validation after all. Maybe the memories were supposed to be both real and flawed, two distinctly opposing threads woven into a colorful fabric, as true as they were false and as common as they were unique.

Maybe it wasn't all about validation, or proof, or having some authority stamp his/her approval on my document of memory. Maybe it was about me accepting it, me validating it, and me moving on, and not moving on, but owning it and doing with it whatever I chose.

It was my choice.

Chapter Thirty-One

RE VERA FACTUM EST ITA

*B*ack into the driveway of my parents' house, Dad asked the three of us to get out before he pulled his car into the narrow spot in the garage. Once he wedged it in, nearly scraping the wall, we walked over to meet him, ascending the two steps up to the back door. Placed ominously to our left was a wheelchair ramp, installed per his specifications when they moved in, in preparation for another future day in our collective lives.

I don't believe that the three of us really took notice of that kind of thing, Mom and Dad's herculean efforts to make sure our future lives were secure and relatively stress free, any more than the younger versions of us noticed how much raw energy and effort went into hosting a Thanksgiving dinner for ten people, some of whom you didn't really like. I can only speak for myself, but I never seemed to fully appreciate what was going on around me, what others were doing to make my life easier. Instead, I liked to think about what *I* was doing, flogging myself day by day to ensure my people had bleached underwear, fresh vegetables and clean, sanitary hot-tub water.

Following Dad inside the door we were greeted by Mom's yapping Pekinese, Chuy Jalisco. Here was a dog who understood that he had landed in a house of old people who didn't mind being put on his schedule. He refused to poop unless one of the elderlies, regardless of their condition, would walk him, at minimum, for thirty-seven minutes. He refused to eat his dinner unless one of my parents sat beside him in the living room, waiting however long it took until he decided to both start and finish the meal. He took naps on top of a $1,250 coffee table, the same one we weren't allowed to put drinks on. And, to top it all off, he barked incessantly at whomever he chose—without ever being asked to stop. In the same way that the US Postal Service didn't stop delivering because of hail, sleet or snow—Chuy J. didn't stop barking because of sleeping babies, important phone conversations, or quiet family gatherings.

"Did he poop, Dick?" was often a side conversation, inserted randomly, when talking on the phone to Mom. There was never any warning. She just blurted it out whenever Dad and "the boy" got back from their walk. "How many?" she would continue, again randomly cutting you off regardless of whether you were relaying mundane life details or announcing that you had just cured colon cancer. What followed next was the inevitable "How big?" to gauge the feces size and "Oh, he's such a good guy, get the boy a cookie."

He never, ever ate table food, except every night when Dad would feed him from his own plate, doling out small, digestible morsels. It was as heartwarming as it was disconcerting. Again, it was their lives, not ours, not our place to comment, but was that damn dog really getting a better childhood than we'd had? And were we really comparing ourselves to that damn dog?

Dodging Chuy, who was excited and mad all at the same time, we passed through the family and laundry rooms until we reached the big kitchen. Mom and Dad had bought the house, an architectural tribute to the '70s, a couple of years before and had completely redone it. It was stunning, in line with Dad's design vision combined mostly with Kim's and, to a lesser degree, Rick's redecoration skills. I was not involved much in this sort of thing, first because I lived so far away and secondly, I wasn't advertised as "on the same page" with the others. I was asked, however, where the giant medieval sword from Spain should be hung. Even more satisfying than watching Dad use the area I so designated for the bulky weapon was Kim being highly offended by both the item and its placement.

Who in the hell did I think I was?

Mom was in the kitchen, pulling a Pyrex dish of bubbling spinach-and-artichoke dip out of the oven. She had already laid out a spread of two other homemade dips and three kinds of chips, but the hot stuff was her signature item. "Here you go, Kimber." Mom motioned to Kim as she placed the dish down on a hot pad on the huge island. "I know you are probably hungry."

"Yeah, thanks, Mom," Kim said, wasting no time in launching in. "The traffic was awful on 45 and I am starving."

Like Dad, Mom looked absolutely ancient, especially since I was gauging her age not from the last time I really saw her, in late June, just five short months ago, but in 1978 when she was forty-something.

"Hi, Mom!" I greeted her, as she literally shuffled around the island.

"Hi, Amy S.," she said, embracing me warmly. "I can't believe you are here for Thanksgiving," she continued, smiling. "We're so excited that the boys and Willie are coming too, that never happens."

"Yeah!" Kim shouted from over the dips, an array that included what looked like a buffalo chicken and a seven-layer Mexican with homemade guacamole. "It sucks when it's just all the rest of us."

"We're so excited too," I said. It was heartwarming, the sucking without us and all. "They'll all be here in the morning, I know they can't wait."

"I'm so glad your dad's meetings got pushed up," Mom said. "Now we get more time with you." Returning to the sink to wash the tomatoes for the salad she continued, "We're having filets, they look good. Well, I guess we'll eat them, someday, when your dad finally starts the grill.

"DICK!" she screamed, causing Chuy J. to lurch violently. "YOU NEED TO GET THE DAMN COALS GOING IF WE'RE EVER GOING TO EAT!"

"When are Rick's people going to be here?" I asked.

"Rick said they were on their way," Kim replied, still grazing.

Joining her at the buffet, I sampled the wares, which were all appealing. One bag of the chips was still icy cold, not long removed from the freezer where Mom also kept dead birds from the yard and dirty diapers, holding both items only briefly before the garbage man came at the end of the week. It all had to do with her being a sanitary czar, keeping things amazingly tidy and clean for someone pushing her late 70s.

"Don't spoil your dinner, Amy S.," Mom warned as I dove into the buffalo dip.

Kim just looked at me and smiled, almost winking. "Yeah, Amy, you better watch yourself."

Just then Rick's people burst into the room, first little Clara, then Otto, then Fiona, then Estelle and then finally, Finn. The group was all part of the ten-and-under crowd, so it hadn't just gotten exciting, it had gotten crazy—all due to my brother's prolific personals, the Phallic Font of Grandchildren. I barely got a chance for a quick hug from everyone, including Finn who now and forever would be little Rick in my mind, before they realized that neither of their parents were in the room. Grasping this, they literally dove into the snacks, elbows and crumbs flying everywhere.

Trying to distance myself, so I wouldn't be culpable for anyone getting overserved, I edged near Mom by the sink. "How's it going, Mom?" I asked as she stood hunched over the cutting board.

"It's going . . ." she answered, almost shouting over the noise. "Yes, I'd say it's definitely going."

I couldn't put my finger on it, but she looked different, almost altered, from the last time I had seen her. She had the same freshly coiffed hair, pressed Capri pants, and pretty blouse, so it wasn't that. Watching her almost dangerously slice an avocado, I continued to look on in total silence, the state we both enjoyed most thoroughly.

"Are you ready for Thanksgiving?" I asked. "It's such a big job with us here and then, well, Christmas is right around the corner."

"Now why in the world do you have to go and bring up something stupid like that, right now?" she asked, stopping what she was doing to look me directly in the eye. "You know how stressed out I get."

"I know, Mom," I repented, "I'm sorry, but it will be fun, and you have Jennifer and me to help you."

Continuing cutting, she nodded. "You're right, you're right . . . I know you're right." Placing the avocado into the salad, she cleaned the knife and wiped her hands on a kitchen towel. "You know I do miss you, Amy S.," she stated, not like she had to, but like she wanted to. "And I'm glad you're here, there is just so much, so much activity . . ."

"I know, I get that, Mom," I said. "But, you don't have to do it all yourself. You have to let us help."

"I do love you, girl." She smiled. "Let's have a bit of the Crisp White! You get the glasses."

"You want one?" I asked Kim, who was busy winding Rick's kids up to a point of no return.

"One what?" she replied.

"A glass of Mom's white wine?" I answered.

"Yes!" she said. "Make it a LARGE."

Grabbing three crystal glasses out of the cabinet, I brought them over to Mom, who was preparing the spout on her five-liter box of Franzia Crisp White. I wasn't really a fan of the "Crisp White," a touch too sweet for my palate, but not unlike my most recent trip to my mom's "other" house and "other" world, I wasn't calling the shots here. I was just having a free drink.

Turning away to provide Kim her glass, Mom's voice trailed off. "I have something for you, A," she said, retreating into the laundry room.

Leaning back against the countertop I sipped my drink, watching Kim regale Rick's kids with hilarious instructions regarding personal hygiene. "You must wash your hands," she nearly screeched, waving her arms about. "After you do the poop."

This delighted the kids, especially Otto, who was chanting, "Pooper Scooper, Pooper Scooper!" over and over again. Finn, on the other hand, was winking at Kim while comically slapping his own butt. This sent her into even higher orbit, making me wonder who was winding whom up.

"Here you go," Mom huffed, returning with several file folders on top of a book.

Flipping through the files, I read the tabs, in Dad's longhand cursive handwriting. "Amy – Texas Tech Grades"; "Amy – Teeth"; and "Amy – Surgery." The first two were pretty self-explanatory, my transcripts from Tech and my dental records. The last, "surgery," intrigued me enough to open it now rather than wait until later, as my surgical experiences had been as limited as my sexual ones.

The documents all referenced a plastic surgeon on FM1960. Wait. Plastic surgery? In 1989? They had the wrong daughter here, maybe Kim got a breast enhancement in '89, but not me. Then I saw it, a heinous black-and-white picture from the side. It was me. It all came flying back . . . my dramatic, emergency plastic surgery. It was the summer of '89 (not '69, apologies to Bryan Adams) and I was a counselor at Camp Olympia. I was playing basketball and wearing earrings when a camper got her finger caught up in the golden hoop I was wearing while we were under the basketed hoop. Somehow, the force of her finger combined with our rapid downward spiral ripped the earring through my earlobe, leaving a wide-open gash. When I had finally called Dad and described the injury, he insisted I come home. He scheduled the plastic surgeon and I was henceforth returned to pristine condition.

I was a plastic-surgery survivor. This meant that I could regale my friends with tales of woe from my "plastic surgery" experience, tantalizingly leaving out the details, leaving them to think my breasts had been reduced due to the strain on my young, collegiate back.

This was a good day, indeed.

With a smile still beaming across my medically improved face, I examined the book. It was my Bible, my green Children's Living Bible. Though I would have recognized it regardless of the time or place, it was even more striking now that I had just seen it, in brand-new condition, in the near past.

"Thanks, Mom . . ." I said as I looked flipped through the creased pages.

"I'm going to go check on the damn grill," she said after taking another a sip of her wine.

"Can I help?" I asked.

"Not unless you can get your father to do his small part, his only part," she said.

I said nothing and watched her walk out of the kitchen, again shuffling, but this time muttering, "You said you would help, but do you? No. You said, 'Now Mama, I'll light the grill' and did you light it? NO!"

After a series of falls, eye surgery, and other health concerns, Mom didn't get around very well. Her balance was off, she was physically weak and her depth perception was compromised. None of that stopped her from going about her regular business, including trips to the hairdresser and the Walmart. Suddenly, I realized that what I had perceived as her transformation wasn't so much due to her sudden aging, but because when I supposedly went back in time, I had seen her in a totally different light.

Not only had I witnessed her treating Little Amy, or me, differently than Rick and Kim—something I guess I knew was real but hadn't ever completely validated my own memory of—I had also seen her as a contemporary, as a mom and wife just trying to survive all the goodness, and badness, until the next day, when it all started over again.

She chafed under the expectations of her own parents, particularly her mother, who could be sweet, cruel, loving and demanding. Next, she was living in a world that expected her to be a domestic goddess, and love it. Did she really want to be a domestic goddess? Some people did, but did she? Did she find satisfaction in folding sheets, preparing meals and taking people to band rehearsal and soccer practice? And what about her marriage? Was that what she really wanted? Sure, she had married one of the best guys I knew, my father, but did that mean he was the right guy for her?

Is that why she drank?

Perhaps a slight buzz made her feel not whole, not invincible, but optimistic enough to feel like she was capable of something significant. It was an impact that wouldn't just be appreciated by others, but more importantly, by herself. In the drink she found self-validation, or at least the tiny roots of it. The only difference between us, her and I, was that I "knew" when to stop, or at least I thought I did. But, if that was true, then why did the most dramatic, awful event of my life, the wrist-slashing, happen while I was completely drunk? Then again, maybe that, and all of my combined experiences, was why I had the self-awareness, as an adult, to know when to stop drinking? I had a built-in sensor.

What if, somehow, someway, she had given me the self-assurance she didn't have, or hadn't been given—the confidence I needed to know when to stop? What if she had pushed me so hard because she knew it was the only way I would be free of what imprisoned her?

I had always thought it was Dad who had given me the tools

to survive real life with a smile on my face, but it made more sense that it was her, because only she could have known how desperately I needed it. Maybe she gave it to me without even knowing it and despite all the things that went terribly wrong.

Maybe it was the best gift of all.

And maybe it was why she didn't like me—because we were so alike, not in the ways I had always feared, but in the best kind of ways, in the heart.

Love was easy; like was far more complicated.

It didn't let her off the hook for making me feel like there was a huge difference in the way that I was loved versus the way Kim and Rick were. I guess it was something that I felt all along, and acted out on, but had never really believed it. Now I did. Regardless, if I could focus on the fact that she loved me, and she truly did, maybe I could find peace, not just for me, but for her too.

It would be almost impossible, in this house where we ran from our real feelings like an Olympic sprinter, but what if I spoke to her about it? Not here, not now mind you, but another time, not the right time, because the truth was there never would be an actual time that seemed right. What if I told her that I remembered all the bad stuff, and rather than giving her some empty promise that she was forgiven, even if she was, what if I explained to her that I thought our sameness, or the way she had raised me, aside from the conflict, had managed to make me strong, and mighty, and stable, and happy?

What if I told her that it was time to be honest, and honestly, we both knew it hadn't been perfect, sometimes far from it, but we were OK? What if I told her I firmly believed she was the mom that God had given me for a reason? And what if instead of honesty ruining everything, telling her the truth, as I saw it— the presence of love, but the absence of like—freed both of us from the burden of remembering it, but not talking about it? Yes, what if by being totally authentic, out loud, in person, I could finally begin to shift my focus, my look back, on all the good that was truly there?

And what if the only way for her to be free of it, for her to feel the forgiveness she needed, the forgiveness we all needed, was for one of us, me, to take that one horrifying step toward honesty?

What if?

What if grace doesn't mean that nothing happened or that everything is magically wiped away, but that you are loved despite the real presence of whatever happened? That's what makes it so powerful . . . nobody deserves it. Not you. Not me. Not anyone.

What if?

What if, like Will had said, love really could fix anything? Could the simple act of choosing to love for the sake of loving mend not only our relationship, but allow us to both experience real peace? Could allowing love to direct everything I did, every choice I made, transform my existence?

And then, what if, like Mary had said, every life really does matter? Just because nobody would ever make a *Lifetime* movie out of all this, it didn't mean that it wasn't important enough to talk about, to take seriously. Just because it wasn't a case of extremes didn't mean it didn't matter. In fact, it mattered just as much as if it was destined to make everyone cry on *Good Morning America*.

In a culture that celebrates exceptions, both tragic and triumphant, have we marginalized the vital significance of regular, everyday life? Do fewer and fewer people find the joys in "regular" living and show less compassion for the struggles associated with it, because we've accepted that only the exceptional, extraordinary life is worth discussing, dissecting and celebrating?

And what does social media do to propagate the process?

What if?

What if I went back in time, at this point in my life, with

Mary, because she was safe and because I was finally ready to confront the questions I was sure I didn't have? The questions that my brief, life-changing conversation with my dad had stirred up. He had said that he failed to "protect" me, but even that wasn't enough for me to believe it. I had to see it for myself. Otherwise, I would have never, ever, in a million years, seriously considered talking to my mom. Out loud.

What if?

What if I went back now because I had finally decided to approach life as something to be thankful for, rather than something to bitch about?

What if?

What if I went back to 1978 not to check off every single item on my emotional agenda, but instead so I could understand how impossible it would be to have one's menstrual cycle while using a belted napkin *and* wearing a snap-crotched turtleneck? Was it my destiny to salute and celebrate the hard-earned technological advancements in adhesives and functional fashion?

What if?

It was too much, I had felt too much. I needed to regroup. Walking back through the laundry room and into the family room I saw Jennifer convening an impromptu one-person meeting with the Black Friday sales ads. "Three-thirty a.m.," she stated as she wrote on an official-looking yellow pad, a sparkle in her eyes, "Macy's doorbusters, seventy-five percent off kids clothing, ladies jeans and small electronics . . . Now WHO needs a small electronic . . ." Out the back door, I went down the two steps into the garage and out into the driveway.

Silence. God, how I loved it. God, how I needed it, and God, how I didn't need it.

Walking down the drive, I noticed how the setting sun mirrored the scene I had witnessed just twenty hours, and thirty years ago, on old Creekview Drive. The majesty of the long, elegant pine trees, loblolly to be precise, combined with the glow of evening caused time to stand still. Yes, clothing and cars could and would change, but some things, like a magnificent orange sky, the shadow of Spanish moss or the low buzz of crickets make it impossible to determine whether it's 1978, 2018, or 1898.

Once out of doors, away from people, their stuff, and technology—the smells and the sounds were timeless. There was a comfort in that, experiencing the same environment that individuals had across the ages. Perhaps time travel is possible, maybe that's where the wrinkle is, the one that allows the transportation between reality and memory.

Standing there in my forty-six-year-old body, destined to sag and wrinkle in the years I knew nothing about, I thought about Little Amy, about Big Amy, about younger Sue, about older Sue and about everyone who had played a part in the last forty-eight hours. Though I was still a long, long way from connecting all my emotional dots, I was closer, and, I knew one thing for sure. Yes, the one nugget of wisdom I could mine from the quarry of confusion was in the form of a desperate hope. I hoped that my own two boys were never, ever transported back to their childhoods.

What would they see there? Me throwing back a few drinks with my friends, steaming mad about my tortilla soup that exploded on the stove, or instead would they see the version of their childhoods that I played in my head, the highlight reel of us playing soccer in the backyard, making a movie trailer or that one time we made Christmas cookies, for seventeen freaking minutes.

The truth is, if they were given one thirty-six-hour window, they might see more of my unfortunate nature—the soup-spilling, cussing one—than the happy-go-lucky mommy, enthusiastically flipping flash cards, from my own mind.

Maybe I really was the decent parent I hoped I was, but the boys, thirty years from now, might not properly understand that, especially given only a few precious hours in the past. But they would understand that, right? They would get that I wasn't perfect and they would love me anyway.

Why couldn't I afford my mom and dad that same courtesy?

Perhaps grace-for-all, love, forgiveness and a fresh perspective was the lesson, or maybe it was about how I raised my kids, or about how I felt about myself?

Or, maybe, just maybe, it was learning that what we see of life, the transparent stuff on the surface, is nothing more than something to distract us from what is really going on.

Real life.

Just as I had almost unhinged the meaning of life, I heard the back door open behind me. Turning from the bottom of the driveway, I saw Rick and Kim coming down the steps and into the garage.

"There you are, friend," Rick said, holding two pipes.

Kim was right behind him. "Sister of mine, we were looking for you."

Retracing my steps up the uneven drive, we reunited at the edge of the garage. Rick gave me one of the two pipes and motioned to Kim, who had hers ready.

"Expect we deserve a celebratory smoke . . ." Rick stated, laying on a thick, yokel-like accent. "We got 'er done today."

"Yep," Kim agreed, mimicking Rick. "We done survived Death Camp Thanksgiving Eve."

Rick lit each of our pipes.

"I can't believe anyone ever said 'we couldn't pipe,'" he continued, referring to an incident on his back porch when his then five-year-old daughter claimed we had no idea what we were doing. The pipes had been purchased as a working prop for our annual summer Brother-Sister weekend, and he'd held on to them ever since. "Yes sir," he said dramatically. "This ain't amateur hour, we are one-hundred percent pro-fess-ion-als. We are certified legit."

Perching the pipe between his teeth, he moved a huge cooler to the edge of the garage. "Have a seat, lady friends," he said, motioning toward the Igloo.

Still holding my old green Bible and the file folders, I turned to put them on Dad's work bench. As I did, a small piece of paper fluttered to the ground. Reaching down to pick it up, I unfolded it and read the scratchy ballpoint handwriting. "*Dear Amy,*" it began. "*Meeting you was the best part of this Thanksgiving. If you are ever wondering what to do, or are having a difficult time with something, here are what I think are the two most important things to remember in life: (1). No matter what the question (ANYTHING), LOVE is always the answer. (2). There isn't anything in the world that LOVE can't fix. I hope to see you again soon! Love always, Big Amy.*"

It was my note. It was Will's words of wisdom. She had saved it. We had saved it. I had saved it. She/We/I had defied her/our/my little ten-year-old freak self and saved it. And as sure I had been that it wouldn't have made one damn bit of difference, I was positive it had changed everything.

"What are you looking at over there, sister?" Rick said. "We got unfinished business over here" he continued, motioning to me with his pipe.

"Yeah," Kim agreed loudly. "This is biscuit-and-sausage time, put your reading materials away."

Carefully placing the scrap of paper back in the Bible, I made a mental note to pick it up on my way back into the house. Then I would shove it, along with the note, into one of Mom's 2000 Ziploc bags, offered up in a dizzying array of sizes and strengths. Then I would zip it carefully into the protective case of my backpack. No scratch that, I would make a copy, or several copies of the note first, upstairs on Dad's 3-in-1 printer/copier and then place one in each piece of my luggage and then mail myself an additional copy. Then I could take a picture of it with my iPhone, back it up on a flash drive and email it to myself for safekeeping. Then I could take a picture of it with the

Bible, and a video of me with all of it, along with a picture of me at ten years old. Then I could . . .

"Let's go, sister! Pronto!" Kim bellowed.

Returning to the cooler, I worked hard to separate myself from the overwhelming number of thoughts and feelings I was experiencing. It felt like electricity. They had left me an open seat, in the middle. Kim fished three cans of Bud Light out of her coat pockets. "A little libation," she said as she passed one to each of us. "Just a little something for your troubles."

Popping the attached tab on the aluminum, low-calorie adult beverage, one I could somehow feel good about consuming, I realized, once again, that I was the widest and broadest of the three of us, taking up the most room between Kim's undergarment-less white jeans and Rick's hot-but-I-don't-believe-it blue jeans. *Crap. I should really try to lose some weight.* Chugging a healthy sip of my beer, I changed my mind. I'd do that tomorrow, or after Thanksgiving. I'd be skinny by the time I went to England for my annual visit with Miss Julia in January. I'd be whole then.

It was all BS, and I knew that, but it felt good to remind myself of how gifted I was at being totally delusional.

Looking at the glowing pines, we sat quietly. Silence. It wasn't that we were afraid to say anything, it was that we were on the same page. As different as we each were, and we were, we loved each other no matter what. And the truth was, we had each gotten here the same way—our very existence relied on just another case of mundane, married sexual relations. It just so happened that, in our case, the same combination of people had done it, and I mean it, for each of us to even be breathing.

I guessed there was something pretty special about that.

"Expect we got a lot figured out today," Rick stated, taking a draw off his pipe. "Yes, sir, I do expect we did."

"We're ready now," Kim said, looking off into the distance, holding her pipe like she was wearing a satin robe and a cravat.

"We're ready for whatever might happen . . . Dick done made sure of it."

Taking another generous chug of my beer, I placed the can precariously between my legs and stuck my pipe in the corner of my mouth. My hand brushed my face in the process. I felt a small abrasion. I put my hand on it, making sure it was real.

"Where did you get that scratch?" Rick asked.

Putting my arms around each of my siblings, I leaned back and grimaced, delivering my words with a delicious twang. "Well, friends, that war wound is a whole 'nother story . . . I expect, well, I 'spect we'll just have to put the whole damn thing, the whole lot of it, right there in our hope chests."

We all laughed. After all, I was pretty damn funny.

EPILOGUE

Though the journey detailed in the pages in this book didn't happen in real life, the impact of writing it was, for me, nothing short of life changing. I went and spoke to my Mom during Christmas of 2016. I used real words and referenced actual events that had never been spoken of. Though we didn't walk away agreeing on all the finer points, we walked away having honestly discussed them. We both cried. Though we will likely never speak of it again, which I am 100% good with, we are forever changed. We are free from acting like it never happened and hoping no one ever brings it up. We are living, together, in the land of honesty. Though it may not change anything we can see, everything we can't is different now.

ACKNOWLEDGMENTS

First and foremost, many, many thanks to the main characters portrayed in this book, who are real-life people. In writing this, I created dialogue that while based on memories and feelings, is fictional. As I neared completion, I went to each member of my childhood family and explained to them what I'd done. In every case they supported me and encouraged me to see the project through to fruition. This emotional blank check was what really made completing the cathartic journey of this book a reality.

Next, an enormous thank you to my editor **Laurie Boris**, who took my million-word first draft and tediously helped me find the book within the non-book. Your careful, considerate deliberation and precise editing made sharing this story a reality. I have no words big enough to cover my gratitude.

To **Mary Jones** – who I called randomly and told she was a major character in my fictional story. Thank you for your enthusiasm and blind faith. If what happened in the book were to happen in real life, I'd want you to play the same role.

To **Rich Thomaselli** – formerly of the Bleacher Report – for seeing something in my writing worth singling out. It was you who made me believe that I had a voice to share on a larger stage.

To **Bill Eichenberger** – of the Bleacher Report – for teaching me what writing standards are all about.

To **Robert Hastings** and **Barbara Streit**—my high school band directors. Though it was crystal clear that I was never going to have a career playing the alto saxophone, thanks for cultivating my love for writing and encouraging me to pursue my non-musical pursuits.

To **Texas Tech University** – From here anything's possible. #iAMaRedRaider

To **Teri Tallant Flash** – an old camp friend who posted "The Creative Process" when I was attempting to complete this project. Without even knowing it, you helped me to reach the finish line.

To **Connie Thompson Cline**, **Deena Rode Weast,** and **Missy Martin Bracken** – three dear friends who, despite our physical distance, have continued to ask me "when are you going to write that book?" This is it.

To the Commune – **Sarah Wilson Vier**, **Virginia Lyons**, **Stephanie Rice Weaver**, **Jane Christenson Wood**, **Mike Roberts,** and the late **Karen Vining**—for a level of friendship that is as life changing from afar as it is in person.

To **Tara Beck Bissonett** – "Kat" or "The Hair Whisperer" —for not only making me look like a well-groomed, stylish, and alluring woman, but for discussing every detail of this book, and my life, at length.

To **Sue Weinland McAfee** – my aunt and friend—for a lifetime of support and for a very honest conversation in my kitchen. I feel privileged to be related to you, Uncle Chris, David, Stephanie and Leigh.

To **Sue Shibley** – my former neighbor—for asking me for a signed copy of my first-ever writing business card. LFATS.

To **Carolyn Bates**—for enthusiastically helping me select the first version of the title for this book. I'd go on a trip with you anywhere.

To **Rye Walsh** – who, after several glasses of wine one Halloween night, got real with me and told me I was going to have to believe in this book if it was ever going to really happen.

To my **Camp Olympia family** – there are too many of you to mention here even if I could use all the pages of this book. That's unfortunate because so many of you, individually and collectively, have shaped who I am. Thanks for being "my people" from age 10 to 50, for loving me and for making me feel like I'm a part of something bigger than myself.

To **Kristi Lamb** – you were the one who convinced me I could be a sportswriter, since then you've treated me like I was totally a legitimate writing force. Thanks a million times over. I can't believe we still have all our NCAA eligibility remaining, we should totally do something about that.

To **Yvonne, Andrew, Louise, Matthew, and Sophie Clarke** – my dear English friends—for loving me and my family and supporting each of us. I doubt we will ever make another connection like the one we share with you.

To **Dawn Oldham Koenig** – my most loyal friend – for loving me, supporting me and being totally honest all in the same breath. And for holding me accountable for my tangled hair.

To **Kelly Hall** – my dear Texas Tech friend—for talking me down when my writing endeavors were belittled at a cocktail party. People don't think they can get a book published without friends who believe in them. Go Tech.

To **Patty Buchanan Lanning** and **Missy Buchanan** – my life-long friends. Your support of me and my writing has made such a difference. A special thank you to Missy, one of the few friends who has read virtually every piece of writing that I have ever shared publicly. Meow and wrap skirts forever.

To **Caroline Morgan Hamm** – my Texas Tech roommate and dear friend. The first thing I ever got published you hung on our dorm room door, announcing, "The famous author lives here." That changed my life. Thanks for encouraging me to be honest, specifically with this story. 2DD.

To **Tommy and Kathy Ferguson** – the former directors of Camp Olympia—for always finding ways for me to use my passions at camp and beyond. You believed in me more than I ever did.

To **Shonda O'Brien Hiers** – for crying when I told you I was being sent to cover the Orange Bowl in Miami. You and Captain Troy have been two of the primary people who have taken me and my writing seriously. This doesn't happen without you.

To **Dana Dugas Rivera** – my pen pal and dear friend. I completed and revamped this book as our in-writing relationship began and then flourished. It was in our communication that I found what I believe is my true writing voice. It's yet another unbelievable result of our deep and meaningful connection. Thank you for writing me back. #CONSTANT.

To **Scott, Clay, Gracie, and Caden Barr** – my Ohio family. My people. My tribe. My squad. Never in my life have I felt more accepted, loved, and celebrated than while in your company. Thank you for believing in me and more than anything for loving me. The headphones are not wireless.

To **Mary Johnson Barr** – my loyal and beloved friend for life—for taking every single aspect of my life as seriously, if not more seriously, than I do. Thank you for discussing, at length, the more revealing parts of this book. Thanks for being the friend everyone else just wishes they had, and for the second edit. See you at Panera. In a booth.

To **Alan, Esme, and Ella Turner** – my English family – for your love and support and for treating me, always, like an actual family member. A special thank you to Ella for a long conversation we had about confidence that can be found within the pages of this book. Love each of you.

To **Julia Turner** – my BFF in England. There is no way to adequately gauge your huge impact on this book and my life. I hope you'll notice how many of our deep conversations are woven into the storyline. More than anything, thank you a million times over for encouraging me to live in the world of honesty.

To **Bill Daughters** – my father-in-law who passed away in

2016. Pops, I know how proud you would be of this even though it's a girl book. I hope you know how much a part you are of this and any other achievements I may reach. We are golfers.

To **Hogan, Morgan, and Jagan Daughters** – my nephews and niece. There are no words for how proud I am of each of you and how much I love living our thug life together. It chose us. Remember, I'm your Aunt. Always.

To **Floyd and Shelly Daughters** – my brother-in-law and sister-in-law. When the in-law truck came around and dropped you two off at my door was one single best moments of my entire life. Thank you for your consistent support and love.

To **Estelle, Fiona, Otto, Clara, and Finn** – my nieces and nephews. I love each of you very much and am proud to be your Aunt. Remember, we got to be Legit! #thebeat

To **Jennifer Weinland** – my sister-in-law. Thank you for a million unplanned, super deep conversations around your kitchen island. Without a doubt, a lot of our life-changing realizations have found their way into these pages.

To **Rick Weinland** – my younger brother. The thing people don't get about you is how wise you are. Having you in my life is just about the best thing ever. Thanks for being my person. Can't wait until we make a man out of Willie again. PS You caught the big one!

To **Kimber Weinland** – my much older sister. Thanks for living this story with me and thanks for never, ever failing to be in my corner. There are no words for what your unconditional love has done for me. I'm still jealous of you, but I can live with that. The reality of my much bigger boobs helps. Love you forever. Mwaaaaaaah.

To **Dick Weinland** – my Dad. This book project is a direct result of your "out of the box" approach, where nothing is ever impossible. Your positive support of everything I have ever done is incalculable. All my results are a credit to you.

To **Sue Weinland** – my Mom. I always knew you were a courageous person, but your attitude and support of this book has taken that opinion to an entirely new level. I have no words for what that means to me. Thank you for always encouraging me to dream big. I'm thankful God picked us to be Mother and Daughter.

To **Matthew Daughters** – our youngest son and such a source of joy. Thank you for coming into my office when you were in third grade and had run out of reading material and saying, "Ok, Mom where's that book you wrote? I need to read for 20 more minutes." It illustrates your beautiful sense of humor, your positive attitude and the total belief you have in each member of your family. I love you more than you'll ever know.

To **Will Daughters**—our oldest son and one of the most intuitive people I've ever met. Thank you for being the first person to read this book and for always believing in each of my crazy projects. I'm so proud of you it literally makes my heart ache. Thank you for teaching me that comfort isn't an art.

To **Willie Daughters** – my first and current husband. The difference between me being a published author and not is you. Thank you for being my full partner in all things. I cannot wait to ride down the road together in the Nicey-Nice. We can bring the book with us. I don't know about you, but I think our marriage is going really well. Love you forever.

To **God** – my life is yours. Thank you for all the seeds you have planted, are planting, and will plant in my life. Can't wait to see what grows next. #SOforreal

About the Author

A native Houstonian and a 1991 graduate of The Texas Tech University, Amy W. Daughters has been a freelance writer, focusing mostly on college football, for the past decade. *You Cannot Mess This Up* is her first published book, meaning she can no longer claim to be "the author of unpublished books." Amy lives in Centerville, Ohio—a suburb of Dayton—where she is a regular on the ribbon dancing circuit. She is married to Willie (a computer person) and the proud mother of two sons, Will (21) and Matthew (13).

SELECTED TITLES FROM SHE WRITES PRESS

She Writes Press is an independent publishing company
founded to serve women writers everywhere.
Visit us at www.shewritespress.com.

Size Matters by Cathryn Novak. $16.95, 978-1-63152-103-4. If you take
one very large, reclusive, and eccentric man who lives to eat, add one
young woman fresh out of culinary school who lives to cook, and then
stir in a love of musical comedy and fresh-brewed exotic tea, with just a
hint of magic, will the result be a soufflé—or a charred, inedible mess?

A Tight Grip: A Novel about Golf, Love Affairs, and Women of a Certain Age by
Kay Rae Chomic. $16.95, 978-1-938314-76-6. As forty-six-year-old
golfer Jane "Par" Parker prepares for her next tournament, she experiences a chain of events that force her to reevaluate her life.

Tzippy the Thief by Pat Rohner. $16.95, 978-1-63152-153-9. Tzippy has
lived her life as a selfish, materialistic woman and mother. Now that she
is turning eighty, there is not an infinite amount of time left—and she
wonders if she'll be able to repair the damage she's done to her family
before it's too late.

Slipsliding by the Bay by Barbara McDonald. $16.95, 978-1631522253. A
hilarious spoof of academic intrigue that offers a zany glimpse of a
small college at a crossroads—and of the societal turmoil and follies of
the seventies.

Arboria Park by Kate Tyler Wall. $16.95, 978-1631521676. Stacy Hallo-
ran's life has always been centered around her beloved neighborhood, a
1950s-era housing development called Arboria Park—so when a massive highway project threaten the Park in the 2000s, she steps up to the
task of trying to save it.

In the Heart of Texas by Ginger McKnight-Chavers. $16.95,
978-1-63152-159-1. After spicy, forty-something soap star Jo Randolph
manages in twenty-four hours to burn all her bridges in Hollywood,
along with her director/boyfriend's beach house, she spends a crazy
summer back in her West Texas hometown—and it makes her question
whether her life in the limelight is worth reclaiming.